The succubus wailed, hi
Malcolm took a step tov
his blade. She hissed and the.. ...
Watching her, Malcolm let out a breath a... ..
body to slump. Demon fire flickered off the alley walls, bathing
them in crimson violet. He spat blood and touched his nose,
wincing. Broken. He swabbed his blood and sweat-streaked
face and wiped it on his already ruined shirt. Blood continued
streaming down across his lips.

"Christ," he panted, his ribs aching with each breath.
Someone had to have heard the gunshots. Police were notoriously slow, but he couldn't risk it. Malcolm eyed the dead demon,
encased in ghostly fire. A moth fluttered around it. Fucking
reckless, he scolded to himself. His own DNA was splattered on
the ground and the corpse's knee. He looked around, hoping for
a faucet, something to wash away the blood.

Movement caught his eye. Far across the empty field, hidden in the shadows but still visible to Malcolm's enhanced sight,
two figures stood watching him. Shorty and Cornrows.

Cornrows smiled then slapped his companion on the side.
The men raced away.

Fuck! Malcolm looked back at the corpse. No time. He
limped from the alley, grabbed Hounacier's bag, and fled.

HOUNACIER

THE VALDUCAN — BOOK 2

BY SETH SKORKOWSKY

For Jesse Sisk, who's been there since the beginning and never stops encouraging me.

Thanks, brother.

CHAPTER 1

ELEVEN YEARS AGO

Malcolm wiped dusty sweat from his face as he made his way up the road. The strip of gray asphalt looked as if it had been poured like a molten river of lava many years ago. Only a few lumpy patches gave any indication the street had ever been repaired. An oncoming rider on a tired bicycle veered away, giving Malcolm a wide berth. A pair of muscular men, leaning against a dingy pickup, looked up as Malcolm approached. Island rap blasted from a little blue radio on the hood between them.

A white face in Haiti always drew attention. Three weeks into his second trip and he still wasn't used to it. White meant foreign. Money. Kidnappings were common, though anyone trying to get money from Malcolm would be shit out of luck.

Beyond the truck, Malcolm stopped beneath a pair of palm trees, enjoying a moment's shade. He glanced again at his hand-written directions. Satisfied, he adjusted his backpack and started up a gravel path.

The music stopped.

Turning, he saw the two men standing straight, watching him. Mama Ritha had guards at her house as well, though a fat woman and a couple pre-teens weren't as intimidating as these two. Malcolm gave them a little smile, hiding his trepidation, then continued toward the squat, white house at the end of the path.

A pair of older men sat under the porch awning, quiet as

Malcolm neared. One wore a pink polo, his skin a deep black. A glimmer of kindness twinkled in his eyes, visible behind the apprehension. The other man was lighter. There was a stillness to him, a weight. Sweeping tattoos decorated his arms and chest, visible through the open shirt and dusting of white hair. A pair of jam-jar glasses, frosted with condensation, stood on the table between them. A horn-handled machete in a wooden sheath rested on the table as well.

"May I help you?" the darker man asked, his thick Creole accent muddling the words.

"Yes," Malcolm said. "Are you Micelo Tavel?"

"I am."

"Sir, my name is Malcolm Romero. I'm researching local religious practices and spent some time with Mama Ritha. She spoke very highly of you."

Tavel frowned. "No interviews. Not after those *National Geographic* boys. Voodoo's not for tourists or to be laughed at. Ritha knows my feelings on that."

"Yes, sir." Gravel crunched, and Malcolm glanced back. The two rap fans were coming toward him. "She told me you wouldn't be interested in talking to me," he said to Tavel, his voice quickening slightly. "My—"

"Then why are you here?" the old priest interrupted. His eyes narrowed. "Why come all this way if she told you that?"

The two young men stopped just a few feet behind Malcolm.

Malcolm swallowed, trying to at least appear calm. "I'm looking for Ulises Belair. I understand he's staying here."

Tavel's brows rose in a curious arch. He turned to the tattooed man beside him.

The man's hand moved to the sheathed machete. "I am Ulises."

"Mister Belair," Malcolm said, forcing a smile, "it's a pleasure to meet you." He stepped forward, offering his hand.

"Stop!" Ulises snapped. He gripped the weapon then threw his left hand out before him. A tattoo of a half-lidded eye adorned the pale palm.

Fear twisted and rose inside Malcolm's gut. He opened his hands out to his side, his gaze locked onto the machete. He felt the eyes of the two guards boring into his back. Bokors were the sorcerers of voodoo, practitioners of both light and dark magic. For the first time since coming to the island, he was truly and mortally afraid.

"Look at it!" Ulises ordered, thrusting his tattooed palm out further.

Malcolm did as he was told.

Nothing happened.

Slowly, Ulises lowered his hand and rested it on the chair arm. His grip loosened on the machete but didn't move. "How can I help you?" His voice was slow and purposeful.

A long, low breath escaped Malcolm's lips. His heart still pounded. "I, um... As I said, I'm researching Haitian Voodoo practices. I've spoken with many priests and heard of you."

"And what have you heard?" Ulises asked.

"That you're a bokor. A very respected one. Mama Ritha told me that you were in Hinche, visiting Father Tavel, and said I should come speak with you."

The old man snorted. "Ritha sent you?"

"Yes, sir."

"Mama Ritha despises me. Despises what I do. Did she tell you that too, white-boy?"

"She might not think much of what you do, sir, but she does still respect you."

Ulises shook his head. He picked up his drink and took a sip. "I don't do interviews. Go back to Borgne."

A heavy hand dropped onto Malcolm's shoulder.

"Wait," Malcolm urged. "She told me that you wouldn't normally do an interview but that I ... I had to tell you that she found the groom."

The grin fell from Ulises' lips. He set his glass back down and touched the machete. Not gripping, almost protective. "The groom?"

"Yes, sir."

Ulises shared a look with Tavel and nodded.

The priest motioned a finger. The hand withdrew from Malcolm's shoulder, and the two guards walked away, gravel crunching as they left. Once they were gone, Tavel stood, extending his hand. "Please excuse our caution. There is a madman in Hinche, and one can't be too careful. Come." Malcolm shook the priest's rough hand. "Thank you, Father. I heard on the bus that the police caught the killer last night." Tavel gave Ulises an uneasy grin. What teeth he still had were very white compared to his charcoal skin. "That's what they said." He gestured to his empty seat. "Please, sit down. I'm sure you two have much to discuss."

Removing his backpack, Malcolm took the battered chair, a bit taken aback at the sudden and complete change in the men's demeanor. Whatever Mama Ritha's cryptic message suggested meant a good deal to them. He wished he'd opened with that instead of hello. "Thank you, sir."

"I'll bring you something to drink," Tavel said then hurried though the house's open door.

Ulises sat silent, his golden-brown eyes seeming to study Malcolm. His fingers lightly stroked the machete's polished wood sheath. He glanced at the open door. "Micelo should thank you for arriving. He's very uncomfortable with me. You offer a good distraction."

Unsure how to reply, Malcolm simply smiled.

"People fear what they don't understand, what they don't want to know about," Ulises continued. "What was your name?"

"Malcolm Romero."

"Romero," Ulises repeated, seeming to roll the word in his mouth, inspecting the flavor of it. "Cuban?"

"My father was. I'm American. Grew up in Baton Rouge."

Ulises nodded to himself. "And you go to college?"

Malcolm turned as Tavel stepped out and offered him a glass of some red-tinged drink. "Oh, thank you." He started to rise from the chair, allowing his host the seat, but the scrawny priest just smiled and shook his hand.

"You two talk. I will be inside."

"Thank you, Micelo," Ulises said as Tavel retreated back into the house. He motioned to Malcolm, urging him to continue.

"Tulane," Malcolm said. "New Orleans."

"I know New Orleans very, very well," almost doleful. "And what do you study?"

The blocky ice cubes clinked as Malcolm lifted the glass to his lips. Freezers were a rare luxury here. He sucked a breath as the strong rum burned his throat. "Anthropology," he coughed. "I'm researching my dissertation."

"An ... thro ... po ... lo ... gee," Ulises said, each syllable almost a different word. "Voodoo?"

"Yes, sir."

"And do you believe?"

"I'm trying to keep personal bias out of my research," Malcolm said.

"So no?"

"Oh, it's not that," Malcolm lied. "I just want to be scientific."

Ulises smiled. "Don't worry. You will believe, Malcolm Romero. That much is certain."

"Well, then." Malcolm took another sip and then set the drink onto the table. He reached for his backpack. "I just have a few questions I want to start with."

"No interviews."

Malcolm paused. "But I thought ..."

"Not yet," Ulises said. "We are having a ceremony tomorrow. I want you to be there. Be my assistant. Afterward, once you believe, I will answer your questions."

"Wow," Malcolm said, genuinely surprised. "I'm honored. What ceremony?"

"One to find a killer."

"You mean the slasher?" Malcolm asked. "Like I said, news was that he was captured last night."

"He was, in a way. But the real killer was not."

Malcolm's eyes widened. "More killers?"

The old sorcerer shook his head. "Just one. The man they caught is not it."

"So they have the wrong man?" Malcolm asked.

"He was the man who did it," Ulises said. "But not the murderer."

"So the real killer is still out there?" Malcolm asked, struggling to understand the old man's riddle.

Ulises nodded.

A chill wormed up Malcolm's spine. The slasher had already

killed and mutilated twenty people in the last two months. "Then why not get him now? What if he strikes again tonight?" "That cannot be helped." Ulises shook his head. "I arrived here only a few hours before you. This ceremony takes time. Tomorrow morning, we begin."

The pungent tang of smoke briefly washed away as one of the mambos rubbed a fluttering chicken across Malcolm's face. The priestess held the bird firmly, brushing its wings down his bare arms and chest.

Once she'd finished the backs of his legs, she said, "Enter," then she and her partner, a priest with a clay bowl of smoldering herbs, turned their attention to the next person in line. Malcolm strode into the near-empty yard, a pair of muscular men on either side of him.

His morning had started early with Father Tavel rousing him from the makeshift bed on the priest's floor. Then, with Ulises and the two rap-fan guards, Seymour and Jean-Luc, they had loaded several boxes into their truck and a forty-year-old Volkswagen then driven them up to a white stucco church just outside of the city. There, in the yard, boxed in by the church, an old cemetery, and a rusted, wrought-iron fence, they'd begun setting up. More helpers trickled in, houngans and mambos, other priests and priestesses in and around the city. Together, under Tavel and Ulises' joint instructions, they cleaned and arranged the yard then erected a thick, painted pole at the center. It symbolized the crossroads. The door to the spirit world.

Worshipers gathered outside the entrance around noon. Dozens at first, but their ranks now filling the street numbered in the hundreds if not thousands. And more arrived still, many carrying gifts of food or sacrifice. Their combined murmurs and chatter swelled together into a rumbling cloud of noise. This was by far the largest ceremony Malcolm had ever seen. More and more of him resented Ulises' demand that Malcolm not bring a camera or notebook to record any of this.

After they had finished the setup, Father Tavel and Madame Hero, the resident houngan asogwe and mambo asogwe, led everyone out of the yard for the cleansing. Once sanctified, they brought in the other priests and priestesses, purifying them before they entered. Afterward, each took up their own birds and smoldering bowls to help usher in the growing crowd.

Ulises stood a few feet inside the yard, his hand on the machete at his hip. Shirtless, his body covered in so many tattoos that it was hard to take them all in. "Stop." The old man thrust out his left hand, its pale, tattooed palm facing Malcolm. He closed his fist and nodded.

The two escorts returned to the gate.

"Come here, Malcolm," Ulises said. "Stand here. Watch me."

Taking position beside the sorcerer, Malcolm eyed the dense crowd outside the fence. Admitting everyone might take a couple hours. Was he to stand here the entire time? And what was with that eye tattoo? Ulises' part in all this was unlike any voodoo ceremony he'd ever encountered. He needed to remember as much of this as he could and write it down the first moment he had a chance.

The two men escorted a gangly woman before them. As before, the old bokor thrust his palm out. After a couple seconds, he nodded. The two men went back to fetch another worshiper, and the woman sauntered off into the yard.

Malcolm motioned to the sheathed machete at Ulises' side. "Do you need me to carry that?"

Ulises' grip seized around the horn handle. "No!" The sudden anger melted from his face. "No. Hounacier is mine to carry."

"But," Malcolm said, choosing his words not to upset the old man, "if I'm your assistant, isn't a laplas supposed to be sword-bearer?"

"I am sword-bearer." He turned toward the next escortee, a man with a thick moustache. He raised his palm, lowered it, then allowed him to move on. "You are my assistant," Ulises continued. "Do as I say. Watch me."

Malcolm nodded. As frustrating as it was, this was a rare if not unique opportunity. Bokors rarely gave interviews, especially ones of Ulises' renown. Best to not irritate the old man lest he lose it. He glanced back at the sheathed blade. Hounacier, Ulises called it. The dark, polished sheath and white grip, etched and carved into the head of something like a strange nocturnal animal, were so pristine, so new in appearance, that they stood out against the rest of Ulises' worn attire.

Keeping straight, Malcolm remained silent as the men brought devotees up one at a time before them. Each time, Ulises held his palm out before ushering them in. After what he guessed was half an hour, a few of the drummers began warming up, their beats echoing though the yard. Turning his head a little, Malcolm watched through the corner of his eye as they played while others milled around. His feet ached from standing so long, and he shifted his weight. The heat from the afternoon sun left him slick with sweat. He barely noticed as the two men brought a round-faced woman before them, her hair hidden beneath a white headscarf. Ulises raised his palm. Malcolm jumped as the woman suddenly let out a hiss. She turned away, shielding her eyes as if from a spotlight. Ulises whipped the machete from its sheath as the two men grappled her arms.

"No!" the woman screamed. "Please. Please don't hurt me!"

The old man gestured with the blade, and the men led the woman, fighting and wailing, to a small, fenced pen not far from the main circle. A ring of mirrors and wooden masks surrounded the little corral, facing inward. Long strands of colored beads draped the wooden fence. People stopped and watched as Seymour opened the sagging gate and the men pushed her inside.

"Please!" she cried. "Please, no!"

Without a word, Ulises tied the gate shut. He dipped his fingers into a shallow dish of white powder and drew a line across the threshold.

"No. There's been a mistake," the woman cried as they turned and walked back toward the entrance. Seymour remained beside the corral gate, his hand gripping his own plastic-handled machete.

"What was that about?" Malcolm demanded.

"Shh," the old man hissed. "No questions. Observe."

Malcolm clenched his jaw, standing silent as Ulises continued his strange ritual, the woman's pleading wails echoing behind them.

Hundreds more passed the old man's test, unfazed at the tattooed hand. Malcolm watched each one, his attention unwavering. Eventually, a bald man with tight, rope-like muscles was presented before them. He stood straight, confident. Then recoiled the instant he saw the bokor's palm.

Again, the machete slid from its sheath, and the two guards dragged the man, kicking and fighting to the corral. Two more men rushed to help, and together, they pushed the terrified prisoner into the pen. He fell to his knees, sobbing. Once Ulises had redrawn the white powder line, the two strangers stayed behind to watch over the captives.

Time crawled as he stood there, watching the old man work, the drums and laughter increasing behind him. Finally, after the line outside had nearly completed, a small, white van and a pickup stopped on the street outside.

Several police officers crawled out of the vehicles. Malcolm looked around, expecting some reaction from the priest. Instead, several of the white-shirted officers stepped in line. When the first of the policemen was presented before Ulises, he stood straight, hands at his sides, aviator sunglasses hanging from his open collar.

Once he'd passed Ulises' test, the officer walked back to the gate as another policeman was brought forward. Afterward, he returned to the yard entrance.

A cluster of policemen circled behind the van, pistols and shotguns drawn. They pulled a man in filthy green shorts out of the back and pushed him into the yard. Once cleansed, the two officers dragged the haggard prisoner forward. Steel cuffs bound the man's wrists and ankles. Swollen bruises and scabby cuts marred his hollow-cheeked face, likely remnants of some terrible beating. Judging by the officers' treatment of him, Malcolm could guess the handiwork was theirs.

Ulises displayed his palm, and the prisoner let out a high, terrible scream. He struggled to pull away, but the officers held him firm. Hounacier out, Ulises marched the cuffed man to the yard and locked him inside with the others.

"Who was that?" Malcolm asked as they walked back to the front.

"The man they caught," Ulises said.

"The killer?" Malcolm glanced back. The man stood, shoulders slumped inside the corral, the two policemen beside it. "You said he was innocent."

"No," Ulises corrected. "I said he wasn't the real murderer, but he did kill those people."

Confused, Malcolm opened his mouth to reply but thought better of it. *Just go along with him. Don't ruin your chance of the interview.*

After several more minutes, the last of the attendees were admitted, and the priests made their way toward the erect post at the yard's center. Wiping the sweat from his brow, Malcolm located a food-cluttered table and fetched some lukewarm water from a white-haired woman. He gulped it down, refilled the cup, then carried it and a fresh one to Ulises.

"I had hoped for more," the old bokor said to Father Tavel. The two men stood beside a row of wooden trunks.

Tavel frowned. "You said you only needed three."

"Three is the minimum for an anchor. Four is preferred."

"Can you still do your magic?"

Ulises pursed his lips. "It will be difficult. The beast will fight. If it is strong enough, it may resist."

Tavel met Ulises' eye. "Then fight it harder," he said, his tone hard, almost threatening. He picked up a brown bottle from a trunk and joined the other priests gathered near the pole.

Ulises let out a long breath then picked up a grimy brown duffel from behind one of the boxes and set it on the lid.

Malcolm offered one of the cups. "I brought you some water."

The bokor accepted it and downed it in three gulps. He dug through the canvas bag and removed a long necklace of tiny shells. A graven bone hung from the end, its curved shape resembling a claw or crescent. Ulises kissed the bone then pulled the necklace over his head. He removed a rolled leather bundle from the duffel and continued to dig. "Here," he said, pulling out a second necklace, a single-strand rather than three. He kissed the bone amulet at the end. "Wear this."

Malcolm lowered his head, and Ulises put it around his neck. "Thank you."

A brief smile tugged the edge of the old man's mouth then was gone. "I am sword-bearer, but a laplas should be armed." He untied the lace around the bundle and unrolled it.

Malcolm swallowed, seeing the ancient, sawed-off Remington. The wooden stock had been sanded down into a curved grip.

"You are to carry this." Ulises drew the weapon from a long, stitched holster and thumbed the lever on the back, opening it. "Do not fire it unless I tell you. There will be many people around, and the spray might hurt someone if you aren't close to the beast."

"Beast?"

Ulises removed a green cartridge from a loop inside the roll and loaded it into the right barrel. "This one is bronze. I suspect it will work." He loaded the second barrel with a red one, a black stripe drawn around its end. "If not, this is a general load. Something in here may hurt it." He snapped the shotgun closed and slid it back into the holster. "Safety is on the back."

"I can't shoot that," Malcolm said, stepping back. "It might kill someone."

The old man gave him a hard glare. "If the time comes to fire it, people will already be dead. You do as I tell you." He offered the weapon. "Put it on."

Malcolm clenched his teeth. He drew a breath then accepted the shotgun. It had a long shoulder strap that crossed his chest and hung at his hip.

"Good." Ulises shoved the roll back into the duffel and cinched it closed. "It's time."

The two men circled around to the far edge of the open ring surrounding the painted pole. Mambos and houngans moved to the music, drawing swirling chalk and cornmeal patterns around the tall post. Malcolm found himself bobbing his head to the beat as he mentally noted as much of the ceremony as he could. Priests blew mouthfuls of liquor onto the pole. The chickens were fed before their heads were twisted from their bodies. The sword-bearers danced in the circle, twirling their blades in mock, rhythmic combat.

The congregation's energy rolled higher. Chanting grew

faster, hundreds of voices merging in song. More dancers trickled into the ring, seeming drunk within the moment. Dust swirled in the air from dancing feet, only adding to the stink of sweat and smoke.

Eventually, one of the dancers, an elderly man, began to shake, his eyes rolling up into his head. He stumbled and bumped into one of the priests. The other dancers moved around him, singing and chanting, and the man suddenly moved with an energy and vigor he hadn't had before. He hopped and shimmied in a unique rhythm.

The first of the loa had arrived.

The priests gathered around the possessed man. One hurried to one of the nearby trunks and fetched a straw hat and a twisted cane, which the old man graciously took.

Malcolm watched the man saunter and dance as Legba, the Gatekeeper. Of course, he knew there was no spirit, no Legba. But obviously, the old man believed it, and so did the others. He wondered what made the old man *believe* the spirit had taken him. Could he have moved in those rhythms before? How much of his new vigor was psychosomatic?

More dancers moved inside the ring, their fervor fueled by the loa's appearance. Others began to shake and twitch as the spirits mounted them. Each time, the priests moved in to greet them, verify the loa's identity, then fetch their signifying totems. Erzulie, Sogbo, and a half-dozen more appeared within the congregation. In his observations, Malcolm had witnessed possessions before but rarely more than three at the same time. Still, more arrived with rolling eyes and sporadic convulsions.

He watched a young man with a wisp of a goatee wearing a pair of sunglasses with only one lens and clutching a rum bottle. The teenager groped several of the women, posing as Ghede. Malcolm grinned to himself, seeing the boy swig the liquor and get away with much more than he could probably ever do otherwise. He had no doubt the boy was enjoying his absolute, if temporary, freedom.

A stocky man leaped past, swinging a black machete. Malcolm scooted away, allowing the man more room. He recognized him as Ogoun, the warrior. Ogoun danced before

Ulises then stopped and began speaking to him. Curious what *wisdom* the *spirit* was imparting, Malcolm started toward them. Then the rum-swilling youth in the one-eyed glasses stepped in his way.

"How you doin', white-boy?" he bellowed. "Enjoyin' yourself?" His breath reeked of alcohol.

Malcolm forced a smile. He'd known it was only time before the *spirits* harassed the outsider. They never failed to. "I'm fine."

"Of course you're fine," the boy said through a wide, toothy grin. "You got yourself a lady. Just need to impress her papa."

"No," Malcolm said, bemused. "Sorry. I don't have a lady."

He tried to step around the drunk teen, but the boy gripped his shoulder firmly.

"Don't you be fibbin' to Papa Ghede," he laughed. "I see you eyein' her. You goin' to watch her dance. See if you can learn the steps."

Malcolm shook his head. "So which lady is it?"

The teen laughed again then pointed the hand holding the bottle toward Ulises. "That one right there. You've been followin' her all day."

"You caught me," Malcolm said, playing along as he tried to slip out of the boy's grip.

"Don't you worry, Milky. I won't tell her husband."

Malcolm froze, his brain reeling in complete surprise. "What?"

"Her man."

"No," Malcolm said. "What did you call me?"

The boy swigged his bottle and grinned. "Milky. That's what your baby sister called you when she was little. Couldn't pronounce your name. Mama thought it was cute. Started callin' you that. She said it in front of your friends one day when you were eleven, and they laughed. Kept callin' you that because it made your ears turn red." He cocked his head a little. "Aren't red now. You look pale, Milky."

Malcolm just stared at him, his mouth open.

The boy offered the bottle. "You look like you need a drink."

Malcolm started for the bottle when the youth slapped his hand away and laughed.

"You can't have Papa Ghede's rum. Get your own."

"How ... did you know that?" Malcolm asked.

The boy's one visible eye squinted mischievously. "Papa Ghede's been watchin' you for a long time. Watched you take you first step, your kiss, first fuck. Now, I'll watch you fall in love." He turned and grinned at Ulises then back at Malcolm. "And she is a beautiful lady."

"Who?" Malcolm asked, genuinely creeped out and curious.

"Hounacier," the boy breathed, the sour stink washing over Malcolm's face.

"The ... machete?"

The boy cocked his head and giggled. "She's no more a machete than I am a seventeen-year-old named Toussaint who abuses himself every mornin'."

"So it's a loa?"

"No, she's something else. Something ..." he lifted his hand like trying to catch a delicate, unseen bubble on his fingertips, "beautiful." He poked Malcolm in the chest with his finger. "You'll see, Milky. You just keep impressin' daddy before you court his woman." He knocked back the bottle then offered it. "To love."

Malcolm raised a tentative hand, and the boy snatched the bottle away. Without a word, the teen sauntered back into the ring, laughing. Malcolm stood dumfounded by the whole encounter. He shook his head. He'd once seen a street psychic dazzle people by revealing things to audience members he couldn't have possibly known. It was a trick, a mentalist hustle. Tavel was too reputable a houngan to have set it up. He was a believer. Ulises? Malcolm didn't know why Mama Ritha had disliked the old bokor. Maybe he was a scam artist.

Still, how had the boy known about the nickname?

Malcolm glanced across to Ulises. The old man nodded sternly, motioning him over, and Malcolm edged through the dancing crowd toward him.

"You were to stay by my side," Ulises quietly scolded.

"I'm sorry."

Ulises sighed. "I believe the loa have all arrived. It's time for us to begin our part."

Malcolm quietly followed as Ulises shared words with several of the priests and the old man posing as Legba. The fourteen loa-possessed worshippers gathered at the central post and began dancing around it, their circle growing, pushing everyone but Ulises and Malcolm away until they'd cleared a forty-foot-wide ring. The dancing loa took the chalk and cornmeal and began drawing the elaborate and swirling edges of the ring save for a narrow gap at one end. The drumbeats continued steadily as the loa worked, and the dense crowd swayed, many with hands raised.

"Stand here," Ulises ordered, and Malcolm took position at the back of the ring.

He felt awkward, the only non-moving person in the entire circle. Unsure what to do with his hands, he clasped them before him but decided it too stiff. He moved a hand to his side to be more casual but found himself holding the wood grip of the gun at his hip. Sliding his hand away, he just tried to focus on the old man slowly pacing the perimeter. Malcolm noticed the drunk teen's one visible eye watching him and couldn't help but wonder if this was about to be some terrible joke at his expense. What the hell was he doing here?

Ulises reached the far side of the ring and thrust his machete high.

The drums ceased, and the crowd parted before the unpainted gap. Priests lined the edges as the white-shirted policemen marched the three prisoners though the open valley.

A pair of loa took the bald man's arms as he entered the ring. Tears stained his dusty cheeks. Searching the crowd desperately, his eyes found a slender woman about Malcolm's age. She put a hand to her mouth as if forcing away her own tears.

The scarfed woman came next. She scowled indignantly as another pair of loa escorted her in. Finally, the beaten man in the green shorts entered the ring. He kept his eyes downcast and clutched his cuffed hands together.

A drum sounded, followed by another, loud and ominous. Ulises backed away from the three captives, Hounacier still raised.

Drums beat again, steadily like a slow pulse. The loa painted the circle closed, completing the ring. Ulises stopped beside Malcolm, and the loa escorts gently pulled their prisoners to the packed ground, laying them on their backs, their heads toward the central post.

Ulises unleashed a loud whoop, and the drums erupted into a rapid beat. A stream of musical chanting poured from the old man, the strange words completely foreign to Malcolm. The loa danced in and around the circle, unhindered by the painted lines.

Holding his machete out, sideways across his open palms, Ulises aimed the length of the blade at the bald man, then the woman, and then the cuffed prisoner. His song grew louder, faster as he repeated the chant, gesturing to each person for several seconds before moving to the next.

Hair and clothing ruffled as if caught in a gust though the heavy, sticky air didn't move. The dancers' fury grew. They jumped and twirled, circling the ring like frenzied sharks. The old bokor's voice was almost a scream as he aimed the side-turned weapon at the bald man. A tremor shuddered through his body and then ceased as Ulises focused on the woman. She began to tremble as well. Ulises continued the sequence, his voice roaring. Each time, whichever prisoner he focused on would shake as if the machete blade were arcing an invisible bolt of lightning.

The spasms became more intense. Legs and arms moved with impossible speed, a blur of skin and cloth. Malcolm jumped as the scarfed woman screamed, her shrill voice cracking into something deep and inhuman. The unseen bolt moved to the cuffed man beside her. His bound hands pulsed like a jackhammer. In the blur, they appeared to swell. A metallic pop, and one of the steel shackles blew open.

Wide-eyed, Malcolm stared in horror as the bald man's head seemed to stretch, his mouth jutting forward. One of the woman's legs elongated for a moment. Her sandal popped free and bounced across the circle. The chanting song raged around him. Malcolm's hair whipped in the unfelt wind.

With a loud rip, the man's shirt split open. A membrane

of dark skin stretched beneath his arms to the base of his ribs. He screamed, the tone deepening as iron-like fangs sprouted from his mouth. Ulises howled, stamping his feet as he kept the machete blade aimed at the writhing form.

Horrified, Malcolm stepped back. Shouts erupted around him as several people in the crowd tried to flee. Policemen drew their weapons, their eyes wide with terror. Ulises continued his chant as loa danced around.

A pair of short horns burst through the top of the bald man's head. He rolled onto his knees. His legs lengthened, feet curling like hooks.

Malcolm took another step, about to run when arms seized him from behind.

"Watch, Milky!" Rum-soaked breath. "Watch her dance."

The woman in the white scarf and the prisoner in broken handcuffs both scrambled away as the beast stood. Brown, bat-like wings extended outward, nearly twenty feet across. Blade-like claws curled from the fingers atop each wing. It opened ruby eyes and shrieked a piercing scream.

Gunshots erupted as one of the officers fired his pistol, not caring about the crowd around him. Bloody holes popped open along the creature's skin then closed. The monster spun and hissed.

Ulises charged.

He swung the machete, but the beast sprung back with a flap. Leather wings ruffled as it swiped its claws. The old man ducked and spun to the side, Hounacier out before him.

"Watch her." The teen's grip loosened and slid away. "Learn the steps."

The beast lunged, snapping its jaws. Ulises lurched back, barely escaping the iron teeth, but one of the taloned wings raked his upper arm, splitting open a pair of long cuts down his bicep. The monster moved in. Ulises raised his wounded left arm, displaying his palm. The lidded tattoo opened wide, and the creature recoiled. Keeping the hand up, Ulises thrust Hounacier forward, but the beast flapped and hopped back, landing atop the painted pole.

Remembering the heavy sawed-off at his hip, Malcolm

drew it and aimed the gun in both hands. He pulled the trigger. It didn't move. He squeezed it harder until his finger hurt.

Ulises ran forward and jumped, slicing the machete down into one of the beast's hooked feet. It screamed and fell backward, wings flailing. It hit the ground with a hard thump, nearly hitting the loa Erzulie. Snarling, it hobbled upright. It snapped its jaws as Ulises dove toward it. He ducked below the attack and hacked the blade into the crook of the monster's neck. Blood exploded from the wound. It thrashed, knocking the flat of a wing hard into Ulises, but he drove the blade up under its ribs.

Brilliant purple and white fire burst from the wound at the creature's neck. It spread like lit gasoline across its body. Malcolm feared it might burn the old man, but Ulises didn't appear concerned about the flames. He wrenched the blade from the corpse and stood, straddling it. No smoke came from the fire. In fact, it didn't even seem to burn.

Panting, Ulises turned and met Malcolm's horrified stare. Burning blood dripped from Hounacier's blade. Stepping over the hideous corpse, the tattooed priest approached. Blood from the wound at his arm ran down to his hand. He reached out and touched the end of Malcolm's still-extended gun, gently pushing it down and leaving a pair of red fingerprints.

Ulises glanced down at the weapon. "The safety is still on."

Releasing a breath, Malcolm let go of the trigger. His lips shook, struggling to form words. "What ... what the fuck!"

Ulises didn't react to the sudden outburst. "Do you believe, Malcolm Romero?"

The loa all circled the flaming monster, cradling it. The young woman from the crowd pushed her way forward. Sobbing, she fell to her knees beside it.

Malcolm sucked a breath, trying to calm himself. His heart still pounded in his ears. "What *is* that?"

"A demon." Ulises glanced back. The loa had laid the crumpled monster on its back. Several were crying. "An asanbosam. Its soul is now burning away." He stared back at Malcolm. "Do you now believe?"

Malcolm nodded.

A smile curled at the side of the old man's lips. "Then I will teach you. I will make you a hunter."

"What?"

"I am old, Malcolm. I feel it. Someone must carry Hounacier. You are her groom, and I will teach you."

A thousand questions whirled though Malcolm's head. He stared at the monster that everything he'd ever known told him shouldn't exist. The white-shirted officers unlocked the broken cuff from their prisoner's wrist. He embraced one of them, tears of joy running down his face. The fire along the demon's body had begun to fade, and with it, its grotesque features seemed to melt back into the body of the dead bald man.

"Do you accept this offer, Malcolm?" Ulises asked.

The teenage Papa Ghede looked up from the beastly corpse. His one eye met Malcolm's, and the boy smiled. In that moment, Malcolm realized the loa was real.

"Do you accept?" the old man repeated.

Malcolm felt himself nod. He lowered his gaze to the machete, seeing a beauty to it he hadn't seen before. There was an intelligence to it. "I do."

CHAPTER 2

PRESENT DAY

"This looks good." Malcolm killed the headlights and backed the SUV onto a primitive drive. Tall grass and weeds scratched against the underside, sprouting from the narrow strip between the two earthen tire trails. He stopped beside a twisted oak, its branches shading them from the moonlight above. Brake lights reflected red off a bullet-ridden "No Trespassing" sign on the gate behind them. Malcolm only hoped the resident hunters weren't there on a Tuesday night. He turned off the engine.

Pale light glowed beside him as Orlovski activated his phone. The knight tapped the screen and peered closer, his eyes invisible behind the glare on his glasses. "Message sent."

Halfway across the world, Master Alex Turgen, unofficial leader of the Valducans, would receive the simple text, "Mission go."

Malcolm kissed the crescent-shaped bone on his seashell necklace and pulled it on.

"Here." Samantha, Orlovski's student, leaned in from the back seat, offering a pair of small, plastic boxes strung on metal bead chains. A square of black electric tape masked the trackers' LEDs.

Malcolm accepted one and put it on. "Thanks." He opened the door and stepped out into a wall of Missouri humidity and around to the rear of vehicle. There, hidden in one of the suitcases, he removed a dark, navy ballistic vest and strapped it on. The shrill hum of a mosquito buzzed past his ear. He cinched on a heavy belt, making sure Ulises' old sawed-off was positioned straight across his back. His fingers found Hounacier's carved handle at his hip, and he gave her a reassuring squeeze. *Ready, baby?*

Malcolm unrolled a slender wire and hooked the rubber earpiece over his ear. He snapped the throat mic on. Turning his back to the SUV, he clicked the knob atop the Puxing. "Testing. Sam, you hear me?"

"I'm right here," she said dryly from inside the vehicle.

Malcolm grinned. The joke was dumb. It was dumb the first time she did it three jobs ago. Now, it was a ritual, a light moment before the storm. "Radio," he said, feigning annoyance.

She chuckled behind him. "Testing. I read you," came through the earpiece. The girl's weird accent was a collected timeline of globe-hopping with her Australian oilman father. Twenty-three, quadrilingual, and versed in a dozen local customs. Master Sonu already had his sights set on making her a Librarian.

Dry grass crunched as Orlovski stepped around beside him. The all-black getup made him look like a disembodied head floating in the night. His short, straw-blond hair only added to the Russian's paleness. He rested a latex-gloved hand on the kukri, Amballwa, at his waist. He nodded to Malcolm's bare and tattooed arms. "You need bug spray?"

"I'm good," Malcolm said, pulling on a pair of thin leather gloves. The open palms made them fit awkwardly but left his tattoos accessible. "Ready?"

Orlovski pushed his ear bud in and nodded. "Hope they don't have any damned dogs."

"Hopefully." Most animals hated demons. Except, of course, demonkind linked to animals. Ghouls and jackals, lamia and snakes, werebeasts and their species' breed. In those instances, animals loved their demonic masters. Malcolm didn't expect dogs with this one, whatever kind it was. "Got your papers?"

The Russian patted his back pocket.

"What's your name?" Like Sam's stupid joke, the drill was ritual.

"Eduard Lukov," Orlovski said, his voice coming in through Malcolm's radio. "I sell picture frames and am on a working vacation. You are Adam Jones, my distributor."

"Good." Shutting the tailgate, Malcolm looked in the side door. Sam hunched in the seat, peering at an open laptop, shotgun resting on the floor. "Sam, you ready?"

She gave a thumbs-up.

"Keep the scanner open," Orlovski said. "Call if you see or hear anything."

Her brow arched. "Understood."

Orlovski shut the door. The dark tinting nearly masked her screen-lit silhouette.

"All right," Malcolm said, excitement tingling across his shoulders, adrenaline priming his senses. "Let's do it."

The two men followed the dirt path back to the road and headed up the rough asphalt. A large sign warning that trespassers would be shot hung from a sturdy pipe-fence gate. They climbed over it and continued on a gravel drive. Gnarled trees hid the moon, only allowing scattered pools of pale light. Their footsteps crunched quietly. The drive turned, following the hill's curve. Malcolm watched the shaded woods for movement as Orlovski led just a few feet ahead.

Seven months ago, Emily Anders, a student at MSU, went missing. Her family, desperate and frustrated at the police's lack of progress, turned to Daniel Hendricks, a local psychic.

Daniel, who was one of the few legitimate psychics Malcolm had ever known, sensed a great and evil power at work. He saw a house, a tiny cell, and an image of a black form with emerald eyes. No one ever found Emily Anders.

Four weeks ago, Tiffany Mayhew walked out of a coffee shop with a grande low-fat latte and never made it home. Two weeks later, her family turned to Daniel Hendricks. After feeling several of Tiffany's personal effects and visiting the parking lot where her car had been found, Daniel told the Mayhews that he couldn't get a good reading and returned their money. Fifteen minutes later, he emailed Malcolm what he had seen.

Orlovski raised a hand and dropped to a knee. Crouching low, Malcolm hurried up beside him. A two-story house sat at the top of the hill, silhouetted against the sky like a castle on some cheap book cover. Pale yellow glowed from three of the blind-covered windows. Bluish light flickered through a fourth, likely a TV.

Malcolm pulled open a Velcro pouch at his belt, careful to keep it quiet, and drew out a black metal tube. He extended a plastic antenna from one end and removed the lens cap from the other. He thumbed the button on the back. "Camera One is on." Malcolm unfolded the rubberized, segmented legs from the bottom and wrapped them around a slender tree. "Sam, you reading this?"

Her voice came through the ear bud. "I have it."

Malcolm peered down the top of the camera, aiming it as best he could. "You have the full house?"

"Yes. Don't see anyone outside," Sam said. "Looks like a motion light at the right corner. Stay clear of it."

"Thanks. We'll head around the side and set the second camera before going in. Let us know if you see anything."

"Okay."

Staying low, they skirted the edge of the clearing. As they passed behind a decrepit woodshed, Malcolm's foot hit an empty paint can, sending it skittering into the brush. *Shit!*

The two men froze in a crouch, watching the house.

Malcolm took five slow breaths then whispered, "Sam, everything clear?"

"No movement."

Orlovski shot a cocked eyebrow at Malcolm. Thirty seconds later, they continued on.

Passing a blackened burn pile, they circled to the rear. Light shone through a back-door window overlooking a narrow deck. A cinderblock building loomed twenty yards behind the house, its only opening a single metal door. A tin-roofed carport stood off to one side, sheltering the dark shape of a cargo van.

Malcolm pointed to the van, and Orlovski pulled out a stubby night scope. He peered through the eyepiece, nodded, then offered it over. Taking the monocular, Malcolm studied the vehicle in shades of luminescent green.

Daniel's vision in the parking lot had showed Tiffany Mayhew being dragged into the same windowless van, a long scrape along its left fender, license plate beginning with "P3Y." He'd seen the emerald-eyed shadow, a dark room, pain.

The van was registered to an Arnold Hobb, whose last known address was a duplex in Ozark, just a few miles outside the city. It had taken the hunters just a week to track him down to the isolated house. Hobb was a hefty man, mid-thirties. Contractor. They'd seen him out with another man, long-legged and thin. Malcolm had gotten close to them at a little burger joint. The cobalt scarab tattooed on his right wrist didn't detect a demon. He could have checked them with the eye in his palm to see if they were familiars. But if they were, it would only guarantee their master would know they were coming for it.

"Sam, do you see this?" Orlovski asked as he mounted his wireless camera to the top of a wide brick grill.

"Little to the right," she said. "Good. I have it."

Studying the house, Malcolm ran a gloved finger across his bristled chin. The back door looked the best. Two minutes, and they could have it swept. Sam could radio if the suspects fled. Still ... they had no proof. He trusted Daniel, but if they were wrong...

Malcolm chewed his lip. He glanced back to the windowless building. It looked more like a bunker than a shed. The hunters shared a look and nodded.

The cinderblock walls stood twelve feet high, slightly tapered to one side along the building's twenty-foot length. The construction was new, maybe a year, and a hell of a lot better made than the house appeared. Malcolm frowned, noticing the bar across the steel door. It appeared even less of a shed. More like a cell. The Russian must have felt it too because his hand moved to Amballwa's handle.

A padlock held the bar shut. Malcolm removed a curved shim from a pocket and worked it down the lock's shackle until it popped open. Careful to keep it from scraping loudly, he pulled the bar aside, nodded to his partner, then inched the door open.

Blackness. The stink of sweat and filth pressed out like a physical force.

Orlovski raised the night scope and let out a long sigh. "Shit." He pulled the door open, spilling a wedge of moonlight across the concrete floor. He stepped inside. "Clear."

Scrunching his nose, Malcolm followed. Dark shapes hung in the shadows, slowly gaining form as his eyes adjusted. Straps and manacles dangled from a gridwork of steel rings. He inspected a sturdy wooden table, angled like a medieval rack. Dark splotches stained the edges and the floor along the bottom. "I think this is the place."

Orlovski grunted. He offered the monocular, its green-lit eyepiece casting a dim glow across the room. Serrated metal hung on the wall beside them. Reluctantly, Malcolm accepted it.

The scene around them was worse than he'd imagined. Various hooks, blades, clamps, and other perverse torture implements covered two of the walls. An acetylene torch stood in the corner. "Jesus."

"What is it?" Sam's voice asked through the radio.

"Sex dungeon," Orlovski replied.

Malcolm's jaw tightened. The description barely did the room justice.

A creak came from the back corner. Malcolm drew Hounacier from her sheath. He set the night scope on a cluttered table and pulled a slender flashlight from his belt. Amballwa in hand, Orlovski flicked on his light, shining a brilliant white beam across the room.

Pegboard slats covered the wall, their metal hooks filled with leather and chromed implements. Malcolm shined his own light, sweeping it along the corners.

Another creak and a whimper. Both lights zeroed in on the right side. A twisted black harness hung to the boards. The two men shared a glance then slowly approached, lights steady and weapons raised.

A metal latch glinted, partially hidden under the harness web. Malcolm followed the seam, seeing a narrow rectangle door beneath the pegboard. Orlovski stepped to the side, nodded. Malcolm twisted the little latch and pulled the door. It opened with a loud creak.

The reek of sweat and urine poured from a shallow closet. A mound of grimy cloth covered the floor. It writhed.

Instinct took hold. Malcolm raised his machete. He saw the tangle of auburn hair and desperate, terrified eyes behind the strands. Tiffany Mayhew was alive.

"Hold," Malcolm said to Orlovski. Hounacier still raised, he pocketed the flashlight and extended his left palm toward the huddled girl.

She pressed herself against the corner, averting her eyes.

"Look at it," he ordered.

Tiffany's blue eyes slowly lifted. She looked at Malcolm then at his palm. No reaction.

Malcolm sheathed Hounacier and knelt. "You're going to be okay, Tiffany. We're here to help."

The girl's dry lips quivered. "Are … they gone?"

"No," Malcolm said. "We'll take care of them. We just need you to stay here for a minute—"

"No!" she screamed. "No! It's a monst—"

Malcolm dove in and clamped a hand over Tiffany's mouth. "Shh! Quiet."

The girl froze save a terrified tremble.

Malcolm wrapped his other arm around her and pulled her close. "It's all right," he whispered. "You're safe now."

"Sam," Orlovski hissed. "Any movement?"

"Negative."

Malcolm let out a sigh. "Tiffany, I need you to stay quiet, okay?"

She nodded.

Slowly, he released her mouth. "Monsters. How many are there?"

Tiffany didn't say anything for several breaths. Finally, "One."

"One," he repeated for Sam to hear. "What does it look like?"

She swallowed and cinched her eyes. "It's … big. Claws. Teeth like … nails. Green eyes."

Malcolm nodded. "What color is it?"

"Gray, like … smoke."

"Smokey? Its head," he said. "Is it feline, like a tiger?"

She nodded.

"That's a yes."

"Looks like we found one of Allan's mist cats," Sam said.

Orlovski frowned, his low growl resonating in Malcolm's earpiece.

A year before, Tiamat, the Mother of Demons, had been summoned in Tuscany. Before they'd killed her, the beast had hatched at least half a dozen new demon breeds onto the earth. Allan and Luc had encountered one in Naples only two months later. Allan, who loved naming the new species, had dubbed it mist cat. Arguably, it was one of his better names. All they knew about them was that they were fast, could leap incredible spans, and silver did fuck-all against them.

The Russian drew his pistol and ejected a magazine. "Switching to brass jacket, amethyst tips." He slapped the new mag in place and racked the slide.

"Tiffany," Malcolm said, his voice calm. "How many men are there aside from the monster?"

She swallowed then shook her head. "I don't know."

"It's important, Tiffany. Try to remember."

"Two," she said uneasily.

"Two? Are you sure?"

"Movement!" Sam snapped. "Back door."

Malcolm and Orlovski shared a look. "Tiffany," he said. "We need you to stay here, all right?"

She grabbed his arm. "No! No!"

He stood. "You'll be safe."

"Coming out the upper front window," Sam said. "Shit, it's big."

Malcolm hurried out of the crawlspace. "We'll be back. Stay here."

Squeezing Hounacier, he followed Orlovski to the open doorway.

Orlovski pressed himself against the wall, Amballwa gripped tight in his hand. "Sam, where are they?" he whispered.

"Man headed your way. Has a gun. Can't see the demon."

"Keep watching." Malcolm replied, voice low.

Leaves crunched outside, drawing closer. Malcolm held his breath.

A long shadow, cast from the house above, grew in the doorway, sealing out even more of the light. The footsteps slowed then stopped.

A bead of sweat trickled past the corner of Malcolm's eye. Slowly, he let out his breath. Through the cinderblocks, his enemy was only three feet away.

The shadow swayed. Leaves crunched, and the tip of a black pistol cautiously poked through the open doorway. It inched further until a hand became visible.

In a blur, Orlovski grabbed the shooter's wrist and yanked. A portly man yelped as he fell through the doorway, his cry cut off as the kukri slashed his throat to the bone. Blood sprayed out in a fan, hitting Malcolm's cheek. Gurgling, Arnold Hobb crumpled to the floor, blood pooling beneath him.

Without a word, Orlovski charged through the open doorway and out into the yard.

Malcolm ran out behind him, cutting wide in case of a shooter. "Sam, where is it?" He scanned the darkened woods for movement.

"Not sure. It looked like it jumped into the trees."

He craned his neck, searching the tangled canopy. Beyond the house, above the drive, a flash of vivid green eyes. *There!* Leaves shuddered as the beast sprang to the neighboring trees and into shadow. "Front of the house!"

Malcolm hurried to where he'd seen the beast, Orlovski a few feet behind. He just had to get close enough for his tattoo to pinpoint it.

They came around the corner when Sam's voice yelled over the radio. "Behind you!"

A gunshot blasted from the house. Malcolm wheeled in time to see Orlovski pitch forward. The long-legged man stood in the front doorway, shotgun aimed.

Diving to the side, Malcolm scrambled behind a giant woodpile. He drew his sawed-off and clicked off the safety.

Orlovski groaned and tried to stand. A second blast hit the Russian's leg, and he crumpled.

"Taras!" Sam screamed.

"Shooter," Malcolm hissed. "Where is he?"

"Still on the porch."

Remington in hand, Malcolm peeked around. The man swung the gun up and straight at him. Malcolm dropped, splinters exploding above him. Logs buckled and rolled off the pile. Keeping low, Malcolm scurried to the other side, hoping the gunman was still trained on where he'd just shot. He rounded the edge, spotted the man, and fired.

The shooter leaped to the side, and the window behind him shattered inward. Some of the shot must have hit because he lurched as he raised his gun back. Malcolm aimed the second barrel.

Four quick shots rang out. The man dropped his gun, staggered, then fell.

Orlovski lay on his side in a haze of smoke, pistol outstretched. Malcolm charged up to his partner. "Taras, hold on!"

Groaning, Orlovski shot the dead man once more before dropping the pistol and clutching his bloodied leg.

Malcolm clambered up beside him and checked the wound. "Shit." Blood soaked the Russian's pants around three large holes in the back of his thigh.

Orlovski let out a long hiss, his jaw tight. "I think it's broken."

"Hold on, brother." Malcolm sheathed Hounacier and flicked open a knife. He slit the black fatigues just above the wound and peeled them open. Blood coated the back of Orlovski's thigh, pouring from the ragged holes.

The Russian's breaths quickened, his eyes clenched. "How bad?"

"You'll live." He sliced off the rest of the pant leg to make a tourniquet.

Orlovski clawed the ground beside him, reaching for his fallen kukri. "Amballwa."

Pausing his work, Malcolm grabbed the holy blade and set it in his partner's gloved hand. "Here."

Orlovski clutched the handle, pressing it against him. "Breathing ... really hurts."

"I'm sure it does," Malcolm said, forcing the dread from his voice. In Orlovski's vocabulary, "really hurts," was somewhere beyond agonizing. "Vest saved you."

"I can bring the trauma kit," Sam offered.

"No," Malcolm said. "Stay there."

"But—"

"No!" He slipped the cloth binding under Orlovski's leg, and the Russian howled. Malcolm started the knot when the blue scarab tattoo on his wrist suddenly scuttled to the side. Dropping the tourniquet, Malcolm spun and ripped Hounacier from her sheath.

A lean creature crept down the trunk of a nearby tree. Smokey vapor wisped off its skin, impossible to differentiate from its gray fur. A low snarl came from behind its bared fangs. Slits of vibrant green shone from the pupils of its cat-like eyes.

Malcolm stood, Hounacier before him. The beast cocked its head and leaped, trailing vapor like a comet's tail. Growling, it circled to the side, pacing like a jungle cat, then stood erect.

Leaves crackled as Orlovski fumbled for his pistol. "Move!"

"Stay down." Narrowing his eyes, Malcolm stared down the demon before him, seven towering feet, claws splayed.

"Move!" Orlovski rolled to the side and fired. Bullets peppered the beast with blossoming puffs of mist. One took it in the face, and the monster roared.

It charged, Orlovski's rounds ineffectively pluming off its body. Holding his ground, Malcolm displayed his left palm. His skin itched as the tattooed eye stretched open. The beast froze, averting its eyes. Smokey mist blew away as if caught in a tempest.

Seizing the opening, Malcolm attacked, hand still displayed. He slashed Hounacier across, aiming for the demon's neck, but the monster stumbled back. It lurched away from Malcolm's next swing but not before Hounacier bit into its shoulder.

It sprang to a tree then onto the porch roof. Hateful green eyes glared down as it paced back and forth, claws clacking on tin.

Malcolm followed, staying between it and his partner. Blood dripped from Hounacier, evaporating before it hit the ground. *Time to end this.* Orlovski's leg needed tending, and he had internal injuries. Malcolm stepped back and knelt, feeling for his sawed-off. Orlovski's brass and amethyst bullets were as useless as silver. Malcolm's loads were iron, bronze, marble, and quartz. He hoped one of those would work. His fingers curled around the grip.

The mist cat crouched on its forelimbs, obviously unconcerned with the shotgun. It leaped.

Malcolm whipped the gun up and fired. The blast caught the flying demon cat in the chest. Yowling, it recoiled and hit the ground just a few feet away. Malcolm dropped the empty sawed-off and lunged, hacking Hounacier down into the wounded creature. The blade bit into its back as it tried to rise. It staggered and snapped its teeth. Sidestepping, Malcolm brought the machete down into the demon's skull.

Yellow-tinged turquoise fire spewed from the demon's wounds, quickly spreading out over its corpse. Its burning blood shimmered along Hounacier's blade. Malcolm stared at the ethereal flames. Mesmerized, he raised the flaming blade up toward his face, the cool metal touching his temple beside his right eye.

No! He fought the machete, struggling to pull it away. "Not there." His arm shook, unable to overcome Hounacier's desire. Malcolm grabbed his wrist and managed to gain some control. The trembling blade moved as a dousing rod, finding an open patch of skin on his left inner forearm. Allowing Hounacier its gift, he loosened control. It sliced along his flesh. Malcolm hissed as flaming demon blood entered the shallow cut.

Hounacier ceased her fight. A trio of pale, golden lines glowed beneath Malcolm's skin for a brief moment then faded.

"Thank you," he breathed.

Orlovski groaned behind him.

Malcolm turned back to his injured partner. Orlovski's waxy face looked ghostly, hued in the demon fire's light.

"What ... were you doing there?" Orlovski moaned.

Malcolm tied the tourniquet and cinched it tight. "Fixing you up."

Orlovski shook his head. "No. Y ... you cut yourself."

"Don't worry about it." Taking a nearby stick, Malcolm

looped it into the binding and tightened the tourniquet down. "We're going to get you out of here."

Samantha's voice yelled though his ear bud. "Mal, scanner got a call on Tiffany Mayhew. She called in!"

"What?" Malcolm looked back at the cinderblock shed, its door still open. "Where is she? Did she leave?"

"I ... I didn't see her. She must have gotten out when I was watching the fight. Mal, police are coming."

Fuck. "*How long?*"

"*Don't know.*"

Malcolm ground his teeth. Orlovski shot, three corpses, police imminent. At a guess, twenty minutes before the first police car. In thirty, every cop in the county would be all over. What had Tiffany told them?

"What do we do?" Sam asked.

A faint light moved within the torture room's door. *There!* Malcolm ran to the building and looked inside. Hobb's body now lay on its back, his blood pool disturbed by bare footprints. Tiffany sat huddled in the corner, clutching a serrated knife, her face half visible in the glow of a cell phone pressed to her ear. "Tiffany?"

She flinched as she saw him then seemed to relax.

He smiled, keeping his voice calm, "Is that the police?"

Tiffany nodded.

Keeping clear of the blood, Malcolm stepped inside. "The bad guys are gone now." He held out a hand. "Let me talk to them."

She seemed to hesitate then slowly offered up the phone, her blood-stained hand trembling.

"Hello! Hello, Tiffany!" said a woman's voice from the speaker.

Malcolm took the phone and clicked it off.

"Why did you do that?" Tiffany yelled, eyes wide.

"We need your help. My partner is hurt."

"But—"

"Tiffany!" Malcolm drew a breath. "Please. Help him."

She wiped her tear-streaked face, smearing a little of Hobb's blood on it in the process.

"Mal," Sam said. "What are you doing?"

"Trust me." He helped Tiffany to her feet and led her out of her prison to where Orlovski lay.

She froze, seeing the demon's corpse, blanketed in ghostly fire. Already, some of its features had begun to melt back into the form of its now dead host.

"Tiffany," Malcolm urged, pulling her hand. "It's dead. But my friend needs you."

"Mal," Sam repeated, her voice strained. "What the hell are you doing?"

Orlovski looked up as Malcolm and Tiffany knelt beside him.

"We've ... gotta go." He gulped air. "The police ..."

Malcolm smiled comfortingly. "Will be here soon. You've lost a lot of blood. Do you remember your name?"

The Russian closed his eyes then nodded. "I'm Eduard Lukov. I sell picture frames."

"Mal," Sam's voice echoed in his ear. "You can't be serious."

"That's right," Malcolm said. "Eduard, this is Tiffany. She's going to stay with you, okay? Tiffany, did you tell the police about us?"

She nodded. "Yes. I told them you let me out and killed one of them."

"All right," he said. "We need you to change your story for us. Eduard saved you. Only him. They brought him in a couple hours ago and tortured him. But he escaped. He killed one, took his gun, then let you out of your cell."

"No. That's not what happened."

He set his hand on hers. "Yes, it is. That's what you need to tell them. He took the man's gun, let you out, and killed the other two. We need you to say that. Do you understand? Will you do that for us?"

"Yes."

"Thank you." He looked down at Orlovski. "You got the story? They tortured you. You escaped. Got it?"

The hunter resignedly nodded. "Do it."

Malcolm punched him in the eye.

Tiffany tried to grab Malcolm's fist before it smashed into

Orlovski's nose, unleashing a stream of blood. "Stop!"
"Tortured him," Malcolm repeated. "Beat him. Now, help me get his gear off."
Carefully, they removed Orlovski's web belt. He stifled a cry as they worked the ballistic vest off of him. An enormous swollen and purple bruise spread out just below his shoulder blade. Several ribs appeared broken, but the impact missed his spine. Thankfully, the individual pellet strikes weren't visible.
Malcolm fished the fake IDs from the Russian's back pocket and took the three spare magazines from his ammo pouches.
Sam spoke in his ear. Panic was gone, replaced by the stone-cold tone of a Valducan. "Mal, we have ten minutes, tops, before we have to be out of here."
"Give me five. Count 'em down." Leaving Orlovski and the girl, repeating their lie again and again, Malcolm ran up the porch and into the house. Trash and grime coated everything in a yellowish film. Empty beer cans and dirty plates blanketed every flat surface, their contents rotting and speckled with roach shit. He dropped the IDs beside a mound of unopened mail atop the dining table. In the kitchen, beside the back door leading to the cinderblock prison, he deposited two of the magazines loaded with specialty ammo in a drawer. Malcolm removed a pair of his own shotgun rounds from his gear and planted them as well. If the police and FBI were going to believe Orlovski got the gun from his captors, they needed to find more of the unique ammo than just inside the dead men's bodies. Buying it wouldn't be too difficult considering everything else they'd find there.
"Four minutes."
Sweat ran down his face as Malcolm hurried out to the cinderblock bunker. Searching the walls, he found a knife with a long, curved blade, its handle wrapped in electric tape. Not a perfect match for Hounacier's and Amballwa's cut marks but close enough. He smeared the blade in Hobb's coagulating blood pool then rolled the body over to hide the disturbance. After slipping the last of Orlovski's magazines deep into the dead man's pocket, Malcolm pocketed the dead man's pistol and ran back out.
"Three minutes," Sam said.

He removed Orlovski's camera from the grill. "Almost done!" The turquoise fire had begun to wane, revealing a stocky man with buzz-cut hair. Malcolm slid the blade into one of Hounacier's cuts and returned to Orlovski.

"Here." He slipped the tape-wrapped handle into his partner's hand. The latex gloves were already piled with his other effects beside him. "This is the weapon you used."

Orlovski only grunted. Maybe he knew what was about to happen. The hardest part.

"Tiffany, you can't tell them about the monster."

"Why?" she asked. "It's real. I did see it."

"I know," Malcolm said. "But no one will believe you. In a few minutes, any trace of it will be gone."

She shook her head. "But …"

"I have a friend. Daniel. He'll contact you. You can tell him everything. He's the one that found you."

"Two minutes, Mal," Sam urged. "We gotta go."

Malcolm touched Orlovski's other hand, still clutching Amballwa's jeweled handle. "It's time."

Orlovski shook his head, pressing the blade flat against him. "No. No, you can't."

"She's evidence," Mal said, prying the Russian's weak fingers open. "We'll keep her safe."

"Please, Mal," Orlovski begged. Tears welled in the blond man's eyes. "Don't take her from me."

"You'll have her again. I promise." He pulled the bloodied kukri free.

"Please!" Orlovski sobbed. "Don't take her from me!"

Malcolm tried not to look at him as he scooped up Orlovski's effects. It was the only way. Without a word, he hurried back down the drive, stopping long enough to retrieve his own camera, then raced to where Sam waited in the SUV.

She didn't speak to him as he threw the gear inside and gunned the engine. She was still too new to understand. After the first mile, he slowed to more reasonable speed. Locals only slightly sped along the Ozark roads. Two hills later, he pulled to the side, allowing three flashing squad cars room to pass. They had no idea what they were in store for.

CHAPTER 3

"Jesus, what a circus," Sam said as they pulled into Cox South Hospital.

Three different reporters stood out front, each meticulously placed so that their cameramen wouldn't catch the others. News vans from across the state cluttered the already cramped parking lot, and even more raced toward Springfield to join them. They already knew the name Eduard Lukov, and while the police and FBI were too busy to dig that far into their victim-hero's identity, the press had nothing else to do but chip into Orlovski's already weak alias.

Twenty minutes after leaving the crime scene, Allan and other Valducans had already begun the elaborate and laborious task of transforming Eduard Lukov into a man that reporters and internet sleuths could easily find and then write off as uninteresting. Malcolm's job now was to get the Russian out of there before anyone cracked the tenuous illusion.

He managed to find a space in the parking garage. They'd rented a non-descript Toyota on the off-chance that anyone might somehow recognize the black SUV from the night in question. How the hell had such a simple job turned into such a world-class fuck up? Media and police attention were one thing. Hospitals and questionable injuries was another. Somehow, on Malcolm's watch, he'd managed to pull them both off. Thankfully, neither of them were dead or holy weapons confiscated. At least, not yet.

He checked himself in the visor mirror and cinched his olive-colored tie. The black, plastic-framed glasses seemed an inadequate disguise, but they'd worked many times before. They also drew attention away from the strip of Sam's makeup, masking the red line from when Hounacier had tried to mark his temple. Long, steel-gray sleeves hid his tattooed arms.

"You ready for this?"

Sam nodded, her jaw tense. She stepped out and shut the door behind her. Malcolm followed. Sam's ponytail bounced ahead of him with each step, its curled end forming it into a long, auburn teardrop.

Dual rows of glass doors slid apart, releasing a gust of air conditioning into the June air. Three uniformed police stood near one wall. They glanced at the newcomers for only an instant before their attention returned to their white Styrofoam coffee cups. Malcolm made his way to the reception desk and waited.

A pale nurse dressed in pastel-molted scrubs looked up. Her hair was cut short, shiny, like a smooth, brown helmet. "May help you?"

"We're here to visit Eduard Lukov."

The receptionist's plastic smile cracked. Her eyes darted to the three policemen and back so fast that she probably didn't even realize it.

"My name is Adam Jones," Malcolm continued. "I should be on the list."

She clicked her keyboard a few times, then the smile returned to her pink-painted lips. "I'll just need to see some identification, Mister Jones."

Malcolm drew the wallet from his back pocket. "I understand." He flipped it, revealing the beautiful, two-thousand-dollar Oklahoma driver's license featuring his face and alias.

She squinted at it, not really appreciating the forger's masterful work. "You'll need to sign in." She offered up a clipboard.

"Excuse me," said a female voice.

Shit. Malcolm turned to see a pretty Hispanic woman in a

mint green pantsuit. "Yes?"

She smiled. "Fernanda Guzman, *Springfield News-Leader*. I couldn't help but overhear. Are you familiar with Eduard Lukov?"

"No comment," Malcolm said, noting the little black recorder in the woman's hand. He scratched his alias onto the log beneath Sam's.

"Do you know of his condition?" Fernanda asked.

"Not yet." He accepted a pair of visitor passes from the nurse, keeping his palm downward to hide the tattoos.

"How do you know Mister Lukov?" the reporter pressed.

Need to move before they bring a camera. Malcolm clipped the plastic badge on his shirt, smiled at the nurse again, and hurried toward the elevator.

"Mister Jones," the reporter said, her heels clacking on the linoleum behind them. "Do you know why Eduard Lukov was abducted?"

Malcolm stepped into the elevator behind Sam and hit the "Close" button.

"Did he see—" The doors slid shut.

"Bloody hell," Sam growled "Thought we were made."

Malcolm fidgeted with his tie. "Just relax."

"Relax? They'll be snapping our pictures when we leave."

"They should have a back door they'll let us use."

She shook her head. "And if they don't?"

"They always do." He squeezed her shoulder. "We'll be fine."

The doors opened to the third floor. White halls, their travelers hesitant to make eye contact, low voices tinged with concern and grief. Hospital smell, the scent of cleaners overlaying the stink of humanity. It was the same everywhere but always a little unique, like different women wearing the same perfume. Malcolm slowed his steps, blending in.

A blue-uniformed security guard checked their badges before allowing them in Orlovski's room.

"There he is," Malcolm said before closing the door behind him.

Orlovski lay stretched out in his bed, his leg encased in a

blue cast. A purple bruise circled his right eye and down along his bandaged nose. "About time you got here."

Sam bent to give the Russian a hug. "We brought you a friend."

"A friend?"

Sam peeled open her laptop satchel's Velcro flap. "She misses you."

Orlovski's mood seemed to brighten instantly. Eyes wide in anticipation, he watched her open the bag like a kid opening a birthday present, its contents known and long coveted. His fingers reached forward as she removed Amballwa. Sam gave him the kukri, and he held it against his chest, eyes closed, his breaths long and relieved. "Thank you. Thank you."

"How are you doing, brother?" Malcolm asked, watching the door in case some nurse might stroll in to find her patient cradling a giant knife.

"Six-hour surgery removing buckshot and putting a plate in. Three cracked ribs but no serious internal injuries." He snorted. "You broke my nose."

"Police interview you?"

Orlovski nodded. "Over an hour this morning before the doctors kicked them out. They'll be back."

"You hear anything about Tiffany?" Malcolm asked.

"Yeah, sounds like she recanted on your little story that I was a prisoner."

Sam's lips pursed. She shot Malcolm a little glare. "I told you she'd crack."

Malcolm shrugged. "That's unfortunate."

"Unfortunate?" Sam asked.

"For her," Malcolm said. "If she told them that there was a monster, then two mysterious men showed up and saved her, leaving one behind. Then say that there was no monster, and Taras was a prisoner who got free, and then back again to the original story, she sounds insane. The story was as much for her as it was for us. Right now, we have enough information out there that Taras' alibi should check out for at least the next forty-eight hours."

"All the more reason to get him out of here," Sam said.

"It's not going to be easy," Orlovski said. "They're not just going to let me go. I killed those men."

Malcolm smiled. "Sure they will. You're a hero. They've got enough in that house to keep them busy for now." He surveyed the cast running from Orlovski's hip all the way down to his ankle. "They give you an idea how long you'll be wearing that thing?"

"A few months." Orlovski's smile drew to a thin line. He glared at the cast like it was some living thing, a parasite that might have latched on to him. "With PT, they estimate a year before full recovery."

"A year," Master Schmidt growled. It wasn't a question; it was a scolding. Malcolm's man was out of circulation during one of the hardest times in the Valducans' eight-century existence. With only thirteen active knights and another four known independents, only seventeen hunters protected a world of billions. Two years ago, it was sixty. Now, they were one less.

"Femoral fractures are tricky," Malcolm said. He'd found an empty waiting alcove nestled on the second floor. Tablet in hand, he scanned his latest field report as Schmidt buzzed in his earpiece. "I suggest we allot eighteen months before active field work."

Schmidt sighed. "Any issues with the story?"

"None. Police found charred bone fragments they suspect to be from other victims. Everyone's attention is on that."

"When can you extract him?"

"Hospital won't release him for another few hours," Malcolm answered.

"Then what?"

He shrugged, still scrolling though the report. "Head down to Chile. Should take us ten days. We can hold the fort there. Sam can continue training, and Master Sonu can start her as a Librarian. Give Luiza and Matt some field time for a change."

Schmidt harrumphed. "Luiza's pregnant."

Malcolm paused. "Really?"

"Announced it Sunday. Needless to say, we'll need to keep

her off the front line for a while. You and Matt will run point while Taras heals."

"I see." Malcolm frowned.

"That's not going to be a problem, I assume."

"No," Malcolm said. A year before, Matt Hollis had been the black sheep of demon hunters. Possessed with an entity no one understood, he'd been invited, against Malcolm's protests, into the Valducans' fold. Words were exchanged. Even after Matt had more than proven himself, revealing that the spirit inside him was that of his holy weapon Dämoren, the two never quite mended. Malcolm didn't hold a grudge. But given the information he knew at the time, he still stood by his suspicion of the outsider. Matt never really seemed to accept that. They were brothers now. But they'd never be friends. "Not at all."

"Good," Schmidt said. Silence. Car noise rumbled in the background. "We think we have another mist cat in Croatia."

Hounacier's cut tingled beneath Malcolm's sleeve. "Already? It's moving fast." Tiamat's broods had taken the form of flying, human-faced eels. Each one unleashed its own unique demonic breed on anyone it attacked. How many demons one could conjure was anyone's guess. Maybe it would just keep doing it until killed, or until every demon of that type was accounted for. Malcolm pictured it like some sort of interdimensional queue, or maybe bullets in a magazine, each spirit waiting its turn. If they didn't kill that eel soon, mist cats might become one of the new dominant species.

"We'll need your report as soon as possible."

Malcolm tapped the screen. "Sending it now. The short of it is, brass and amethyst are ineffective. One of the loads in my shotgun worked, but I don't know which. List is included. Judging by the two men, I'd say Allan's theory that they can make familiars is valid."

"Do you think them werebeasts?" Schmidt asked.

"Nothing suggests transformation." Malcolm scanned his other inbox. He'd neglected it the past month since Daniel had first contacted him. He noticed two emails from Ulises. One titled "Great News" from three weeks ago. Six days later, "Call me." They hadn't spoken in months. Once this business with

Orlovski was settled, he'd give him a call. Malcolm saw another message from an unfamiliar address but recognized the name. Natasha Luison.

The title read, "Important: It's Tasha."

"Uwe suspects the recent attacks along the coast are from a new lycanthrope," Schmidt said. "Something aquatic."

"Really?" Malcolm said, not really listening. Four years. How had she found him?

"If so, it's going to make them very difficult to track." He opened the message.

Malcolm,

It's been a long time. No one knew how to contact you, but I managed to find this address in some of Ulises' things. There's no real easy way to say this, but I have some terrible news that you need to know.

"Ah," Schmidt was saying, "Your field report came through. I'll make sure Allan reviews it. Expect a call from him once he does."

"Always do," Malcolm said, still reading. A horrible dread welled in his stomach. *Oh shit.*

"Fine, then. Call when you leave the hospital or if anything changes."

Malcolm pursed his lips. "Master Schmidt, I won't be able to go to Chile."

"What?"

"I just received a message." Malcolm drew a breath. Held it. "Ulises … my mentor … is dead. I need to go home."

CHAPTER 4

Lush tree canopy blurred past the windows as Malcolm's bus barreled down the I10 toward New Orleans. Home. The rhythmic thumping of spacers in the seemingly endless bridge through the swamplands sounded like a metronome keeping time. Counting down the miles. Brackish water glistened in the trench between the east and west spans. The occasional fisherman floated through the treeless lane. Malcolm peered down as they neared the next mile marker. Someone had written a name on the window glass with black marker, its stylized letters impossible to read. Through the scrubbed and faded scrawl, he could almost spot the place where Ulises and he had sunk two dead familiars nine years earlier. Now, a limbless log floated there, its barkless surface encrusted with sunning turtles.

After the hospital had released Orlovski, they'd loaded him into the back of the SUV for Sam to make the five-thousand-mile drive to the Valducans' wind farm in Chile. Malcolm didn't envy the infinitely shitty roads the Russian and his broken leg would have to endure. Once they were off, Malcolm drove to Jackson, Mississippi. Any FBI in search of what might have happened to their now missing witness would find the Toyota rented by his only known associate, Alex Jones, returned to the rental car company, sending them off in the wrong direction. The next morning, Malcolm purchased a bus ticket and, with only a suitcase, a locking guitar case, and a backpack, had started the last leg of his journey home.

His response to Tasha's email had been short.
Thank you for letting me know. I'm on my way.
I'll call you when I arrive.

-Mal

The long drive had afforded a good deal of time to think, only fueling his need to get there. During his night in Jackson, he'd searched for news articles about the murder. The most he'd found was a short blurb, detailing the briefest of facts. Ulises Belair, 81, found murdered in his home. His house was ransacked, and his head was missing. Police had no suspects.

Malcolm, however, did have a suspect. Tiamat's cultists, the ones who had killed dozens of his fellow hunters and their holy weapons, had taken the heads of any knights they hadn't offered as sacrifice. Hounacier had helped kill their god. This reeked of retribution.

Ulises' two last emails had been brief. They always were.

Malcolm, you need to come home. There's something you must see.

Ulises

The other simply said, "Call me," and his phone number.

Malcolm had messaged the Valducans what he knew. Ulises was never a Valducan, but he was a hunter. An attack on one was still an attack on all. The full strength of the Order would come down on who or what had murdered him.

The balmy stink of humidity rot, diesel fumes, and urine greeted Malcolm as he stepped off the bus. He breathed deep, savoring the all-too-familiar smell. It carried memories. Some bad, most good. An unwashed woman, her face speckled with tiny scabs, sauntered past, pushing a yellowed stroller piled with bags. New Orleans held its own special breed of homeless residents. The city was a magnet for demonic energy, and many former familiars, their masters long dead, were drawn here as well. Most never knew why they felt the calling. A few managed seemingly normal lives. The rest were simply insane. Junkies looking for a fix they didn't know or understand. San Francisco was the same way.

He booked a room at a hotel on Canal Street. Not knowing how long his stay would be, he paid cash for the first week. The clerk, a pretty girl with a tattoo of an eagle on her neck and about ten pounds of braids piled atop her head, didn't seem the least put out when Malcolm didn't give her any ID.

"That'll require a two-hundred-dollar security deposit," she said, her perfectly sculpted brow sharply arched.

Malcolm handed her the money, took his plastic pass-card, and headed up to the third floor. Room 318 smelled of cheap potpourri spray and old cigarettes. He removed a photograph of himself, Nick, and Colin grinning outside Notre Dame Cathedral. Out of the three knights, Malcolm was the only one still alive. He propped it up on the bedside table, making sure it faced both the door to the hall and to the adjoining room. A tiny motion sensor hidden in the grooved frame would activate a micro-camera and notify his phone. The unit itself was worth more than anything else Malcolm planned to leave unattended, but theft wasn't what concerned him.

After a quick shower to wash off the bus film, Malcolm changed the bandage on his left forearm. What little scarring the razor-sharp blade left would soon be concealed beneath a new tattoo. Three golden lines, their ends tapered to points. It bothered him that Hounacier kept trying to place her blessing on his face. The eyes on his palms were difficult enough to conceal. Either she didn't understand the social issues a facial tattoo would cause, or she simply didn't care. The marks were his gifts, like medals or merit badges, tokens celebrating special kills, each one bestowing a power. His first demon kill marked his left palm: the warding eye. A triple-kill earned him his blue scarab. A jorogumo's fire gave him stamina. Whatever the mist cat's death would bestow, Malcolm didn't know. First, he needed to find an artist, one who worked in the old way. Maybe AJ was still in New Orleans. She'd inked two of his marks before.

Once dressed, Malcolm picked up the brown guitar case

with his Remington and Hounacier strapped inside and headed out.

He made his way to the Quarter. The drone of traffic calmed, gradually replaced by music. An enormous accordion player sat shoehorned into a wheelchair, his plump fingers gliding across the keyboard. Eyes hidden behind neon green sunglasses, the musician smiled as Malcolm passed.

Parked cars cluttered one side of the street, leaving little room for drivers. The wall of vehicles, combined with the overhanging balconies, formed a tunnel along the shop fronts. Glitter dust sparkled between the concrete bricks, too deep for brooms or wind to dislodge. Tourists shuffled past, nursing kitschy plastic drinking glasses. Locals, dressed in an eclectic carnival of styles, glided along like sharks amongst tuna. Suited men stood before strip clubs, wearing black earpieces like they were Secret Servicemen, pimping the pleasures inside. The streets stank of body odor, exhaust, and beer. Occasional whiffs of oily ganja smoke wafted through, their origins impossible to pinpoint. Malcolm found himself grinning. He was home.

"Excuse me, sir."

He turned to see a short, bald man in a hole-speckled polo smiling at him. Another man stood behind him, grinning around a stubby cigarette.

"I really like those shoes," the bald man said.

Malcolm glanced down at his slightly worn hiking boots. "Thank you."

"What would ya say if I could tell ya where and what street ya got those shoes?"

Smirking, Malcolm rubbed his chin. *I guess I don't appear as local as I'd thought.*

The man with the cigarette seemed to notice Malcolm's tattooed arms. Eyes widening, the grin fell from his lips.

"I'd say," Malcolm started, "that I got my shoes on my feet on Royal Street."

The bald man laughed and snapped his fingers. "Aw, that's right! On yo feet on Royal Street!" He turned to his friend, still standing like a wax statue. "Man here knows his lines."

The friend shook his head tensely, almost unnoticeably. His

lips tightened, as if trying to pass some important, unspoken danger.

"Say, man," the bald man said, turning back to Malcolm. "Since ya already got my line, ya think you can spare a dollar?"

"Don't know. Got any other lines?"

Baldy's smile widened. Two of his bottom teeth were missing. "'Course I got more. Tell ya what—"

His friend thumped him hard in the back. Baldy snapped his head around. The guy with the cigarette gave a quick gesture with his head, stabbing his nose toward Malcolm's hands. Baldy turned back to Malcolm, quizzical. Then his gaze lowered.

Malcolm slowly rolled over his open palm, like a stage magician revealing a materialized ball.

All joviality vanished from Baldy's face. "Uh ... um ... shit."

"You know these marks?" Malcolm asked.

Baldy gulped. "Yeah."

"You knew Ulises, then?"

Both men nodded.

"We was real sorry to hear what happened to him," Smoker said. "Papa Ulises was a good man."

"Do you know who I am?" Malcolm asked.

"Yeah," Baldy said. "You're his boy, the Doctor. He talked about ya. Said ya was off ..." he glanced at the worn case in Malcolm's other hand, "... killin' evil."

So much for anonymity. "You men have any ideas who might have killed him?"

They shook their heads.

"Don't know," Smoker said. "I hadn't spoke with him in a while. Always real nice. Helped me out with some stuff when things got bad. He did that. Helped folks."

Malcolm nodded understandingly. "Well, I'm going to be around for a while. If either of you gentlemen hear anything ..." He extended a folded twenty from his previously empty fingers.

Baldy held his hands up, like the money was trying to arrest him. "No, no, man. That's all right. Ya ain't got to pay us. Papa Ulises was a friend."

"You sure?" Malcolm eyed Smoker.

He didn't seem to want it either.

"Well, thank you." Malcolm withdrew the bill into his palm again. Ulises had spent long hours, and quite a few drinks, teaching him some basic sleight of hand tricks. Real magic was less obvious, at least until it became dangerous. "I'll owe you one. My name's Malcolm."

"We know that, Doctor," Baldy said. "I'm Julian." He motioned to Smoker. "This here's Dwayne."

"Pleasure to meet you. You know Alpuente's?" Malcolm nodded to the shop just half a block away.

"Jim Luison's place," Julian said.

"That's right. You two hear anything, just let him know." He offered his hand.

Julian looked at it as if maybe the tattoo had teeth. Reluctantly, he shook it. "We will."

Smiling, Malcolm turned and continued on. By tomorrow, everyone would know Ulises' pupil had arrived. A vengeful bokor was nothing to take lightly. He passed several antique shops until coming to one, its walls the color of wet terracotta. A suit of archaic armor stood in one of the windows beside a Victorian divan, upholstered in shades of scarlet and cream. "Alpuente's Antiques" it said above the door in golden letters.

He stepped inside, the stink of the city immediately giving way to the aroma of fresh lilies bulging from a blown glass vase atop the counter. Furniture from different eras filled most of the shop's floor space, nestled around dark wood and glass cases, their contents brimming with treasures. Not seeing anyone right off, Malcolm took a step toward the counter. His right wrist began to itch.

His cobalt scarab tattoo shuddered. Three of its legs twitched nervously, as if unsure what to do. The beetle warned him of demons, even in human form. When near the possessed, within about ten feet or so, it scuttled around to the side opposite. The only time it had ever moved like this was in France, in the Valducans' chateau.

Malcolm looked around. There. A black stone mask, like a skull or withered face, leered from a support column ahead. Brow furrowed, he stepped closer. A semicircular table rested against the column, making it hard to get too close. He leaned in, gazing at the shriveled eyes nestled deep within their sockets. The scarab shuffled like a child needing to pee, causing the hair on Malcolm's arms to stand on end.

The Valducans once owned a pair of Oriental jade masks that housed the essence of demonic lions. Ancient, their secrets of creation long since lost, the masks repelled demons, possibly even familiars. He'd never seen them work, but he had witnessed the catastrophic result when those masks were pressed to faces of two of his friends, possessing his Valducan brothers. He'd had to kill them. If this mask was as those, it was powerful. Powerful and dangerous. There was one way to be sure.

Transferring Hounacier's case to his other hand, Malcolm tentatively raised his palm. While the tattoo on his left hand could repel demonic powers, the one in his right could sense energies, sometimes more than he wanted. He winced as the lid parted, revealing the blue iris beneath. Hovering his palm inches from the mask, he closed his eyes.

Hatred. Rage. Withered hands peeling a screaming child's skull like a grapefruit. Crushing blackness, like ice. The sweet taste of a corpse riddled with—

Malcolm yanked his hand back, nearly stumbling into a chair. Gritting his teeth, he released a long breath, fighting nausea. *God damned ghoul,* he thought. How the hell did it end up in there, and how did Jim get it? Did he have any idea what he had? Rubbing the apprehension from his fingertips, Malcolm flipped over the little white tag hanging from the demon mask.

"Not for Sale."

Looks like he did.

"Can I help you?" a creaky voice asked.

Startled, Malcolm turned to see an old white man sitting in a chair behind the counter, nearly hidden behind the enormous bouquet. A silver haze of hair tufted from the sides of his bald head. A slender air hose looped up over his ears and down below his nose, resting just above a thick moustache.

"Now that piece there isn't for sale," the old man said.

A mulatto woman peered around one of the shelves near the back, her dark curls brushing her shoulders. "There you are."

Malcolm smiled. Aside from her hair, she looked exactly the same. Beautiful. "Hi, Tasha."

She set a carved opium pipe inside the case and closed its wood-framed door. "It's been a while." Tasha turned to the old man, watching them curiously. "Pawpaw, it's Malcolm."

The old man stared at her for a moment then turned to Malcolm, eyes wide. "Mal?"

"Hi, Mister Alpuente."

"Well God damn, son, why didn't you say somethin'?" He winced as he stood up. "Finally cut off that damned hair."

Malcolm grinned. "Yes, sir."

"I liked you better with it." Tasha strode up and gave Malcolm a hug. "I'm sorry, Mal."

He squeezed her, catching the scent of citrus. He missed the spiciness of her old perfume. "Thank you."

She met his eyes. "You look like hell."

He snorted. "Been busy."

She halfheartedly smiled, her cupid's bow lips parting as if about to say more but deciding against it.

"So where you been?" Mister Alpuente stepped around the counter and offered a hand. "Ulises said you were off in Europe."

Malcolm shook the old man's bony hand. "I was. Been stateside a couple months now." He glanced at the oxygen hose leading to a black pouch at the old man's waist, bulging like an enormous fanny pack. "How are you doing?"

"Can't complain." He gave a little cough then added, "I was really sorry to hear about Ulises. Terrible."

Malcolm nodded. "Yeah."

"Just a matter of time though. People he saw. I *warned* him."

"What people?" Malcolm asked.

Alpuente frowned. "Dregs. People tryin' to cheat. Buyin' curses and amulets. 'Don't let those people in your house,' I said." He shook his head. "Terrible."

Malcolm's lip twitched. Alpuente's opinion was harsh, but he had to agree. Even Malcolm had expressed his concern about Ulises' continued work as a bokor.

Tasha touched Malcolm's shoulder. "Come on. Daddy's

upstairs."

Malcolm nodded to the old man and followed Tasha through the back of the shop.

"Forgive him," she said, starting up a tight staircase. "You know how he gets."

"It's fine." The steps creaked loudly as he followed her up. A decade before, he'd mastered sneaking up and down them in the dark not to rouse her family. "Tasha, I noticed a stone mask down there. Do you know anything about it?"

"That? That's Daddy's. It wards off evil."

Yeah, the same way Vlad Tepes warded off Ottoman invaders by impaling thousands of their predecessors outside his capital. "Do you know where he got it?"

"You can ask him," Tasha said without turning. She led Malcolm down a short hall and knocked on a door at the end. She opened it without waiting for a reply.

A broad black man sitting at a cherry wood desk turned from his computer monitor. A spark of recognition flashed in his curious eyes. "Malcolm!"

"Hi, Jim."

"It's good to see you." Jim stood, towering at six and a half feet. He offered a giant hand, which Malcolm shook. "Please, have a seat."

Setting Hounacier's case down, Malcolm took one of the leather-backed chairs, noticing the candle shrine in the office corner. "Thank you."

"Daddy, can I get you anything?" Tasha asked, still standing beside the door.

Jim looked at Malcolm, who only shook his head. "No, Boo, we're good."

"All right," She motioned her head back. "I'll go keep an eye on Pawpaw. Let me know if you need anything."

"Thanks."

She looked at Malcolm, almost an afterthought. "We need to catch up."

Malcolm smiled. "We do."

She shut the door, and Jim gave him a look of a father trying to hold his tongue.

"How have you been?" Malcolm asked, breaking the momentary tension.

The huge priest grunted. "I've been good. The store has been doing well. My father-in-law has been killing me." He rolled his eyes then chuckled. "We keep trying to tell him to enjoy retirement, but every morning, he's down the stairs and unlocking the door like clockwork."

"How's he doing?" Malcolm asked, thinking of the oxygen tank.

"He'll outlive us all. So how about you, Malcolm? Last I heard, you were off in Europe."

"Yeah, I spent a few years there. Mostly France. Couple months in South America. Got back to the states in March."

"And you're only now coming home?"

Malcolm swallowed. Whatever paternal deficiency his own deadbeat father had left, Ulises and Jim both made up beaucoup. "Got busy."

The priest nodded, his expression deafening. *You should have made time to visit before he died.* "With your ... Order?"

"Yes, sir. I'm one of the senior knights now. We had an incident last year. Left us pretty shorthanded."

"I heard."

"You did?" Malcolm hadn't told Ulises much about Tiamat. The old man never approved of Malcolm joining the Valducans.

Jim grinned, white and broad. "Papa Ghede tells me about you from time to time. He favors you, I think."

"I've heard," Malcolm said, suppressing his discomfort with a smile. The smile faded. "What happened?"

Jim sighed. "Neighbors noticed his door open. No one thought much of it. Then sometime after lunch, a young woman came by. She went inside and found him."

"Who is she?"

He shrugged. "Local girl. Prospective client, probably. Police came. Neighbors called me. Had my number from when Ulises would get onto one of his tears." Jim must have seen the question in Malcolm's eyes. "He'd been drinking a lot more the past few years."

"I see." The old man always loved his rum, but after

Hounacier bonded to Malcolm, the drinking only grew. It was part of what made neglecting his mentor so easy, but that didn't help with his guilt.

"Furniture was knocked around. Looked like a robbery, but ..."

"They took his head."

Jim nodded.

"Any suspects?"

The priest sighed. "Police don't have any yet."

"What about you?" Malcolm asked.

"Ulises spent much of his time with ... questionable people. Maybe one of his gris-gris didn't work as expected. Maybe they thought they could steal his magic."

"A good bokor spends as much time in the darkness as they do with the light," Malcolm said, reciting Ulises' words. "Someone has to help those who've strayed too far. They go into the darkness to save them."

"And sometimes, they don't want to leave. I know this is hard, Malcolm, but you must admit that Ulises was spending a lot of time with very troubled people. Dangerous people."

Of course, it was easy to say that. Houngans and Mambos could afford to live like respectable people if they wished. That's why they needed Ulises. It wasn't all just weddings and blessings. He dealt with the ugly side. "But no suspects?"

The priest shook his head.

"Did you ask the loa?"

"I did," Jim answered.

"And?"

"They told me to find you."

Malcolm snorted.

"Ulises had no will we know of, but everyone knows you're his heir. His house, of course, is yours. Courts won't take very long to decide that."

Malcolm frowned. "Don't know what I'd do with it."

Jim's brow rose. "You're not moving back?"

"No. I'll stay as long as it takes to find his killer, but I have other obligations."

"What did Maggie say to that?"

"I haven't talked to her yet."

The huge man straightened in his chair. "You came here first?"

Malcolm nodded.

"Mal, if the other priests learn you spoke to me before her, they'll become suspicious. A new bokor needs to follow protocol. Especially one of your ..." He glanced down at Hounacier's case. "... lineage. You need to pay respect to the queen first."

Malcolm chewed his lip. Voodoo politics didn't interest him. Catching Ulises' murderer was all that mattered. Still, he couldn't afford to be making enemies. "I'll go see her next. Pay my respects."

"You need to go now. I'll be here."

"But—"

"Go."

No use arguing. "All right." Malcolm picked up Hounacier's case and stood. "One thing first."

"Yes?"

"I noticed an obsidian mask downstairs. Where did you find it?"

Jim leaned back. Swallowed, like maybe he didn't want to say. "It belonged to Ulises."

Malcolm thought of Ulises' cryptic email. "How did *he* get it?"

"Wouldn't say. He showed it to me maybe three weeks ago."

"Where did he keep it?" Malcolm asked. "Was it in his house?"

"It hung on the wall facing the door. His body was found beside it."

Malcolm's brow creased. *A demon couldn't have gotten inside with that thing guarding the door.* "Do you know what that thing is?"

The priest nodded. "Demon mask. Keeps them away."

"Did you know there's a demon inside it?

"He told me that too."

A trio of laughing children ran past, clutching homemade popsicles, as Malcolm made his way down the cracked sidewalk.

Tiny, wooden houses lined the street. Layers of brightly colored Mardi Gras beads hung from porch rails and picket fences, like coral, growing thicker every year. He eyed one strand draped prominently along the top of a car gate, its beads composed of tiny shells and colored glass. Real beads like those were a rare treasure indeed. At least for those who didn't know better than to avoid them.

Local spiritualists, whose clientele wished to free themselves of some emotional pain or anxiety, would have them project all their negative energy into a small stone or glass bead. Anyone accepting the bead would, in effect, take on the burden of that negative energy. Many found their way onto necklaces that tourists fought and competed for before taking them home, far away from the city. Ulises had found such bitter amusement in how many women exposed and degraded themselves to proudly earn a mantle of the pain of scorned lovers and grieving parents.

Malcolm stopped at a simple yellow house, its porch buried within a jungle of potted flowers. He followed the wooden steps up and knocked on the door.

It creaked open, revealing a man's tattooed face. Tight braids hung down over his shoulders. Suspicious eyes met Malcolm's, wandered down his tattooed arms to the case in his hands. "Can I help you?" Three red teardrops traced from the corner of one eye, and a tiny black cross decorated the space between his brows. This wasn't a man to take lightly.

"Is Magdalena here?" Malcolm asked, a little worried he might have come to the wrong house.

"And you are?"

"Malcolm Romero."

A female voice with a pronounced drawl called from inside. "Darius, who's at the door?"

"A Mister Romero, ma'am," he said over his shoulder.

"Mal? Well, let him in!"

Darius opened the door the rest of the way. "Come in."

Maggie's house smelled of candle smoke and lemon Pledge, and the AC was about two notches too low. Wooden masks and framed photographs filled the beige walls. An offering-cluttered shrine to Simba dominated one corner. It looked the same as it always had, save for the flat-screen television where the old, wood-cased set used to be.

"Malcolm Romero," said an old black woman in a floral-print chair. Bright eyes sparkled out from a nest of fine wrinkles. "It has been a while."

"Hi, Miss Maggie," Malcolm said, suddenly feeling like a kid in the priestess' presence. She'd always had that effect on him. New Orleans' Voodoo Queen never forgot a name or a birthday. Though the title was one of respect rather than actual power, she carried it with the dignity of a woman born to lead. The old matriarch served as an anchor among the city's otherwise disjointed population of mambos and houngans.

"Come on in," she said. "Sit down."

Malcolm took a seat on the green sofa beside her. "Thank you."

"Malcolm is a doctor," Maggie proudly said to the thuggish man now closing the door.

Darius just nodded. He took the chair opposite the old woman.

"Let me think ..." tapping her lip. "Archeology?"

"Anthropology."

"Oh, that's right. Anthropology. He's Ulises' boy."

The man's posture straightened a little, his confidence seeming to shrink a bit.

"Darius, sweetie, could you bring Doctor Romero some tea?"

"Yes, ma'am." He stood and went into the kitchen. The subtle bulge of a pistol poked beneath his shirt. Malcolm wondered if that was the gun that had earned the facial cross. The mark symbolized at least five kills.

"That's all right," Malcolm said.

Maggie just set a hand on his knee. "You're sweatin'. Help cool you down."

Malcolm nodded. No one ever escaped Maggie's house without at least one glass of sweet tea.

"You cut off that ponytail, I see." She leaned closer. "I like you better without it. Look like a young Martin Sheen. Anyone ever tell you that?"

"Yes ma'am," Malcolm chuckled.

Ice cubes tinkled as Darius stepped back in. He set a tall glass of golden tea on the table, making sure to move a coaster there first.

"Thank you, Darius," Maggie said, withdrawing her hand. "You can go on home now."

"Are you sure?"

Maggie nodded. "Doctor Romero and I have a lot to catch up on. He'll take care of me; don't worry."

The man glanced back at Malcolm and nodded. "A'ight. I'll be back tomorrow."

"Tell your mama hello for me."

"I will. Good to meet you," he said to Malcolm.

"You too."

Maggie waited until Darius had left. "He's a good boy."

Malcolm smiled. The old woman could find the good in anyone. She could also charm the most hardened criminal with just a wink. Grandma magic, Ulises had called it.

"I'm terribly sorry for your loss, Malcolm," she said. "He was a good man."

"Thank you," Malcolm said. For some reason, Maggie's condolences were the only ones that really mattered, not Jim's, Tasha's, even the other Valducans'. Grandma magic. "Do you have any idea who could have done that to him?"

She frowned. "I last saw him a few weeks before he died. He was workin' with a man who had been a servant to demons. Ulises was tryin' to pull him back to the light."

"A familiar?"

"I believe so but not just one. He'd served several during his life."

Demon addict, Malcolm thought. People who had been bound as a familiar were broken human beings. Someone that served more than one would be shattered, desperate to find a new master. "Did you get a name?"

"Marcus. Never heard a last name. They met at that jazz club Ulises liked on Frenchman." Her eyes looked up, searching her memory. "Brass Sax."

It's a start. A demon hunter's head would make a good offering to a potential master. "Anyone else he'd been seeing?"

Maggie pursed her lips. "I heard he'd been visitin' with Atabei Cross."

"Who?"

"Atabei Cross. She's some root worker down in the Ninth. Leads a little congregation down there, I understand. Met her just once." She sipped her tea. "Pretty thing, little older than you."

"She doesn't pay respects to you?" Malcolm asked.

The Voodoo Queen snorted. "Most of the local priests don't do that. Never have. No, she keeps to herself down there."

"That reminds me," Malcolm said. "I saw Jim Luison before coming here. He was worried people might gossip if they found out I saw him first."

Maggie smiled, revealing a mouth of pearly dentures. "They'll gossip no matter what you do, Boo. If any say anything to me, I'll tell them truth. You were visitin' Natasha. Jim just happened to be there." She met his eye. "Everyone knows about you two."

"That was a long time ago." Malcolm tried his tea. Suddenly realizing how thirsty he was, he gulped it twice more.

"That's your perspective." The old woman winked. "Tasha's grown quite a reputation the last few years. She's one of Erzulie's favorites."

"Must run in the family." Her father was also favored. Instead of the loa of love and beauty, Jim was the preferred vessel of Baron Samedi, the loa of the dead, the darker half of Papa Ghede.

"You've never been mounted, have you?" she asked, eyeing Malcolm over the rim of her glass.

"No, ma'am."

"Hounacier always claimed you. Told them, 'Back off. He's mine.'"

"I guess she did," he chuckled

Maggie motioned to the rectangular case at Malcolm's feet. "Is that her?"

"Yeah."

"Well, bring her out. I haven't seen her in years either."

Malcolm fought the hesitation, not wanting to offend the old priestess. Once, before he was born, Ulises and Maggie had been a bit of an item. Then Hounacier appeared. Malcolm always suspected the queen regarded the holy blade with an air of resentment. The other woman. "Of course." He thumbed open the latch and lifted the lid, revealing the wood-sheathed machete strapped inside beside the shotgun and row of shells.

"There she is," Maggie said. "Bring her closer."

Malcolm tore the Velcro back with a loud *scritch*. Pulling her free, he slid off the polished sheath.

Maggie leaned closer as Malcolm presented the blade before her. She peered over the weapon, like an artist inspecting the work of a master. She nodded as if to herself. "Welcome home." Maggie leaned back in her chair and nursed her tea, her gaze distant, almost regretful.

He set the blade across his lap.

"Let me know when you're ready to move into Ulises' old home," she said, her tone suddenly businesslike. "My boys can help you get things set up."

Malcolm hid his apprehension behind a final sip of tea. "It's not necessary, but thank you. I won't be staying that long."

The queen's brow arched pointedly. "Why not?"

"I have obligations I need to attend. My Order needs me too much."

Maggie drew a patient breath. "Malcolm, Hounacier is part of this city. She belongs with her people. Your only obligation is to her. With Ulises gone, you must take his place."

He shifted under the old woman's gaze. "It's not that simple."

"Yes, Mal, it is. It's time to move home." She nodded to Hounacier. "Ask her. She'll tell you where she needs to be."

Following the walk alongside a white concrete wall, Malcolm mulled over the voodoo queen's words. He'd never wanted to upset the old woman, but trying to explain himself was useless. She'd lived in the city her entire life. It was the world to her. Malcolm had seen the world. He knew how big it was. Hoarding Hounacier in just those pockets that practiced her religion was selfish. Too many people needed her.

The wall opened to a black, wrought-iron gate, and Malcolm stepped through into Saint Roch cemetery. Following the necropolis' streets past moss-dusted tombs, he found his way to a large mausoleum. White marble sealed each of the four vaults. Two were so old and weathered, their graven names were but memory. The third denoted Edith Moore, who died in 2003. Ulises Belair's name marked the fourth and newest slab. Fresh and wilted flowers lay on the ground before it, alongside dozens of coins and colorful trinkets. Several more coins clung to the vault's face, affixed with candle wax. Burned stubs lay scattered about as well. Malcolm ran a finger along a triple-X scratched into the marble. Four more similar marks adorned the façade—one in charcoal, another in blue paint pen. Long ago an over-dramatic tour guide had started the tradition of defacing Marie Laveau's tomb with the same mark as a means of gaining luck. The practice took off, and the lines between fantasy and religion blurred and melted as more people subscribed to the ritual. Belief made the magic real, and now, it seemed the city was canonizing Ulises as one of the voodoo kings to be paid tribute. Malcolm snorted, wondering if the old sorcerer would have ever imagined it.

He pressed his hand against the smooth stone. A moment of pain as the tattoo-lid opened. Malcolm closed his eyes, hoping, praying to feel his old friend inside.

"I'm sorry," he muttered. "I should have called … visited more. I should have been here." Guilt coiled and balled in stomach. It was too late for apologies. "You used to scare the shit out of me, you know?" He chuckled. "You were so damned intimidating. So serious. Then… then you became my fucking dad." Malcolm cleared his throat, fighting back tears. "I never told you that. I never knew my own father, and then once I had one, I fucking neglected him. I'm sorry. I'm sorry we fought so much. I … I'm going to find who did this to you."

The tattooed eye stretched wider until it felt as if the skin might rip. "I love you … father."

The tattoo faintly throbbed. Love. Malcolm couldn't tell if it was real or imagined, but accepted it nonetheless.

Malcolm closed his hand and wiped his eyes. Glancing

around to be sure he was alone, he opened his case and removed the machete. Reverently, he slid Hounacier from her sheath and pressed her against the old man's tomb. "We'll make this right." Malcolm drew a breath. Held it. "I promise."

After a few silent moments, he returned Hounacier to her case and snapped it shut. Next time he visited, he'd mark his own XXX with the blood of Ulises' murderer.

Trapped in thought, he stepped out of the cemetery yard.

"Welcome home, Milky."

Malcolm spun.

A disheveled white man with irregular dreadlocks squatted against the cemetery wall. His eyes were rolled back like veined, white orbs. He grinned at Hounacier's case. "And to you too, beautiful lady. Welcome back." The man shuddered then blinked. He looked around then, suddenly noticing Malcolm standing right in front of him, eyes wide.

The man smiled sleepily. "Hey man," the Creole accent now replaced with a southern drawl. "Those are nice shoes you got."

"That so?" Malcolm asked.

"I bet I could tell you the street you got those shoes on."

"I bet you could." Malcolm handed the guy a five.

"Wow," the guy said, accepting the money. "Thanks."

Malcolm turned and continued on. The loa knew he was back. It was time to get to work.

CHAPTER 5

Malcolm sipped tea from a porcelain cup decorated with roses and skulls. Dull pain buzzed along his arm as AJ inked his newest tattoo out with quick jabs. He winced, her needles hitting the still-tender machete cut.

"I told you," she said, not looking up. "You should let that heal first."

"Just do it." Malcolm pressed his tongue against the roof of his mouth as the artist worked.

Jim hadn't heard of Marcus, the demon-addict that Ulises had been seeing. Last night, Malcolm had gone to the Brass Sax, hoping to find him. He didn't. But one of the regulars, a redhead named Liz, knew him. After a few Vodka Sours, she revealed that Marcus was a stocky man with kinky hair. She didn't know his last name but said he showed up every Saturday night. Tomorrow.

AJ dabbed away the blood and ink with a wet paper towel. "That's two."

Malcolm checked the pair of tapered golden lines stretching across his forearm like claw marks. Hounacier's cut connected the bottom tip of the left line to the top of where the third one would soon be. He opened and closed his fist, watching the marks ripple. "Lookin' good."

"Thanks," AJ said. "You sure you have to run now? I can finish the last one in just a few minutes."

"Sorry. Got an appointment."

AJ shook her head, her bone-plugged earlobes wobbling. "Suit yourself." She dropped the needle-tipped sticks into a metal tray. "You know the drill, Mal. No direct sun. No swimming. Keep the bandage on." He drew a breath as she smeared a cold film of antibiotic gel onto his am. "Tomorrow then?"

"Three o'clock." She wrapped the fresh tattoo before finally peeling off her latex gloves.

Apologizing for the reschedule, Malcolm tipped her a few extra bucks and left the shop. Finishing Hounacier's tattoo was important, but so was his next appointment. Leather case in hand, he hurried six blocks to Puffy's. The painted image of a fat-cheeked man grinning around a cigar decorated the restaurant's plate-glass window.

He checked his watch. 10:46.

"Just one?" asked a young waiter with a bright red shirt and sculpted black hair.

"Two."

The man nodded. "Sit wherever you like. I'll bring your menus."

The restaurant consisted of small, semi-separate rooms. He remembered when it had been an insurance office a decade before. Malcolm found a little corner table that gave him a good view of the front, ordered a sandwich, and waited.

Fifteen minutes later, a thin, black policeman stepped inside. Seeing Malcolm, he approached the table.

Malcolm stood, offering a hand. "Corporal Duplessis?"

He shook his hand. "Doctor Romero?"

"It's good to meet you," Malcolm said, taking his seat. "Jim Luison speaks very highly of you."

The officer nodded and slid into the opposite chair. "Call me Louis." He glanced over his shoulder. "Jim told me about your... problem."

Malcolm nodded. "I've hit a dead-end not being related to Ulises Belair. Jim said you could help me with that."

Duplessis' lips tightened. He ran a hand along the back of his shiny bald head.

"I understand this is a big risk," Malcolm said, his voice low.

The policeman nodded. He opened his mouth, but Malcolm held up a silencing finger.

"I see your guest has arrived," the waiter said. He set an amber, plastic water glass down before Duplessis. "Are you ready to order?"

"Yeah." Duplessis picked up the laminated menu, barely looking at it. "Um ... roast beef po' boy. To go."

"Anything else?" the waiter asked, not writing the order.

"That's it."

"All right. I'll get that right out."

Malcolm waited until the waiter left before nodding the officer to continue.

Duplessis reached into his pocket and set a bright green flash drive on the table.

Malcolm palmed it. "Thank you."

The policeman nodded. "Not much on there. Think the cut was a machete. Common in these kind of killings."

These kind? Malcolm ran a finger across the table's edge. "Any suspects?"

"Several prints. But he had a lot of people that visited. With records. Detectives are still interviewing them all." He swallowed. "It's all in there."

"Thanks again." Malcolm folded a pair of hundreds beneath a paper napkin and slid them across the table.

Duplessis pushed them back. "That's all right."

He eyed the napkin. "Are you sure?"

"Not money."

Malcolm hid his trepidation behind a bite of his sandwich. "What then?"

The officer leaned closer. "My wife. She's up for a promotion at her bank, but there's another guy the manager likes. He's probably going to get it instead."

"I'm listening."

His dark eyes traced up Malcolm's arms. "I was thinkin' you could help her out."

"How?"

"A gris-gris."

Bitter relief washed up Malcolm's spine. For a moment, he'd

thought the policeman was requesting a hit. "That's possible."
A little smile twitched at the edges of Duplessis' mouth.
"I'll need her name, of course, and a picture. Help me focus."
He sipped his water. "And something of hers. Personal effect."
"Her name's Rochelle." He pulled a battered black wallet
from a back pocket. Flipping it open, he wrestled out a little
photograph then hesitated.
"I just need it to focus," Malcolm assured. "You'll get it back
when I deliver her gris-gris."
"How long will it take?"
"Three, maybe four days."
Duplessis' brow creased. "That long?"
"I'd prefer a week, but you look like you need it now. Look,
I owe you. I owe you a lot. This is going to be real hoodoo, not
some knock-off shit from a tourist trap. It takes time."
Reluctance faded from the officer's face. Drawing a breath,
he handed Malcolm the picture. From a shirt pocket, he removed
a tightly rolled plastic bag and offered it over.
Malcolm unrolled it to see a ball of black hair inside, likely
pulled from a comb. "Don't worry. I learned from the best."

Lunchtime tourists wandered the French Quarter's dingy
streets, snapping pictures and watching performers. Lost in
thought, Malcolm followed the sidewalk past shop fronts,
their painted stucco façades artfully decayed, revealing the
old brickwork beneath. There were two methods to making
Rochelle Duplessis' gris-gris. This first was a simple blessing,
granting luck toward her career. It gave her an edge. The second
was more sinister: a curse on her rival. That was more effective,
but Malcolm preferred not to take the darker path.
He came to a sea-green shop. Multi-colored curtains hung
in the window, framing a display of various candles and tiny
cloth pouches. A wooden sign hung above the door, depicting a
coiled, rainbow-colored serpent around the name, "Crossroads
Voodoo Boutique." He stopped, allowing a bearded man
clouded in patchouli and clutching a black paper bag to step
outside.
A tiny bell jingled as he closed the door behind him. Wooden

masks ran along the tops of the light-colored walls. Below them, assorted candles and pouches, encased in crinkly plastic, rested atop cloth-draped cases. An enormous shrine dominated one corner, cluttered with offerings. A blue ribbon of spicy incense twisted and curled out from a clay holder.

A thin white woman with a steel-gray bob leaned behind the counter. Her ring-encrusted hands waved before her as she spoke with a clean-cut black man in a cream suit with no tie.

"Well," the woman said, her face brightening, "Doctor Romero, I presume."

"Paula." He offered a hand to the suited man. "Mister Warren."

"Good to see you, Mal," Earl Warren said with a firm shake. "It's been a long time."

"Too long," Paula said, walking around the counter. Her long, flowing clothes did little to disguise the fact that she was built like a stick insect. She gave Malcolm a hug, the top of her head only coming to his chin. "Good to see you."

"Good to be seen."

"Maggie had said you were in town." Earl's gaze lowered to Malcolm's case. "Nasty business with Ulises. I hope they find who could have done that."

"They're working on it," Malcolm said.

"And you're here to pay your respects?" Earl asked. "Maggie said you don't intend to stay."

"I'll be here until justice is done for Ulises."

"Ah," Earl said. "Be careful what you do, Malcolm. Things could cause problems for our community if you interfere with police business."

Malcolm's eyes narrowed. "Worse than someone killing an old man in his home and cutting his head off?" Earl never approved of Ulises. His congregation met in a church, resembling, in most respects, any other. The voodoo priest was a businessman. Real-estate. Image was everything to him.

"That was a tragedy," the priest said. "Senseless. But blood should never beget blood. I can only hope you understand that. Ulises never did."

"Ulises understood the world in ways you couldn't,"

Malcolm said, his anger rising. "He didn't hide from it."

Earl's jaw tightened, the muscles undulating. "If you think I'm going to sit back and let you set our religion back a hundred years, you're mistaken. Best keep Ulises' dusty old sword in that case of yours."

Malcolm met his eyes. "Or what?"

"Gentlemen," Paula snapped. "Now, this is my shop. If you two want to fight, then get out. Measure your dicks somewhere else."

"You're right," Malcolm said, backing down. "I'm sorry, Paula."

Earl sighed and raised a hand. "Apologies." He gave Malcolm a plastic smile. "We can discuss this at a more appropriate time."

"Yeah."

"Again, I am very sorry for your loss, Malcolm." He turned to Paula, still glaring at them like a pissed off den mother. "We'll continue our talk later. Take care."

"You too," she said, the anger melting a little. She waited until he left, door tinkling behind him, before she took a breath. "So," she said cheerfully, "how can I help you, Mal?"

"I need some supplies," he said. "I'm making a gris-gris."

A question ticked in the mambo's eye. Apprehension.

Pretending not to notice, Malcolm scanned the glass herb jars nestled in a corner rack. "A friend's wife is up for a promotion at her job. I wanted to give her something that could help."

"Ah, career," she purred, nervousness gone. Paula glided over to the jars, her long fingers moving across their labels. "What does she do?"

"Banking."

"Money, then." she plucked one of the jars. "We can do that. What all will you need to make it?"

Malcolm grunted. He hadn't made a gris-gris in five years. "Everything."

An hour and sixty-two dollars later, Malcolm left Crossroads Voodoo Boutique. He'd fit the two bags of ingredients inside Hounacier's case, not realizing how off-balance it would become. The finished gris-gris itself would weigh under two ounces. Unfortunately, all the materials to make it weighed a couple pounds.

Hip-hop blared out from an enormous, wheeled speaker as a team of dancers in matching jogging suits worked a pack of tourists. Shoulder to shoulder, the audience clogged the sidewalk, watching the performance though their cameras and phone screens. It was a pickpocket's dream. Paying attention to his surroundings, Malcolm scooted though the sweat-stinking crowd.

A man in a grungy, yellow bucket hat glanced at Malcolm's tattoos and quickly stepped out of the way. "Excuse me, sir," he mumbled.

Malcolm nodded as he passed. The sudden and almost fearful respect from the local hustlers felt strange. His life as a demon-hunter had been spent either in Ulises' shadow or as under the radar as possible. Anonymity was slipping. What troubled him more was that part of him enjoyed the attention.

Emerging from the crowd, Malcolm noticed a piecemeal bicycle chained to one of the cast-iron hitching posts. A yellowed raccoon skull rested just behind the seat rack, affixed with rusty wire. The skull was a ward, a totem to keep evil spirits from following the rider. Malcolm wondered where it was the owner went that evil might follow them home. He'd seen the type of ward before in Haiti and Jamaica but never stateside. Malcolm glanced around, wondering if maybe the owner was watching him. No one was. Disappointed, he continued on.

Maybe before he left, he'd have a chance to meet this cyclist. Maybe glean a bit of insight on the custom's migration.

Four blocks later, he arrived at Alpuente's Antiques. The scarab tattoo itched as he stepped inside. Malcolm quickly moved past the ghoul mask's uncomfortable gaze.

Mister Alpuente stood behind the counter, talking to a fat man in a hideous Hawaiian shirt. A pair of silver coins rested on a black, velvet mat between them. The old man glanced over. "Tasha's in the back if you want to go give her a hand."

"All right," Malcolm said. "Thanks." He made his way past the ornate furniture toward the dark, double doors in the back of the shop. Something banged, followed by a metallic clatter.

"Damn it," Tasha cursed as Malcolm entered the hall. Four claw-footed chairs rested outside an open door.

Peeking into the windowless storeroom, Malcolm spotted Tasha atop a stepladder, heaving a box onto a shelf. "Need some help?"

She turned. A curly wisp hung across her face. "Sure thing, Desperado." Tasha nodded to a wide chandelier of swirled white and purple glass hanging behind her. "Daddy wants me to pull this thing down, but I need to make room to move it first."

"Desperado?"

Tasha brushed the hair back. "Guitar case. Really?"

He frowned. "What's wrong with it?"

"Do I really need to tell you?"

Sighing, Malcolm slid Hounacier's case beside the door. He moved an oaken pillar to one corner so he and Tasha could carry a narrow table out into the hall.

"Careful," she said as Malcolm unhooked the chandelier from a thick ring set in the ceiling.

"Got it?" Malcolm grunted, lowering it.

"Yeah."

Still bearing the brunt of the weight, Malcolm stepped down the ladder as she guided it onto a thick, foam pad atop a dolly.

"Slowly." Tasha adjusted a heavy blanket beneath the fragile arms. "Slowly. There."

Malcolm let out a breath, flexing his arm a couple times to return the feeling.

"Don't get worn out just yet," she said. "We still gotta put it up in the showroom."

"I'm fine."

She stood up. "Thanks for the help. I'll owe you dinner tonight."

"That's all right." He needed to start on the gris-gris, maybe even spend a few hours with Duplessis' files.

Her lip twitched. "Well, maybe another night then."

She's asking you out, you idiot. With his tattoos, Malcolm could detect poisons, go without sleep for days, and even smell three times better than any human. But none of Hounacier's blessings could help him talk with a woman. "No ... I mean ... I'd love to do dinner tonight. But the first one's on me."

Her almond eyes narrowed. "First one? Little presumptuous."

"No ... no. I meant I wanted to take you out."

"So it's a date?"

Malcolm's face grew hot. "Well, it's a dinner. Give us a chance to catch up?"

Tasha's lips pursed into an amused smile. "Okay. I'll let you buy me dinner. But one condition ..."

"What's that?"

She motioned to Hounacier's case against the wall. "*That* stays at home."

A cold weight fell in Malcolm's stomach. "I can't do that. Hounacier has to come with me."

She sniffed, amusement vanishing from her face. "I see."

"It's just ... there's no one I can trust her with." He thought of Ulises and Maggie. Hounacier had killed their chance for happiness. It wasn't coincidence that most Valducans never married. They already were.

"What about Daddy? You don't trust him?"

"I do. It's just ..." He balled his fist, searching for the words. "Someone killed Ulises. What if they come after me? What if I left Hounacier with Jim, and they come after her? They'd kill him. It's too much of a risk."

Tasha swallowed. "All right." She looked back at the case. "But you're not carrying that ugly thing with us. Deal?"

He chuckled. "Deal."

"Perfect." She nodded toward the chandelier. "Let's finish this."

Taking the front, Tasha pulled the awkward dolly, mostly steering as Malcolm pushed. One of the wheels wobbled, making it pull to one side. Together, they guided it though the hall and out into the showroom as Mister Alpuente repeatedly warned them not to bump into anything.

"Here we go," Tasha said, stopping beside a life-size carved lion. A sturdy steel ring hung from a beam above. "I'll grab the ladder."

The bell above the front door tinkled as Malcolm carried

the stepladder in from the back. The scarab at his wrist crawled around to the other side. Something growled. Pulse quickening, Malcolm looked up to a spikey-haired man in the doorway, eyes wide, lips peeling away from lengthening teeth. The growling hiss deepened.

Malcolm froze. It was like when a demon saw his warding palm, but more powerful. The man's dark eyes turned bright yellow, transfixed on the obsidian mask. His cheeks and jawbone shifted beneath the skin, lengthening his face, and his ears slid higher up his head. The ladder clattered to the floor.

The stranger's head snapped toward him. His skin rippled in pimpling waves. Werebeast.

"Tasha!" Malcolm yelled. "Move!" He ran to the storeroom, popped the latches on Hounacier's case, and flung it open, spilling Paula's bags across the floor. He tore Hounacier from her straps and charged back to the showroom.

The front door stood open. The demon-man was running across the street, knocking pedestrians aside. Squeezing the wooden sheath, Malcolm chased after him.

He dashed through the traffic. Tires squealed. A car horn blared. The man's head was barely visible, bobbing though the crowd. He turned at Conti Street beside the giant courthouse building. Malcolm raced after him.

Malcolm turned the corner in time to see the man vault the black fence encircling the courthouse lawn, clearing the iron spikes. "Son of a bitch," Malcolm spat, stopping.

The demon's speed was incredible. Onlookers stopped to watch, their eyes cold, curious. Some pointed. A teenage girl tracked the man with her pink-cased phone. He sprinted across the manicured grass then leaped over the other side.

Malcolm clenched his jaw, watching him disappear behind a row of parked trucks. A demon now knew he was here. It knew of the mask in Alpuente's shop. Neither he nor Tasha's family was safe until it was dead. Malcolm just had to find it first.

CHAPTER 6

"You know," Tasha said, sipping her wine, "when you said you were taking me out, I expected something a little less fancy."

Waiters in matching vests glided though the restaurant, their accents perfect as they recited Italian entrees. Soft music played from unseen speakers, audible only during those few moments when every conversation took a simultaneous pause.

"I'm full of surprises," Malcolm said. "What were you expecting? Greasy burgers and beer?"

She shrugged. "Something like that."

"We'll do that next time then."

"There you go, talking like this is going to happen again." She smiled then quickly covered it with another sip of wine. "Though I admit the tie does help your case."

Unconsciously, Malcolm tugged the silk tie. Most of the other well-dressed diners wore suit jackets. He stood out. That was never good. Though he suspected the disapproving glances were more aimed at the black, tubular bag resting beside him. Mister Alpuente had lent the oxygen tank bag as long as he needed it. It wasn't large enough to fit a sawed-off as well but big enough that Malcolm had to wrap Hounacier's sheath in a hotel towel so the machete wouldn't be as obvious inside the black nylon.

"Still," Tasha continued, "you should have told me we were coming here. I'd have worn something nicer."

"Ruin the surprise." He gestured his wine glass toward her striped lilac dress. Honey-colored stones sparkled from her matching pendant and earrings. "Don't worry about it. You look great." The fact Tasha had spent so much effort making herself up when expecting a greasy spoon told him a lot. Maybe she wasn't as over their former relationship as he'd thought.

A waiter arrived, refilled their glasses, and took their orders. After he left, Tasha reached for her wine but stopped. Her finger tapped the narrow stem. "Mal ... that man at the shop. Was he...?"

Malcolm rested his elbows on the table, lacing his fingers. It was inevitable. He was surprised it had taken this long before one of them broached the demon at the shop. They both had questions, but asking them would spoil the evening. "I have an idea."

"What?"

"I say that until our dinner is through, we forget about Ulises' murder and what happened today. We just pretend that we are simply old friends catching up. What do you say?"

Tasha nodded, apprehension melting with a warm smile. "I think I can agree to that."

"Good." He picked up his glass. "Last time we spoke, you were finishing up school. Marketing, I remember."

"Yeah." She sniffed. "Moved to Atlanta. Got a buying job at a retail chain. Got engaged."

An unexpected tinge of jealousy tugged at Malcolm's chest. "Engaged?"

Tasha shrugged. "Not anymore, obviously. It just didn't ... work out."

Malcolm nodded understandingly, feeling a bit guilty in his relief.

"Then Pawpaw got sick, so I moved back two years ago."

"You still play?" he asked.

"Some." Tasha smiled. "A couple friends have a band. They ask me to jam with them every few weeks or so. Not as much since Jeff had his daughter, but enough to feed the need. Other than that, I just work at the shop, do a little volunteer work with some of the elderly. Bring food, help around the house, that type of thing." She drew a long breath. "And what about you, Mal? What have you been up to the last four years?"

"Oh, you know," he said. "Working."

She cocked her head, telling him he wouldn't get off so easy.

"Europe, mostly. Spent a little time in India, South Korea. We have a wind farm down in Chile, so I had a few weeks down there."

"And what exactly do you do?"

He ran a thumb back and forth across the white tablecloth. "Acquisitions. I verify the authenticity of holy weapons."

"And what makes one authentic?"

Malcolm suppressed his trepidation. *Why shouldn't she know? She saw a demon.* Still, it felt wrong to discuss it. "A holy weapon is possessed by an angel," he said finally.

Tasha's golden eyes flickered down to where Hounacier rested beneath the table. "An angel?"

"Well … angelic being would be more accurate. They're what gives weapons their power."

"So they're loa?"

He shook his head. "No. Loa are different. Think of them as… cousins."

She nodded then sipped her wine. "And you verify if weapons are mounted by these spirits?"

"Yes." He rolled over his right palm, showing the tattooed eye. "This can sense them. It's how I knew what the mask in your shop was. Some of the people in my … company research different reports and records, trying to locate holy weapons. Once they find one they suspect to be real, they send me to authenticate it."

"So how many of these mounted weapons are there?" she asked.

Malcolm's jaw twitched at the question. "Forty," he said, counting the suspected one in China. It was easier than saying the full truth.

"I thought there would be more than that."

"There were. A lot more. Something happened last year. Many of the weapons were destroyed, and a lot of good people died. We're still recovering from it all."

"Oh."

The waiter arrived with their food, offering a much-appreciated distraction. Malcolm enjoyed a particularly good duck marsala while he and Tasha talked of lighter things, people they knew, places they'd gone, and memories of older times. Malcolm made a point not to mention any of the more sinister aspects to his travels, which still left him with plenty of stories. It was by far the nicest meal they'd ever shared together, including when they went to the wedding of their friends, James and Keisha, who were now living in New Jersey and divorced, according to Tasha. Of course, when Malcolm and she had dated, his income had been next to nothing. Finishing his doctorate while spending his free time apprenticing under Ulises didn't pay. So their dates were always pretty simple.

Tasha had told him once that he'd been her first love. She wasn't his, but she was his greatest. They'd had two wonderful years together, then Malcolm had been recruited into the Valducans. Everything changed. Five years later, they're sitting, enjoying a meal they once could have only dreamed of sharing.

"Would you care to see a dessert menu?" the waiter asked, gathering their plates.

Tasha gave Malcolm an unsure look.

"Please," Malcolm said.

They split an enormous, ice cream and brownie concoction drizzled in raspberry cream. Malcolm wondered how exactly one person was supposed to eat it by themselves. Trepidation rose as he watched the rich dessert whittle away. Once they were done, the agreement was over. Questions would be asked, and the moment of light happiness would die.

"Okay." Tasha scooped a melting wedge of ice cream into her spoon. "I can tell you're waiting for it."

"What?"

She motioned to the bowl between them. "You stopped eating."

"Just taking a break."

Tasha pointedly glanced at the spoon still in Malcolm's hand. "You're stalling it."

"No, I'm not," he lied. Malcolm set the spoon down and

sighed. "I take it you're ready?"

She nodded. "That man at the shop. What was that?"

"That was a demon," Malcolm said plainly. "Werewolf, I think. Probably didn't know about the mask—at least not until it saw it. I doubt it would have just strolled in otherwise."

"A werewolf?" She sat back a little more, posture straightening.

He nodded.

Not really looking, Tasha stabbed the last dollop of ice cream with her spoon, scooting it around the bowl. "It's strange. This morning, if you'd told me werewolves were real, I wouldn't have entirely believed you. I believed in demons, possessions. How couldn't I? But actual monsters?" She shook her head. "You and Ulises, even Daddy. You all told me about them. I just ..."

"I know," Malcolm said.

"How many?" Tasha met his eyes. "How many demons have you killed?"

Malcolm rubbed his chin. He scanned the nearby tables, making sure no one was listening. "Sixty-three."

Tasha blinked. "Wow. That many?"

"A third were from that *incident* I told you about. The demons got together and attacked us. They had this cult of demon worshipers and were trying to summon a goddess. To get us out of the way, they hunted us down."

"You think that might be linked to Ulises?"

"Possible. There's also a guy he was working with. Former familiar to multiple demons. He might have done it to serve a potential master."

"What is a familiar, exactly?" she asked.

Malcolm finished the last of his wine. "A demon can mark a victim's soul. Usually a bite, but there's other ways, depending on the breed. Once marked, a demon can possess that person whenever they want. Time, distance, doesn't matter. But until it takes them over, they can lead seemingly normal lives. Some breeds, though, can do more than that. They can put a bit more of themselves into a victim, making them slaves. Killing the demon will free the souls they marked, but familiars ..." He shook his head. "They're never the same afterward."

Tasha's lips pursed, like maybe she still didn't fully believe him. Finally, "That werewolf ... Will it come back?"

"I don't know," Malcolm said. "It won't get in the front door. Not as long as the mask is there. The bars over the windows will keep it out, but the upper floor windows ..." He shook his head.

"It can get up there?"

"Easily. Keeping wolfsbane around, even dried, will help, but it's no guarantee."

Tasha rubbed her fingers nervously. "What do I do? Buy silver bullets?"

"Those will just kill the host. The demonic spirit will simply move to another body whose soul it marked. Besides, you can't really *buy* silver bullets. But, um ..." Malcolm winked. "I got connections." He smiled.

It didn't help. She reached for her glass then stopped, seeming to decide against it.

Malcolm set his hand on hers, calming her fidgeting. "Just hang tight. You've got one of the best demon hunters in the world on your side." He squeezed it lightly. "I won't let it hurt you."

"The plan was that I'd come pay my respects, take care of any affairs," Malcolm said as they strolled the cracked sidewalk back to apartment. "But with the nature of the murder and the obsidian mask, he's heading up now." A warm breeze coursed lazily down the nighttime streets, washing away the sticky air.

"Because of the mask?"

Malcolm nodded. "There's a demon inside of it."

"It's alive?"

He nodded again. "A ghoul. That's what gives it the power to ward back demon-marked. As far as we know, it's the only one in the world."

"Does Daddy know?"

"Yes. Ulises had told him but never said where he got it."

Tasha turned to him. "Is it safe?"

"No," Malcolm said flatly. "But ... it did keep the demon out. But if anyone stole it or put it on ..."

Her face darkened. "What if it broke?"

Malcolm shrugged. "I suppose its essence would escape, searching for a host."

Tasha's eyes widened, a question forming on her lips.

"It can't mount you by force," he said, placing a hand on her arm. "Don't worry."

"Are you sure?"

"They have to be invited or summoned," he said. "Only after they have a body can they mark unwilling victims."

"Oh," she said with a relieved smile.

They continued down the sidewalk. Malcolm hadn't mentioned that the number of former demonbound in the city might give the ghoul spirit several willing hosts. Though if she already knew the loa's affinity for mounting them at will, which she likely did, Tasha might figure it out.

Glancing back as they turned onto her street, Malcolm noticed a pair of men walking half a block behind them. One was short and wiry with a squarish face. The other was tall and broad, his cornrows visible as they passed under a streetlamp. Hadn't he seen them outside the restaurant? Were they following them? Paranoia itched along the back of his neck, but Malcolm didn't turn for a second look. If they were following him, they'd know they were made.

"What'd you say his name was?" Tasha asked.

"Who?" Malcolm asked, his line of thought broken.

"The man coming up from South America."

"Matt Hollis."

"And he's like your partner?"

Malcolm strained a look at a parked pickup truck's back window, hoping to see the two men in the reflection, but couldn't make anything out. "Yeah. I'm the senior knight though. It'll take him a few days to get up here. It's a long drive."

"He's driving?"

"Most of the way. He'll have to ferry across the gap, and if he can't catch a ride on a freighter in Panama, he'll drive the rest of the way. Matt's not too fond of airplanes."

"Jesus, that sounds like Hell," Tasha said. "How long does it take?"

Malcolm stole another glance back as he turned into her

complex. The two men weren't there. He sighed in relief. *Just paranoia.* "Ten days if the roads are clear. Hard to know this time of year."

A group of teens laughed and cavorted around a bench in the apartment's courtyard. The stink of cheap cigars and pot wafted from their direction. A chunky boy met Malcolm's eye as they passed, his eyes a little too hard for someone so young.

Tasha led him up a flight of stairs to the second floor. "Mal, I was thinking. I don't think that cult you met last year is to blame for Ulises' murder."

"Why's that?"

She stopped before her dented maroon door and turned. "If they were demon worshipers, wouldn't they have taken the mask?"

Malcolm paused. "Maybe they didn't know what it was."

"Do you believe that?"

He chewed his lip. "No."

"Same with that guy you were talking about, the one that was a familiar once," Tasha said, fishing a bulbous key ring from her purse. "Wouldn't he have taken it?"

"Probably," he said. Ghouls couldn't make familiars—not living ones anyway. Still, she had a point. A demon that sent him there, because the mask prevented it from entering itself, would have wanted the ghoul freed or the mask destroyed. Why hadn't he seen this?

She unlocked the door and looked at him, a question in her eyes. "So what do you think?" he asked.

Tasha cocked her head. "About?"

"Who killed him."

She shook her head and sighed. "I don't know, Mal. I just … I just think it was someone else."

"Like who?"

"I don't know." Tasha opened the door. "But I don't think it was someone who loved demons." She met his eyes, a faint smile at the edge of her lips. Invitation.

Malcolm swallowed, already regretting his next words. "I enjoyed tonight. I have a big day tomorrow."

"I enjoyed it too," she said. If there was disappointment, she hid it well. "It's been too long."

He smiled. "So you think I can get that second date? I promised you burgers."

"Yeah," she chuckled. "You got it."

"Good." He leaned in. She met his lips, soft and tender. She tugged on his lower lip as she ended the kiss. "Goodnight, Malcolm."

"'Night."

Tasha stepped inside and smiled warmly as she closed the door. Malcolm stood there for a moment after the bolt clicked, old, forgotten emotion welling up as if they'd never left. Damn it, he thought, unsure if the curse was for his desires or for his refusal to act on them. Malcolm balled his fist as if to knock on the door. No, he *did* have things to do. He had a gris-gris to finish, a police file to read, and a werebeast to find before it hurt anyone.

The teens paid him no mind as Malcolm passed, headed back to his hotel. Tasha's theory troubled him. If a demon or vengeful cultists hadn't killed Ulises, then who? Maybe Jim was right. What if the killer's intention wasn't based on the old man's past but on the present? If it was some former customer, unhappy with their hex or gris-gris, or even some misguided fool hoping to steal the bokor's power, then where did that leave Malcolm?

A woman screamed. Malcolm spun, instinctively dropping Hounacier's shoulder strap to his hand.

A blonde with tiny, pink shorts squealed a few feet behind him, her arms wrapped around a tall man.

"When did you get here?" the man asked, adjusting his wireframe glasses.

"This morning," she gushed.

Tourists, Malcolm thought, annoyed. Returning the strap to his shoulder, he turned back around, but not before he spied the two men he'd seen earlier. They were a half block behind him, strolling his direction. His pulse quickened. No way it was chance. Drawing a breath, he continued, trying not to appear that he was on to them.

He turned at the next street, following the noise toward the more populated areas. Malcolm passed a crowded cafe entrance and braved a look behind him. Shorty and Cornrows had fallen back but were still following, not looking his direction. Shorty sucked on a cigarette, watching his feet, while his tall companion peered into his phone. Who was he talking to?

Malcolm hurried across Canal Street and went left, away from his hotel, once he reached the opposite side. Pulling Hounacier's bag to his front, he unzipped the top. After another block, he slowed, allowing his pursuers time to see him before he turned beside a towering building. Near the back, he tucked into a wide, loading garage.

Dim fluorescents flickered above. A pair of giant blue compactors sat along one side. Malcolm ducked into the shadows between them, nearly stepping into a pile of human shit. Trying to ignore the awful stink of refuse and feces, he watched the street outside and waited.

The two men came into view, walking at a quick pace. Malcolm slunk behind the steel bin, holding his breath. He slid his hand into the bag and gripped the machete tight. Attacking them outright was out of the question. Too many witnesses, and he didn't even know their intentions. They could have guns, something he lacked. If they saw him, he was trapped.

The scarab tattoo didn't move as they passed just eight feet from him. Their footsteps faded. Malcolm waited a count of ten, emerged from his hiding place, and peeked around the corner.

The two men stood at an intersection, scanning up either side. A squarish lump bulged at the back of Shorty's waistband. Pistol. Malcolm tensed, ready to draw back in case they turned toward him. Finally, Cornrows committed to a decision. He nodded and hurried across the street, his small partner at his heels.

Malcolm quietly stepped out and doubled back to Canal. Trying not to run, he hurried four blocks up to his hotel. He looked back, making sure he didn't see his pursuers before he headed inside.

The young man behind the counter didn't even glance up from his computer screen as Malcolm passed and went straight for the elevator. Jaw tight, Malcolm watched the front door, impatient for the slow elevator to come. He suppressed the urge to push the already lit button again, as if that helped. Eventually, it dinged, and three seconds later, the metal doors slid apart. Malcolm pressed "5" and kept his eyes on the front door until the elevator lazily closed. He let out a long, slow breath as it started up. Who were those men? Not demons. Maybe Earl Warren's men, sent to keep an eye on him. Maybe Ulises' killers. If he'd had Orlovski here, they could follow the men, see where they were going. With Sam, they could run a three-point tail, which was preferable. But Orlovski was out of commission for the next year. Sam was with him, and Matt was nowhere near the country yet. Malcolm hated working alone. He'd always had Ulises or another knight watching his back. Now, he felt naked. Alone. He was always the hunter, not the target, hiding in dark alleys, wondering who his enemies were.

The elevator stopped at the top floor then waited its customary eternity before finally opening. Malcolm smiled at a middle-aged couple waiting before the door. He took the stairs back down to the third floor, checking that the hall was clear before stepping out.

The "Do Not Disturb" tag still hung from his door. Malcolm scanned the halls, verifying he was alone, then slipped into his room.

The room was dark, the only light being the red LCD alarm clock. One hand inside Hounacier's bag, gripping the handle, he flipped the lights.

Empty.

Malcolm checked the closet, the bathroom, and bed. All as he had left it. The unsewn leather pouch and packets of herbs that would become Rochelle Duplessis' gris-gris was still atop the desk. His phone blooped loudly. Checking it, he saw video of himself searching the closet five seconds earlier. The hidden camera was still working. No one had been in his room.

He let out a sigh, finally allowing some of the adrenaline to cool. Releasing his grip on Hounacier, Malcolm reached behind the picture frame and pressed a little button, cutting the feed. He felt under the side chair and peeled the green jump drive from where he'd taped it. Police evidence was nothing he wanted to be caught with, and leaving it out was equally stupid. Malcolm opened his laptop and jacked the drive in. Hopefully, the Valducans had found something in the files he'd sent them. Regardless, he intended to finish reading them, maybe even continue on that damned gris-gris. He eyed the cheap, single-serving coffee pot resting in the corner. It was going to be a long night.

CHAPTER 7

"Beautiful lady, beautiful lady, Filomèz take my gift and bring prosperity." Malcolm kissed the curved needle and looped a single stitch in the leather. Once tight, he looked at the small photograph of Rochelle, lit by the seven candles on the table. He closed his eyes, holding the image of her smiling, round face in his mind. "Beautiful lady, beautiful lady, Filomèz take my gift and bring prosperity." Malcolm made another stitch.

The gris-gris bag was coming along much faster then he'd expected, though he did have a few setbacks along the way. It had taken several attempts before he'd successfully burned the intricate loa's symbol into the light green leather that would face the pouch's interior. The fourth try, he'd managed to sketch the glyph with a red-hot needle without a single mistake. A tight, black coil of Rochelle's hair ran alongside the white cotton thread, making each stitch a part of her. It also had a tendency to kink and break if he wasn't careful. A lazy priest might spread the stitches out, taking a fraction of the time, but Malcolm was a perfectionist. The stitches needed to be tightly spaced to hold the loa's blessing. Ulises' reputation as his mentor was at stake if Malcolm cut corners.

"Beautiful lady, beautiful lady, Filomèz take my gift and bring prosperity."

Malcolm looped the stitch through and rubbed his eyes. Still wired after avoiding his pursuers, and with the power of Hounacier's blessed tattoo, he'd stayed up too late reading the police file. He'd studied over a hundred pictures of the scene. Graphic close-ups of Ulises' headless corpse, the carpet beneath soaked red, and the black ghoul mask leering from the splattered wall above. Malcolm had seen many bodies, even of friends, but was that so much different than seeing the old man like that. Shots of the tattoos they both shared, a deep gash at his shoulder, the camera flash reflecting white off the still-wet blood. No defensive wounds. Ulises had either known his killer or was taken by surprise. The amount of blood suggested it hadn't been quick. He'd suffered there, on the floor of his house, beneath the photos of his adopted son who never called and the trapped ghoul that hated him. Autopsy results would be weeks away. Malcolm doubted the report was priority. The cause of death was easy to guess.

As Duplessis had said, there were a lot of fingerprints, but there were also hairs. On the furniture, in the carpet, and stored in dozens of clay jars around the old man's work area. Unfortunately, DNA tests would also be several weeks. Still, many of the prints came up in the police database. Ulises' home had been a veritable halfway house for New Orleans' worst. Among them, a Mister Marcus Fisher. His photo matched Liz's description perfectly: Mid-thirties, stocky, though the hair in the most recent photo was shaved. Malcolm had his demon-addict. Marcus was familiar with addiction, it appeared. Amphetamines, mostly. He also liked knives. He'd served five years for stabbing a man.

NOPD had already ruled Marcus Fisher out as a suspect. The night before Ulises' murder, Marcus had been found with three grams of meth and a bottle of non-prescribed Adderall after he'd robbed a taxi driver—all three being clear violations of his parole. Marcus had been, and still was, in Orleans Parish Prison. OPP was a demonic paradise. Malcolm suspected that Marcus would have little problem finding a new master there. Still, he planned to pay him a visit. Maybe see if Marcus might know anything about Ulises' murder or the mask.

Malcolm set the half-finished pouch down and checked the clock. 2:38.

Shit. AJ.

He quickly put everything away, careful not to damage the drying flowers, grabbed his bags, and headed out.

"Police arrived at the scene to find the victims, their throats cut."

A short, teal bus sat out front of AJ's shop, its roof sawn off like it had been sliced with an industrial laser. A man in a ridiculous pirate getup stood at the front, recounting the gruesome tale of a long-dead murderer who had once stalked the streets. What truth the story held was buried beneath a crust of lies and exaggerations. But the nearly twenty tourists ate it up, snapping pictures of the now empty lot across the street, where the bodies of two women were found three decades before.

"Incredibly, there was no blood at the scene," the guide said, his voice booming from a mounted speaker, "and no explanation as to where it had gone. It had rained that week, leaving the ground soft, but police found no footprints aside from their own, as if the killer had simply floated down like an angel of death ... or a vampire."

He got that part right, Malcolm thought, shaking his head. Ulises had killed the demon back in '88. He eyed the cheap, brass-hilted sword hanging at the guide's waist, tucked beneath a red, polyester sash. How was it that he could get away with wearing that all over town without a problem while Hounacier had to hide inside an oxygen tank bag? *Maybe if I dressed like a cartoon too.* Grinning, Malcolm checked over his shoulder one last time, making sure his new friends Shorty and Cornrows weren't around, then pulled open the tattoo parlor door.

Rock and roll music echoed off the art-covered walls, nearly masking the buzz as a pudgy man with a ponytail inked a woman's already colorful sleeve. AJ sat behind a glass counter, its shelves laden with glistening body jewelry. Seeing Malcolm, she looked at the dragon clock on the wall and gave an exaggerated sigh.

"I know," Malcolm groaned.

AJ set her tablet down and sniffed. "You're late."

"Sorry. I got—"

Her pencil-thin brow shot up, silencing him. She jabbed a thumb toward the empty booth behind her. "Get in the chair."

His tongue pressing the roof of his mouth, Malcolm eyed a photograph of a woman's tattooed back. A bright phoenix emerged from blue flames at the base of her spine, its fiery orange wings stretching across her shoulder blades.

"Almost done," AJ said, jabbing the spiked stick along his arm.

Blindness. Malcolm couldn't see, as if his eyes had simply winked out. He froze, panic rising. He still felt and heard rapid, meaty jabs as AJ worked, but he couldn't see. It wasn't blackness. Blackness would have been something. It was just ... nothing. The new tattoo tingled like electricity, then sickly, intangible globs of light, like when he rubbed his eyes in the dark, and the room emerged before him.

"There," AJ said.

Malcolm sat still, wondering what in the hell had just happened. Hounacier's blessing had obviously taken effect, but ... what did it do? He watched as AJ wiped and cleaned the golden mark. The three tapered lines were exactly as Hounacier's vision, their edges outlined in hair-thin red. She hadn't drawn that part. Already, Hounacier had begun her own modifications to the now blessed mark.

"Everything fine with it?" AJ asked, her voice tinged with artist's doubt.

"It's perfect," Malcolm answered, hoping she wouldn't notice the faint but growing metallic sheen.

"Good."

AJ slathered the fresh tattoo with ointment, cool on his angry skin, and wrapped it with gauze. Malcolm massaged his eyes with her fingertips. What had the blindness meant? Hounacier's gifts never came with instructions. Some he knew from Ulises' own marks. The rest, he had to figure out. Most revealed themselves naturally as he noticed changes in himself. Others, like the empathic eye, gave an instinctive urge when to use them.

He paid AJ for her extra time. Her work was among the

best he'd had. She was still young enough that she could easily become a master. Movie stars and the elite would seek her out to offer themselves as her canvas.

The tour bus was gone by the time he left. Malcolm checked the streets, searching for his two new fans or Spiky Hair, though the demon could have easily changed bodies by now, maybe even hopped to one across the world. He doubted that. New Orleans' demonic gravity was too strong for the creatures to resist even when they knew they should. It was here somewhere. Satisfied, Malcolm shouldered Hounacier's bag and the backpack holding his sawed-off and made his way to Alpuente's.

Sweat trickled along the back of Malcolm's neck, soaking into his already damp shirt. He entered his hotel, grateful for the cool blast of air conditioning. Tasha wasn't at the shop, but Jim had been eager to speak with him about the werebeast.

"What the hell were you thinking, running out of here like that?" Jim had scolded. "We can't have people seeing you chasing after some guy with a machete."

"I'm sorry," Malcolm said. "I wasn't thinking."

"Damn right you weren't. Ulises taught you better than that. We're just lucky no one called the police." He shook he head. "What exactly were you planning to do if you caught him? Kill him in the street? In front of a hundred people?"

Pursing his lips, Malcolm looked away, unable to answer.

The priest sighed, shook his head. "You can't be gettin' emotional like that, Mal. That puts all of us at risk. You, me, Dad, Tasha, even Hounacier. You know better."

Jim was right of course. He nearly always was. Malcolm *did* know better. Master Turgen would have lost his mind if he'd known about it. Master Schmidt probably would have demoted him. "It won't happen again," he said, to himself more than to Jim.

"I know this is tough for you," Jim said. "Just use your head. You're a hunter, Mal. Be one."

Malcolm had given Jim two of his 12-gauge shells for protection: one silver, the other a mixed load for anything else that might wander into the mask's protective gaze. He didn't have that many to give, but he felt better knowing Jim had them. He'd told him about the two men the night before, but Jim didn't have anything more to give than to mirror Malcolm's own theories.

Forgoing the elevator, Malcolm took the stairs up to his floor. Still grumbling about Jim's deserved scolding, he opened his hotel room and froze.

He'd left the lights off, but the room was now lit. Malcolm reached into Hounacier's bag, drawing her out. The lights were still off and the heavy curtains closed, but he could see the room clearly.

No, not clearly. The colors were ... wrong. Muted.

Swallowing, he closed the door behind him with his foot and scanned the room. Colors pinched off as the door shut, leaving everything cast in shades of red, like a crimson spotlight shone from the bed. Malcolm stepped forward, seeing the clock. How was it illuminating the entire room?

He now noticed how much light spilled through and below the curtains, adding its own orange and white hues, far more than he'd ever noticed. Cautiously, he flipped the wall switch. The light drowned out the colored haze, returning the room to normal.

Son of a bitch. He turned the light off, plunging himself into a moment of blackness before the glow from the curtains and red-lit clock filled the room. A crazy laugh erupted from his lips, and he flipped the lights on and off again. *Hounacier, you beautiful angel, you didn't?*

His phone blooped in his pocket as the picture camera messaged him. Ignoring it, excitement tingling along his skin, Malcolm stepped into the dark bathroom beside him and shut the door. The impossibly faint light from beneath the door seemed to swell, illuminating the narrow room enough for him to see most of it. The visibility rivaled most night scopes. Hounacier's new gift was a great power indeed. Malcolm laughed again and kissed the machete's blade. "I love you, baby. Thank you."

Rochelle Duplessis' gris-gris was nearly finished, well ahead of schedule. After several hours stitching and powering it, the growing need to try out his supernatural sight had become unbearable. Malcolm hadn't slept in nearly thirty-eight hours. His blessed stamina could keep him up long enough to enjoy his newest gift.

Malcolm sat at a tiny table against a wall, enjoying a beer and watching the dim bar with more clarity than he could have imagined. The five-piece jazz band had stopped for a quick break, abandoning the Brass Sax into murmurs and inebriated conversations.

He sipped his drink and scanned the crowd. The illuminated faces of customers peering into their phones lit the room like torches. Liz, the redhead from the other night, leaned against the bar, her tits bulging from the top of her shirt as she chatted up a bearded man, working him for drinks. Neither Shorty nor Cornrows had shown themselves yet. *I wonder if anyone here is messaging them.* If the two men were working for someone else, there might be other eyes following him. Pushing the paranoia out of his mind, he finished his drink. *No need to make up more problems than I already have.* Still, Malcolm searched the room for anyone watching him.

Malcolm ordered another beer and headed to the restroom. With no one to watch his table, he carried Hounacier and his backpack with him. Standing in line, he found himself wondering about Tasha. He'd called her earlier that day. Left a voicemail. She'd texted that she enjoyed their date and would see him tomorrow. Why hadn't she called? More so, why did it bother him so much?

It might be a good idea to swing past her place on the way home, just to be sure she was fine. Those men might not have only been following *him.*

No. He stepped into the scummy bathroom, its floor glistening with piss. *She'll kick you in the teeth if you just drop in this time of night.*

Malcolm came back out, alcohol-fueled thoughts pushed aside, and maneuvered through the impatient crowd toward his table. He saw his beer sitting there already and gave it thirty seconds before someone took it. As he made his way closer, the scarab at his arm scuttled around beneath his skin.

He spun, searching the direction opposite the tattoo. A tall, broad-shouldered man walked toward the exit, arm in arm with a long-haired woman with caramel skin. They stepped through the open door and turned. The tattoo itched, moving away until they walked out of range.

Heart thumping, Malcolm pushed his way toward the outer wall. The scarab moved again, sensing the demon on the sidewalk outside.

"Excuse me," he said, nearly walking into a crowded table as he tried to follow the demon's path.

One of the patrons mumbled some insult behind him as Malcolm neared a window. The tattoo inched along, tracking the creature. As expected, the couple strolled into view.

Malcolm ducked back before it could see him. *What now?* One of them was possessed, but which? What of the other one? Familiar? Potential victim?

The scarab moved back to its normal position once the creature was too far away for it to feel. Malcolm checked the window again, seeing the couple continuing on. Did the demon know who he was? Maybe the werebeast had switched bodies and was trying to lure him out. If so, its victim was bait. Someone would die if he didn't act.

Anger flared in his chest. Ulises dead, Orlovski down, people following him, and now a fucking demon strolling by, flaunting its next meal. Malcolm clenched his jaw, watching them cross the street. "Not tonight you don't." Clutching Hounacier's strap along his shoulder, he hurried out into the sticky night.

He dashed between a pair of slow-rolling cars. Once across the street, he peered down the corner where they had turned and spied the couple a block ahead, her arm still looped through his. Before, the shadows might have obscured them, making them difficult to see, but not anymore. A little grin pulled at Malcolm's lip as he followed.

Keeping his distance, Malcolm studied the pair, searching for any telltale sign of which one was corrupted. The man was built like a linebacker, muscled arms bulging from his sleeves. But the strength of the host rarely correlated with the demon's.

The petite woman on his arm could be it just as easily. Instead of size, Malcolm watched their motions. She moved with a dancer's grace, fluid and quick. The man walked tall, confident, his shoulders back. It told him nothing. They turned right at Elysian Fields. The woman's arm slid down and took the man's hand. Malcolm held back, watching from the shadows. Once they were two blocks ahead, he braved following down the well-lit street. The few pedestrians offered little cover. One paused as the couple passed, turning back for a final look. Then the next did the same.

Charmed, Malcolm thought. The demon's power had caught their interest even with only a passing glance. Vampire? Succubi? Malcolm hadn't seen their faces. Maybe the demon's eyes would betray it.

They crossed at Chartress and continued down the narrow street, walled with tiny houses. Unzipping the top of Hounacier's bag, Malcolm positioned it under his arm, hoping it didn't look too obvious. He remained at a distance, allowing his new sight to pierce the shadows. The demon and its companion kept their lazy pace, never slowing or looking back. The homes gave way to shitty buildings. Shops and offices, most of them abandoned. No one else was on the streets. Beyond a railroad track, brick and steel warehouses, crusted with graffiti, loomed silent and dark. Malcolm picked up his pace lest he lose them in the industrial maze.

Headlights turned onto the road ahead, killing Malcolm's night vision. The sedan's engine roared. Malcolm averted his eyes as it neared, rap blasting from the open windows. The bass' boom hit his chest as the car rolled past.

Malcolm looked up again and froze. The couple was gone.

Pulse thumping, he scanned the streets. Tailing a demon was dangerous. Losing one even more so. Had it seen him? Was it now stalking him, alone, on a dark, empty street?

Where's the human? he wondered, fighting back paranoia. *If it saw me and fled, where did its companion go?* No demon could transform itself in the time he'd looked away. Morphing bone and musculature took a few seconds to complete, as did sprouting fur and horns. The companion would have reacted, run, or screamed. *Unless they were a familiar.*

He looked back. The street was empty. Malcolm unzipped his backpack and removed the sawed-off. Holding it against his side, he cautiously approached where he'd last seen them. A damp breeze rustled his hair. He passed a parking lot, walled behind chain link. A scrawny calico watched him from the shadow beneath a van. Malcolm came to the brick warehouse where the demon had last been. White, rust-stained bars covered the windows. Keeping an eye on the roof, he passed the building to see a litter-strewn field to the side. The demon and its companion where nowhere to be seen.

Two more warehouses stood beside his, one brick, the other blue sheet metal. Beyond them, he heard the chugging of a ship making its way up the Mississippi, invisible behind an earthen berm. Malcolm swallowed, squeezed the shotgun's grip, and slowly made his way around the building, careful to stay quiet on the broken seashell gravel. He peeked down the alley between the first two buildings and froze.

The bald man stood thirty feet away, his back against the metal wall. The woman knelt before him, naked, her head slowly bobbing before his crotch. Enormous, caramel-colored wings spread open from her back. Succubus!

Unsheathing Hounacier, Malcolm let the oxygen bag fall from his shoulder. He stepped out, clutching the machete and the sawed-off. The gun could hurt her enough to prevent her flying away, but he couldn't risk injuring her victim.

Gravel crunched beneath his feet.

The man looked up, seeing Malcolm across the alley. His lips curled into a wicked smile.

The succubus pulled back, and Malcolm's eyes widened. A grotesquely huge cock slid from the demon's throat. He saw now that the man, too, was naked. No discarded clothes littered the alley. The chiseled, ebon man wasn't a victim. He was an incubus. His clothes, like his lover's, were nothing more than glamoured illusion.

The succubus moved to stand. Malcolm raised the sawed-off and fired. Blood exploded from her arm, and amethyst shot peppered her wings. The incubus whipped his arm around her, pushing her aside as he charged. Malcolm fired the second barrel, taking it in the chest. The demon roared. Unfazed, it hurtled toward him like a rampaging rhino. Malcolm dropped the smoking Remington and brought his palm up. The tattooed lid barely parted before the demon was on him. Malcolm lurched to the side, swinging Hounacier as he spun. The blade scratched the incubus' back. The beast turned, blood pouring from its open pectorals and onto the white gravel. Backing away, Malcolm brought his palm up. The incubus' eyes narrowed, but it stood firm. Leather wings rustled. The scarab moved. Malcolm wheeled as the succubus sailed toward him, claws splayed. He aimed his warding palm at her, blasting her in its power. She shrieked and fell back as if hitting a wall. Seizing the opening, the incubus charged.

Malcolm ducked the beefy fist and it smashed through the metal wall behind him. He tried to dive, but the demon's knee slammed into his face with a sickly crack. Blood exploded from Malcolm's nose. Blinded with pain, Malcolm thrust Hounacier upward. He felt her hit. The incubus bellowed and leaped back, wrenching the machete from Malcolm's sweat-slicked grip.

Fighting to stay conscious, Malcolm scrambled to his feet. The incubus pulled at the blade jutting up though its belly. Weaponless, Malcolm stepped back. Outrunning them was impossible. He eyed the discarded shotgun. Even if he could reach it, the shells were in his bag.

Snarling, the incubus kicked the Remington, spraying gravel. Malcolm jerked to the side, the gun barely missing him before it sailed out into the darkness. The incubus charged again. Malcolm dove toward it. As he hit the ground, he grabbed Hounacier's handle and yanked. The demon's foot slammed into his ribs like a sledge. It stumbled over him, falling to its knees.

The succubus shrieked toward him. Malcolm rolled to his feet, grunting as he stood. He swiped the blade, but she flapped backward, buffeting Malcolm with a hard gust. The incubus staggered to its feet and turned. Malcolm lunged, spun, and hacked. Blood sprayed across the alley, igniting mid-air in purple-red fire. The incubus crumpled, its nearly severed head lolling to the side.

The succubus wailed, high and shrill. Clutching his side, Malcolm took a step toward her, fiery blood dripping from his blade. She hissed and then flew up into the night.

Watching her, Malcolm let out a breath and allowed his body to slump. Demon fire flickered off the alley walls, bathing them in crimson violet. He spat blood and touched his nose, wincing. Broken. He swabbed his blood and sweat-streaked face and wiped it on his already ruined shirt. Blood continued streaming down across his lips.

"Christ," he panted, his ribs aching with each breath. Someone had to have heard the gunshots. Police were notoriously slow, but he couldn't risk it. Malcolm eyed the dead demon, encased in ghostly fire. A moth fluttered around it. *Fucking reckless,* he scolded to himself. His own DNA was splattered on the ground and the corpse's knee. He looked around, hoping for a faucet, something to wash away the blood.

Movement caught his eye. Far across the empty field, hidden in the shadows but still visible to Malcolm's enhanced sight, two figures stood watching him. Shorty and Cornrows.

Cornrows smiled then slapped his companion on the side. The men raced away.

Fuck! Malcolm looked back at the corpse. *No time.* He limped from the alley, grabbed Hounacier's bag, and fled.

CHAPTER 8

A piercing screech jerked Malcolm from a restless sleep. Hand still resting on Hounacier, he glared at the alarm clock. 6:30. Grimacing in pain, he stretched his arm and turned it off.

Malcolm was pretty certain the incubus had fractured at least one of his ribs. The whole side stung with every movement. Broken or not, doctors wouldn't be able to do anything about that, and walking into a hospital just after an alley decapitation wouldn't have been a good idea. Still, Malcolm sure wished he had something for the pain. What few meds he'd had were given to Orlovski for the drive.

Gingerly, he crawled from the bed and checked his phone. Allan hadn't messaged. Hopefully a good sign. Not bothering to turn on the light, Malcolm shuffled to the bathroom.

A pathetic sight greeted him in the mirror. White gauze encased his nose, a rust-brown spot along the bridge, framed by a purplish pair of black eyes. The bleeding had finally stopped around 2:00. The dark bruise along his side had spread to maybe six inches across. Tiny nicks and gravel scratches marred his back and knees.

You deserve this, he thought. *Dumb fucking move.* Malcolm had lectured novice hunters countless times never to do the exact thing he'd done. New Orleans was a demon well. No Valducan was to ever hunt here alone. He was lucky to be alive. Hounacier was too important. If he'd died … Malcolm shook his head. *No excuse.*

Drawing a breath, he carefully peeled the tape back to inspect the damage. The swelling had gone down some, and the cut across his bridge wasn't as bad as he'd thought. Still, it would be a while before he didn't look like he'd gotten his ass beaten. *Should have seen the other guy.*

The shower was a welcome refresher despite its lack of pressure. He stood trancelike, letting the water hit his shoulders and run down his back while he replayed the previous night.

"All right," Allan had said over the phone. "We have one headless corpse, two witnesses, possible DNA, a pissed succubus, and a werebeast somewhere about?"

Malcolm dabbed the bleeding cut. "Definite DNA." The two wads of toilet paper screwed up his nostrils made his voice nasal. "There was no time to sanitize the site. Also fingerprints on the gun. Didn't have time to search for it either." Losing Ulises' sawed-off pissed him off as much as everything else. If only those two assholes hadn't seen him.

The Englishman's groan echoed through the cell's speakerphone. "You sure leaving town isn't an option?"

"Not yet," Malcolm said, still fighting the seeping wound. "There's too much at stake. The werebeast knows about the mask."

"Mal, you might need to collect that mask. You know how dangerous it is. And how valuable."

"I'm not stealing it from them," he growled. "And if I did, nothing could stop that beast from coming in there and killing everyone. Besides," Malcolm added. "I need to find out where in the hell Ulises got that thing. What if there are more?"

"Mal ... you were ambushed by two succubi. You're in danger."

"One of them is gone. They won't try that again." Malcolm hated lying about how he'd encountered the two demons, but it was better than the truth. Not that Allan wouldn't have understood. It was just too hard to admit his own stupidity out loud.

"But that succubus could move to a male body and come back," Allan said.

"I'm not leaving, Allan," he said flatly.

Silence. Eventually, Allan spoke again, his tone all business. Cold. "All right, then, damage control. No cameras at the yard?"

"No."

"Are you sure? It was dark."

"There were no cameras," Malcolm said. "I'd have seen them."

"Clothes? Shoes?"

Malcolm glanced toward the lumpy bag beside the toilet. Pink smears shone through the white plastic. He'd liked those shoes. "Bagged. I'll dump them once we're off the phone."

"Change hotels?"

"Same thing."

"I'll start now," Allan said. "Uwe's on assignment for the next several days, and my hacking is dreadful. But I'll see what I can dig up, find out what police have."

"Thanks."

"Mal," Allan said, voice tinged with apprehension, "are you sure you don't want to report this to the Masters? It's not like you."

"I will. Just not yet. You know how Schmidt and Sonu are."

Allan snorted.

"Just buy me a couple days."

"I'll do what I can. Just … don't make me regret it."

"Thanks, brother. I owe you." Malcolm had tapped the phone, ending the call. "I owe you a lot."

The pipes in the wall groaned, and water belched suddenly from the showerhead. Missing his old, shitty hotel, Malcolm finished his shower.

It was 7:00 when he stepped out of the bathroom, a fresh bandage on his nose and a film of AJ's tattoo antibiotic cream on his more serious cuts. He wrestled a strangely narrow ironing board from the closet and flipped on the iron. As it warmed, he fished the dress clothes from his hastily packed bag and tossed them onto the bed.

Shorty and Cornrows might not have seen the whole fight, might have missed the succubus, but they definitely saw Malcolm above a corpse sheathed in demon-fire. None of the suspects in Duplessis' file matched their appearances. If they weren't linked to Ulises' murder, then they were following him for another reason. It was time to lay the cards on the table and visit their suspected employer.

A pair of dueling mockingbirds chirped furiously back and forth in the early morning. From the shade of their tree, Malcolm watched well-dressed worshipers entering the almost-glowing white church across the street. Aside from the main entrance, framed by an old man and a chunky teen serving as greeters, Saints of Light Church had smaller doors on either side. Malcolm had taken position near the packed, gravel parking lot, surveying that side door and the front. From that position, he could also watch the cinderblock-and-metal building behind it, which looked like a school gymnasium but white with dark, wooden doors. He felt odd just standing there, half-hidden behind a parked pickup. If he'd had a car, he could watch from inside. Or if he was smoking a cigarette, maybe he wouldn't look as strange. However, Malcolm didn't smoke, and he didn't have any cigarettes to pretend that he did.

Black eyes hidden behind sunglasses, he searched for familiar faces. By all accounts, nothing looked unusual among the churchgoers. Maybe there was a bit more white in their clothes and the women's scarves than at other churches, but it wasn't overly obvious. Most people would never guess it was a voodoo congregation. It was as inviting and warm as any Christian church.

Traffic through the doors slowed to a trickle, and Malcolm checked his watch. 8:57. Adjusting his collar, he strolled across the street.

The old black man was closing the entrance but smiled broadly when Malcolm started up the five concrete steps. "Welcome," he said, offering a folded paper. His gaze locked onto the white bandage across Malcolm's nose then was politely averted. "Beautiful morning."

"It is." Malcolm accepted the program, his palm down to conceal the tattoo.

"We're just about to start. Have a seat, brother."

Malcolm stepped inside, removing his glasses. Low

murmurs filled the cozy chapel. Several fans hung from the vaulted ceiling, spinning lazily. Sunlight shone through the three colorful windows on the left side, each painted to look like stained glass. They appeared almost like Catholic saints, though a few differences, such as the yams and avocado in Saint Isidore's bounty, revealed them as the loa they truly represented. Malcolm slid into one of the rear pews, setting Hounacier's bag beside him. He scanned the crowd, hoping to see either Shorty or Cornrows.

A minute later, voodoo houngan and real-estate agent Earl Warren stepped up to the front, draped in vestments reminiscent of an episcopal minister. Earl raised his hand, and the congregation rose. Leading songs and prayer, Earl preached with a passion and charisma most priests could only envy. From the back, Malcolm joined the song and prayers while still scanning the audience.

As the service continued, he grew more and more impressed at what Earl had accomplished. Not only was his flock meeting in a well-made and modern building, they were by far the most diverse group of voodoo practitioners he'd ever witnessed both financially and racially. Earl's dream of bringing a legitimacy to voodoo was well on its way to becoming a reality.

And that's what made him dangerous.

For twenty years, Earl had fought, campaigned, and even risked his life to pull his religion out from the shadows of superstition and racial hatred. He'd combated gang wars, homelessness, drug abuse, and domestic violence, all while preaching his faith. People like Ulises and Malcolm represented the darkness and sinister underbelly that, in Earl's mind, demeaned everything he stood for. Earl would die for his dream. Would he kill for it?

Today's sermon discussed the importance of family. Earl had only begun when his eyes met Malcolm's in the audience. A flash of concern, maybe surprise, then the houngan smiled. His gaze returned to Malcolm several times during the remainder of the service. Malcolm watched for any subtle signs of concern or warning signals the priest might relay to anyone in the room, but Earl didn't seem the least concerned at all. His church was a sanctuary. Reputations on both sides had to be maintained, and Earl knew as well as Malcolm, that they were both safe here. At least for now.

After two more songs and a closing prayer, the service disbanded. Earl stood at the main doors, chatting and saying farewells. Malcolm remained seated as worshipers shuffled past. Some glanced his way. Most fixated on the bandage and black eyes, but a few looked at Malcolm himself. Curious. Fearful. One plump woman pulled her boy closer to her side as she saw the bokor. Malcolm wondered what all they'd heard about him. Surely, Earl had warned them. Ulises would have been honored to have such looks. The old man had reveled in his mystique.

Earl gave a small nod as the last of the congregation finally left. He closed the door and returned to the altar, robes swishing. "That's all right, Cedric," he told a young teen extinguishing candles with a long douter. "I'll take care of that. Go on to class."

"Thank you, sir," Cedric said, handing Earl the cone-tipped rod. He tugged at his black tie and hurried through a side door.

The priest stepped onto the platform and snuffed a yellow taper. "Happy you came, Malcolm." He extinguished another and turned. "Pleasant surprise to see you there. Ulises never visited."

"I love what you've done here," Malcolm said, slipping out of the pew. He stifled a grunt as his ribs protested the movement. "Impressive."

"Thank you." Earl shook his head. "You look like shit."

Malcolm laughed, winced. "Rough night."

"You okay?"

"I'm fine."

Earl set the douter in a corner and brushed an unseen blemish off his robes. "I heard there was a murder down in Bywater last night. Man got his head cut off."

"Really?"

The houngan nodded sadly. "Burned him up in a dumpster," he added, gaze probing.

Malcolm paused. "I can honestly say I don't know anything about that." He searched Earl's face for any sign he knew more than he'd said. Nothing.

"Probably drugs. Lord knows." He tapped his nose. "So you goin' to tell me about this?"

"I had a momentary lapse in judgment."

Earl's lip twitched like he was going to say more, but he just shook his head. "So what brings you here, Malcolm?"

"A pair of men have been following me since Friday. I wanted to know if they're yours."

"Mine?" Earl's nostrils flared, insult mixed with confusion.

"Yeah. Black. One's tall, cornrows. The other is short, square little face."

"I don't know anything about this. Are they who did this to you?"

Malcolm shook his head.

"Why would you think I sent them?" he asked slowly.

"You had some strong words back at Paula's shop. Few hours later, those men started following me."

Earl straightened, chest rising. "That's not how I work, Malcolm. Now, I'm not gonna lie; I have asked about you. It's only fair. But I haven't sent anyone to follow you."

Malcolm studied the priest's eyes. If he was lying, he was good, but Malcolm had no doubt the businessman was superb.

"You should tell the police about this."

"No," Malcolm said. "I'll find out who they are."

Earl's brow arched. "And how do you intend on doing that?"

"Just talk to them. Say hello, find out who sent them?"

"Mal, if these men are dangerous, if they're related to Ulises' murder ..."

"I can take care of myself," Malcolm assured.

"I know you can do that. I have ears, and I knew Ulises. But this is a job for the *police*, not you." He clasped his hands before him and squeezed. "I know what Ulises did. And he took care of a lot of bad people, troubled people. But demons, monsters?" He looked around, then whispered, "He *murdered* those people. You know better than that. That talk scares folks. Zombies and demons and all that Hollywood trash. I turned a blind eye once, but *never* again. I so much as suspect you hurtin' anybody, I swear you will go to prison."

Malcolm's jaw tightened, anger boiling in his gut. "If you don't believe in them," he growled, "you should ask the loa about them."

"The loa talk in riddles, Malcolm. Symbols. You know that as any of us do."

"Not on this. They're real."

Earl shook his head regretfully. "I'm sorry you believe that." Malcolm chewed his lip. *Damn fool.* He drew a breath. Held it.

"Well, thank you, Earl. I assumed wrong. My apologies."

Earl looked at him, as if unsure Malcolm was insulting him or not.

"You have nothing to worry about." Malcolm shouldered Hounacier's bag and turned. He slipped a five into the donation box beside the door. "I really do like what you've done here." He pulled open the oaken doors and stepped out, leaving Earl standing at the altar.

"Malcolm!" Tasha exclaimed, putting a hand to her lip. "What happened?"

"Can I come in?"

"Of course." She opened the apartment door. Tasha wore a curve-hugging, green dress, likely from the morning's mass.

Malcolm glanced back, searching for his tails. Not seeing them, he stepped inside. Dark wood furniture, too large for her modest place, dominated the apartment. Tattered paperbacks, ranging from theological to cheap spy thrillers, packed a single bookcase. Antique cameras and framed photos filled the cherry shelves on the opposite wall. Two of the pictures were of Malcolm: an artistic black and white of him, long hair framing a crooked smile, and another with his arm around Tasha's shoulder, their faces frozen in laughter after one of her performances. A tangle of various plants surrounded the one large, barred window. It smelled earthy, tinged with her perfume and a faint burnt odor, maybe two days old. Tasha had never been a skilled chef.

She closed and locked the door and reached for his bandaged nose. "Who did this?"

"Incubus." Malcolm tugged at his unbuttoned collar,

allowing some of the air-conditioned air to flow under his shirt. "Incubus?"

"Yeah." He brushed away her concerned hand. "Big bastard. Like a bodybuilder on PCP."

"Did you ... kill it?"

He nodded.

Tasha picked her guitar off of a wine-colored couch and placed it on a black stand. "Sit down. You want something to drink?"

"Yes please." He grunted, stiffly lowering himself into the seat. "Found him over in Bywater behind some warehouses. There was a succubus too." He pressed a palm against his side. Somehow, the pressure made it feel better despite the pain. "It got away."

"So ... are you all right?"

Malcolm sighed. "I don't know. Succubi usually don't retaliate. At least not directly. Might charm a victim to do it for her. But ..." He shook his head.

"What?" She offered him a tinkling glass of tea and sat down beside him.

"I think it was mated. When I found them, they were ... occupied with one another. Demon packs are common, but sex ... never heard of it between them."

"Why not?"

"They don't reproduce." Malcolm sipped the cold tea.

Tasha shot him a little smirk. "We weren't trying to reproduce."

He chuckled then winced. "Yeah ... you got me there. It's just that the incubus, it tried to protect her." Malcolm pursed his lips. "That doesn't happen."

"It was protecting its mate from the big bad bokor." She winked.

"But they don't mate."

Tasha shrugged. "Obviously, *they* did."

Demons mating? The idea of it was ludicrous. Still ... the way the incubus had thrown its arm across her. The archives told that cambions, half-breed children of succubi and humans, were possible. But if they could breed with each other? What would that union beget?

Malcolm gulped his tea, the blocky ice cubes clacking. He set the glass on the table and met Tasha's golden eyes. "There's more. Your dad tell you about the guys that were following me?" She nodded.

"They saw me kill that demon last night. Probably saw the succubus too. Ran away when I spotted them, but," he shook his head, "I was standing over a headless corpse at the time, Hounacier in hand."

Tasha nodded as if to herself then swallowed. "Well, means they're not cops."

"It does. Probably not reporters either. Evidently, someone moved the body after I left."

She cocked her head back. "What?"

"Paid a visit to Earl Warren this morning. Maybe see if those men were his. He said they weren't."

Tasha snorted, her full lips curling into a smirk. "He'd say that if they were."

"True. But he also asked me about a murder down there last night. Said someone burned the body up in a dumpster."

"But … you didn't?" she asked.

Malcolm shook his head. "I left it in an alley. Some of my blood in it. Once I saw those two run away, I just got out of there."

"So you think they moved it?"

"Don't know. Swinging by the crime scene wouldn't be a good idea right now. Not if it's still there. And especially if Earl suspects me. No telling how many cops he knows." Malcolm ran a finger along his jaw. "But if you could give me a ride, we could drive past, casual, let me get a peek to see if the police are around."

Tasha's brow furrowed into a glare. "So you want us *both* to go by a crime scene that you *just said* the police might be watching out for you?"

"Yeah, but we'll be in a car. I'll keep low. Better than walking down the street with the murder weapon on me."

Her glare didn't waver. "Uh huh. Speaking of which, if I were to do this, which I'm not saying I will, Hounacier stays here."

Malcolm opened his mouth, but her finger shot up, silencing him. "No. I'm not getting pulled over by the police with a suspect and a murder weapon inside my car. Period."

Malcolm closed his mouth and nodded slowly. "Agreed."

Chartress Street looked even shittier during the daylight hours than it had at night. Boarded and broken windows peered out from a quarter of the building. Neglect and decay had consumed the rest. Many so afflicted with peeling paint, crumbling brickwork, and unkempt vegetation, Malcolm preferred to think of it as some grand, intentional art piece rather than the sad and rotting truth. The big exception was the two steel warehouses, immaculate and the color of freshly fallen snow, safely walled off behind high chain-link topped with coiled razor wire.

A few cars travelled the narrow street. Malcolm sat low in the seat beside Tasha, searching for any sign of police, finding none. "Up here." He motioned to the row of small warehouses beside the empty lot. "Keep slow. Not too much though."

He peered at the alley entrance where the demons had been. No yellow police tape. No officers or reporters. Nothing. Malcolm tried to twist for a better look as they passed but hissed, the sharp pain in his ribs stopping him.

"You all right?" Tasha's death-grip on the wheel revealed just how much she truly hated bringing him here.

Malcolm sniffed, forcing away the pain. "I'm fine."

"You gone to a doctor?"

"No. Picked up some ibuprofen this morning, but ..."

Tasha laughed. "Jesus, Mal. You're thick sometimes. You know that?"

"Doctors ask questions. Turn around up here. Give it one more pass."

She pulled into the tiny parking lot for an abandoned eatery, and wheeled the little hatchback around. Malcolm studied the alley as they neared, seeing the black hole where the incubus had punched through the metal wall. The corpse was gone. *Son of a bitch. Who moved it?* He strummed the gray armrest. *And why?*

"That it?" Tasha asked after another block.

Malcolm nodded. "That's all I needed. Thank you."

"Good. Now let's get your fool ass something for the pain."

"No hospitals," Malcolm said, desperate to get back to Hounacier. They'd left her hidden in Tasha's apartment, locked in an old armoire. What if someone broke in? She needed protection.

Tasha shot him a sidelong glance. "Who said anything about a hospital?"

"What?"

She blew out an exasperated breath. "Seriously, Mal, have you forgotten where we are?"

"Tasha," Maggie said, opening the door. "How are you doing?"

"Good," Tasha said, hugging the voodoo queen. "How are you?"

"Irritated. Guest comin' tonight. Louis insisted on cookin' for it. Kicked me out of my own kitchen." Maggie looked at Malcolm standing on the porch behind Tasha. "Boo, what happened?"

"You know ..." He plucked a dead leaf off a hanging plant. "Fighting."

She nodded, a knowing look on the old woman's face.

"He won't go to a doctor," Tasha said. "I was wondering if you could help him out."

"Of course, baby. You know I will." Maggie's gaze lowered to Malcolm's empty hands. "Just the two of you, I see," a subtle smile to her voice. "Come on inside; we're lettin' the cold out."

Malcolm followed Tasha inside. A pair of women sat on the couch, talking to a bald man with a thick, gold hoop dangling from one ear. A trio of kids, Malcolm guessed between the ages of five and nine, sat on the floor, watching cartoons. The smell of sautéing onions awoke his empty stomach. Through the open kitchen doorway, he saw a hefty, olive-skinned man in an apron working above a sizzling skillet.

"Come back this way," Maggie said, closing the front door.

Malcolm smiled hello to the seated strangers, their faces familiar but names forgotten, and followed the old woman through the hallway.

"Here we are," Maggie said, opening a bedroom door. "Little

privacy. Sit on the bed there."

Malcolm did as he was told. He scanned the collection of old photographs and decades of shadowboxed Mardi Gras memorabilia.

"Okay now," Maggie said, pulling a wooden chair up before him. "Let's see what we got. Open your shirt up."

Malcolm gave a surprised look.

"I saw the way you walked in here. Been doin' this since before you was born." She stabbed a slender finger toward him and twirled it around. "Open it up."

Tasha frowned as Malcolm peeled open his shirt, revealing the hideous purple bruise. Maggie's expression remained neutral. "Fightin'? Looks like you were on the losin' side." Her fingers traced along his ribs, earning a pained wince. "Don't feel broke. That's a blessin'. So Malcolm, you spend some time in Bywater last night?"

"Rumors get around fast," Malcolm said.

Maggie shrugged. "People tell me things. It's my job to know where all my kids are. Tasha, could you go to my bedroom closet and bring me back the red first aid kit? Also the little box under my nightstand. You know the one."

Tasha hurried off, and Maggie started removing the bandage from Malcolm's nose.

"Earl Warren came by this mornin'. Checks in on me every Sunday. Said you was at his church today."

"Yes, ma'am."

"Isn't that a nice place? Very proud of him."

"It is," he said.

Tasha came back in carrying a huge, plastic first aid kit, nearly the size of a small suitcase, in both hands. A carved, wooden box sat atop it. She pushed the door shut with her foot and set them down on the bed beside Malcolm.

"Thank you, sweetie." Maggie popped open one of the clear side doors and rummaged through the kit. "Earl's got his eye on you. Best be careful with him."

"I will be."

"He can be a strong friend if you make him. But you got a long way to go for that."

"Is he the only one who told you about Bywater?" Malcolm asked.

"Mm-hmm. Said you denied it but don't believe you."

"I wonder who else he's told."

Maggie fished an amber prescription bottle out from the case, its contents scrawled on a strip of masking tape. "He's only gonna tell people he trusts. He won't go blabbin' to everybody. Makes us all look bad." She snapped the lid shut and opened the wood box packed with various charms and pouches. "But ... folks are gonna ask me about it. So tell me, Malcolm. What happened last night?"

"Nothing," Malcolm said. "Just went to a bar. Had a disagreement."

The old woman gave him a flat stare. "Don't you lie to me, Malcolm Romero. I know what you do. Ulises shared more than a fair share of his stories in this very room. Now ... is that your story? Or is there more to it?"

Malcolm glanced away from Maggie's brown eyes, ashamed. *Grandma magic.* She was right. She already knew about Hounacier, about the monsters. Life with the Valducans had made him forget that unlike the other weapons, Hounacier was known. Celebrated. Feared.

"No," he said finally. "There's more."

She set a delicate hand on his knee and patted softly. "Tell me about it. What happened?"

"Christ, Malcolm." Tasha turned the hatchback into the motel's tiny lot. "This is where you're living?"

"I was in a hurry last night. Needed a place that didn't require ID." Over her shoulder, he eyed a pair of men sitting in a dark blue sedan. Its huge, chromed wheels cost as much as the car if not more.

"Why didn't you call me? You could've stayed at my place or even daddy's. This is a shithole."

"It was late. Besides, I need to be able to come and go."

Tasha brushed a spiral of hair behind her ear. "I have a spare key."

Malcolm shook his head. He watched a girl with a tiny skirt

and bad weave lean through the sedan's window. "Thank you, but I've put you in enough danger as is." The girl held up a clear bag, smiled, and pocketed it. She strode back to the building, having just completed one of the least subtle drug deals in history. No one seemed to care. Malcolm let out a sigh and met Tasha's eyes. "I think it would be best if you stayed with your dad at the shop."

"What?"

"At least until I've got this werewolf and find out about those men following me."

She pursed her lips. "I can take care of myself, Mal."

"They saw us together at least once," Malcolm said. "People know about our history. They could go after you to get to me."

Tasha shook her head. "I'm not moving back in with my dad. Period."

"Then do me a favor."

"What?"

"Find a silver knife. Make sure it's the blade and not just the handle, sharpen it, and carry it on you."

"Okay. But you do me a favor."

"Name it," Malcolm said.

"Move out of here."

"Deal." Malcolm leaned across toward her. She moved to meet his lips, but he kissed her on the cheek. "Thank you." He gathered Hounacier's bag and got out of the car.

"You be safe."

"I will." He watched her pull out of the narrow drive before he headed up the peeling metal stairs to the second floor. The pain in his ribs was noticeably less. He wasn't sure how much of that was Maggie's gris-gris now hanging around his neck or the Vicodin she'd given him. The pills rattled in his pocket with every step. Sleep. That's what he needed most. Not that he could. His brain hadn't slowed since he got here.

Near his door, he spotted a folded, yellow piece of paper hanging beside it. He pulled it from the clip and unfolded it.

Mr. Hebb,
There is a package for you at the front counter.

Malcolm looked around, heart thumping. No one seemed to be watching him. Allan and Tasha were the only ones who knew he was here. He'd messaged Allan the alias he'd used this morning. No way could he have sent something this fast.

Paranoia rising, Malcolm made his way down to the front office. The television playing for the empty lobby showed a map of Springfield, highlighting the location of the grisly murders discovered the week before.

A paunchy man with thinning, brown hair sat behind the desk, engrossed in his computer. He looked up as Malcolm approached.

"There's a package for me," Malcolm said, holding up the yellow note. "Room two thirty-four."

The man sighed heavily and fetched a brown cardboard box wrapped in clear tape. "Here you go."

"Thanks," Malcolm said, accepting the package. It was heavier than he'd expected. He turned it over, feeling something big shift inside. "Did you see who brought it?"

The man shrugged, returning to his chair. "Black kid. Fifteen, maybe sixteen."

"Anything else?"

He scratched his cheek with the back of his fingers. "Not really. Had a Saints hat on."

That narrows it down, he thought sarcastically. "Thanks."

Malcolm headed back to his room, keeping an eye out for anyone watching him. Once inside, he set the box down. There were no markings save "For room 234" written atop it in black, flowing marker script. *Female?*

Most package bombs detonated when the box was opened. And while the contents did move, which usually wasn't the case, he for damned sure wasn't opening it from the top. He flicked open his knife and carefully poked the blade into the side, rotating it wider to a pencil-sized hole.

Leaning closer, he closed his eyes and sniffed. Newspaper. The acrid stink of tape adhesive. Oil. Malcolm inhaled again, long and deep. Gun oil. He peered through the hole, seeing crumpled paper. He punched another hole on the opposite side, allowing airflow, and sniffed again. Definitely gun oil. Beneath that, powder solvent.

Cautiously, he cut alongside the box, careful not to stab anything inside. He cut a three-inch incision and another, forming an "L." Holding his breath, he peeled the cardboard open.

No wires. Just crinkled balls of newsprint. He cut it open further and tentatively reached in. Something hard was wrapped inside. Round and long, like a pipe. There was another beside it. He felt further and paused. *No way.*

Malcolm pulled the object out and unwrapped it. Ulises' sawed-off. Someone had thoroughly cleaned it. There was a fresh gouge and chip in the wooden forend, likely from when the incubus had kicked it, but it was otherwise fine. He thumbed the latch open. The spent shells were gone.

Puzzled, Malcolm tore the box open the rest of the way, finding a white envelope against the top. The first thing he'd have seen if he'd opened it correctly. "Dr. Malcolm Romero" it read along the top in the same feminine handwriting.

He opened it and removed a single-page letter.

Doctor Romero,

I apologize that my boys startled you last night. They meant no harm. They have cleaned the scene and removed any evidence for you. There is no need for you to worry.

I was a friend to Ulises and was deeply saddened by his death. He spoke very highly of you. My sincerest condolences for your loss.

I would very much like to speak with you about something he and I were working on. Please come to my house tomorrow for lunch, and we can discuss it in person. I look forward to finally meeting you.

Sincerely,
Atabei Cross   -

CHAPTER 9

Malcolm sat outside a crowded cafe, nibbling a toasted sandwich. A trio of young men chatted at the table beside him, framed backpacks slung over the backs of their chairs. The faint breeze wafted their cigarette smoke his direction, bathing him in the stink. He sipped his five-dollar coffee and watched the street.

As he'd expected, Allan hadn't found any suspects on the flaming John Doe NOPD had pulled from the dumpster. Shorty and Cornrows had done their job well. The question was why? Why did Atabei have him followed? Why had they gone to such lengths to protect him?

Allan had also dug into Atabei Cross, the voodoo priestess who didn't tribute the local queen, and someone whom Ulises had been visiting before his death. Thirty-nine years old, she'd emigrated from Haiti two years ago. Unmarried, but considered herself a widow. She owned half a block down in the Ninth Ward, three houses connected by empty lots leveled in the wrath of Hurricane Katrina. She also owned a couple acres down by Saint Bernard, a few miles outside the city. No criminal record. Clean driving record. Paid her bills on time. And, according to their website, the most recent "Volunteer of the Month" at the New Orleans Homeless Shelter.

Nothing in her records seemed terribly unusual, and that meant he didn't trust her. Haitian records were terrible at best. There was no telling what kind of life she had lived before becoming a model citizen.

That morning, in keeping with his promise to Tasha, Malcolm had moved out of his shitty hotel and into a spare bedroom above Alpuente's Antiques. While it might not have been exactly what Tasha had intended, moving in with her wasn't a good idea. She deserved someone who could give her all his heart. It hurt, but it was best.

When asked, Jim had called Atabei a "shifty root worker" who sold love powders and lottery charms. Malcolm thought of the negatively imbued Mardi Gras beads. Jim didn't have anything specifically against her; he just didn't trust her. But he would have said that about anyone who didn't acknowledge Maggie's rulership. Malcolm didn't have such scruples about charm makers. Someone had to do it. He needed to know what type of woman she really was. And the best person to ask was one who bought charms and stayed out of voodoo politics.

A white and blue police car rolled up the street, slowing as it approached. A sudden hush and silent tension rose from the men at the neighboring table when the squad car stopped.

Malcolm rose from the uncomfortable chair, shouldered Hounacier's bag, and downed the last of his coffee. He strolled up, nodding to the bald policeman sitting in the cruiser and circled around to the passenger side.

"Corporal," he said, slipping into the seat. In all the years spent trying to avoid being in a police car, he never thought he'd be in the front seat of one.

"Doctor," Duplessis said. "I hadn't expected to hear from you yet."

"Under promise, over deliver, they say." Malcolm held out a clear, plastic bag containing a small pouch of light green leather with a braided cord. "She should be the first to touch it. Tell her to wear it around her neck, if possible, touching her skin. She can take it off to shower but should keep it on her all the time until after the promotion is finalized."

The officer took the bag, examining the gris-gris inside. "It'll work?"

"I can't make a promise. Free will is always a factor. But I can promise that this is one seriously potent gris-gris. Possibly the best I've ever made. Tell her not to wear any others for the promotion. Loa can get a little touchy if you try to stack too many on."

"All right," Duplessis said with a little smile. "Anything else?"

"That's it as far as the gris-gris. But I do have a couple questions if you don't mind."

The policeman looked up from the bag. "What questions?"

Malcolm scratched his bristled cheek. "I heard they found a body in a dumpster, head cut off. I was wondering if it might be related to Ulises."

Duplessis frowned. "Where did you hear this?"

"Here and there," Malcolm said with a shrug. "Word got around. Got to me."

Duplessis slipped the bag into a little console between the seats. He flipped the little plastic door shut but not before Malcolm spied an etched brass disk inside. A policeman's charm. Paula had sold them for years at her shop.

"Head wasn't cut off," Duplessis said. "Not all the way. They stripped it, burned the body. Still no ID, last I heard. So far, we don't think it's related."

Malcolm nodded. "Okay." The officer's openness likely meant Malcolm wasn't a suspect. "Can you let me know if anything does look similar?"

"If it does."

"Thanks. One more thing," Malcolm said. "Do you know anything about Atabei Cross?"

The officer's brow rose. "Cross? I know her." He paused. "Of her."

"Tell me," Malcolm said.

"Priestess. From Haiti," he added as if it compared to an Ivy League law degree "She makes a lot of charms for folks. Potent. Real popular."

"So why didn't you go to her for your wife's gris-gris?"

Duplessis' lips twitched. "Price."

"What does she charge?"

"Depends. Sometimes a percentage. Like five percent of her raise. Other times, it's just a favor, but you never know what till she asks."

"Five percent? One-time fee?"

The policeman shook his head. "Forever. And if you break it, she'll curse you."

A cold weight settled in Malcolm's stomach. Haitian and African priests often used favors as payment. Many were too poor to pay with money. Most of the time, they were small. Barters or little chores. Other times, they far outweighed anything money could buy. The percent fee might explain where the money for all her properties had come from. "You say she's real popular?"

Duplessis nodded.

"A lot of people owe her favors?"

Nodded again.

"Other policemen?"

"Yeah." There was a warning in his dark eyes.

"You owe her any favors?" Malcolm asked carefully.

"Not me." Duplessis snorted a little grin. "Jim would have my ass if he heard I was dealing with her."

Malcolm chuckled. "Thanks. Good luck to your wife."

Duplessis offered his hand. "Good luck to you too. I hope you find what you're looking for."

White- and purple-flowered weeds filled the empty trash-strewn lots that once contained the many houses in the Lower Ninth Ward. More and more homes appeared every year, built atop the gravesites of their former selves. Many were contemporary suburban in style, brick or contextually designed, their architects lacking even the most basic understanding of the city's soul. Malcolm followed the sun-faded street; the asphalt crackled like the bottom of a dried creek bed or some artist's giant mosaic. There was no sidewalk.

Wind chimes rustled on a nearby porch as if to signal his passing. A heavyset black man with a deeply receded hairline, wearing a T-shirt with its sleeves cut off, watched him. Malcolm thought of the guards outside Micelo Tavel's home so many years ago. That had been the last time he'd felt unease visiting a priest's home. Once Ulises had taken him under his wing, he was the one feared. Now, the old, familiar tingles started up the back of his neck.

No. He was a Valducan knight. Protector of Hounacier. No root worker was going to scare him no matter how many favors she was owed.

Malcolm crossed the street. A fence wall encircled the lot, boards overlapped, leaving no gaps to see through. The lack of graffiti on the white-painted wood was striking. The wall wrapped behind a pink little house and continued on. The fence turned alongside the next street. Ahead, a giant red and white house rose above the surrounding neighborhood like some ancient castle overlooking its lands. Elevated on an eight-foot base of vine-coated stone, the first floor stood completely above the walled yard. A pair of broad stairways swept up from street level, culminating at the porch. Six thick, square columns stood along the front, thrusting up through the wide balcony running the width of the home.

Shoulders back, Hounacier's bag where he could reach it, and hiding any sign of being impressed by the imposing home, Malcolm walked up the steps and knocked on the oaken door. Furious barking erupted on the other side. Two dogs at least. Big by the sound of them. Orlovski would have hated this place.

"Down!" shouted a woman's voice.

The dogs silenced.

A bolt snapped, and the door creaked open. Malcolm pretended to scratch his shoulder, his fingers only inches from the open top of Hounacier's bag.

"Doctor Romero," said a tall, lean woman, her hair pulled back tight. There was a smooth shine to her ebon skin, testament to years spent baking beneath a hot sun or working too close to a fire. She had an elegance to her, the sharp lines of her face giving an air of strength rather than hardship. She wore a colorful skirt of some silken material the color of pomegranate and a dark blouse with bell sleeves. Several beaded strands hung from her neck, ending at a white disk, like a piece of polished whalebone. A pair of Rottweilers sat attentively beside her, eyes curious, cautious. "It's a pleasure to finally meet you." Her accent was the smooth Haitian Creole he hadn't heard in years. She extended a slender hand, rings on three of her fingers. "Atabei Cross."

Malcolm stepped back and extended his palm. "Look." He

clicked his tongue, drawing the dogs' eyes as well.

"Of course," Atabei said with a cool smile.

Nothing happened.

"Thank you," Malcolm said, accepting her still extended hand. Rough. Worker's hands.

"Ulises did the same when we first met. Always with that eye." She shook her head regretfully. "Please, come inside. Sogbo and Bade won't bother you."

Malcolm glanced at the two huge dogs named after the loa of wind and lightning. One looked back, still wary. The other seemed more interested in Malcolm's feet. He stepped inside onto a dizzying, multi-colored rug that looked like interlocking rings in four shades of green. Over the scent of dog, the house smelled of fresh jasmine, sage smoke, and old wood. A huge mirror, wrapped in an antiqued gold frame, dominated the side wall, reflecting the crucifixes and straw-maned wooden masks along the other. It reminded him in some ways of the Valducans' chateau back in France. They'd only just moved the new European headquarters to Belgium, but he hadn't visited it yet.

"Would you like something to drink?" Atabei asked, leading him down the hall. Dog nails clacked along the wooden floor behind him.

"Please." Refusing the offer could be as dangerous as accepting it. He'd learned early never to insult a voodoo priestess.

"Sadie," Atabei stepped into a room with a pair of plump couches and several large chairs. Everything was new and high-end. "Please bring us some lemonade."

"Of course, ma'am." A chubby woman with tight braids and eyes just a little too close together rose from a chair and hurried into an adjoining room.

Atabei gestured with a long hand. "Have a seat, Doctor."

"Thank you." Malcolm took the chair opposite hers, a small rectangular table between them, its polished surface interlocking insets of exotic woods. He rested Hounacier's bag across his lap. A huge shrine dominated the side wall where a television might normally be.

"I would like to apologize for Quentin and Errol frightening you the other night. That was not their intention."

"I appreciate their help rectifying it." Malcolm's thumb slid along the bag's black canvas. "But why were they following me?"

She smiled, almost embarrassed. "They were ... looking out for you. Ulises was a dear friend, and I didn't want anything to happen to you," she looked at the bag, "or to Hounacier. May I see her?"

Malcolm ran his tongue across the backs of his teeth. If he did need her, having her out would be to his advantage. "Of course." He reached inside the zippered maw and pulled the machete free.

Atabei leaned forward, brown eyes transfixed on the sheathed holy weapon. She touched her plump lips. "I remember seeing her, many years ago when Ulises was travelling Haiti. Beautiful. Her own loa."

Ulises had always said that too. Called Hounacier the loa that lived only within the blade. In a way, he was right.

"He loved her," Atabei continued. "He spoke of her quite often." She smiled. "And of you."

The door opened, and Sadie walked in carrying a pair of glasses.

"Thank you," Malcolm said, accepting one.

She handed the other to Atabei. "Can I get you anything else?"

Malcolm shook his head.

"No," Atabei said. "That's all."

The plump woman smiled and left. Before the kitchen door closed behind her, Malcolm spied a familiar face leaning against the counter, eating. Shorty.

Atabei sipped her lemonade, watching him over the rim. Malcolm lifted the glass to his mouth and sniffed. It smelled real. Not the powdered crap. He touched it to his lips, allowing only a drop through. He tensed, waiting to see if the serpent tattoo encircling his bicep tightened. It warned him of poisons. Satisfied, Malcolm took a long drink and set the glass on a little wooden coaster.

"Now, you said you were looking out for me. Do you know who killed Ulises?"

The priestess let out a long breath and shook her head. "I don't. But I do know what stalks our streets. Once I'd heard of Ulises' murder, I went to check on the mask of his, hopefully retrieve it before someone took it. But Mister Luison had already rescued it."

Malcolm straightened, pressing into the soft chair back. "You know of the mask?"

"Of course," she said with a smile. "I made it."

"You?" Malcolm blinked. "You made that?"

"I did."

"How?" he asked, the first of a dozen questions suddenly whirling through his mind.

"I can draw ... exorcise the demon out then transfer its essence into another vessel."

"Not just masks?"

Atabei shook her head. "No. Demons can possess animals too. Or jewelry. Even a weapon. Just as long as the animal or material is one linked to the demon."

An unholy weapon? A nameless chill wormed up Malcolm's spine. *What could such a thing do?* "So, obsidian for the ghoul."

"Yes. One of the reasons I sought out Ulises was to learn about the different minerals and how they work. I hadn't known how many breeds there were until after I'd made my first masks. He taught me a lot. I only wish we'd had more time together."

Malcolm blinked. "Masks? There's more than one?"

"Of course. I couldn't kill them, so I had to put them somewhere."

"How many?"

"Three." She licked her lips. "I was in Port-au-Prince. After the earthquake, there was talk of creatures eating the dead and stalking the camps. Three of them. It took some weeks to get them all and ... two of my friends." She sipped her lemonade, washing away the mournful expression.

A weight formed in Malcolm's stomach, heavy and familiar. Ulises had wanted Malcolm to go after the quake, but Malcolm had been chasing down an itwan in Armenia with three other knights. It was eight months before he'd finally made it to Haiti. It had been his last visit. Ulises never forgave him for that. *They were hunting them themselves,* he thought. *Untrained. No holy weapons.* Surely, he could have gone. Helped out. *No.* If he hadn't been in Armenia, two knights might have died. Being in Haiti alone, especially during the aftermath, would have been too risky. They had to work as teams. It ensured survival for them and the weapons. Malcolm realized his grip had tightened around Hounacier's scabbard. He drank some more of his lemonade, swallowing back the regret. "How did you learn to do this?"

"It wasn't easy," she said. "My husband died many years ago because of a demon. I wanted to know how to destroy them. Save others from his fate. I spoke to priests, learned hoodoo. I met an exorcist once. He explained how faith can draw the spirit free. Consulted loa. It was years. But all I could do was trap them. Destroying them ..." She shook her head.

"So you came to Ulises?"

"Yes. Ulises was like the baron." She lifted a finger, moving it with each word like a conductor's wand. "When he came to your town, you knew ... death was with him."

"But also life," Malcolm added.

"There were many funerals before he'd come. Then, only one. The last."

"Do you know why anyone would kill him?"

Atabei shook her head. "No. Ulises was loved but feared. I don't know who could have done it."

"Anyone you suspect?"

"A few," she said with a reluctant shrug. "As long as his killer is out there, none of us are safe."

Dishes rattled, muffled through the kitchen door. Footsteps echoed from somewhere above.

Malcolm tried to keep track of them. Four people at least. "Then why did you wait until now to contact me?"

She glanced down at her hands in her lap, fingers twisting. "I did not know you. And after some of the things Ulises told me, I did not know your convictions."

"Convictions?"

"Your ... dedication. How far you will go to kill these monsters. It was difficult to approach you with my proposal until I knew your dedication."

Malcolm cocked his head. "What proposal?"

"There is a killer on the loose in this city. A monster. I want you to help me. With your help, I can draw it out, put it into an animal, and then you can kill it. No one has to die. I will do all in my power to help you find Ulises' murderer, but I ask this first before more people are killed."

Malcolm drew a long breath, studying the woman's face. She seemed sincere. His instincts told him not to trust her. But she was connected. She claimed a power that the Valducans had only ever heard of. What if she really could do as she claimed?

"You said there were three ghoul masks."

"Yes."

"Can I see them?"

She smiled. "Of course. But they are not here."

"Where are they?"

"They are protecting others that the demon is after."

Malcolm swallowed. Demons didn't usually single out a specific victim. Not without reason. "After them how?"

"It wants their souls." She drew a heavy sigh. "We do not know where the monster is. I need you to summon it as Ulises could."

Malcolm frowned. He hadn't performed a summoning in years and never without Ulises' guidance. "It's not that simple. I need at least three souls the demon has marked."

"Is that all?" she asked as if it was something mundane, like he'd asked for a Coke.

He suppressed a snort. "No. But that's the hard part. Three demonbound are nearly impossible to gather. And that's the minimum just for a lower breed. Vampire would need four. Rakshasa six. After that, I'd require a sanctified ring. And no one to bother us."

Atabei seemed to look through him, contemplating his words. She traced a finger along her jaw, stopping at her chin. "I think it would be best if I showed you something."

CHAPTER 10

Malcolm sat in the back of a pearl-colored SUV, Hounacier's bag across his lap. Outside the window, the sprawl of tiny homes gave way to industrial complexes, giant fuel depots, and then county highway. The quaint, suburban houses eventually yielded to the lush, green forests of the bayou. Shorty, whose real name was Errol, sat beside him, watching the trees though his own window. He stank of some cheap, vanilla-scented cologne. Still, it was better than the lingering reek of cigarette smoke that had clung to Malcolm since back at the cafe. He wondered about that pistol he'd spotted at Errol's waist the other night. If he was wearing it, he didn't show. Sitting in a car seat with a gun in your spine was real uncomfortable. He was either very experienced with the hard discomfort or wore it somewhere else. Malcolm seriously doubted that Errol wasn't armed, and there was plenty of room under that triple-extra-large jersey of his.

Cornrows, now Quentin, drove. Quentin was soft-spoken, his country Creole accent somehow impervious to the modern media that had diluted so many others. There was a hard wariness to his blue eyes. They made an unsettling contrast to his dark skin. It had been Quentin who had carried the near-headless corpse to that dumpster and burned it. Errol had been quick to mention that he'd been the one that hosed the blood off the kill site as if that were somehow comparable. Police usually didn't shoot at you for spraying water and kicking gravel around like they did for incinerating naked corpses.

Atabei sat in the front, hands in her lap, fingers laced. Several bracelets circled her wrists, heavy with charms: beads of bone and ceramic, a couple silver coins, and other talismans. Malcolm thought about her claim of demonbound jewelry. What would that do? *Nothing good,* he thought. Would she risk wearing something like that?

After a few minutes, they turned at a trailer park and continued down a narrow strip of road. Tree branches arched above like the rafters in some ancient cathedral, draped with tattered banners of Spanish moss. Through the blur of tree trunks and foliage, Malcolm could see patches of brackish water coming nearly to the edge of the elevated road. His ribs panged with each bump and bounce. Eventually, Quentin pulled the vehicle onto a dirt drive. Errol hopped out and opened a rusty gate. He closed it behind them then climbed back in.

Malcolm shifted on the leather seat. Whatever surprise Atabei had was coming, and he wasn't really sure what to expect. Before they'd left, he'd gone to the restroom and sent a text to Allan, letting the Valducans know what was going on, just in case.

The road turned, and the forest opened up into an enormous field. Two other vehicles sat parked in the grass to one side. On the other, at least a dozen shipping containers of various colors formed a giant ring, nearly filling the open span. A few looked as though someone had taken a scrap torch to them, cutting windows and doors. Wooden ladders and even stairs connected to the upper stacked boxes, forming a second story on some. It reminded Malcolm of a training course Nick had once made in order to prepare knights for raids.

A slender woman in a straw, wide-brimmed hat looked up from a fenced garden just outside the ring and waved. Malcolm noticed the black shotgun leaning against the post only a few feet away. Beyond it, chickens pecked and strutted inside a wide, caged coop.

Quentin parked the vehicle beside an old Saturn.

"We're here," Atabei said, and opened her door.

Malcolm tongued the back of his teeth, drew a breath, then opened his own door. The sticky, Louisiana heat came down like an enormous hand. Black-and-red insects buzzed around, flying between the flowering weeds. Letting the others take the lead, he followed Atabei to where the gardener stood.

"Nice to see you, Miss Cross." The woman pulled a pair of grimy gloves from her hands.

"How are you today, Keisha?" Atabei asked.

"Oh, I'm doin' fine. Tomatoes are comin' along real good," Keisha said, sweeping her hand with an air of gardener's pride. "Started some leeks over there."

Malcolm half-listened while the two women talked. Over Keisha's shoulder, he spied the back of a crude figure like a scarecrow made of lashed straw and animal bones, facing outside toward the woods. He guessed its face would be a painted wooden mask. Glancing to the left, he spotted another one far to the side. It, too, stood at a man's height, bright string holding it to a carved post. Although he couldn't see them beyond the container village, he knew he would find two more, also facing the cardinal points. Standard hoodoo ward for protection, just larger than he'd normally encountered. Maybe later, he'd get a chance to have a closer look, see the specific totems used.

"So, the others around?" Atabei asked.

"Nah," Keisha said with a shake of her head. "Gabe and Peewee went into town 'bout half hour ago. Should be back soon."

Atabei motioned her head toward the container ring. "And our guests?"

"Oh, they're fine." She lowered her voice. "Leigh Ann's been cryin' for her mamma."

Atabei sighed and nodded. "Nothing we can do about that. At least not yet." She gestured to Malcolm. "This is Doctor Romero. He's Ulises' boy."

Keisha's baggy eyes widened. "Oh! Oh, it's so good to meet you, Doctor." She offered a hand. "Keisha LaFargue."

Malcolm displayed his palm.

She looked at it, forehead crinkled in a confused expression.

"Pleasure to meet you, ma'am" he said, shaking her hand.

"Keisha's one of the people taking care of our guests," Atabei said, like that was supposed to mean something to him.

She turned back to the gardener. "Can we see them?"

"Oh course. Of course," Keisha gushed. She moved toward the leaning shotgun, but Atabei stopped her.

"That's all right. We've got it."

"Are you sure?"

The priestess nodded. "We'll be fine. Doctor Romero is here if we have trouble." She gave Malcolm a cryptic smile. "Thank you, Keisha."

Malcolm nodded goodbye to the woman and followed Atabei and the two men past a dingy green container and into the ring itself. The ground inside was packed flat, devoid of vegetation save weeds alongside steel boxes. A thick post jutted from the great ring's center, standing over ten feet high. Carved animal and human faces adorned the dark wood like a totem pole, but more African in design.

They crossed the arena to one of the boxes, a red one, sun-faded to a mottled pink. A small window air-conditioner hummed at its back end, dripping condensation into a tiny mud puddle. Someone had built a tight cage around the unit with rebar, the silver weld points glinting new in the sunlight. Beside it, a steel winch, like the kind used to pull a fishing boat onto a trailer, was bolted in place, its blue, plastic-coated cable running inside through a little slit. There were no windows in this box. Only a pair of window-shaped clusters of cut holes, each about as big around as a finger.

Quentin lifted the side of his shirt and reached for a pistol tucked at his hip.

Shit! expecting a trap, Malcolm's hand slid into Hounacier's bag, gripping her handle. Quentin, not seeming to pay him any attention, drew a black snub-nose and strolled around to the container front. Malcolm looked at Atabei.

The priestess saw his hand in the bag. "You might need that." She nodded in Quentin's direction, urging him to follow. Errol was approaching the winch. He slipped his hand up the front of his jersey and drew a pistol out from the front of his huge shorts. Nick used to call people that did that idiots. Said they would panic, grab the gun, and squeeze the trigger in excitement or get it tangled in their clothes and blow their dicks off. Guaranteed way to spot an amateur.

"Go on," Atabei said.

Malcolm drew Hounacier from her sheath and followed Quentin, trying to keep his eye on Errol and on the black little holes drilled into the air-conditioned container. He rounded the corner, and the scarab tattoo itched, starting its dance.

A pair of black, obsidian masks stood maybe neck-high atop a post, dead even between the container and the one opposite. They were just like the one in Jim's shop. Withered, leering skulls, their eyes tiny orbs set in deep sockets. They were attached back to back, each facing a container door.

Quentin stood there, his pale eyes on the holy machete, revolver down at his side. "Be sure not to get in front of the mask."

"What is this?" Malcolm asked.

"It's for our safety." He banged lightly on the steel door and peered through a slot cut eye-level. "Coming in. Against the wall." After a couple seconds, he called, "Okay!"

Ratcheting clicks came from the back of the box as Errol worked the winch. "Locked!"

Quentin nodded to Malcolm. "Don't get in front of the mask." He popped open the door.

The stink of humanity, unwashed and oily, wafted from the open door. A mattress lay in one corner near a table bolted to the wall, a few books atop it. A small radio sat on a white, plastic chair. Closer to the door, a shower curtain hung from a ring. The stink of urine and feces emanated from the blue, plastic toilet visible inside.

Malcolm's jaw tightened as he saw a young man, maybe twenty, his clothes crumpled and stained, standing against the far wall, his head turned away and eyes scrunched. "What is this?"

Grass crunched as Atabei came around beside him. "He's marked. Found him a couple weeks ago. Bitten. We patched him up and brought him here. Gary," she said with a mother's voice. "Gary, this is Malcolm. He's going to help you."

The man's eyes, hidden behind greasy brown hair, glanced up at Malcolm for only a moment.

Malcolm stepped closer, Hounacier out front. His hair rustled in the window unit's cool blast. Atabei followed. He noticed the round, white, metal collar around the man's neck, just below the unkempt beard. "Silver?"

"Yes."

"Gary," he said, stopping just a few feet from the trembling man. Gary grunted pathetically.

"Look at me."

The man shook his head.

Malcolm sidestepped, coming between the prisoner and the mask outside. "Look up."

Immediately, the man's shivers stopped. He drew four deep breaths and opened his eyes. He lifted his gaze, wide eyes pleading and desperate.

"Is this true? Did you see a monster?"

"I don't know. They say I did. It was dark. Some animal came out the woods. Attacked me. Tore me up real good." He showed his arms, striped with pinkish scars. "Say I'm infected. You gotta help me, Mister."

Malcolm raised his palm.

Gary winced and turned away, his collar rattling.

"I see." Malcolm met Atabei's eyes, pursed his lips, and walked back out to where Quentin stood.

"You've kept him here, prisoner, for weeks?" Malcolm asked once the door was shut.

Atabei nodded. "We hadn't expected it to be this long. Ulises said he'd get you back here, but then ..." She shrugged.

Malcolm thought of Ulises' cryptic messages. Of course, the old man wouldn't have shared anything like that in them. He died waiting for a phone call that never came. Pushing back the regret, Malcolm nodded to the second container, the other mask guarding its door. "Who's in there?"

She smiled weakly. "That's Leigh Ann."

"Show me."

Errol released the winch, allowing slack in Gary's leash. As before, Quentin knocked and ordered the prisoner inside the other box to move to the wall.

Malcolm eyed the big man's revolver. "You know, bullets

won't work on that thing if it transforms."

A faint grin tugged at Quentin's lips. "These will." He swung open the cylinder and drew out a single shell. Silver. Two deep slices formed a cross across the slug's nose. It wasn't religious. The cuts would peel the bullet open like a flower once it hit flesh. Very nasty.

"Locked!" Errol called.

Quentin slid the bullet back into the chamber, clicked the cylinder shut, and popped the door handle open.

Malcolm stood ready, Hounacier in hand. The door groaned open, releasing a fresh waft of foul air. The sparse furnishings were like the other except … toys. Stuffed, brightly colored toys littered the floor. A sickening wave rolled through his stomach. Standing at the back wall, a young black girl, maybe nine years old, clutched a dirty, sea-green, plush elephant, her eyes downcast.

Son of a bitch. Malcolm's mouth dropped open for only a moment. He wanted to tell Quentin to shut the door, pretend he didn't see the terrified child locked in a steel box and held to a wall. *No. I need to check her.*

He stepped inside. Again, Atabei followed. They stopped about eight feet away.

"Leigh Ann," Atabei said, her voice tender. "Leigh Ann, this is Doctor Malcolm. He's going to make you better."

The girl shifted, still refusing to look up at them.

Malcolm stepped between her and the mask and crouched down. No matter what this girl was, he couldn't let himself forget what she might become. "Hi, Leigh Ann. Look up for me."

Her big, brown eyes lifted, partially hidden beneath a frizzy curtain of oily hair.

Slow, as to not startle her, he raised his arm and opened his palm.

Leigh Ann screamed, shrill and horrible. The stuffed animal fell to the floor, and she pressed her hands over her eyes.

"I'm sorry," he muttered. Malcolm stood and walked out, trying to ignore her sobs.

"Do you understand why I need you?" Atabei asked as the door squeaked shut behind him.

Malcolm closed his eyes. As horrible as keeping them was, letting them live endangered even more lives. They were innocent, victims of the demon inside. Once it was bound or dead, their souls would be free. Until then, they were damned. He turned to the priestess. "Are those collars solid silver?"

"Yes."

"Even the hinge pins? If those things transform, the silver will hold, but even a hardened, steel pin will snap."

She nodded. "Ulises was very specific about that."

"Good." If the werewolf did try to take one, the collar would strangle it, maybe even break its expanding neck. "You can't draw it out of them? The demon?"

"No. It has to be formed for that." She gazed off in the woods, her eyed focused on nothing in particular. "The ghouls had only one form. They were either monsters or they weren't. Werewolf that can hide in a human it's possessing. Even if you caught every single person it had bound, it could still hide." She turned back to him. "I need it to manifest, become *real*. Then, I can draw it out."

"I see," he grumbled, disappointed. Holy weapons worked the same way.

"We have a wolf caged in one of the other boxes. Sent down from Montana," Atabei said. "Once I can draw the spirit out, I'll put it in there. Then, you can kill it."

"Can you put it in a mask instead?"

"A silver one. Yes." Atabei cocked her head. "So will you help me? Help them?"

"And you're sure the same monster bit them both?"

"Yes."

If the demon was smart it, would run. It could have been watching through those prisoners' eyes. Might be listening to them right now. But New Orleans' gravity was strong. It was likely trapped. Cornered. No telling what it might do. Malcolm nodded. "I want the mask once we're done."

"I will agree to that."

"We still need to find a third victim," Malcolm said. "And we need to be fast."

She smiled, revealing those tiny little teeth. "I know where to find him."

CHAPTER 11

Quentin pulled the Lexus into a tight space outside of Alpuente's Antiques.

"Thanks." Malcolm picked up Hounacier's bag and opened the door.

Atabei turned to face him. "Are you sure you don't want us to wait?"

Malcolm shook his head. "No. I have a few things I need to do. I'll meet you at your house at ..." He glanced at the green, dash-mounted clock. 4:43. "Seven o'clock."

Atabei's mouth tightened into a momentary frown. "I will let my people know. Call me or Errol if you need anything."

"I will. Just make sure the site is prepared for when we arrive. We won't have much time once I catch it. If it has a fourth body in the area, it might jump to that one and attack us or one of its captured victims so that we no longer have three."

"Don't worry about that," she said. "If it knew where its victims were, it would have attacked us by now. They don't know, so it doesn't know either. Just be careful. Don't let it see where you take it."

Malcolm nodded and stepped out. As he closed the door, he noticed Jim watching them through the shop's plate window. The priest's stony expression was the same one he'd given back when Malcolm and Tasha had broken up.

That's not good.

Jim was already by the door by the time Malcolm stepped

inside, his enormous frame nearly filling the doorway. "Looks like you made a new friend."

Malcolm glanced back in time to see the pearly SUV drive away. "Yeah." The scarab tattoo itched under the ghoul mask's hateful gaze.

"Did you learn anything?"

"A lot." Malcolm stepped to the left, away from the mask's stare. He noticed Tasha near the far wall, opening a case, a pair of obvious tourists ogling the contents. Mister Alpuente sat behind the counter. A disapproving frown tugged at the old man's lips.

"Mal," Jim said. "You need to be careful with her."

"I'm figuring that out." He nodded toward the rear door. "Can we go upstairs?"

"Of course." Jim led him through the back and up the creaking stairs to his office. Opening the door, he offered Malcolm one of the leather chairs before taking his own. A fat, lemon-yellow candle burned in a glass jar atop Jim's altar, surrounded by silver coins and a fresh chicken's foot. He'd been praying for someone's protection.

"So what is it?" Jim asked, leaning forward over his desk.

"Atabei claims she made the demon mask," Malcolm said.

The huge priest snorted. "I'm sure she does. With Ulises gone, no one can say otherwise."

"I believe her. She has two more just like it."

Jim paused, his head cocking to the side a little. "Really? Two?"

"Yeah. She says she can make more and is willing to teach me how."

"Mal, be careful. You don't want to end up in that witch's debt."

"I'm not. She *needs* me."

Jim scratched his chin. "How's that?"

"She needs me to call the demon in. She can't do that on her own. My payment is a demon mask and getting to seeing her do it."

"Just be sure she sees that as an even trade," Jim said. "She has a reputation."

Malcolm thought about that, strumming his fingers on the armrest. He hadn't mentioned the little detail about hunting a werewolf down and keeping it prisoner somehow. The yellow candle came to mind. Probably best he didn't tell him. Jim was worried enough. "I want to ask you a favor. Big one."

"Anything."

He plucked a pen from an upright desk stand and drew one of Jim's business cards from a little wooden holder. "If you don't hear from me by noon tomorrow." Malcolm wrote an email address on the back of the card and slid it across to Jim. "Send a message here. Tell them everything."

Jim took the card and studied it. "This is your Order?"

"Yes." He stabbed the pen back into its brass sheath.

"If you're giving me this, you're worried. What's going on, Mal?"

"Just playing it safe."

Jim shook his head. He set the card down and tapped it with his finger like some stage magician about to perform a trick. "If you're so concerned, why are you going?"

"The Order has been searching for the secret of making those masks for over a century. This could be huge. It could save lives."

"But tonight? Why not wait for your friend?"

"I have to."

"Why?"

"Because people will die if I don't."

The big priest nodded and leaned back. "I see."

"Just don't worry about me," Malcolm said.

Jim smiled. "I can't ever promise you that."

Long shadows stretched across the street by the time Malcolm made it back to Atabei's house. The sun would be down in an hour. Malcolm used to hate hunting at night. Populated areas made it necessary. But now, with his newest gift, he looked forward to it. The three-strand seashell necklace hung from his neck, its bone crescent bouncing against his chest as he hurried up the front steps.

No dogs barked when he knocked.

Errol opened the door almost instantly. No telling how long he'd been standing there waiting. "Ready, Doctor?"

"Did you get the things I asked for?"

Errol smiled broadly. His yellowed teeth seemed too large for his head. "Sho."

Malcolm stepped inside. "Atabei here?"

"Left an hour ago," Errol said, closing the door. "Meet us there."

He led Malcolm into the living room, where Quentin sat stooped over the table, winding silver chain from a clear, plastic spool onto a six-inch dowel rod. The spool looked like the kind found at a mall shop that also sold gaudy medallions like the diamond-encrusted gold cross hanging from the big man's neck. Two more rods rested beside it, each wrapped with what looked to be several feet of chain and ending in a silver ring. Also on the table were five Motorola radios, several empty battery packages, and Quentin's snub-nose.

Malcolm picked up one of the rods, inspecting the chain. As he'd instructed, the links were fused shut, not butted. "Solid silver?"

"Yeah." Quentin picked up a pair of flat-nosed cutters and snipped the chain from the spool.

He flipped over the ring. Fleurs-de-lis lined the outer edge. Likely from the same jewelry place. A bulbous knot held it to the chain. Malcolm tugged it. "Looks good."

"Merci." Quentin reached into a shiny, red paper bag by his feet and removed another ring.

Malcolm set the dowel down and picked up one of the burgundy and black radios. Cheap. Maybe a two-mile range in ideal conditions. They weren't encoded, so anyone on the same frequency could listen in. *Better than nothing.* "Who are the others for?"

"Atabei has one," Errol explained, his voice peppy. "Other two are for Sammy and Issach. They're already out there keepin' watch."

"And the masks?"

"Over there," Errol said, pointing to a cardboard box on a plush, white chair. Crumpled newspaper poked out of the open top. "Did you get the third one?"

"Jim Luison wouldn't let me have it," Malcolm lied. No way was he going to let Atabei have it. Not until she proved she could do what she claimed. He'd instructed Jim to lock it securely in place so no one could run in and steal it. Malcolm pulled the paper aside, revealing one of the obsidian ghouls. The scarab at his wrist wiggled under its sudden gaze. He picked it up and found its mate wrapped up beneath it. "We'll just have to do it with these two."

Errol let out a little grunt.

Malcolm turned. The little man's eyes were wider than normal. Quentin looked up at Malcolm as well, half-wrapped dowel in his hand.

"That worry you?" Malcolm asked.

Errol nodded. Quentin's flat-mouthed expression revealed his answer.

"Good," Malcolm said, his tone cold. "Because I'd be worried if you weren't. Overconfidence will kill you. We're about to put this monster in a corner and if you make one mistake, it'll rip you in half. Just do exactly what I say, and this will work. Get cocky, think that mask will keep it off you, and it'll be *your* corpse we're burning in a dumpster. Understood?"

They nodded.

"Good. Two masks will work."

While Quentin finished with the fifth and final chain-wrapped rod, Malcolm and Errol gathered their gear and carried it out the back to the SUV. A lush garden lined the northern side of Atabei's enormous back yard with a glass greenhouse on one end. The rest of the manicured grounds were meticulously laid out, all encircling a grassy ring at its heart, lined with chalky stones. A fifteen-foot tree trunk thrust straight up from the middle. Half-finished carvings decorated the pole, reminiscent of the one in the woods.

Once Quentin made it to the vehicle, Errol tapped his phone and pressed it to his ear. "Hey. He still there?" A pause. "Yeah. We're on our way. Let Issach know. A'ight?" He thumbed the screen and jammed the phone back into his pocket. "They're ready."

Quentin pushed the black remote hanging from the visor, and the gate opened. Malcolm patted Hounacier's bag reassuringly as they pulled onto the street. *Ready, baby?*

Twenty minutes later, they pulled into an alley and slowed beside a white sedan. A baby-faced black man with round, wire-framed glasses sat in the driver's seat, arm outside the window, clutching a cigarette. He nodded, and Quentin pulled up behind him and parked.

"We're here." The big man killed the engine and stepped out.

Malcolm followed, backpack with the supplies over one shoulder, Hounacier's bag under his arm.

The driver came out of the sedan and bumped fists with Quentin then Errol.

"This here's Issach," Errol said with a little snap of his head.

Issach gave Malcolm a short nod.

"So what are we lookin' at?" Malcolm asked.

"He's in there," Issach said, pointing across the street with his chin. "Lives up on the third floor. Three forty-one."

Malcolm eyed the six-story apartment building. "Cypress," it read in bold, white letters. "Air Conditioned," beneath it.

"He's there now?" Malcolm asked. Taller buildings framed the apartment, their walls connected.

"Yeah. He left 'bout two hours ago. Went to the corner store. Came back." He removed a black-and-gold phone from his pocket and handed it over. "This is him. Name's Shane Gruss."

Malcolm smirked, seeing the spiky-haired man's picture on the screen, the image captured while he was standing in a checkout line. *Hello again, asshole.* He handed the phone back. "This the only entrance?"

Issach shook his head. "Sammy's coverin' the door in the back."

"Show me."

Leaving Quentin out front with a radio, Issach led Malcolm and Errol across the street and around to a parking lot behind the buildings, protected by a wrought-iron gate. One of the pointed, vertical bars had been broken free, allowing them to sidestep though the gap. A skinny man with a lumpy Afro and a neatly trimmed beard sat on a metal box near the building. He looked up as they approached. "Hey, boys."

"Hey." Issach stabbed a thumb toward Malcolm. "This here's the man Mama Atabei told us 'bout. Malcolm."

The man hopped off his box and extended a hand. "Sammy. Real pleasure to meet you." A faint whiff of alcohol tinged his breath.

"Good to meet you," Malcolm said, shaking his hand. He nodded to the oversized malt energy drink resting on the box. Another can lay discarded in the narrow gap between it and the building. "Been drinking?"

Sammy shrugged. "Been a long day."

"Well, it's about to get a whole lot longer. You're done drinking for now. I need you sharp."

Sammy made a sour face, his head going back a little.

"I'm not fucking around," Malcolm snapped. "We're about to do something so damned dangerous it'll be like catching a rabid grizzly with kite string."

Sammy gave a little laugh.

"You think I'm fucking kidding?" Malcolm's eyes narrowed. "I've seen people better trained and better equipped than you guys get killed doing this, and I'll be damned if anyone's dying under me. Atabei said I'm in charge?"

Sammy nodded. "Y ... yeah."

"Then do what I tell you. You don't, people die. Maybe you. Got it?"

"Yes, sir."

"Good." Malcolm drew a breath and nodded to the red brick building. "Now, what do you know about this guy?"

Sammy, seeming real happy at the change of subject, gestured up the flat wall. "He's the fifth and sixth windows up on the right, closer this way. Third floor." The dark windows were difficult to see this close to the building. On the bright side, it meant the demon wouldn't see them either.

"He have a car back here?"

Sammy nodded. "Blue one over there. One with two flat tires."

Malcolm's brow cocked. "You do that?"

"Yeah. When we got word you were comin'."

"Good job." Malcolm looked around, scanning the area. No cameras. No entrances but the one gate and the apartment itself. There was an alley beyond the fence on the far side of the lot, near a dumpster. It looked to go for two building lengths before splitting at a T-intersection, each headed to a different street. There was another broken-off pole there where people had obviously been cutting through, evident by the worn trail through the strip of weeds. He'd done raids in complexes before, but those were search and destroy jobs. Taking a prisoner, especially a possessed one, was going to be a hell of a lot harder.

"So what's the plan?" Issach asked, adjusting his glasses.

"Depends," Malcolm said, still scanning. "It's too busy to nab him until late. Around midnight might be safe. I'll want a look at the building layout to be sure where everyone needs to be. Back door's probably best to get him in the car." He gestured to the alley beyond the fence. "I'm thinking through there. Gives two points of escape." He turned to Issach. "Can you get me inside?"

"Yeah."

"Then let's have a look around."

Malcolm sat in the front seat of the SUV, his skin sticky with perspiration. They'd parked in the T-alley behind the apartments, facing the northern street. Using the AC was pointless for such a long wait, so they'd opened the windows, but the heavy, humid air didn't move enough to make any difference. He'd made Quentin smoke outside, but the stink still drifted in.

He checked his watch.

11:44. *Sixteen more minutes.*

He hated the waiting before a job. Time slowed to a painful crawl as the tension only raced higher and higher. Over all the years, it had gotten better, some, but it never went away.

Malcolm slid his hand into the oxygen bag and touched Hounacier's handle. She could always calm him. Tracing his fingers across the smooth grip, he petted the carved animal head curving from the end. He never had figured out exactly what type of animal the crude carving was supposed to depict. Panther, he suspected. It felt like a panther, sleek and menacing. It would help if anyone knew where exactly Hounacier originated, but no one did. Ulises had said stories of her first appeared in Les Cayes in the late nineteenth century. Then in the 1920s, a New Orleans bokor named Papa Peyroux carried her back to Haiti. If he had known what the animal was, he took it to his grave.

Malcolm remembered the way Ulises had touched her handle the day they'd first met. Protective. She was his love, and along came some half-Cuban American from some big university with big ideas and no faith. He couldn't imagine how that must have felt. But Ulises took him, trained him, and eventually gave his greatest love over to that same arrogant boy he now called his son. A son that never called, rarely visited so that Ulises could see him, see Hounacier, be in the room with her again.

Would that be his fate too? Would the day come when some pompous shit would appear, inherit Hounacier, and leave Malcolm to loneliness and booze as his only company? He'd deserve that.

Pushing the thought away, Malcolm checked his watch again.

11:51. *Close enough.*

He took the radio from console and thumbed the rubberized button. "Check in. Issach, you got anything?"

"Nothin'."

"Sammy?"

"Just sweatin' my balls off," Sammy replied.

"Well, get ready. We're going in in five minutes. Remember the plan. Issach, we'll meet you up on three."

"Got it," Issach said.

Malcolm picked up the black wire earpiece and plugged it into the Motorola. Taking Hounacier's bag, he stepped out of the vehicle and clipped the radio to his belt. "Quentin, you ready?"

Quentin sucked a final drag off his menthol and dropped it. He nodded, blowing a long stream of smoke.

"Errol, go ahead and start the car." Malcolm slipped the silver-chain-wrapped dowel in his back pocket. "Call Atabei. Let her know."

The little man nodded and stuck the key in the ignition.

Before closing the Lexus door, Malcolm slipped the sawed-off into the holster along the back of his belt, beneath his untucked shirt. He kissed the crescent bone pendant then slung Hounacier's bag across his back. He nodded to Quentin, and they started down the alley.

His shoulder tingled with the familiar excitement, adrenaline trickling through his veins. His senses heightened, even beyond normal. He could smell every piece of mildewed garbage, the burger joint half a block away, even the lingering traces of Errol's cheap cologne behind him. Each scrawled graffiti picture and word was clearly visible in the dim light. They turned at the intersection and continued twenty yards toward the broken fence. Sammy was already by the door, rocking on his heels, antsy, looking over his shoulder.

Malcolm gave a quick scan, verifying no one was around, and slipped through the narrow opening into the parking lot.

Sammy nodded to him.

"You cool?" Malcolm asked.

"Yeah," the thin man said a little too eagerly.

"Good," Malcolm said. "Just stop bouncing." He motioned to Quentin, and the big man unwrapped the obsidian mask and offered it over.

Sammy accepted it like it was radioactive or something.

"Just stand at the door with this at your chest," Malcolm said. "That'll keep him inside if he gets past us. Just hold it tight, and for God's sake, don't drop it or put it over your face."

"Okay."

Malcolm pressed the radio button. "Going in." The metal door squeaked as he pulled it open. Flickering fluorescent tubes, their light yellowed by dingy covers, lit the hallway beyond. The men stepped in, passed a broken elevator, and turned up a tight stairwell that stank of vomit.

They came up on the third floor. The long hallways stretched from one side of the building to the other lined with numbered doors. Black pads of hardened gum and cigarette burns speckled the brown carpet. Issach stood at the other end, by the second stairwell, the other demon mask in his hands. He gave a little nod then headed toward them.

They closed in on unit 341. Malcolm put a finger to his lips. The muffled sound of a TV blared from a nearby apartment. Malcolm drew Hounacier from her sheath and pointed the two men where to stand. Issach took position before the door, the black mask at neck level. Quentin pulled his revolver from under his shirt and took position just behind and to his side. Taking a breath, Malcolm put his back to the wall beside the door handle. He held up a hand and counted down on his fingers.

3 ...2 ...1.

Cocking his knee, Malcolm mule-kicked back, smashing his heel just below the handle. Wood popped, and the door burst open.

"There!" Issach shouted.

Malcolm spun in a crouch, his head below the mask, Hounacier out before him. A black remote control flew into the wall near his face, spraying him with broken plastic. Silhouetted in the light of a flickering television, Shane Gruss, the man from the antique store, now shirtless, scrambled over the back of a couch and through an open door. The door slammed shut.

"Go!" Malcolm ordered.

They moved into the room, Malcolm to one side, Issach and Quentin moving together to the other. Glass crashed in the other room. Metal *thunked.* A man screamed.

Malcolm raced to the door and kicked it open. Torn blinds hung out a smashed window. He scanned the bedroom. Empty. He ran to the window.

Below, shattered glass and twisted window frame littered the dented top of a white van. Sammy was on the ground, crawling away on his back, mask against his chest. Lengthening, gray hair whipped along the demon man's skin as if he were in a wind tunnel. He growled, his face rippling in the phantom gale. It pushed its way toward Sammy.

Fuck! "He's outside!" Malcolm slashed the machete across the bottom of the windowsill, knocking out the broken shards.

Sammy released one hand from the mask, jammed his hand down his pants, and pulled out a pistol.

Pop. Pop. Pop.

One of the rounds hit the monster in the gut. It staggered back.

"No!" Malcolm screamed.

Sammy kept firing. Blood exploded from the beast's shoulder. "Stop!" Malcolm climbed through the window. Holding the edge, he swung down. Searing pain shot through his ribs as he caught his weight. Stifling a yelp, he dropped the rest of the way onto the parked van. He landed with a loud *thunk* and went to his knees. Glass bounced and tinkled around him.

The half-formed beast whirled. Growing circles of hairless skin widened around the bleeding wounds. Its eyes narrowed, seeing Malcolm. It fled toward the alley.

Gritting his teeth, Malcolm slid off the roof onto the asphalt. The injured monster squeezed though the broken fence and loped off down the alley.

Malcolm hit the radio button as he started after it. "Errol! It's coming your way." He ran to the fence, Sammy behind him, and slipped though the blood-smeared opening. Ahead, the monster turned the corner, headed toward the SUV.

Fighting through the pain, Malcolm squeezed Hounacier's grip and hurried after it.

Over the sounds of their pounding feet, glass shattered ahead. Errol's scream was cut off.

"Errol!" Malcolm rounded the corner. The monster, now mostly formed, crouched below the Lexus' open door. Blood splattered the pearl paint as the beast tore into Errol's stomach, his face the serene, distance-eyed calm as the demon claimed his soul.

Malcolm charged.

The creature's head snapped around, its lengthening maw caked in chunky red. The blossomed silver slug pushed itself out from the creature's shoulder and fell to the ground. Gray fur sprouted from the bald spot around the now-closed wound, and the beast swelled to its full size.

It stood. Bloody and split blue jeans hung from the werewolf's waist.

Malcolm threw his left palm out, and the tattoo stretched wide. The beast winced, backing half a step into the open door.

With a roar, it sprang, landing on all fours and charged with incredible speed, its bloody jaws wide.

Hand still extended, Malcolm braced for the attack.

The beast leaped, its claws stretched before it.

Malcolm whirled to the side, allowing a clear line of sight from the beast to the demon mask in Sammy's hands behind him.

The airborne monster jolted back. It slammed into a brick wall and fell.

"Stay on it!" Malcolm ordered as the scrambling beast tried to rise.

Holding the mask out front in both hands, Sammy moved to the side, trapping the werewolf between the wall and the mask. Fur whipping, it tried to crawl forward along the edge, but Malcolm moved in its path, warding palm out.

The beast gave a whimpering growl and clenched its eyes. Not looking at the tattoo protected it from the effects, but not from the mask. Head down, it tried crawling back, but Sammy adjusted his position, keeping it pinned.

Bones popped and shifted beneath the werewolf's skin. Its snout undulated and flattened and lengthened. The gray fur thinned, thickened, thinned again.

Footsteps raced up the alley behind them. Malcolm glanced back to see Issach and Quentin running toward them. Issach froze, eyes locked on Errol's bloodied form.

"Issach!" Malcolm snapped over his shoulder. "Mask!"

Issach jumped. He looked at Malcolm.

"Mask!"

Nodding, he ran up beside Sammy, his own mask out before him. The demon wailed beneath the combined assault, its bestial voice cracking to human. Its fur shrank away, revealing pinkish skin as the body shifted and shrank to normal.

Shane Gruss lay trembling in the scummy alley corner, crushed beneath the power of the masks.

His palm still out and Hounacier ready, Malcolm looked to Quentin. "Tie him up."

The big man just looked at him, terror in his wide, pale eyes.

"Now, God damn it!"

Quentin pulled a dowel from his pocket and approached the demon man.

"Get his hands first," Malcolm said.

Shane didn't struggle as Quentin pulled one of his hands behind him and looped the chain around his wrist. He pulled the other arm back and wrapped the rest of it tight, finishing with a crude knot.

"Make sure that'll hold." Malcolm lowered his palm long enough to fish the chain-wrapped dowel from his own pocket. He tossed it underhanded. "Now his neck."

Malcolm looked around. They needed to move. Someone had to have called the cops about the shots. Errol moaned on the ground, his fingers fumbling with the gruesome wound as if trying to push the blood back in.

Malcolm's enhanced eyes caught movement along the far side of the alley. A homeless man lay in a dark corner beside concrete steps, his mangy beard hanging like Spanish moss. The man was caked in filth; Malcolm couldn't even guess his race. He shivered and twitched, eyes rolling like a crackhead in withdrawal. The man's eyes snapped to attention and met Malcolm's with a sudden and strange familiarity.

The loa looked at him, seeming curious, a question on his crusty lips. He glanced to the demon and back to Malcolm and shook his head. Pity? Warning?

"Got it," Quentin exclaimed.

Malcolm turned from the mounted man. *Sorry. No time for your riddles.* "All right, get him to the car. Sammy, go around to the other side. We'll pin him in the middle with Errol between you two."

"With Errol?" Sammy asked. "Can't we call him an ambulance?"

"He's marked," Malcolm said. "The demon's inside him now. We'll wrap his neck and take him with us." *I just hope he survives until we reach Atabei.*

CHAPTER 12

"Oh, God," Errol blubbered. His silver-bound hands pressed Issach's red-soaked shirt against his stomach. "I don't wanna die." Passing lights slid across the bloodied white leather seats as Quentin sped down the highway.

The overpowering reek of the open gut wound made Malcolm's eyes tear. He crouched in the back of the SUV's storage area, clutching Hounacier, ready to strike either of the prisoners before him if they tried anything. Sammy and Issach were crammed awkwardly on either side, masks ready. Sitting closer to Errol, Sammy gulped, looking like he was about to throw up.

"I don't wanna die. I don't wanna die," Errol sobbed.

"You're gonna be okay," Issach mumbled, not looking at him.

Malcolm clenched his jaw. This was his fault. Errol was under his command, and now, the demon had him. Even if Atabei could exorcise it, Errol might still die.

"I'm … thirsty," Errol panted.

"Be quiet," Malcolm growled.

"It hurts," Errol cried.

"I know. But you're just losing blood by talking. Shut up."

A long, weak whine resonated from Errol's closed mouth. At least he'd stopped talking. Every word, every plea, only cemented Malcolm's guilt. How many people were going to die under him? Their dead faces flashed through his mind. Nick.

Erika. Kazuo. So many now gone. He'd failed them. *Stop. Focus, damn it.* Errol couldn't die too.

Tires squealed as Quentin slung the SUV off the highway and turned onto the dirt road past the trailer park. The vehicle trembled and shook, hurtling down the dark tunnel of woods.

"Almost there," Quentin said into his radio, his voice coming though the bud in Malcolm's ear.

"We're ready for you," Atabei responded.

"I'm dying," Errol moaned to no one in particular.

"Quiet," Malcolm growled. "You're going to be fine."

Shane Gruss, who hadn't spoken or moved since they caught him, turned his head. He looked at Malcolm from the corner of his eye.

Malcolm tensed. "Head down."

"I know where we going," Shane said, his lips barely moving. "I know because he knows." The demon nodded toward Errol.

"Head *down*," Malcolm repeated, moving the blade into the demon's line of sight. His spine tightened. The demon hadn't manifested but was talking. They weren't supposed to do that.

"He's not going to be okay." Shane looked back down toward his lap. "Neither are you."

The rumbling SUV slowed and turned into the primitive drive. A bald man by the open gate waved them on. The vehicle bounced down the narrow path. Light flickered through the trees ahead. The woods opened up into the field. Dozens of oil torches surrounded the shipping containers, bathing them in orange fire. Silhouettes hurried out, and the SUV slid to a stop. Bade and Sogbo jumped against their chains, their barks filling the silence.

"All right," Malcolm said as they opened the doors. "Let's get them to the pen." He crawled out of the back and around to where they were pulling the prisoners out the side door.

"Help me," Quentin said, trying to gently pull Errol out. Two men came in around him and carried the injured man away, his blood staining their pristine, white garments.

Atabei watched Errol, eyes tense in horror and worry. "We need to do this now! Get the collars."

"Are we ready?" Malcolm asked.

"Everything is as you said."

He eyed the two concentric bands of white powder nearly filling the container ring, broken by only a small gap. Three steel rings, the kind used to tie a dog in a yard, were screwed into the ground on one side of the central post. A trio of ropes ran from outside the circle, each threading through a different steel ring and ending in a metal clip. Summoning the loa would take too long. They weren't necessary for his part, and Atabei had said she didn't need them for hers. Still, tradition demanded that they call them.

Errol's pained wail sent birds fluttering from the darkened trees.

Malcolm swallowed. No time for tradition. "All right. We need a fourth ring."

"Karri," Atabei snapped to a mulatto woman, her thick curls spilling out beneath a white scarf. "Set a new ring."

"We don't have any more."

"Make one. Check with Peewee."

The woman hurried off.

"What else?" Atabei asked.

"We'll need a rope for him. Just like the others. Once this is done, we need to get him to a hospital."

Atabei nodded. "Take a moment to gather yourself while we prepare."

She walked away, and Malcolm drew a long breath. He held it, trying to calm his pounding heart. Slowly, he released it and drew another. *Keep it together. Keep it together. He's not going to die.*

Malcolm wished he believed that. He needed to. Blowing it out, Malcolm sheathed Hounacier then peeled off his sweaty shirt. He dabbed his face and tossed the crumpled shirt onto the Lexus' hood. "Ready, baby?" he asked aloud, drawing the machete. He kissed the blade and marched into the fire-lit ring.

Despite Atabei's insistence that it wasn't necessary, Malcolm demanded cleansing by a live chicken before anyone entered the circle. She wasn't as priestly as he'd imagined, but Malcolm was, and by God, he was going to have something holy about this. No way was Malcolm locking himself inside a ring with a demon and his sins and negative energies still coating him. Bitterly, she agreed.

Once cleansed, he took the fluttering bird by the ankles and rubbed it over Atabei, Quentin, Issach, then Peewee, the broad-shouldered bald man who had opened the gate. That complete, he entered the ring, the annoyed bird still twisting against his hold. Oily citronella smoke from the near fifty torches filled the air. A faint hint of other herbs, including sage, accented the lemony smell.

He circled the central post, stopping at each cardinal point and holding the sin-laden chicken before it. On the fourth pass, he knelt. "I offer this to you. Protect us."

Malcolm drew Hounacier and cut the bird's head free with a quick chop. It fluttered and writhed, blood squirting from the tiny hole ringed in brown feathers. He stood and rubbed as much blood as he could onto the post before the animal went limp. Malcolm laid it at the base, just below a long-faced carving, and turned back toward the circle's opening.

Slowly, he walked, his neck and shoulders prickling with that all-too-familiar tingle. He was a bokor. The groom. Husband, father, and child to the nameless angel that was Hounacier. Other holy weapons had their gifts, but hers was power. He reached the edge and thrust the machete high.

A drum thumped.

Issach and Peewee stepped through, escorting young Leigh Ann into the ring. A thick choke chain encircled her neck, just above the silver collar. She looked at Malcolm. Terrified tears framed her pleading eyes. Backing slowly, Malcolm led them to the first staked ring. The two men took the rope that ran through the ring and clipped it to the long end of the chain.

Peewee drew a screwdriver from his pocket and removed the silver collar's locking pin. It was like pulling the pin from a demonic grenade. The werewolf could now take form. If it did, the choke chain leash was all that held it. The men guided Leigh Ann to the ground, face-up, her head toward the central post. Outside the ring, Sammy pulled the rope, taking out the slack. The chain rattled through the steel ring as it tightened.

Their work complete, Peewee and Issach left the ring and

fetched the next prisoner, Gary. The lone drum sounded again as he came inside. His escorts led him to the second rope and attached it to his chromed choke chain before removing the silver hoop. Gary's eyes never left Hounacier's glinting blade. They laid him down beside Leigh Ann. Sadie, the chubby woman from the house, pulled the rope taut.

Next came Shane Gruss, entering with an ominous drumbeat. Peewee and Issach led him at arm's length, obviously more afraid than they had been with the others. Issach snapped him in then fidgeted with Quentin's knot for a full two minutes before finally unwrapping the slender, silver chain. A burly man, who looked like he might have been a professional fullback fifteen years ago, pulled the rope as they lowered Shane to his back, head facing the post.

Finally, they carried Errol in on a crude stretcher. Malcolm clenched his jaw, struggling to keep the stoic face. Blood soaked the tight-wrapped cloth around Errol's waist. He rolled his head toward Malcolm, eyes glassy and pained, breath shallow.

Lacking a fourth choke chain, Issach looped the rope directly around Errol's neck. It ran through a crude arch of bent rebar pounded into the ground like a croquet hoop. For an instant, Errol's eyes snapped to attention. A devilish smile curled his lips then was gone.

Just keep fucking with me, asshole, Malcolm thought, anger rising.

In taking Errol, it had taken his knowledge. It knew what it was in for. Death or eternity in a silver prison. *We'll see how you're smiling then.*

The two men turned to Malcolm. He nodded, and they left. They took position on either side, just outside the ring, each holding an obsidian mask shrouded beneath a crimson cloth.

The drum sounded again, and Quentin stepped into the ring, carrying a wood platter. A long, silver mask, vaguely resembling a wolf's head, rested atop it. The lights of the torches shimmered off its hammered surface. He skirted the inner edge of the ring until reaching the opposite end behind Malcolm.

Another drum beat. Atabei entered. She carried a small bowl in one hand. She knelt, dipped her fingers into it, and drew a pair of lines, sealing the circle. Setting the bowl down, she stood and followed the inner edge and stopping at the northernmost side.

The drum thumped again, followed by another. Hounacier still raised, Malcolm backed away from the four prisoners, the slow drum marking each step. He stopped beside Quentin.

Malcolm gave a loud whoop, and the drums erupted into a rapid tempo. Holding Hounacier out, flat across his open palm, Malcolm unleashed a streaming chant. "Ohma sarri ayi ah. Oonu karri na. Ohga narrifischtoo. Tikki ahsa ah."

He didn't know the words he spoke; they simply channeled through him. He'd never heard anyone but himself and Ulises speak the musical language until last year when Tiamat's followers called their demonic goddess into this world. Matt had called it the First Tongue, the language of God.

His voice rising, Malcolm aimed the flat of the blade at Leigh Ann. "Ohma sarri ayi ah. Oonu karri na! Ohga narrifischtoo. Tikki ahsa ah!"

Malcolm moved his chant to Gary, straining his bound neck to watch, eyes wide. "Ohma sarri ayi ah. Oonu karri na! Ohga narrifischtoo. Tikki ahsa ah!"

The verse complete, Malcolm moved to Shane and then Errol before starting back again with Leigh Ann, his voice rising.

"Ohma sarri ayi ah! Oonu karri na! Ohga narrifischtoo! Tikki ahsa ah!"

His hair rustled as if in a breeze, but the humid, smoke-filled air didn't move. The chanting grew faster, and the drums sped to keep pace. The second sequence complete, Malcolm stamped his foot and began again. Sogbo and Bade started howling.

"Ohma sarri ayi ah! Oonu karri na!" A sudden tingle vibrated up his body, through his bones, and into his hands. Hounacier's blade warmed against his palm. "Ohga narrifischtoo! Tikki ahsa ah!" The little girl trembled at the last words before Malcolm moved to Gary. Like Leigh Ann, Gary spasmed just as Malcolm ended the sequence and started on Shane.

Hair and clothing flapped in the ghostly wind as Malcolm began the fourth pass, his voice a scream. Hounacier vibrated against his skin like a hot guitar string, her unseen power arcing to the prisoners. Leigh Ann shrieked and shook, her high voice undulating with the tremors. Gary's legs shook side to side in an impossible blur, kicking up a cloud of dust. Shane wailed, his head pistoning back into the ground like a pneumatic hammer. Fresh blood trickled down Errol's legs as his back arched under the invisible bolt's fury.

"Ohma sarri ayi ah!" Leigh Ann's hands shook, seeming to change shape in the blur. "Oonu karri na!" Ohga narrifischtoo! Tikki ahsa ah!"

A howl exploded from Gary's mouth as his teeth stretched out from his peeling lips. Pimpling hairs rolled up his shaking body.

Almost there. He switched focus to Shane.

The white man's skin grayed as rolling fur spread out from his chest. His legs lengthened, forming long-toed paws.

The sequence complete, Malcolm moved to Errol. The little man bounced and writhed. His face lengthened, and an inhuman roar burst from blackening lips. Blood exploded out from the bandage, squirting across the ground and onto Shane beside him. Someone in the audience screamed. The two dogs yelped and cried. Shifting organs hemorrhaged and squeezed though the red-stained bandage and out onto the ground.

Shit!

The three prisoners all erupted in cackling laugher as Errol fell still.

You son of a bitch! He moved back to Leigh Ann, rage fueling his chants. Her filthy shorts split open as canine thighs swelled beneath then. A black, wormlike tail slithered out from between her legs and sprouted fur. Furiously, Malcolm focused the power harder on her. Spittle flew from his lips as he roared the streaming mantra, but the demon refused to take hold.

Gary's body instantly swelled as Hounacier's arc hit him.

"Ohma sarri ayi ah!"

His face lengthened, fangs filling the growing jaws.

"Oonu karri na!"

Thick, black hair burst from his skin, ribs shifting beneath it.

"Ohga narrifischtoo!"

Gary's pulsing legs contorted and changed, and his hands stretched into long-fingered claws.

"Tikki ahsa ah!"

The werewolf roared and yanked against the chain at its neck. The other prisoners screamed as the beast thrashed beside them.

"Now!" Malcolm shouted.

The people holding the ropes released all but the demon's. They fumbled to help Sadie, who was sliding forward as the beast fought its leash. Their ropes slack, Shane and Leigh Ann rolled, scrambling away from the thrashing monster. Shane stumbled on his tattered pants, no more than a skirt of denim ribbons. The werewolf slashed his leg. His left calf peeled from the bone. Screaming, he fell onto Errol's broken form.

Malcolm lurched forward, Hounacier up and warding palm ready. Before he reached them, Issach, standing on that side of the ring, yanked the shroud from the ghoul mask, and the werewolf recoiled away. Shane dragged himself out of the beast's reach before collapsing face down in the blood-soaked earth.

The team holding the werewolf's rope heaved, yanking its head back to the ground. Malcolm noticed Atabei standing a few feet behind it, lips moving. He hadn't heard her over the screams and snarls. Face calm and hands outstretched, she recited a low chant.

"Mayas karri notem."

Malcolm strained to hear her. The flowing words sounded like the First Tongue.

"Holloo mreshti. Mayas karri notem. Ohma ahsa ah rae." She stepped closer, her voice rising.

Malcolm's chest tightened as she drew near it. If the rope didn't hold, he wouldn't be able to save her. Issach and Peewee stood at the edges, eyes transfixed, masks ready.

"Holloo mreshti. Mayas karri notem. Ohma ahsa ah rae." Atabei's right hand rose above her head as she stepped just outside the monster's reach.

Mouthing the words as she spoke them, Malcolm watched in awe as Atabei lunged like a striking viper and touched the

demon's head with the flat of her palm. The werewolf froze as
if paralyzed.

Atabei continued her chant, the words flowing in steady
rhythm. "Holloo mreshti. Mayas karri notem. Ohma ahsa ah
rae."

Glowing red smoke, like liquid fire, wormed from the beast's
nose and mouth and streamed up toward Atabei's upturned
hand. Its bestial features deflated, fur and claws retracting.
The burning smoke poured from its eyes and shortening ears,
gathering into a twisting ball hovering just above her fingertips.
More strands peeled from Shane's unconscious form and Leigh
Ann, now hunkered behind one of the containers, adding to the
pulsing light.

Malcolm stood mesmerized as dozens of other tendrils
stretched out from the ball, as every soul the demon had ever
marked was released. The crimson fire rolled and seethed, over
two feet across. Gary lay on the ground, naked, his shredded
clothed lying around him. He stared up at the glowing, smoke-
like ball, eyes wide.

Atabei nodded, and the team holding Gary's rope released
it.

"Go," she uttered quietly, her face taut in concentration.

The man scooted away and hurried off, the still-attached
rope trailing behind him.

Quentin stepped forward and set the platter and mask on
the ground before Atabei. Hounacier relaxed in his grip as
Malcolm came up beside him, his mouth open in awe. How had
she learned this?

She met his eye. "It's time."

Malcolm licked his lips. His eyes transfixed on the swirling
demon fire, he hadn't noticed Quentin come behind him until
the huge fist slammed into the side of his skull.

He stumbled, head swimming. Another fist hit Malcolm's
kidney, and Hounacier fell from his hand. He tried to reach for
her, but the big man was on him, his thick arms wrapping up
under Malcolm's and around to the back of his head, pinning
him in a half nelson. Quentin yanked him back, away from the
mask, away from Hounacier.

"What the fuck?" Malcolm screamed.

Atabei's lips curled into an evil sneer. "This is for my husband, Hercule."

"What?" He pulled against Quentin's hold, his busted ribs screaming in pain, but couldn't move. "Who?"

She stepped closer, the swirling fire still aloft. "You killed him." Malcolm's anger turned to terror as her slender fingers reached toward him. He tried pushing himself back but couldn't. "I don't—"

Her fingertip touched his skin, and the crimson sphere surged down her arm and hit Malcolm like a wave. Quentin threw him down, and Malcolm collapsed as the icy cold flames surged into his eyes and mouth, choking and blinding him with furious power. It flooded though his veins, filling them with hopeless dread. He tried to scream, but more of the phantasmal fire poured inside him.

"You do not deserve Hounacier!" Atabei screamed. "Murderer!"

Malcolm tried reaching back for the sawed-off at his back, but his muscles wouldn't move right. His numbing fingers found the leather holder. Empty!

He rolled himself over to see Quentin above him. The big man grinned, eyes cruel but tinged with fear, the Remington in his hand.

A brilliant, unfathomable light of alien memories exploded behind Malcolm's eyes, and the demon erupted, roaring though him. It was too late.

Searing pain burned his left palm and right wrist as the warding eye and scarab tattoos boiled and steamed from skin, crackling and hissing. Malcolm screamed.

Bones crunched and popped. His skin painfully stretched near the ripping point. He thrashed and spasmed, trying to fight it, trying to hold it back, but couldn't.

"He didn't have to die," Atabei said.

Malcolm twisted and saw her moving toward Hounacier, lying on the dusty ground near the ring's edge. The witch intended to kill him with her. *No you don't!*

Gritting teeth that shifted and moved inside his mouth,

Malcolm swept his leg at Quentin's feet. It whipped with more force or power than he could have imagined. The big man fell, the sawed-off roaring with a deafening crack and flash. Peewee, who stood with the demon mask not far from Hounacier, leaped back and ducked as the shot flew over his head. The black mask fell from his fingers.

Forcing every ounce of will he had left, Malcolm scrambled, his body stiff and fighting him. His right leg and arm wouldn't move, but still he crawled.

The demon was inside him.

Hounacier could kill it.

Atabei stumbled, backing away as he squirmed and clambered toward her.

Malcolm clawed Hounacier's bone handle with his now-fleshless palm and pulled her toward him. Unable to thrust her back into himself, he rose onto his knee, her handle on the ground and blade to his stomach. Darkness swirled at the edges of his vision, closing in. With his last act of defiance, Malcolm dropped his weight onto the blade for their final embrace.

I

A salty breeze caresses Gulmet's face, rustling his fur. He smells the goats over the hill ahead, their blood and meat and filthy pen. The mortals' stink also fouls the wind. His mouth moistens at the thought of their screams and flesh. Above, a brilliant white crescent, framed in countless, colored stars, casts a brilliant glow over the rocky landscape.

Rajik moves silently beside him. She always was quieter than Gulmet. He looks to her. Moonlight flickers across her golden-brown fur. A female body always suited Rajik best. It is only fitting, after so many millennia, that she be the one to finally bear the children of their union. With the blood moon only weeks behind them, Gulmet can already sense the six new souls forming within her. It will be five more moons before next lunar eclipse heralds their birth. Five moons that Rajik must maintain her wolven form lest the pups die. Five moons until the merging of their spirits becomes a new generation. All they must do now is wait.

They stop at the hill's crest. Below, beyond olive and cypress trees, smoke rises from a tiny, flat-roofed cottage. The valley is fertile, sown with the deaths of six thousand soldiers. Their blood and pain shimmers in every plant that now grows on the long-forgotten battlefield. It is here that Gulmet has chosen for her. Waves lap the shores beyond the building where a small craft rests on a beach. Rajik loves the water.

She nuzzles him, and his flesh tingles at her touch. "It's perfect."

Pleased, Gulmet says, "Everything you desire, I shall provide."

Rajik nuzzles him again. "As I for you." Desire glints in her eyes, though not for him. She desires the hunt. He shall give it to her. New blood shall cleanse their home.

Keeping to the shadows, they descend the hill. Slow. Quiet. Their caution is unnecessary. Mortals could never escape them. But the hunt is a ritual.

A male is visible through the cottage window. Slender, his black beard thick and curly. A child laughs behind him.

They move closer. Gulmet catches the scent of the woman and girl inside, but then the wind slows and shifts.

The goats shuffle uncomfortably, smelling their deaths. They cry and bleat, gathering in the far corner of their lashed cage. They are the first to know their fate but will be the last to die. The thought of it brings more water to Gulmet's tongue. Yes. The humans die first. All but one.

The bearded man yells out the window. But the goats continue to panic.

Gulmet crouches beneath the shadow of a tree. Rajik circles around to the far side.

The man yells again then retreats inside. A moment later, he emerges from the door, a flintlock in his hands. Eyes squinting, he scans the darkness. Gulmet's open mouth curls into a smile as the mortal's gaze passes over him. To the side, he sees Rajik charge from the shadows. She crosses the open ground and springs through the open window.

A pot shatters. A girl screams.

The man whirls around. Eyes wide in terror, he raises the gun.

Leaves rustle as Gulmet charges.

The man turns. In three bounds, Gulmet closes the distance. The gun fires as he springs, its leaden ball passing harmlessly though his ribs. His forepaws strike the man's chest, bringing him to the ground. The man screams and smashes the barrel against him, but Gulmet only bares his teeth and continues pressing the human down.

Inside, the child wails. Her screams are not enough to drown the sounds of her mother's crunching bones and tearing flesh. A string of saliva drips from Gulmet's fangs onto the man's cheek. He waits until his prey hears his daughter die, then Gulmet snaps down onto the man's shoulder, savoring the blood and terror. They sweeten the taste of the mortal's soul. Gulmet holds the bite for only a moment, his teeth scratching the bones, then he pours himself into this new host.

CHAPTER 13

Malcolm woke to the twitter of birds. He was fetally curled in the shade of a large tree. Disoriented, he swatted a mosquito on his arm. Twigs crunched and poked his naked skin as he pushed himself up to a sitting position. A heavy weight shifted in his stomach at the movement, reminiscent of the overfull feeling after a holiday meal.

Squinting in the morning light, he looked around. Woods. No … bayou.

Where am I? He licked his lips, tasting blood. Malcolm touched them, brushing away several dried flakes, now melting against his sweaty skin. He peered closer, seeing tiny holes and hollow tubes perforating the rust-colored chips.

A sudden terror gripped him. Fur. There'd been fur there when the blood had dried. Now, only holes remained.

Memories of the ceremony came flooding back. Atabei had betrayed him. Hounacier was gone.

Panicked, he looked to the spot where he had plunged Hounacier's blade. A hairline scar traced along his abdomen too far off-center to be a quick mortal wound. He'd been too late. The demon had taken him.

But if the beast had healed its wounds, that meant it had killed. It had fed. Malcolm thought of his over-stuffed stomach then vomited onto the leaves. Blood and stringy chunks of meat poured from his mouth. Seeing it, he retched again then again.

Eyes watering, he spat out the bits clinging to his teeth and cheeks. He fished a broken fingernail from behind a molar and dropped it. There was still skin along the back. Curly black hairs ran though the bloody soup. He wondered whose they were. Leigh Ann's kinky hair came to mind and Malcolm vomited again until it was only dry heaves. Panting, he rolled on his back, away from the horrible slop. He desperately wanted to wash the taste from his mouth, but there was nothing but stagnant pools of swamp water.

The scarab and warding tattoos were gone, only faint, scarred shapes from where the artist's needle had pierced his skin, but the ink was no more. Not that it mattered. They required Hounacier to work, and the bond, the comforting warmth in the back of his mind that had been his one rock no matter what else had happened, was gone. He was corrupted, and she'd turned her back on him. Malcolm had failed his highest duty. He'd lost the angel's love. An anguished scream welled from inside. The birds flew away as he roared in pure, unfettered rage.

Malcolm lay there for several minutes, eyes unfocused on the tree above him. He was a monster. He'd killed. He'd fed. He'd do it again. The only release was death. Maybe the demon hadn't marked any other bodies. What if he was the only one? Malcolm's death could cheat it of a body. Even if not, Malcolm couldn't allow it use him as its vessel again. Malcolm had to die.

No, he thought, snapping out of his trance. *No, I have to tell the Order. They need to know about Atabei. About Hounacier. She murdered Ulises. She has to pay.*

Anger fueling him, Malcolm rose to his feet. Flies had already found the half-digested remains. He scanned around, searching for any kind of landmark. Not finding one, he closed his eyes and listened. Wind-rustled leaves. Insect and bird song. The swish of a turtle diving into water. No cars. No sound of civilization all. With nothing to go on, Malcolm opened his eyes and headed north.

Mosquitoes swarmed around him, biting and feasting on his exposed flesh. Mud and grit squished up between his toes. Malcolm climbed fallen trees, hidden twigs poked his bare feet, and green briar tore at his legs. After a few hundred feet, he stopped and listened. Hearing nothing, he continued on.

Five minutes later, he listened again. Nothing.

A clump of scarlet caught his eye, stark against the greens and browns. He headed for it, crawling through a tangle of briars until he came to a small clearing of high grass less than thirty feet across. Malcolm picked up a bundle of cloth hanging from the nook of a low branch. It was a shirt, half-rotted and caked in dark silt. It crinkled like an over-starched shirt as he opened it and shook out a family of tiny insects residing in the folds. "Belle Chasse High School Basketball," it read in white letters. He had clothes, sort of.

Holding it, Malcolm noticed an empty green beer bottle lying a few feet away. The sudden image of him breaking the bottle and slashing his wrists with the glass flashed though his mind. It'd be easy to do. The pain of his failure would end. The demon would lose its anchor to this world.

He shook it away. *No.*

If school kids can find their way here, I'm close. Malcolm tore the shirt in two and wrapped the filthy rags around his feet. With his homemade shoes, he searched the clearing, finding a blackened fire pit and several bits of trash. A rough trail led away into the woods.

Malcolm followed the narrow path. Sweat wetted his hair and ran in rivulets down his back. The old pain in his left knee, a leftover from when he'd slipped between the bars of a cattle grate one night when he was seventeen, was gone. He'd lived with it so long that it was just part of him. He only remembered it on days when it was acting particularly pissy. But now that it was gone, he noticed it. Not just his knee, but other familiar aches were noticeably absent. His constantly knotted back, the big knuckle of his right middle finger, his cracked ribs and broken nose, all gone. His eyesight was better too. Colors were sharper and everything perfectly focused. His sense of smell, previously boosted by Hounacier's gift, hadn't diminished since … since the betrayal. Malcolm wondered if his long-missing appendix was regrown. Sick and terminal people, completely and hopelessly incurable, often sought possession. Malcolm now understood the appeal that drew so many to seek new masters once their old owners were dead.

The trees ahead ended. Beyond them, an unpainted, wooden fence ran to either side, standing just over six feet high. He slowed as he neared the tree line. Black-shingled rooftops stood visible beyond the wall. Many of the cheap panels sagged while others, obviously newer and better made, extended the lengths of individual properties. Malcolm scanned the cleared fifteen-foot strip alongside the wall. Not seeing anyone, he crept across.

Staying low, Malcolm peered through a gap between two of the graying boards. A white mutt laying on the back porch of the house lifted its head. It hopped to its feet, hackles raised, then erupted in furious barking.

Shit!

The dog charged, and Malcolm hurried down the fencerow, the barks raging behind him.

Three houses down, he noticed the black metal lever of a gate door protruding from the fence. A foot-worn trail extended from the entrance. The dog's barking continued in the background. Malcolm only hoped the racket was a common occurrence every time the dog saw a squirrel or any other animal. Still, it posed a threat. Creeping naked behind houses with torn T-shirt booties would be hard to explain.

He peered through the fence gaps, seeing a small yard about two weeks past the need to mow and strewn with mismatched lawn furniture. A rusted swing set with no swings stood near one side. The house itself had several rear-facing windows, most without blinds. It looked dark. No lights. No TV playing. The beige AC unit on one side was silent.

"Buddy!" a man yelled, causing Malcolm to jump. "Shut up!" The dog went silent.

Ready to run, Malcolm watched for any sign the owner might investigate. After a minute of silence, he returned his attention to the house. Sweat ran down his back, warmed in the morning sun, as he waited. After what he guessed was half an hour of being eaten by mosquitoes and not seeing anyone inside, he slowly opened the latch.

The gate hinges squeaked louder than he'd expected. Careful not to open it more than necessary, Malcolm squeezed through the tight opening and hurried up to the house, weeds crunching beneath his wrapped feet. He crouched beside a window, counted to ten, then peeked inside. Empty living room. A haphazard mound of mail cluttered the coffee table before an inactive television. The fan was still. Staying aware of the neighboring houses that might have a view, Malcolm stepped to the next window. Kitchen. Dirty dishes filled the sink below. Still no sign of occupants. Malcolm moved to the back door and checked the handle. Unlocked. Holding his breath, he inched it open. No dog barked. No alarm dinged.

Inside was cool. The sweet stink of floral plug-in air fresheners filled the kitchen. Beneath that, a faint, rotted odor emanated from the blue trashcan along one wall. He licked his dry lips, seeing the faucet, but didn't dare turn it on. Not until he knew he was alone.

Room by room, Malcolm checked the house. The parents' bedroom was mostly clean, the queen-sized bed slept in but empty. Their son, Jamie, according to the shelf of baseball trophies, wasn't home either. His bedroom smelled like a locker room, dirty socks and teenage pheromones. Malcolm peeked out of a front window. A white Ford Taurus, at least twelve years old, sat in the drive.

Satisfied he was alone, Malcolm washed the grime and sweat-melted blood from his hands and face then drank straight from a bathroom faucet. There was a dirt-taste to the water, but he didn't care. After, he checked the mirror. The black eyes and broken nose were fully healed. Even the old scar on his chin had faded, visible only because he knew what to look for. He scratched the black, two-day beard, but using someone else's razor seemed wrong somehow, as if breaking into these people's house wasn't as bad as using their toothbrush and razor. The memory of the liquid remains came to mind, and Malcolm quickly got over the etiquette of not using their toothbrush.

Raiding the closets, Malcolm found a pair of rust-colored shorts, a gray T-shirt, a pair of hunting boots, and socks. The boots were a little large, so he shoved some wadded paper towels into the toes. Inside the mom's jewelry box, he found $40 and a sterling ring. It was thick with a cross-shaped cutout as the face. Malcolm slipped it onto his right ring finger. If the demon tried to take him, it'd break if not cut off the expanding digit. *Enjoy it, motherfucker.*

Inside a nightstand, Malcolm discovered a well-used 1911 and two magazines of hollow points. He took them.

A narrow rack of keys hung in a hall closet. He found one labeled "Ford" then took an olive cloth and net fedora hunting hat and pulled it on. After checking though the window one last time, Malcolm stepped out, carrying a water bottle raided from the fridge. Keeping his head low, he unlocked the car. A blast of trapped summer heat hit him in the face. Without hesitating, Malcolm slid into the hot seat and stuck the key in the ignition. *Please work.*

It clicked and tried to catch. Fear knotted in his chest. Malcolm tried again, and the car sputtered to a start. He backed out onto the residential street and drove away before anyone could notice. The small subdivision consisted of thirty old houses set on a U-shaped street that emptied onto a two-lane highway. With no sign and not knowing where to go, he chose left.

Fortunately, the gas tank was half-full. Gas stations had cameras, and filling a stolen car wasn't something he wanted to do. Unfortunately, the car's air conditioner didn't work. The spongy clutch forced him to mash the pedal against the floor for every gear change. It reminded him of his first car. It was a piece of shit too. Though his didn't stink of French fries and cheap, pine tree air freshener made worse by the heat. Malcolm opened the window, solving both those problems.

Two miles later, Malcolm spied a familiar trailer park. His heart pounded with excitement as he turned down the little road alongside it. Anticipation quickly gave way to nervous dread. He'd killed the night before. How many? All of them? Atabei? And if he'd killed her, what became of Hounacier? How many were still there?

He rolled past the entrance drive.

The gate was closed.

Malcolm continued two hundred more feet until he found a dry strip large enough to park the car. The familiar tingles of adrenaline dancing along his shoulders were different, coupled with an inert weight in his stomach. The last time he'd felt that was when he'd driven to the Valducans' chateau from Limoges, two hunters dead, another critical, two weapons lost, and the fear that what he'd find at the end would be so much worse. He drew a breath, checked that the pistol was loaded, and stepped out.

Gun in hand, Malcolm cut through the woods. Soft earth squished beneath his large boots. Once he'd broken though the shrub line along the road, the bayou opened up. He climbed through a rusted, barbed wire fence strung between tree trunks and rotting posts. Ahead, through the trunks and tangled branches, he spied the colored shipping containers.

Keeping low, Malcolm snuck closer, moving from tree to tree. Cicadas droned around him, their constant buzz rolling higher and lower like surf. He stopped behind a gray oak and peered across the grounds. No movement. No cars. Indigo dragonflies lazily hovered above the grassy field. *Where the hell are they?* Obviously, someone had survived.

Malcolm skirted behind the tree line, scanning for signs of life. As he passed a clump of narrow trees, he jumped, coming face to face with a lean figure. Enormous, red, white-pupiled eyes glared out from a smooth face. Its lips were curled into an exaggerated frown. Bleached white bones ran down the straw-bundled arms and legs, bound with brightly colored string. Animal rib bones encased its grass torso.

Shaking his head, Malcolm let out a breath and bypassed the warding totem. Whatever power the figure had, it was useless on him. Had he not already known where the ceremony ring was, it might have worked in misdirecting him.

He continued on. Keisha's garden was as he'd last seen it. Chickens still sauntered around their caged coop. But there was no sign of Atabei or her followers. Once he'd circled past another of the creepy totems and almost to the next, Malcolm emerged from the woods. He crossed the open span to the nearest container and listened. Hearing nothing, he peeked around to the inside of the ring.

The circle was empty, the post and metal stakes exactly as he'd last seen them. Unlit torches ringed the area. Errol's body was gone. Arcs of brown, dried blood splattered one wall of a powder blue container. Malcolm stepped out, searching the murder scene, the scene that he had perpetrated, but was unable to recall. Insects swarmed atop a red pool near the ring's edge, the blood so thick that it hadn't fully dried. He saw the stains where Errol and Shane had lain and the smeared trails from when they'd been moved, ending at tire tracks. Dread mounting, Malcolm crossed the smudged white ring and stopped above a small spackling of dried blood. The long drag marks from when he'd crawled to that very spot and attempted to kill himself on Hounacier's blade were still there, partially hidden beneath newer footprints. One was an enormous paw, big as his hand.

What did I do?

The closest bloodstain that wasn't Errol's was just outside the ring. Malcolm approached it, noticing a glint on the ground. He picked up a nickel-sized chip of smooth, black glass, one side tapering to a keen edge. The ghoul mask. Peewee had dropped it. The drying splatters told what had come to poor Peewee. Injured, Hounacier inside it, the werewolf would have gone for the closest target. Atabei had been nearing the other mask at the time of the transformation. Peewee was unprotected. Others would have tried to save him. Maybe shot it. Issach would have moved forward, his own mask pushing the rampaging demon off the man. So the werewolf would have gone for the next target. Malcolm moved his gaze up to the blood-sprayed wall. Leigh Ann had been hiding there.

Malcolm approached the gruesome site, remembering the hair he'd thrown up. More blood stained the area, pooled and splattered. Bullet holes peppered the box's side. They'd kept firing while it attacked her. Judging by some of the splatter-lined holes, a few of them had hit. But where did it go after?

Malcolm looked left and right, seeing no other holes. He raised his eyes. More shots traced upward. Deep claw marks marred the roof lip where the beast had scrambled over. A wooden ladder on the far side of the container led to the top. Malcolm holstered the pistol and followed it up. He spotted the trail of sun-cooked drops along the roof running fifteen feet before going over the far side. From his vantage, Malcolm could see out over most of the clearing. With Atabei and her followers still possessing one mask, Hounacier, and silver bullets, the werewolf would have run. Malcolm scanned the grounds, not seeing any other blood pools. It had either dragged someone with it or found a new victim somewhere else in order to heal. Its spree had ended beneath that tree where Malcolm had woken, but what happened between the ring and the tree was still a mystery. How many more innocents had died from Malcolm's failure?

He shook his head. It was time to tell the Order. Jim needed to know. With one ghoul mask gone, the one in the shop was even more precious. Atabei had killed for Hounacier; killing for the mask wasn't a difficult leap especially now that the demon and the man who it possessed would be coming after her. Jim was in danger. Tasha was in danger. Malcolm needed to warn them. He needed to be stopped before he killed again.

Malcolm climbed back down and headed toward the car. The site was compromised. No telling what Atabei had done with the bodies, but she wouldn't be stupid enough to bury them here.

He'd just passed the container ring when he heard rapid scratching on metal followed by an animal's whine.

Remembering Atabei's Rottweilers, Malcolm drew the pistol and spun. The ring was empty.

It came again, something scraping one of the boxes.

Just keep walking, Malcolm thought. Still, he moved toward it, gun ready.

He rounded a container, its once-yellow paint rust-stained to a dull, splotchy orange. Someone had removed the doors, replacing them with a welded rebar cage. A scrawny gray wolf paced back and forth before the metal gate. A cut length of water hose ran through the bars to a large and empty bowl. A blue, plastic funnel capped the other end, held up with zip-ties. The box stank like a kennel, and Malcolm stifled a sneeze.

The animal stopped its pacing and looked at him with amber eyes. Tongue lolling, it rolled onto its back, exposing its belly.

Unsure what to do, Malcolm just stood there, nose itching,

watching the animal roll side to side in total submission. Atabei had said she'd gotten a wolf before Malcolm had requested a mask instead. They'd left it here, cooking in a metal box. "You thirsty?"

The animal stopped rolling and just stared at him.

One of the other containers held water. He'd seen them using it the night before, but what good would it do? Atabei's people might not be back for days, maybe weeks. He considered the gun in his hand but quickly pushed that thought away. There wasn't any food he could see inside, and opening the gate on a hungry, wild animal probably wouldn't end well for either of them.

The wolf rolled onto its stomach. It extended its front paws and pressed its chin to the floor.

"You like chicken?" he asked, remembering the coop.

The animal whimpered.

He could fill the bowl then push one of the birds though the bars. While it was distracted, Malcolm could just open the latch and walk away. Then what? Let a wolf, an animal completely foreign to this area, just roam free? "This is a waste of time." He turned to walk away but stopped. This thing was a victim too. Atabei's victim. *Screw it.*

Hand tight on the pistol, Malcolm reached up, twisted, and flipped the latch.

The wolf sat up onto its haunches.

"You be good. Stick to the bayou, and no one will bother you."

The animal cocked its head.

Leaving the door shut, Malcolm backed away. "You just stay in there until I'm gone, buddy."

The wolf didn't move.

Malcolm rounded the corner and sneezed. He heard the metal gate creak open, and he sneezed again then again. Paranoia of a hungry wolf on the loose rising, he wiped his eyes and hurried back to the car, glancing over his shoulder the entire way. Jesus, that was stupid.

Something fell from his pocket when Malcolm fished out the car keys. Puzzled, he looked down, seeing the silver ring in the weeds. When had he taken it off? An icy chill ran up his spine. Could it have...?

No. It must have slipped off when I put the key in there. Malcolm picked it up and shoved the ring on his middle finger, forcing it over the knuckle. No way would it fall off now.

The Taurus took two minutes to start. It just had to get him to the city. He managed the car around on the narrow road and headed back.

Atabei's declaration came to mind as he drove. She'd called him a murderer. Said he'd killed her husband. Herm ... Hercule. That was it. He didn't remember any Hercule. Then again, he rarely knew the names of those he had killed. No ... set free. He'd never murdered. Not until ... not until last night. But Atabei had told him a demon killed her husband. So how...?

No. Because of a demon. She never said the demon killed him. He died *because* of it. After that, she'd learned how to transfer their essence, move them to an animal or other vessel. The demon hadn't killed him. It had possessed him.

He remembered her words. There were many funerals before Ulises came. Then only one. The last.

They'd killed her husband with Hounacier's blade. She'd spent years plotting revenge. Now, Ulises was dead, killed with a machete. Malcolm was damned, and Hounacier was hers. She'd coaxed their trust with masks and promises of power, and he'd fallen straight for it.

The Order needed to know. By his own code, he should die. The monster inside him had to be stopped. Atabei had to be stopped.

The car coughed and slowed. Malcolm pressed the gas. The needle revved, but the Taurus only slowed. *Fuck!*

He steered the coasting vehicle to the shoulder of the road. *Please, God, not now.* Malcolm turned the car off. After a minute of cursing, he managed to get it restarted, but the car wouldn't go into gear. Malcolm rubbed his forehead. He was still a couple miles outside the city limits, maybe a dozen from Alpuente's. Pushing the frustration aside, he turned off the car, pulled on his ugly hat, and got out. It was only time before the demon took him again, and it was only time before a cop stopped to find him in a stolen piece of shit car and packing a stolen gun. He needed to get moving.

He walked, the sun beating down on him. There were no trees along the road and nothing to shade him. The oversized shoes rubbed with every step. The thought of popping out his thumb to ask for a lift came to mind, and if he wasn't a living time-bomb waiting to kill and eat, he would have. But being alone in a car with some Good Samaritan wasn't something he could do. Demons loved hitchhiking about as much as they loved picking up hitchhikers. No, he couldn't risk that. The urge only mounted as the blisters formed along his heels.

He passed a bank of graffiti-caked pay phones outside a gas station and considered calling Tasha or Jim for a lift. But being alone with them was just as bad as hitchhiking. He needed to get to the shop. The mask would protect them from him. After his warnings to Jim, Malcolm knew the priest wouldn't just bring it to him, not after Malcolm hadn't come home the night before. He'd told him to lock it up and not move it for anyone or anything. The big priest wouldn't unless he was one-hundred-percent sure it wasn't some trick of Atabei's.

Pinkish hues tinged the sky by the time he made it to a bus stop. Malcolm took the bench and waited. A busload of people would be safer than one-on-one in a car. Demons weren't that reckless. Ten minutes later, a flat-faced bus rolled up, and Malcolm got on. His sweat-slick skin goosebumped at the rush of air conditioning. A woman near the back fanned herself, evidently not appreciating the cool air as much as he did. The bus stank of body odor, and Malcolm wondered how bad he must smell. He slid into a narrow seat and blew out a relieved sigh as the bus began to move.

Malcolm watched the streets roll past, and new dread began to form. Atabei knew he was staying at Jim's. What if she had spies watching for him to return there? How many eyes did she have? He needed to be careful. Maybe approach slow, mingling with a crowd of tourists.

A sudden realization broke his thoughts. Malcolm looked down to see that he'd been fiddling with the silver ring and had pulled it off. Swallowing, he shoved it back onto his finger and closed his fist. He needed to get to Jim's fast.

The sun had set when the bus let him off three blocks from the shop. His fist clenched, Malcolm followed the streets, searching for any overly interested faces in the crowd. The nervous weight in his stomach continued to swell. Cold sweat broke out along the back of his neck. He hurried across the street, the fully formed blisters stinging with each step.

Two more blocks.

His face grew hot, and the sudden feeling like he might throw up came down on him like a wave. A quartet of tourist women clutching neon-green, plastic glasses laughed at the mouth of an alley, all peering at a phone screen.

"Excuse me. Excuse me," he panted, pushing past them. The heavy weight in his stomach roiled and shifted. He continued down the narrow alley, not much wider than his shoulders.

Wait, he thought. He hadn't chosen to come down here. He'd just done it. Malcolm watched himself turn into a small alcove mulched with cigarette butts and torn wrappers. The sick feeling receded, and Malcolm, not controlling his own body, lifted his clenched hand. A scream erupted deep inside him, unable to escape his unresponsive lips.

The silver ring was gone.

Malcolm felt himself smile as the walls of his mental self tore away like tissue, revealing a wide, open sea of memories far larger than anything he could grasp. His consciousness plunged beneath the sticky waves of other thoughts and emotions. They pulled him deep into hopeless darkness as Malcolm continued his inward scream.

"Not yet," a smooth, somehow familiar voice whispered through his mind. *"You're mine."*

II

The stink of fish and assorted feces permeating the village curls Gulmet's nose. He wishes to leave it as soon as possible and return to Rajik, but first, he must interact with these disgusting humans. The supply of goats lasted far shorter than they'd anticipated. Rajik's hunger is insatiable. Gulmet had found a pair or travelers on the road and brought them home. They lasted two days. But there is too much risk in hunting humans while Rajik is unable to transform. If anyone were to go looking for a missing family, they might come by the cottage and find her.

So for the next three months, he shall play Iosif, the human that Gulmet wears. Husband, father, unable to hold his alcohol, and deathly afraid of serpents. He will purchase provisions and act as a human until the birthing. While Rajik craves only meat in her wolven form, Gulmet plans to find some breads and fruit for himself. The diversity in palate is one of the few advantages in wearing a human. Leading his mule and two-wheeled cart, he follows the steep road down to a pen of snorting pigs.

"Iosif," says a mustached man beside the pen. His face is pitted with scars. "I haven't seen you in weeks. How have you been?"

"Hello, Pavlos," Gulmet says, recalling his host's memories. "I am well."

"And your family?"

"Very well. Melina is growing fast." Gulmet smiles. "She

takes after her mother. Stubborn."

Pavlos grins, revealing a chipped front tooth. "That's all women, my friend."

Gulmet laughs. The men chat of the weather and gossip. Pavlos' eldest will marry in three weeks' time.

"I'll see you at the wedding," Pavlos says as Gulmet loads a pair of sows into his cart.

"Of course." Gulmet must maintain appearances. He'll find an excuse for Efimia and Melina's absence. Sickness? Death? No, death brings mourners and well-wishers. Efimia's sister lives in Patras. He'll tell them she has grown ill and his wife and daughter went to be with her. The lie decided, Gulmet wishes Pavlos farewell and leaves the stinking village behind. Once the cubs are born, they will raze it and its filthy inhabitants.

CHAPTER 14

Malcolm woke, his cheek resting against cool, red bricks. Scrunching his eyes, he tried to grasp the tattered remnants of the dream he'd had, buying pigs from an ugly man with an enormous moustache. It was important somehow. But then it was gone.

Black iron legs of patio furniture stood just a few feet before him. Shards of broken glass lay scattered about, edges glinting in the sunlight. Cars rumbled nearby. Birds twittered somewhere behind him, and in the distance, bells tolled. A faint breeze slid across his naked skin, stirring a wind chime.

Where the hell am I? He sat up, and his cheek peeled off the worn paving. His stomach lurched at the movement, so full it hurt. Malcolm saw the partial face-print of drying blood on the brick, and the icy horror took hold. Feeling it come, Malcolm rolled onto his knees as his stomach heaved. Blood, strings of chewed flesh, and grayish chunks sprayed out across the paving.

Panting, Malcolm wiped his mouth and looked around. He was inside a small courtyard with potted flowers and moss-coated walls. A balconied, two-story house loomed above him, making up one and a half sides to the yard. Its large glass doors stood a few feet behind him, cream-colored curtains blocking the view inside. Above a stone wall, crowned with broken, upthrust colored glass, stood a neighboring house. A gunmetal gray BMW sat on the far side, beneath a copper-roofed carport, and facing a green sliding car door. He was in the French Quarter, but where?

There were no exits but the curtained doors and carport. The glass-topped walls posed no difficulty for a werewolf, but for him, naked, was a different matter. *Now you're just fucking with me, asshole.* But the tall, defensive glass appeared too complete to account for all the shards scattered about. None of that was colored or from curved bottles. He looked up. Mint-green curtains hung out from a broken, second-floor window, framed in jagged glass. The demon had been inside that house.

Malcolm stood, careful not to step in the bloody mess now running in little streams between the paving bricks. Inside was dark. Only a faint square of light from a distant window was visible through the curtains, their folds patterned in a colorless floral design. He checked the knob. Locked.

Shielding the sides of his eyes, he pressed his face against the glass, seeing no more than the shapes of furniture. Malcolm glanced up at the neighboring house that overlooked the small yard. He didn't see anyone. He hurried over to a window. It was also locked. *You're really just fucking with me.* He wondered how the werewolf had removed the ring without his knowledge. Why hadn't he noticed? He remembered the voice right before he lost consciousness.

"Not yet. You're mine," it had said.

A shiver ran though him. They'd always assumed demons couldn't control hosts until they manifested. Until then, they could only watch through their eyes. He remembered Shane on the drive. The demon talked through him. They'd been terribly wrong. Was it in control now?

No. It was dark. The sun had gone down when it took me. It was night when it spoke though Shane. Malcolm checked the sky. Still morning. They sun hadn't yet crested the top of the courtyard wall. If he moved, he could get to Alpuente's before they opened.

Brown spots speckled the curtains. Malcolm peered through a slender gap between them and saw a crumpled form lying face-down on a blood-smeared kitchen floor. Oh God.

He'd seen werewolf victims before, their throats torn and

bodies ripped open, allowing access to the tender insides. But ... but he had done this. He had killed them.

It, he corrected. *It killed them.*

The thought didn't help. How many more victims were inside? Was anyone alive? How many more would die by him before he grew the balls to do what he had to do? He had to die.

No. First, I have to tell the Order.

Anger mounting, Malcolm headed back to the curtained French doors. He picked up a small clay bunny standing in a planter, its huge, upturned eyes shyly hopeful. With a hard throw, he smashed the figure through the plate window. It caught in the cream curtain and slid to the floor with a heavy thud.

Careful not to step on broken glass, Malcolm pushed the curtain aside and stepped through. The sharp, unmistakable stink of entrails hit him, almost pushing Malcolm back. Arcs of drying blood splattered the wall and a blue ultrasuede chair. Beside it, the shredded corpse of a man, his featured lost to claw marks and hidden beneath red-caked hair, lay on the ground. Loops of mangled intestine spilled across the floor in dark puddles. Malcolm could see up into the man's chest cavity. Werewolves almost always ate the heart.

Bloody footprints, paw-like but too long for any natural animal, stained the rug and shiny, pale tiles. Malcolm's eyes followed their path from the chair to the adjoining kitchen. It had leaped onto the back of a sofa, its claws tearing the fabric. One set of tracks led to the back door, their short stride and full print suggesting a simple walk. He turned, seeing bloody prints on the lock.

The werewolf had locked the door then escaped out the upper floor into the courtyard intentionally, leaving him to scale glass naked or to find this house of horrors. It was fucking with him.

Stomach churning at the scene laid out just for him, Malcolm walked into the kitchen. A woman, her right arm torn free, lay sprawled on the glossy tile; her blood had run down the grout, forming a gridwork away from the carnage. A steel butcher's knife lay among the gore and scattered shards of a broken plate.

The woman's gnawed and fleshless arm lay discarded in the adjoining hall, the carpet matted in wet blood. He pictured the monster sitting there on its haunches chewing the limb like a dog with scraps. Malcolm's stomach lurched, and he dashed to the sink, nearly slipping in the sticky blood, and vomited what little remained in his stomach.

He wiped his mouth and turned on the faucet, gargling and rinsing it out before drinking. Pink chunks swirled in the bottom of the stainless sink. Malcolm slapped a wall switch before him, and the disposal chewed and ground the bits away.

Eyes teary with sick and hatred, he turned his head, seeing the faces of the family he'd eaten smiling out from a digital picture frame. A young couple, standing against a metal rail, the sun setting behind them on an ocean horizon. The picture changed. Now, they were posing with another couple around a table, late thirties it appeared, the men's features so similar it suggested relation. It changed again. A young boy grinning up from a pile of torn wrapping paper, a shiny cardboard box clutched to his chest.

A cold dread seeped into his empty stomach, filling it like lead. The picture dissolved into a photograph of an older couple dressed in Sunday best. Malcolm turned to the refrigerator near him, its black surface buried beneath crayon drawings on colored paper.

Not another child.

The digital picture slid aside to show a new photograph of the now dead mother and father posing with a sandy-haired boy, maybe five, and fat-cheeked baby in the mother's arms.

Malcolm gripped the counter behind him, his knees nearly buckling under the weight inside him. He clenched his eyes. The picture's image still burned in his mind. Their smiles, their joy, gone.

He drew a breath, counted to five, then released it. He needed to know. Malcolm followed the paw prints out into the hall, past the stripped arm, and up the stairs to the second floor. "Brian," read a plastic street sign on one of the doors. Clothes and brightly colored toys littered the floor. Malcolm winced as he stepped on a gray Lego.

The nursery was empty as well.

Maybe they weren't here. Maybe they were off at grandma and grandpa's, he hoped, remembering the old couple in the photograph.

His tenuous hopes died as he entered the parents' room. The cracked closet door hung open, clothes and plastic hangers strewn about, soaking the blood from the red-stained carpet. They were inside. Most of them. The boy, Brian, wore shredded cartoon-print pajamas, his body nearly torn in half, mouth open, his face somehow almost completely clean save a pair of thick, dried drops beneath his left eye. The infant, whom he had hidden in the closet with as a monster ate their parents, was only pieces. A tiny, pale leg, broken off at the thigh, was the only part not gnawed and shredded.

Malcolm's head swam. Staggering, he caught himself against the bed and closed his eyes. He was a monster. He needed to be stopped. The fallen butcher's knife in the kitchen came to mind. One quick motion, and he could finish what the terrified mother had tried.

But the demon wouldn't die. Only Malcolm and the knowledge of what had happened to Hounacier. Malcolm wiped his mouth and nodded. He knew what he had to do.

Careful not to be seen, he peeked out the window. He scanned the street, noticing a familiar white building on the corner. Ursulines. He was on Ursulines. Jim's shop was a dozen blocks from here. Malcolm glanced at the bedside clock. 7:21. Alpuente's opened at 8:00. He could make it before they did.

Avoiding the closet, Malcolm found a pair of jeans and a T-shirt in the laundry. He'd never worn Armani before. He knew they were the last pair of pants he'd ever wear, the jeans of a dead man. Unable to pull on the husband's tiny shoes, Malcolm settled on a pair of rubber flip-flops tucked under the bed. Scouring drawers and the wife's jewelry box yielded a slender silver ring set with a purple stone and a silver cross fashioned like a trio of fused nails.

In the office, Malcolm tore a thick page from a notepad and wrote,

Jim,

*I am possessed with a werewolf. I have killed and will kill again
unless you do exactly what I say.*

Malcolm quickly jotted his instructions, including how to
contact the Order. That complete, he folded the paper once and
secured it to his shirt with a safety pin.

He eyed the now discarded pen. His fingerprints were on
it. His prints were all over the house now. Not that it mattered.
He'd be dead long before the police could catch him. No telling
how many cops Atabei owned. Once word about the killings
got out, she'd know it was him. She could tell them what to look
for. She could point them to Alpuente's.

Standard procedure was to burn a kill site. Destroy any
evidence and save the family the terrible truth as to how their
loved ones had died. But the French Quarter was too populated.
Too much risk of other houses catching and even more innocent
deaths.

Malcolm wiped the pen with his shirt as well as the office
door handle. He swabbed other obvious spots he'd touched
as he made his way downstairs, and then wiped his bloody
footprints off the kitchen floor. DNA tests would take too long
to identify anything, if there was anything recoverable from the
putrid mess he'd vomited outside. He'd just let the police draw
their own conclusions from the paw prints.

Malcolm slipped on a baseball cap and a pair of sunglasses
he'd found. He checked the clock. 7:42. *Only one thing left.*

The dainty ring could only fit onto his left little finger.
Malcolm slipped it on then wrenched the joint back. It popped.
Clenching his teeth, Malcolm held back a scream. Cheeks
puffing with each breath, Malcolm clutched the spiked cross
in his other hand. He closed his fist, pressing the point against
his flesh and wrapped the black, cotton necklace around it.
Not allowing time to think about it, he slammed his hand
into his thigh, driving the nail into his palm. Malcolm yanked
the necklace end with his teeth, clenching his fist closed. The
werewolf couldn't fully form if silver penetrated him. Now, he
just needed to get to Jim's.

Dizzy with pain, he opened the door and left, keeping his
head low. The morning streets were mostly clear, and Malcolm

hurried down the road. *Eighteen minutes.* Rounding the corner, he broke into a jog, the molded heel of the small flip-flops digging into his feet with each step.

Blood oozed between his clenched fingers. Pain shot through his hand with each movement, but Malcolm squeezed harder. He wove though tourists and pedestrians on their way to work. The left flip-flop came free as Malcolm hurried across a street. He was halfway to the shop now. He kicked the other sandal off and ran.

"Hey, Doc!" someone yelled.

Malcolm looked back to see Julian, the bald street hustler, hand raised in greeting. *Shit.* He kept running. *Four more blocks.* A sudden terror swirled in the back of his mind. Jim couldn't help him. Going back would only endanger them.

No. That was wrong. He had to get to Jim's.

The fear grew, his legs faltered, and he stumbled. The demon was fighting.

Fuck you. Malcolm pushed himself harder. He had to get to the shop. Concrete and ill-fitted paving stones tore at his soles. He turned a corner, nearly colliding with a woman. "Sorry." He ran past wrought-iron pillars and shop owners sweeping the night's partying from their curbs. *One more block.*

The silver ring bit into his swelling, broken finger. It throbbed with each pounding heartbeat. Malcolm reached the shop. Lights already burned in the cases behind the windows. He pulled the door with his unbroken fingers.

Locked.

Inside, Mister Alpuente shuffled behind the counter, setting out coin-laden trays.

Malcolm pounded on the door. Searing pain shot through his maimed finger with each impact. Scowling, the old man looked up then smiled. Malcolm shifted uncomfortably. His breath came in desperate gasps. The mask. Its gaze penetrated the glass, pressing his bones. Malcolm crouched below the window, shielding himself from its stare.

The door rattled and clicked. Another click, and it swung open, hitting Malcolm in the knee.

"Mal?" Alpuente asked. "What are you—wait!"

Malcolm scrambled through the open door, pushing past the old man's legs. The full force of the obsidian mask came down on him like a tidal wave, pushing every cell in his body away. He hissed, his teeth and eyes pressing against their sockets. He rolled into the corner beside the door, pinning himself.

"Mal?" Alpuente said reaching for him.

"Back!" Malcolm snarled, his voice strained and bestial. "The door! Lock the door!"

His ribs popped as if trying to crush inside him. Malcolm rolled and tightened into a ball. His flesh rippled in rolling waves, each crested with lengthening and shortening black hairs. The pressure mounted. His brain felt as it if might crush against the inside of his skull.

"Help me," he gasped. He tried to move his head, but instead, it whipped down in the gale, slamming against the floor. For an instant, the onslaught slowed. Then it mounted again with growing ferocity. It was if his very soul were a sail, threatening to rip and blow away. "Help me!"

Malcolm slammed his head into the floor again. His vision blurred, but the tormenting pain thinned. "Jim." He slammed it again. "Get him here now." Malcolm's balled knees creaked and popped as if the bones no longer knew how to fit. Malcolm slammed his head again, leaving blood. "Get Jim!"

He wasn't even sure if Alpuente was still there or had left. He just kept hitting his head, screaming Jim's name in those fleeting respites.

"Jim!"

Claws or hands grabbed at him. He swatted them back. "Jim!"

"Malcolm," a distant voice shouted, barely audible above the whooshing in his ears.

"Jim!"

Blood ran into Malcolm's cinched eyes. "Ji ..." Consciousness failed him before he could finish.

III

Insect song fills the warm night air. Moonlight shines through the trees, painting the ground in silver ribbons. Two more moons until the eclipse. Rajik's swelling has increased. The pups kick and stir within her, ever hungry. They have sapped her, draining her essence. Few of their kind survive birthing, and Gulmet wishes he could take her burden even if for a few short days. But Rajik is strong. She will endure. He has no doubt. Motherhood will command her respect in the Legion, ascend her above her birth status. Siring the brood will elevate Gulmet as well, but motherhood is sacred. Until then, he must protect her. She hungers.

Keeping to the shadows, he moves toward a clearing. High grass ripples in the breeze like ocean waves. The musky scent of his prey grows stronger. He raises his head, eyes watching across the meadow.

There. A herd of deer grazes at the far side.

His mouth moistens. Lowering, Gulmet stalks toward them, slow as to not disturb his cover.

He circles around, hoping to herd them into the fields when they break. The wind stills, and he crouches, muscles taut. His unsuspecting prey continue to eat.

The breeze begins anew, granting cover in the undulating grass. Gulmet lifts his head. They are near. He could take one easily, but Rajik's hunger is too great. He must get closer.

Keeping low, he creeps, his chest nearly brushing the

ground. The air is thick with their scent. The grass thins, and Gulmet stops just behind the edge, his keen eyes watching.

A red doe turns from her grazing. Her brown eyes scan the darkness, passing over where Gulmet waits. She takes a step closer and freezes, nostrils flaring. Muscles tighten.

Gulmet bursts from his cover then springs. His jaws catch the doe's neck as she turns to run. Hot blood gushes into his mouth as he rips into her.

The other deer scatter. Three dive into the cover of trees. Two more bound across the field.

Gulmet releases the dying deer and charges out after them. A male breaks left, and Gulmet follows. The stag weaves predictably, hoping to evade him. Centuries of hunting have taught him their patterns. Gulmet closes the distance. He leaps, landing on the deer's back. His jaws find its neck, and vertebrae crunch with a pop of sweet blood.

He rises, seeing the last deer near the tree line. He can't catch it in time. Two are sufficient.

Gulmet picks up the felled deer, still trembling as it dies, and throws it over his shoulder. Licking the blood from his muzzle, he returns to the doe and heaves it up onto the other side and carries them back from where he's come. No longer caring for stealth, he strides up the rocky slope and between the trees. A rabbit dashes away from the shadows, but Gulmet controls the urge to give chase.

Up the hill and beyond the trees, he comes to the empty cart. The mule, like the fat sows, a casualty of Rajik's hunger. The animal was needless. Gulmet has more than enough strength to pull the cart. He drops the dead deer into the back. Bones pop, and fur shrivels, returning Gulmet to human form. Colors and scents fade as touch and taste heighten. The doe's blood appears purple in the moonlight. He licks the dribble from his arm, savoring it, savoring the fear it had felt as it died. Rajik has not eaten today. He must be quick.

Naked, he stoops to lift the cart handles.

A faint yelp comes on the wind.

Gulmet cocks his head. A cry?

He turns and peers the direction the noise had come. There.

Across a slope, a round head peers above an outcrop, its hair ruffling in the breeze. It is too far to make out the features, but it is human.

The head drops from sight. Could it have seen him at such a distance? He cannot risk it.

Gulmet leaps and runs down the slope, his body transforming as he bounds. He dashes between shrubs and sharp rocks. Pebbles roll and fall in miniature avalanches behind him. Reaching the bottom, he jumps a dried creek bed and bounds up the opposite rise. The slope is difficult. More pebbles loosen under his paws.

Gulmet's tongue lolls out as he nears the top. He bounds onto a boulder then jumps to where the human had been.

Gone.

He sniffs the grass, finding the scent. Male.

Gulmet circles, his nose to the grass until he locates the trail. He races along the ridge's spine until it dips toward a basin. He stops and scans the moonlit ground. Empty. The human couldn't have gone far. He runs down, following a runoff trail. It ends at flat, gray rock.

He sniffs again but can't find the scent. Anger mounting, he doubles back to the rise. He finds it again but can't tell where it leads. He circles, furiously searching, but the scent is lost. Anger welling, he snarls and howls in frustration, the sound echoing through the hills.

Someone has seen him. Gulmet only hopes they couldn't recognize his body.

CHAPTER 15

Malcolm awoke, his head pounding with each heartbeat. The light between his half-closed lids stabbed into his brain. He tried to bring his hands up to shield his eyes, but his wrists and waist tightened with a soft rattle. He looked down. A thick chain belted his waist, sealed with a padlock. It had about an eight-inch lead to a pair of antique handcuffs. He recognized them from the shop: 1920s, their patina of rust polished to a dull, brown shine. Strips of white tape held a fat gauze pad against his right palm. Plastic splints encased his left little finger.

Malcolm lay on a folded, multi-colored quilt against the back wall of Alpuente's storeroom. They'd cleared it out save a pair of chairs on one end, one supporting a white and blue baby monitor, and a copper chamber pot beside him. A pair of chains hung from the rings in the ceiling down to his neck. The weight of a metal collar pressed against his shoulders. Hunkering so he could reach, he felt along the rolled metal. Solid. Thick as ChapStick tube. He only hoped it was silver. His instructions to Jim had been very specific.

Groaning, he felt the bandages over his aching forehead. He winced as he touched the hard knot beneath them.

Should have seen the other guy. He tried to laugh at his own pitiful joke but couldn't force the humor.

The brilliance from the two bare ceiling bulbs burned like twin suns. Squinting, he looked around, hoping they'd left him a bottle of water or something for his dry throat. There wasn't one. He needed food. He hadn't eaten in … Images of the bloody vomit came to mind. He needed food. Real food.

"Hello?" His voice was much weaker then he'd expected. How long had he been here? Had Jim reached the Order? Malcolm wondered where Hounacier was. Had she bonded to Atabei? Atabei, who had murdered Ulises and made him a monster? Not likely. The Order was going to come down on her like the fucking reaper. She'd pay. He wondered how long Hounacier would go before she found a new groom. He imagined her beneath glass, paraded through the museum circuit on one of Master Turgen's "recruiting tours." She was alone. Malcolm had failed her.

The door thumped, followed by a scrape. It swung open, and Jim stepped inside. Something red sloshed inside a milky Tupperware bowl in his hands. A strong whiff of citrus perfume preceded Tasha behind him, the demon mask clutched backwards against her chest, arm positioned to flip it around.

"You're awake," Jim said. Fear tinged the corners of his eyes.

"Water?" Malcolm croaked.

Nodding, Jim set the bowl on one of the chair seats and left. A moment later, he returned, carrying a liter-sized water bottle and a push broom. "Here." He laid the bottle down and scooted it across the floor with the broom.

Malcolm took it. Gritty dust coated the cold condensation. Fighting the handcuffs, he unscrewed the lid and gulped the water down.

"Don't drink it too fast," Jim said.

Malcolm squeezed a final mouthful before coming up for air. Panting, he savored the coolness of his throat. A single drop ran down the corner of his mouth to his chin. "Thank you."

"You gave Dad a big scare."

"Sorry about that." He squinted up at the big priest. "I'm sorry." He met Tasha's eyes. Fear. Tears quivering at the corners. Malcolm looked away. He didn't want her to see him. "I'm so sorry."

"We got the blood up," Jim said. "Cut that ring off your finger. I'm pretty sure you got a concussion or something, banging your head like that. Thought about calling Maggie, but … decided against it."

Malcolm nodded, still not meeting their eyes. "Thanks."

"So you going to tell us what happened?" Jim asked.

"Atabei. We called the demon. She drew it out. Then she … she ambushed me. Took Hounacier. Put the demon inside me. I got away, but … I should have let her do it." His skull throbbed as Malcolm looked up. "She killed Ulises."

Jim's lips drew into a flat line. The muscles in Tasha's jaw flexed tight. Her tears still hadn't come, but she couldn't meet his eyes.

Jim drew a breath and removed the Tupperware's lid. "I talked to your friend Allan Havlock. Said you should eat this to help your wounds." He set it down and pushed it with the broom.

The smell of blood lit Malcolm's sinuses like a eucalyptus, opening wider to take more in. Soft cubes of raw meat filled the plastic bowl like hospital Jell-O. Malcolm's stomach lurched in disgust, but his mouth wetted. "Got a sandwich?"

"I'll bring you whatever you want. But your friend was real insistent you should eat that first."

The sweet, coppery scent grew stronger. Malcolm's gut rumbled, overpowering his revulsion. Almost without realizing it, he reached tentative fingers into the bowl. The meat squished at his touch, raw and room-temperature. Licking his lips, he slipped one cube into his mouth.

The sweet, salty flavor filled his mouth, seeming to course through his entire body as he slowly chewed. Tasha hissed a grimace, but Malcolm didn't care. He swallowed, savoring the sensation as it slid down his throat. The pain in his head and hands dulled. He took another and another, licking his lips to keep the bloody saliva from escaping.

He swallowed the last cube and sighed, feeling better than he'd have thought possible. Only a tingle remained of the pains. He eyed the blood at the bottom of the dish, fighting the urge to drink it like the sugar-sweetened milk left after a bowl of cereal.

"Feel better?" Jim asked.

"Yeah."

"I'll let him know it worked."

Malcolm nodded. After witnessing several possessed and what food they kept in their homes, Allan hypothesized that some demonbound might heal with raw meat. Now, with an actual live specimen, he'd tried it. Malcolm's last contribution to the Order was being a guinea pig. Sickening anger boiled in the back of mind. Who for? Allan for suggesting it? Jim? Himself for getting into this? All three? He tried to push the anger away but couldn't.

Malcolm picked up the half-empty water bottle. "About that sandwich?"

Jim nodded. "Of course."

"How long was I out?" Malcolm asked as the priest turned.

"All day," Jim said. "It's Thursday."

Tasha met his eyes for only moment before looking away. "Mal, I ... I'm sorry." Clutching the flipped mask to her chest, she backed through door. It creaked shut, followed by scraping and a thud.

Malcolm sat quiet, eyes unfocused on the plaster wall, its surface scuffed from decades of moving inventory. How long could they hold him? Until Matt got his ass up here from Chile? That smug bastard was probably itching to do it. He'd grown up on the road. Motel television had been his biggest education. The man had single-handedly ingested more TV than anyone Malcolm had ever met. Never gone to college. He had a high school equivalency and was now a Valducan Librarian. Shameful. Malcolm's lips curled. He should have killed that freak the moment they met.

Wait. What am I thinking? Matt was a little arrogant, but death? He'd proved himself time and time again. He was a brother. Where was this anger coming from? He thought of the hatred he'd felt about Allan's test, still boiling in his gut. It was wrong. He didn't feel that way.

A wave of guilt extinguished the rage. He should hate himself. Should have slashed his wrists in the woods. That family would still be alive if he'd just done it. He should have lifted his throat for Atabei to strike.

The guilty weight pressed harder, crushing down like a

giant hand. Malcolm slouched forward, felling the collar's pull. Maybe he could hang himself with it. He closed his eyes, imagining his blue-faced corpse suspended, toes brushing his soured piss on the floor.

Wait! He opened his eyes and sat up. Never once, not when his friends died, not when his own failures had cause death and pain, had he ever considered suicide. Master Turgen had once told him that no Valducan had ever done that. He'd said it was one of the traits weapons sought when choosing their owners. He wasn't wired that way. Why was he contemplating it constantly now?

A slender finger of terror slithered up his spine. The demon. "You're fucking with me, aren't you?"

The finger scratched in his brain, an impossible itch.

"Is that you?"

It scratched again.

A sickening terror welled in his skull, coursing down his veins. It was influencing his thoughts.

What actions had been his? He remembered the ease with which he'd found his way back to the ceremony site. Did he come here, or had *it*? How much danger had he put Tasha's family in?

A sudden thump startled him.

The door cracked open.

"You need something?" Tasha asked.

"No." Nervous sweat beaded his forehead.

Her golden-brown eyes searched his face. "We heard you talking."

Malcolm glanced to the baby monitor. "Just talking to myself."

She nodded but didn't seem to buy it. "Okay." She opened the door the rest of the way.

"Don't come in here," Malcolm blurted.

Tasha's brow arched quizzically. "You still want that sandwich?"

Malcolm noticed the obsidian mask clutched under her arm. Jim stood behind her, a paper plate and a pair of water bottles in his hands. "Oh. Yes, please."

She scanned the room as if expecting to see something then came in, the mask against her breasts.

Jim followed and set the plate down. A second plate rested upside down atop it as a makeshift lid. He picked up the broom. "Brought you some more water." He hooked the broom around the Tupperware dish and pulled it back.

Hungrily, Malcolm watched the scarlet contents sloshing with the movement. His fists clenched, wanting to beat the son of bitch for taking it from him.

Stop! He relaxed his fist. *That's not you.* "I appreciate that."

Jim only grunted and pushed the plates toward him. The smell of pickles and wheat suddenly overpowered Tasha's perfume.

Malcolm lifted the top plate. Lettuce skirted the edges of a thick ham and cheese sandwich. A pair of green pickle spears rested to one side, their juice soaking into the paper. Nothing about it appealed to him, but somewhere, as if a thousand miles away, he felt the hunger.

The two bottles came next.

"This collar," Malcolm said, lifting the sandwich. "It's unbroken silver, right?"

Jim nodded. "Soldered it shut."

"Good." Malcolm took a mouthful. The sudden flavors of real food—bread, spicy mustard, smoked ham, and moist tomato—flooded his senses. He tasted each with acute clarity, savoring the individual parts and how they blended in his mouth. He'd never tasted anything as incredible. Still, it couldn't fill the hungry pit desiring raw meat.

The sudden image of Tasha screaming beneath him, his teeth diving for her throat. Blood and terror burst across his tongue as she futilely hit him, her closing death weakening her arms. Malcolm coughed, nearly choking on his second bite. She and Jim watched him, a moment's concern in their eyes.

Malcolm forced a swallow. The fantasy of her terror and blood still lingered. "Thank you."

"Call if you need anything," Jim said.

Malcolm only stared at the floor as he listened to them leave. The door closed, and he dropped the sandwich back onto the plate.

"Fuck you," he whispered to the demon.

The little finger itched into a smile.

Malcolm sat cross-legged on the crumpled quilt, his gaze moving across the back wall, counting the red bricks. He wasn't counting them himself; his eyes merely moved row after row, pausing at each one for only a moment before moving on. A window had been there once, the square shape of it left behind like a dinosaur's fossilized footprint, an outline of what had been. He'd tried meditating, but the little itch still whispered its dark thoughts. It wasn't his to control, and the emptying of his mind only gave it more room to sling its rage and self-hate, fantasies of murder and tasting his loved ones' terror.

Footsteps moved across the floor above. It had been his room. Malcolm wondered what Atabei had done with his phone. Was she now trying to unlock it, to see the message his camera frame was sending?

Malcolm didn't need the video feed to know who was now going through his things. The steps were too light to be Jim's, too purposeful to be Mister Alpuente's shuffle. He thought he could even catch the citrus scent of her perfume over his own sour stink. Surely, his olfactory senses weren't that acute. He had to be imagining it. The little itch returned, reminding him of the vision.

He tried to ignore it. *Go to Hell.*

The familiar scrape came from the door. Malcolm turned, expecting Jim with refreshment or some further experiment of Allan's.

The door inched open, and Mister Alpuente stepped inside, an open, over-under shotgun tucked in the crook of his arm.

Malcolm straightened, eyes on the gun.

The old man drew the shell from the upper barrel. The red and white stripe of the silver load Malcolm had given to Jim was unmistakable. Mister Alpuente pushed it back in and clicked the gun closed. Without taking his eyes off Malcolm, he reached back and closed the door behind him.

The old man's pale lips curled downward. The oxygen hose to his nose emphasized the deep frown lines. Slowly, he reached down and clicked off the baby monitor.

Malcolm sat still, meeting the old man's cold stare. After several quiet seconds, Mister Alpuente spoke. "Just heard that police found a family murdered. Husband, wife, two children: five and fifteen months."

Malcolm looked away.

"Think it was some kind of animal did that to them. Tore 'em to pieces."

Malcolm closed his eyes, trying to push out the shame. There was no use denying it.

"Ulises ever tell you how we met?"

Malcolm shook his head. "Always thought it was through Jim."

"No. Jim came along later. My ... wife, Rachel ... she died." Alpuente swallowed. "She was drivin' back from Atlanta. Antique auction. Police called, said they found her truck in Mississippi, antiques still in the back, but she was gone." The old man's slender fingers tightened on the shotgun. "Week later, they found her. Cut up. Police suspected some Manson copycat did it. Took her liver... Cut out her womb."

"She was pregnant," Malcolm said. Ulises had told him about hunting an aswang back in the 70s. He'd never mentioned Tasha's grandmother.

Alpuente nodded, anger burning in his gray eyes. "We'd just found out. Our daughter Jill had just started college. She came back home to be with me. I was lost. Couldn't get up in the morning. I couldn't do anything. Jill brought me to Maggie. Said she could help. Maggie introduced me to Ulises." He shook his head, a faint grin pulling at his lips. "He was all tattooed. Had this dumb-ass hair. Not the type of person I normally associated with, but he wanted to hear the story. So I told him."

There was no question where this was leading. The old man's twisting hands on the gun, the quickening breath as he spoke. Psyching himself up for what he intended to do. The footsteps continued moving above. If Malcolm called out for Tasha, the old man would kill him before she even reached the stairs.

Keep him talking. "What did he say?"

"He told me about demons. Sounded like bullshit to me."

Alpuente scowled and shook his head. "He was so sure. But I didn't believe him. Then police found a second body."

"Another woman?" Malcolm asked, risking his voice a little louder than normal.

Alpuente nodded. "Twenty years old. My daughter's age. After that, I told Ulises I'd help him any way I could."

Tasha's footsteps stopped. Maybe she heard them talking. *Why do I care? He's doing me a favor.* Malcolm had given his report. The Order knew what Atabei had done. This was the final piece. They both knew it.

The old man's jaw twitched. Resolve was cementing. *Not like this. This isn't his burden to carry.* "What did you do?"

"We drove out to Jackson County. Spent three weeks there narrowing it down. I started thinkin' I was going crazy, me and this voodoo priest and his magic machete. I didn't believe in a god back then, but I wanted to. Demon or not, I wanted to find the son of a bitch that took my wife from me."

"Did you?" Malcolm asked.

"Yeah. Tracked it down to an old fire tower. We saw it flyin' out after sunset, silhouetted against the sky. So we went up there and waited." His pink tongue ran across his upper lip. "It had these little poppets up in there, made of grass. Three of 'em. One was Rachel. Just before dawn, we heard it land on the railing outside. I've never been so scared. Ulises though, he did what he had to. He put his finger to his lips and waited beside the door."

Tasha's footsteps hurried from the room above.

Alpuente didn't seem to notice. "Before it even knew we were there, Ulises was on it, chopping that machete of his until it burned. He avenged my wife. I saw it." The old man raised the gun. "I saw the monster. I know what you are. I know what you did!"

Malcolm met the old man's gaze over the top of the twin barrels. "You don't have to do this."

"Yes I do!" The old man closed his eyes, the gun still trained on him. "I'm sorry, Mal."

Running footsteps clapped up the hall. Malcolm braced for the blast.

The storeroom door swung open.

Alpuente whirled as Jim stepped inside.

"Dad!"

"Close the door!" Alpuente yelled, bringing the gun back toward Malcolm.

Jim dove toward him, grabbing the barrel and pushing it away. "Dad, stop it!"

"No!" Alpuente yelled. "You don't know what he is. What he's done."

Malcolm sat motionless as Jim wrestled the shotgun from the old man's hands.

Tasha stepped in, eyes wide. She looked at Malcolm then at the old man clawing at Jim.

"He has to die!"

"Pawpaw, please!" Tasha wrapped her arms around the old man and pulled him away.

"No!" Alpuente shouted.

She hugged him tighter.

"You don't understand." Alpuente's voice cracked, and tears began to form. "You don't know what he is."

Jim looked at the shotgun in his hands. "Take him out of here."

"Come on, Pawpaw," Tasha said as she led the sobbing man out.

"He's a monster ... a monster!"

Malcolm looked at Jim, still staring at the gun. "Thank you."

The priest looked up at him like he was a stranger. Anger boiled in his eyes. The muscles in his jaw flexed. "I'll bring you some food in a bit." He turned and left.

Malcolm let out a long, slow breath as the door thudded closed. His heart pounded against his chest, urging him to move, get up, walk around, and burn off the tension. But the chains held him. The old man had nearly done it. Malcolm couldn't help but wonder if the relief he felt was his or the demon's.

Hours dragged by. Malcolm counted the bricks again. Slept. Twice, Jim had brought food and taken away his piss pot, never saying a word. Without windows or a clock, time became lost. He heard no voices in the shop. No sounds at all but the occasional footsteps outside the door or distant, unintelligible conversations. Malcolm guessed they'd closed the shop, maybe fearing he might yell for help. Smart.

Even the dark itching had abandoned him.

Malcolm lay on his side, eyes unfocused across the scarred, wooden floor. He knew this was the last floor he'd ever see. His mind replayed the long journey that had led to this. He remembered that first meeting with Ulises, how a golden opportunity for his dissertation had changed his life so suddenly. It was almost a trap. Mama Ritha had sent him there knowing perfectly well where it would lead: Faith, Horrors, Love, finally Death.

Everyone knew but him. All the followers at that first ceremony knew what Hounacier was. They knew he was Ulises' protégé. Papa Ghede had told him, but Malcolm hadn't believed in loa. Then the monster and the complete terror he'd felt. His faith was born in terror. How else could he have expected it to end?

He remembered how the loa had circled the dead demon, cradling it as it changed back to human. They'd wept and mourned the man who died so that it could be destroyed. He'd been given a hero's funeral. Malcolm remembered the woman at the ceremony, the way the possessed man had searched the audience for her when they'd brought him into the ring, the way she'd wailed at his death.

The woman!

Malcolm's eyes opened, but he watched the scene replaying across his mind. The slender woman in the crowd. Atabei Cross.

A crazed chuckle rose from Malcolm's throat. He remembered her now. The day he'd found love and faith, she'd found loss and hate. There was a perverse symmetry in how it now ended.

The door thumped and creaked open.

Still chuckling, Malcolm rolled, expecting Jim with food. He stopped as he saw the black leather boots, their toes scuffed to a bluish gray. Malcolm's gaze moved up to see a lean man with a sandy mop of hair. He held a plastic water bottle in one hand, its label torn away. A red bead pressed against the back inner wall, toward the mask in Tasha's arms behind him. The man's other hand held an enormous, black and gold revolver. Bronze wolf heads capped the ivory grip. A thick, Bowie-style blade extended below the barrel, its silver edge gleaming to a fine point. He trained the gun on Malcolm.

Malcolm met the newcomer's tight-jawed face. "Hi, Matt."

CHAPTER 16

The thin, sandy patches of Matt's week-old beard resembled a teenager's first attempt at facial hair. He swallowed, lips moving as if trying to find the words. Finally, "Hi, Mal," his voice devoid of emotion.

"Congratulations for you and Luiza. That's … that's really good news."

"Yeah, we're real excited." Matt's voice didn't contain that familiar Louisiana twang Malcolm had always heard before. Everyone described it differently. Luc said it was eastern French, Allan pegged it as Estuary, and Master Sonu said it was definitely from Mumbai. The familiar accent was always calming, but unsettling when he thought about it. But now … Now, it was gone. Was this his real voice? The idea that he could now hear Matt as he really was somehow creeped Malcolm out more than the chameleon accents ever did.

Malcolm maneuvered his cuffed hands, pushing himself into a sitting position. Chains tinked and rattled with the movement. "You have a due date yet?"

"January." Matt looked at the water bottle in his hand. The red bead tracked the mask's movement as Tasha stepped up beside him. He gave her a nod.

Tasha met Malcolm's eyes. Apprehension shadowed the corners of her lips. Malcolm gave a resigned sigh, and Tasha flipped the mask toward him.

The sudden blast knocked Malcolm onto his back. Pain

rippled through his body. The metal collar tightened and loosened against his undulating neck. Rage and hatred and fear washed though him as an inhuman whine rumbled from his chest.

Then it was gone.

"Thank you, Miss Luison," Matt said. "Can you leave us alone for a bit?"

Catching his breath, Malcolm pulled himself back up in time to catch Tasha's sad, apologetic look as she closed the door.

Matt shook his head. "I've never liked those masks."

Malcolm suppressed a snort. "Didn't expect you here so fast."

"Caught a ship in Panama. Just got in."

"I figured as much. You look like hell."

Matt's brow arched. He eyed Malcolm's chains, chuckled, then they both started laughing. It wasn't funny, but the release of tension just exerted itself. Dämoren's barrel didn't move despite the knight's laughter.

Matt set the bottle on the floor. Keeping the revolver trained, he pulled one of the chairs from the wall and lowered into the seat. From a pocket, he withdrew a rectangular black recorder and set it on the floor beside the bottle. He stared at Malcolm long and hard before shaking his head. "You know ... back when I first met Clay, it was like this. I was on the floor, he was in a chair holding Dämoren on me trying to decide what to do."

Malcolm ran his tongue across the back of his teeth. The bastard was loving this. *What are you waiting for?* The image of his head knocking back, blood and brains splattering the bricks behind him. He shivered at the horror and excitement of it. "What's to decide?"

Matt glanced down at the blood compass. "It's not in you right now. Killing you won't kill the demon. But you'll still be dead."

"But I'll be free. I won't have fear of it taking me again. I won't have to wake up realizing what I've done and who I've killed. I won't have to ..." Malcolm took a breath, the words caught in his throat. "I won't have to live knowing that I lost Hounacier."

"And that's what it's really about, isn't it?" Matt asked. "Hounacier?"

A hot spike of anger twisted in Malcolm's chest. "You wouldn't understand."

"Wouldn't I?"

Do it! Shoot me! Malcolm regarded the holy revolver. "No, you wouldn't."

Matt's lips pursed as biting back a retort. "Does Hounacier still live?"

"Yes." Malcolm twisted his cuffed hand around, revealing the faded scar where the warding eye had once been. "But she's turned her back on me."

Matt's hard expression softened for only a moment. "How did it happen?"

Malcolm snorted. "The eye and the scarab react to demons. With one inside me, they pushed the only direction they could. Straight out."

"That's not what I mean," Matt said, straightening in his chair. "The possession. Tell me how this happened."

Finally. Malcolm motioned to the half-full water bottle by his knee. "May I?"

Matt nodded.

Keeping his hand open to show no threat, Malcolm took the room-temperature bottle and finished it off. He drew a breath then began his final debriefing.

"So I broke my finger to keep the ring from coming off then stabbed the nail cross into my other hand and ran to the shop. The rest ..." He lifted his cuffed hands until the belt-chain rattled taught and displayed the now unbroken finger.

Matt nodded. He hadn't spoken once during the entire story. Malcolm had shared it all: the mask, the gris-gris for Duplessis' wife, the succubus blowing an incubus, the return of his sawed-off, everything. The gunman swallowed and nodded his head. Dämoren's aim hadn't moved from Malcolm's heart once, even when Matt had rolled Malcolm a fresh water bottle. He held it with a casual elegance, the same way a master carpenter might hold a hammer, as if it were not a thing he held but some hyper-evolved extension to his hand. All hunters held their weapons in that manner, but the fact that his was a gun and not a sword or axe gave it a more intimidating edge.

"How many followers would you estimate she has?" Matt asked.

"Based off the ceremony, I'd say at least a dozen devout. Duplessis said she has leverage on many more. Cost of her lifestyle, I'd guess easily a hundred." Malcolm clenched his jaw. "No matter how many there are, promise me ... promise me you'll kill her."

"You don't have to ask that, Mal," Matt said. "She'll pay."

"And if ... for some reason Hounacier has bonded ..."

"Don't worry." Matt glanced down at the little recorder. "No weapon has ever bonded with their protector's killer. We know Hounacier won't do that. Atabei will pay."

Malcolm closed his eyes. "Thank you."

"And you're certain she has only one mask left?"

"If she'd had more, they would have been at the ceremony." Malcolm picked up his water and awkwardly took a swig.

Matt nodded. "And you're sure you can't recall any of the words she used to draw it out?"

"If I did, I'd tell you. Sounded like the same thing those cultists in Italy spoke. First Tongue."

"Any thoughts on how she learned it?"

Malcolm shook his head. "She said she trained with priests, an exorcist, the loa, but I don't know."

"Loa?" Matt asked, brow raised.

"Voodoo spirits, like angels or local deities. But I doubt they shared the secret with her."

"Why's that?"

"She didn't want to call them to the ceremony. If the power came from them, she would have. Also," Malcolm added, "If they knew how to do that or were inclined to share it, they would have told me or Ulises long before then."

"So you've met them?"

"Many times."

Matt's lips tightened, seeming to chew on that.

"You don't believe me?" Malcolm asked.

"With everything I've seen?" Matt's brow rose. "You say it's true, it's true. I was just … thinking."

Malcolm finished his water. The interview was nearing its close. Not much time now. He wondered how they were going to move his body out and hoped Tasha wasn't around to hear the shot, to see his blood. Would she ever enter this room again? Maybe she'd choose to block it out, think of their date as their last meeting. He hoped she would. He hoped she'd find someone and forget about him.

Matt continued gnawing his lip, stalling the inevitable.

Malcolm eyed the revolver. Dämoren 3.0, Allan called it. It was sleeker than its predecessor, streamlined, the barrel bored straight through the thick upper blade. Had Matt killed a demon with it yet? Would Malcolm be its first? His gaze followed the smooth form down to the bronze wolf heads. Anger writhed and bristled in his chest, blossoming like a poisoned thistle. Of course he'd be its first. The wolf. He could almost see the silver slug watching him through the barrel, the spirit inside it shivering with anticipation of tasting his blood. He remembered the first time he'd ever seen those bronze heads. He should have killed him then. In that moment, Malcolm hated that gun more than Atabei, more than anything.

"Why did you have to break your finger?" Matt asked, the sudden question surprising Malcolm.

"What?" He tried to shake off the dark thoughts, but they clung like sticky grease.

"You broke your finger to keep the ring on," Matt said. "I get piercing yourself with silver, but why break your finger?"

Malcolm's brow furrowed in confusion. What a stupid question. He'd just told about how the demon had removed the ring. So why … wait… Malcolm mentally ran through his story. He hadn't told Matt about that. How could he have forgotten that? He opened his mouth to tell him, but instead of what he intended, he said, "I was worried it might fall off. If somehow the cross came out of my hand or maybe wasn't in deep enough. Contingency."

No! Malcolm screamed inside his mind. *No!*

Matt nodded, seeming to accept the lie.

The little itch that had been quiet for so long tickled Malcolm's brain. *"You thought you were in control?"*

"Also," Malcolm added, his face not revealing the least trace of his own horror, "I think I just wanted to punish myself, you know? For what I'd done."

"Yeah," Matt said with a sympathetic frown. "I understand."

Malcolm's gaze flicked down to the blood compass. The single bead had elongated but hadn't split. Matt hadn't checked it in half an hour anyway. He wanted to scream, tell him to look at it, but he couldn't. He could only watch and listen.

Matt sighed, the lax muscles in his arm tightening, preparing. "Mal … I know we haven't always gotten along." He licked his lips, resolve cementing. "I wish this wasn't how it ended."

"You don't have to do this," Malcolm said plainly as the he screamed inside, *Do it!* How had he let this happen?

Hardness formed in Matt's eyes. "We both know I do."

"No." Malcolm shook his head. "There's another way, Matt. You can save me."

The hardness seemed to crack. "How?"

"Atabei. She can take it out. She can free me."

"Do you really think she would?"

The red bead stretched more, growing heavy at either end. "I think you could make her. She'd do it to save herself." Malcolm's invisible reins loosened just a bit, and the blood sphere compressed back to normal.

Matt's lips pursed. The corners of his eyes tightened, the dilemma playing across his face.

Seizing the opening, Malcolm blurted, "Ki—" The reigns snapped taut, and Malcolm coughed, cutting off the words. "Killing the demon and recovering Hounacier is all that matters. Atabei is the key to both." He coughed again as if clearing his throat. He took a breath then met Matt's cautious stare, his eyes pleading and sincere. "I remember how you hated me when I'd killed those demonbound in Limoges. You'd told me once how I'd never understand. I do, Matt. You were right." He shook his head. "I couldn't have understood. But I do now. There is *another* way."

Do it, Matt! Do it! Please, God, see through this.

Unmoving, his face unreadable, Matt looked at him for nearly a full minute. Finally, he nodded. "All right."

A defeated weight sank in Malcolm's heart.

Matt licked his lips. He drew a breath, the gun barrel lifting with the movement. "I'm going to clean up. Bring you some water. I need to think about this."

"Do that," Malcolm said. "No knight would decide right now. Just ... if you decide to put me down, don't let Tasha see it. We, um ..." He looked away. "I love her."

"I understand," Matt said. "I promise."

Fantasies of Matt's screams and terror flashed though Malcolm's mind, interspersed with Alpuente's and Jim's dead and bloodied faces, the pain of betrayal in their eyes. Excitement sizzled though his veins. But he didn't move, didn't say a word as Matt rose and left. He saw himself rooting his muzzle up beneath Tasha's wet and sticky ribcage, seeing up between her breasts to the dead and frozen scream, then biting down on her stilled heart, hot blood bursting in his mouth.

The door shut and locked.

"And to think I resisted coming here. No, Malcolm, we're going to be together for a long time."

Malcolm lay on the floor, a prisoner in his own body. The demon had released its hold only enough for him to adjust his position, but he could feel the tethers' presence, ready for any disobedience. No longer hiding its presence, Malcolm experienced the full extent of his heightened senses. The stink of his own body filled the room like syrupy fog. Still, he could smell the wood and leather of the furniture no longer in the room, the food in the distant kitchen, even the wafting scents of whoever passed near his cell's door. He could hear them too, murmurs and footsteps outside and across the house.

"You know, I've been here a few times before," Matt said maybe two rooms away. "Used to sell antiques."

"That so?" Jim asked.

"Yeah. My, uh, stepdad and I used to swing through at least once a year. There was an older gentleman here. They used to spend hours talking shop about coins."

"My father-in-law," Jim said.

"Really?" Matt asked around a mouthful of something.

"He's staying at a friend's right now. Doesn't want to be here with ..."

"You want to see him?" Tasha asked. "Pawpaw might like the company."

"I'd love to," Matt said. "Maybe after ..."

The waist chain dug into Malcolm's side beneath him and he rolled to stare up at the ceiling, his eyes following the two chains suspended on either side. How much had he been in control in the last few days if the demon could manipulate him without his knowledge?

"You never had control," it purred through his mind.

Malcolm tried to ignore it. He had to have had some control. It fought him when he came here.

"You only thought that because I let you. You're nothing. Just a body."

But that couldn't be true. It had said it resisted coming to Alpuente's. If it had resisted, then Malcolm had beaten it. It wasn't— Without warning, Malcolm's hand slid down and grabbed his balls. Blinding pain shot up into his stomach, but he didn't react. He remained stone-faced, wishing he could scream but instead only grinned. The grip tightened, his testicles feeling like they might crush under the pressure. *"You have no control. If I wanted, you would pluck out your own eyes and eat them without protest. Then smile at your future killer when he walks in, blood pouring from your empty sockets."* His hand released.

The demon's reins loosened, allowing Malcolm to groan in pain.

Tears welled in his eyes, but he still couldn't scream.

"You're nothing but meat."

Malcolm clenched his teeth, biting until they hurt. The demon could hear his thoughts. There was no place safe.

Eventually, footsteps clomped down the wood-floored hall and stopped at the door.

"Are you sure about this?" Jim whispered.

"I don't really see a choice," Matt answered.

Malcolm turned his head as the door groaned open. Dämoren in hand, Matt walked inside. He'd shaved and changed clothes. The waft of his musky cologne wrinkled Malcolm's nose.

A sickened knot roiled in Malcolm's gut, seeing Tasha follow Matt in, mask clutched to her chest. Bastard promised she wouldn't see this.

Jim came in last, dwarfing the other two. He clutched a key ring in his fist.

"Time to get up," Matt said. "We have work to do."

The knot tightened. This was worse than Tasha witnessing his execution. He crawled to his knees. "And the Order is okay with this?"

"Haven't told them."

"Why not?" Malcolm asked.

Matt's brow arched. "You think they'd agree to it?"

Malcolm didn't answer.

"Consider this limited freedom," Matt said. "You do what I say, when I say. You'll sleep in chains, and that collar stays on at all times. If you do anything that risks anyone, I'll do it. Understood?"

Idiot! "Understood."

"Good. Let's get you out of here." Matt stepped to the side, securing a clear line of fire as Jim slowly approached, keys in hand.

The stink of Jim's aftershave and coffee breath made Malcolm look away. He lifted his hands, allowing the priest to unlock the cuffs then the chains.

"So what's the plan?" Malcolm asked.

"First, we'll get you showered and cleaned up," Matt said. "Then a drive past Atabei's. Then, we'll see."

"You going to watch me shower?"

"That a problem?"

Malcolm grinned. "Hope you like the show." He turned his head, allowing Jim access to the chains at his collar. Metal rattled as their weight fell away. "Thank you, Jim."

Jim grunted then backed away as Malcolm pushed himself up to his feet, his joints aching at the long-missed movement.

Stretching his arms, Malcolm rolled his wrists. He pulled at his oily and sweat-ripened shirt, the dead man's shirt from the house. "So about that shower?"

Malcolm stayed in the water until the hot began to fade out. He turned it off and just stood there dripping, his dark skin reddened from heat and scrubbing. Reaching past the half-drawn curtain, he grabbed a towel, momentarily meeting Matt's bored eyes though the mist of steam. The hunter leaned against the counter by the door, his hands crossed in front. Malcolm glanced to the twin wolf heads protruding from the shoulder holster. Seething hatred boiled behind his smile. "Can't tell you how good that felt."

"I'm sure."

After a quick dry, Malcolm wrapped the towel around his waist and stepped out of the antique tub. Matt moved aside to allow access to the sink.

"So what exactly is the game plan? Just drive around Atabei's all night?" Malcolm wiped a hand cloth over the foggy mirror. He scratched the thick, black whiskers along his neck, his eyes studying the silver collar. Twin globs of solder fused both sides of the scalloped, twisting hoop, one for the hinge and the other the latch. Malcolm picked up a can of shaving gel and squirted a thick glob into his palm.

"I'd like to get an initial look," Matt said. "I have two of the wireless cameras. Maybe we could hide them somewhere for surveillance. You said you went inside the house?"

"Twice," Malcolm said, lathering his face in over-scented menthol. "Didn't see much of it. Only a few rooms on the first floor, back yard."

Matt shrugged, his features lost in the wet mirror. "It's a start. We'll draw a map, figure out any weak spots so we can slip inside. Then recover Hounacier, grab the mask, and get her out of there without her followers coming down on us."

"We'll need to prepare a place for the ceremony." Malcolm removed the razor from his bag and ran it under the sink.

"You're in charge on that detail," Matt said. "How long does it take?"

"She took just a couple minutes last time." Lifting his chin to shave, Malcolm continued his inspection of the collar. The two solder points appeared smooth, solidly fused. Jim's decades of jewelry repair had taught him well. "Hard part will be getting her to do it. That might take some time. She spent years plotting her revenge."

"I'm sure we can motivate her."

"Whatever you promise her, Matt, I'm still killing her once this is done."

"I wasn't planning on stopping you."

Once Malcolm was cleaned and dressed, Matt slid Dämoren into a soft-sided laptop bag. From the other side of the padded divider, he drew a Mac-10 Ingram and racked in a magazine of silver hollow points.

"No gun for me?" Malcolm asked with a little smile.

"No." Matt slipped the machine pistol back into the bag, positioned so he could reach through the slit in the side and grab and fire either gun, then clicked the top flap shut. He pulled it over his shoulder, right hand near the slit, and picked the blood compass up off the counter. "Let's go. You lead."

Downstairs, Tasha and Jim were in the hall, moving furniture and boxes back into the storeroom. Seeing them, Jim nodded and led them to the door.

Malcolm smiled to Tasha as he passed, the fantasy of eating her heart flashing though his mind.

She glanced away, fear or shame darkening her eyes. "Be careful."

"Don't worry," he said. "I'll be back."

They entered the showroom as Jim was draping a cloth over the remounted ghoul mask facing the entrance. "Let me know if something happens or you need anything."

"We will," Matt said.

Jim's lips tightened. "You call before coming back here. Just a little warning."

"Understood."

Jim unlocked the front door and stepped aside.

"Thank you, Jim," Malcolm said.

The big priest only nodded.

Sticky, warm air greeted them as they stepped out into the

early evening. Malcolm had never expected to smell the city's stink again, and he breathed deep, part of him savoring it, the other part, his part, horrified that he was free. Tourists and the bar crowd shuffled down the French Quarter's streets, the voices melding into a single noise, accented by music from a dozen different places.

The lock clicked behind him.

Malcolm scanned the crowd and parked cars, searching.

"So where's your rental?"

Matt motioned to the left. "This way."

Malcolm's eyes continued their search. There! Issach stood on the opposite corner, partially concealed behind a T-shirt display. Green light from a nearby sign glinted off his round glasses, hiding his eyes. Without reacting, Malcolm turned left as Matt had told him and began to walk.

They made their way through the sea of bodies, many already drunk or racing to it. Malcolm stole a quick glance back. Issach was on a phone, keeping pace.

"Down here," Matt said when they reached a side street. "Silver sedan."

The car's lights flashed as they neared it. Malcolm cursed Matt's trust—his trust in him, his trust in that damned compass. It was coming. He didn't know what, but he felt the demon's mounting excitement, the quickening heart, the dilating pupils. He stopped beside the passenger door and looked back. Issach was behind a yellow Ford, phone to his ear.

The man froze, realizing he'd been spotted.

Malcolm smiled and winked. "Matt!" he hissed and pointed. "Atabei's boy. Gun!"

Matt wheeled, keys falling from his hand as he shoved it into the bag. Issach dropped behind the car. Seizing the moment, Malcolm kicked Matt hard in the back. He pitched forward, and the compass flew away. His gun went off as he fell, blasting smoke and black nylon. Someone screamed. Malcolm closed in, ready to stomp the fallen hunter, when Issach popped around the Ford, revolver outstretched. He fired.

The car window beside him exploded, spraying glass cubes. Malcolm ducked as the second shot hit the wall behind him.

Groaning, Matt rolled.

Seeing Dämoren swing his direction, Malcolm scrambled around the car and sprinted away. People were on the ground, hunkered behind cars or diving into buildings as Malcolm raced past with superhuman speed. Another shot echoed behind him, followed by more screams. He prayed to feel one hit his back, but it never came.

Head low, he turned at the first street. Panicked pedestrians looked around in confusion, mouths open. He leaped, running right across a rolling BMW's hood then wove between a pair of cars, horns blaring around him. Four blocks later, he slowed to a brisk walk. Blending into a herd of people, he crossed Canal. Three more blocks, then he ducked into a narrow alley and grinned.

Freedom.

Deep beneath the demon's exhilaration, Malcolm only hoped Matt wasn't hurt.

"*He's fine*," the demon answered. "*Now, we hunt.*" Excitement shivered though his veins. He'd waited so long for this. Rajik's killer was here. But first … Malcolm gripped the cursed collar. It warmed beneath his fingers. He pulled and twisted, muscles swelling. His arms trembled under the strain, but the silver loop wouldn't give. Clenching his teeth, the demon yanked and yanked. Skin stretched as his arms and shoulders expanded to lend strength. The silver grew hot, burning where it touched his flesh, but it still held fast.

Defeated, the demon released it, and his swollen muscles deflated. He looked at his palms, examining the red, blistered line across his fingers. Frustrated, he balled his fists then winced.

Malcolm smiled inwardly. As long as Jim's solders held, he had a foothold.

Sirens blared in the distance. He needed to go. There was hunting and revenge to plan. The demon moved deeper into the narrow alley, knowing where it emptied. He knew this city, watched it grow, fall, and rise again. Its allure had drawn him back many times, and he loved it more than he fully understood. He was known here, a legend himself. He was the rougarou, and this city was his.

"Milky?" asked a high, crackly voice.

The demon spun to see a filthy, unkempt man crouched beside a gap in the wall. Yellowed eyes, their irises only dark slivers fluttering below sleep-dusted lashes.

"Milky, what's wrong with you?" His eyes rolled back forward and widened in dawning terror. "Oh no, Milky."

To Malcolm's horror, he lunged, grabbing the mounted man by the throat. The pitying eyes rolled as the loa fled, replaced by horror and pain. The man's arms flailed and latched onto Malcolm's wrist. His larynx crunched beneath the demon's grip, squelching off the sudden scream. He slammed the man's head into the wall, reared back, and slammed it again with a meaty *thwak*. The begger's grip loosened on Malcolm arms, but the demon held tight, squeezing until his fingers broke through the skin. Breath quickening, he watched the life fade from the man's eyes, then released him.

The demon licked the blood from his fingers, savoring the sweet terror within it. The blisters faded from his burned fingers. Kneeling, he moved in, taking a bite of the still-warm flesh, but a sudden tingle prickled his neck, like someone was watching him.

Turning, he looked back down the alley. Empty.

The feeling heightened. He sniffed. Above the stink of salt, exhaust, urine, and blood, he caught the scent of female.

A shadow swept down the alley walls. Looking up, he glanced black hair and rustling wings before claws tore his shoulders and threw him across the damp asphalt.

"You," a fierce voice hissed. "How dare you!"

The demon looked up to see a dark-skinned succubus standing above him, her outstretched wings blocking off the alley. The dim light reflected off her naked, perfect skin, making it almost glow.

Her violet, gold eyes narrowed. "This human is mine, dog. How dare you mark him as your own. Leave it now."

Clutching his teeth from the pain of torn shoulders, the demon rolled to his knees and bowed. "My apologies, Mistress, but I did not mark this body of my own volition."

Her brow rose. "Explain."

"A sorceress, Atabei Cross, wrenched me from my anchors and thrust me into this, the body of her enemy."

The succubus lifted her chin, mistrust tightening at the corners of her plump lips.

"I speak the truth. The sorceress can tear us from our bodies and imprison us in whatever vessel she desires."

"Then we will deal with her," she said. "First, I want to punish the mortal you inhabit. He murdered my mate, Suseel. Do you have other vessels?"

"Yes, Mistress. I have marked one other."

Black dread sank in Malcolm's heart. The werewolf had marked another. When? That first night? Before murdering the family? He wasn't its only body. His death would have meant nothing, and now, a vengeful succubus wanted her pound of flesh, and he had no warding tattoo or Hounacier to protect him.

"Then go to it," she snapped. "This one is mine."

"To beg your forgiveness, Mistress, there is more. Atabei possesses Kuquo, the oppressor who murdered your mate. But I do not believe they have formed the bond."

Kuquo! Malcolm finally knew Hounacier's true name. Somehow, finally knowing it shone like a single fleeting ray, a final joy before the end.

Her lips drew into a mischievous smile. "We could destroy them both."

The demon nodded. "Yes. But there is also another oppressor. Urakael, the killer of my own mate, is in the city. Its child, Matt Hollis, hunts me now. He and this ..." His bleeding shoulder panged as he gestured to himself, "... Malcolm Romero were close. They murdered the Great Mother together. I was toying with them."

She drew a sharp breath. "I see."

"It would be a pity to kill this body now when there are such torments to give it."

The succubus remained silent for several heartbeats. "What is your name, dog?"

"Gulmet," he answered.

"Gulmet, you have taken a body that belongs to me. But for what you have told me, I allow you to keep it until the Great

Mother is avenged. I conscribe you to my service until I deem otherwise. Stand."

Gulmet rose, suppressing his anger. He did not owe this creature a debt, but it was her right of rank.

She stepped closer. Her intoxicating scent of lust enveloped him. She stood no higher than his eyes.

"I am Vimiya." She placed one hand against his chest, caressing the muscles. Her other hand slid down her body and between her legs. She brought it up and smeared warm, wetted fingers beneath his nose. The sudden smell of pure carnality took his breath.

He hadn't felt anything like it since … since Rajik. The guilt from betraying her memory with this desire made him hate this Vimiya even more.

Deep inside him, Malcolm twisted, repulsed and aroused by the unimagined sensuality, and Gulmet grinned at his torment. The succubus nodded approvingly, mistaking his pleasure in her.

"That is my scent. Know it. Know your place, Gulmet."

"Yes, Mistress." The act was unnecessary. It was an expression of dominance. She owned him, and he was helpless.

Vimiya tugged the silver collar. "What is this?"

"It was put on me to prevent my true flesh-form." Each breath brought more of the intoxicating scent, strengthening her hold.

She smiled. "Then come. Let us remove that. We have vengeance to take."

IV

Gulmet walks between olive trees, a pair of dead rabbits swinging from his hand. He's grown bored with this place, the cottage, the fear of taking his true flesh-form. He hadn't told Rajik of the human that had seen him. She would worry. Rajik worries much at late. Three weeks until the eclipse. Then, they will worry no more. They will teach their pups to hunt, to move bodies, and to blend in among mortals. They will be gods to their children, and they will teach them to be strong.

A sharp smell wafts on the breeze. Gulmet sniffs. Smoke?

Quickening his pace, he emerges from between the trees. A dark column of smoke billows beyond the next hill. The cottage!

Fear crackles through his veins. Gulmet drops the rabbits and runs. He crests the first rise. The smoke is definitely coming from the where the cottage is. Bones pop and shift as he leaps down the slope, landing on all fours. He races down then up the next rise, his paws slipping on fallen leaves.

He reaches the top and freezes. *No!*

Orange flames pour out the door and windows, melding with the black smoke. A pair of mounted men sit nearby, their horses shying nervously from the blaze. A third man stands before the flaming doorway.

Where is Rajik? Gulmet races down the hill.

"Tomas!" one of the horsemen yells, pointing at Gulmet.

The man at the door wheels about. The long sword in his hand gleams in the sunlight. Tiny red gems sparkle along its blade. A pair of bronze wolf heads cap its pommel. The man takes three steps away from the fire and draws a pistol in his off hand.

Snarling, Gulmet charges. How dare these mortals come here. The men draw their own guns and fire. The bullets whiz past as Gulmet closes in.

The swordsman stands ready. He fires his own pistol, unleashing a cloud of smoke.

The silver ball slams into Gulmet's breast with a hard *thock*. His foreleg crumples, and Gulmet tumbles. The cursed metal burns in his lung. He tastes his own blood. Fear tinges it.

"Prepare thyself for hell, demon!" the man cries. He drops the smoking pistol and grips the sword before him.

Gulmet hobbles to his feet. The two riders are dismounting, drawing their own weapons. He sees their faint glow. Oppressors!

The swordsman takes a step, murder sparkling in his eyes. Beyond him, through the smoke and blaze, Gulmet spies a brilliant crimson fire inside the cottage.

No! Ignoring the Oppressors, Gulmet runs toward it, his weakened leg threatening to give with every movement. The murdering swordsman readies for the attack, but Gulmet races past him and leaps through the door.

His fur crackles and melts in the hot flames. Smoke stings his eyes. Rajik lies on the floor, cleaved open, flaming organs spilling from the wound. She is gone, her crimson essence burning from this world. The cubs, his children, dead before they ever were.

Gulmet's skin burns, his fur now completely melted away. He crawls to her, taking Rajik in his arms. The one thing he's ever loved, his one single dream, is gone. Gulmet screams.

Fire burns his eyes, stealing his sight. He pulls Rajik close, feeling her against him before his burning nerves surrender to the flames. Through the sizzling of his flesh and crackling of wood, he hears the killers shouting outside, congratulating themselves on his pain.

Finally, his charred arms, no longer able to hold her, drop, and Gulmet slumps atop her corpse. His left eye hisses and pops. His essence breaks free of the now useless vessel and rises into blackness. Crimson strands hold him to this world like a spider's web. One by one, he searches his anchors, hoping one will take him far away; somewhere that holds no memories of him and Rajik.

One, the most distant, a female whose soul he had marked when she was but a child, now grown. She sits at a window, watching a nighttime storm. Her husband dead in the recent war. The lingering suffering of fighting men still stains the lands. Gulmet has never visited this new land across the ocean. It is a wild place, and no one notices a new or missing face.

Gulmet pours himself down the strand and into his new vessel.

CHAPTER 17

Sweat trickled down Gulmet's spine. Even hours after the sun's setting, summer's heat lingered in the balmy air. A silent prisoner in his own body, Malcolm watched himself move through Tasha's poorly-lit complex.

Air conditioners and box fans hummed from many of the windows. Several residents sat on their narrow balconies or in breezeways, chatting or staring at their phones. Gulmet passed behind her unit and glanced up without turning his head. The windows were dark. Her air conditioner was silent.

Malcolm inwardly smiled, praying she wasn't home. *Looks like you missed her.*

The image of her blood-soaked face flashed though his mind, her eyes pleading and pained.

"We'll taste her soon enough," Gulmet purred.

Malcolm cursed himself for thinking with words. The demon could hear his thoughts and see his mental pictures. He had to think without words or images. Even then, he wasn't completely sure the demon wouldn't know his thoughts.

Gulmet continued to the next building and circled around. Raised voices, a man and woman, came from a window above. He stopped beneath a dark awning and looked around.

Vimiya strolled through the courtyard, her wings and nudity masked beneath a shimmering glamour, like summer heat escaping a hot car. Shoulders back, she followed the steps leading up to the second floor and knocked on Tasha's door.

Tasha wouldn't expect the succubus. She might even open the door for her. But if Matt were inside, sitting in the darkness, blood compass beside him, he'd have seen a crimson bead pass behind, dissolve, then re-form and approach the door. Vimiya's glamour wouldn't hide her from him.

Malcolm imagined bullets exploding out the door, the succubus' shocked face as the demon fire consumed her. Gulmet smiled at the thought as well. "*One could only wish.*"

Malcolm winced internally; he'd forgotten not to think visually.

Vimiya knocked again.

Movement caught Gulmet's eyes. Quentin, his cornrows hidden beneath a green cap, strolled past one of the other buildings. Scratching his neck, he gave Vimiya a casual glance then turned the corner.

Gulmet followed, the excitement of a hunt tingling his veins. He slipped across a well-lit breezeway then ducked up a shadowed path leading toward the building Quentin had gone behind. Staying off the cracked concrete walk, he hurried along the grass, his footsteps silent. He peeked around the corner to find his prey turning back toward the courtyard. Gulmet followed.

Keeping a safe distance behind, he watched the big man casually stroll past again. Unlike Issach, who foolishly stood in one place, making himself obvious, Quentin was circling. A predator. Gulmet's lips pulled into a toothy grin. He had no doubt Quentin carried his silver-loaded revolver. He was hunting too. Gulmet's muscles tensed with the thrill of it. A dangerous quarry was always the sweetest kill. Vimiya turned from the door. She glanced to where Gulmet should have been then turned to leave, her eyes immediately finding Gulmet mid-movement without the least trace of effort.

Always knows where her dog is.

"*Shut up.*"

Quentin stopped at a bench, facing away from Tasha's door, and casually reached into his pocket.

A spike of adrenaline shot through Gulmet's senses, priming his muscles.

Lazily, Quentin drew a pack of cigarettes out. The tension receded. Gulmet sidestepped beneath a paint-flaking stairway and waited. Tingles writhed up his back like a hundred worms, signaling Vimiya's approach.

"Who are you watching, Gulmet?" she whispered in his ear.

Gulmet started in surprise. *"So silent."* He motioned to Quentin smoking against the bench. "One of the sorceress' disciples. Quentin. He helped trap me in this body."

"Hmm," she cooed like a child discovering a new favorite sweet. "Then we do have a kill for tonight. Follow us when we leave." Vimiya slipped out from beneath the stairs and strode toward Quentin.

"Excuse me," she said once she was a few feet from him. The glamoured air distorted around her, enveloping Quentin as he turned. "Can I bum a smoke?"

He smiled warmly then drew a fresh cigarette for her. Accepting it, she let him light it, and then they began talking. They laughed, and she touched his bicep. Seeming impressed, she told him to flex, and she touched his chest with a gentle caress.

Gulmet ran his tongue along his teeth as he watched the ease with which she ensnared her prey. She dropped her finished cigarette on the concrete slab and ground it out with a glamoured heel Malcolm knew was but a bare foot. Once the illusion faded, succubi could always be identified by their footprints.

That done, she took Quentin's arm and he led her away.

A few seconds later, Gulmet stepped from his hiding place and followed. They strolled leisurely ahead, their pace slow but purposeful, reminiscent of the night Malcolm had killed Vimiya's mate. They crossed several streets, talking and laughing, both encased in a bubble of glimmering air. Malcolm wondered what it was that Quentin saw and where he might think he was.

He had to stop several times to keep himself from catching up, not that it mattered. Quentin was hers. It would take something more dramatic than seeing Malcolm at a glance to break the hallucination. They walked for blocks, so far that

Malcolm began wondering how Quentin had even gotten to Tasha's apartment. Had he forgotten his car there? Probably.

They passed under the I10 overpass, congested with trash and vagrants. It stank of piss and acrid smoke. On the ground, behind one of the concrete pillars, a pair of men smoked from a broken light bulb. Voices stilled, and hungry eyes watched the succubus' passing.

The pungent stink of lamia greeted them one block later. Niriffo ruled the Mid-City area. She'd told Gulmet she'd kill him if he ever entered her territory again. Vimiya could offer no protection. He only hoped he might pass through before she or her ghouls noticed.

Eventually, they turned at a small, avocado-colored house and started up the porch. Quentin fumbled with his keys, unlocked the door, and they both stepped inside.

That too-familiar excitement returned. The chase was done. *"Time for the kill."*

Gulmet slowed as he closed, allowing a pair of teens to pass. The narrow house looked no more than fifteen feet wide, but deep. The barred windows were still dark. He stepped onto the tiny, concrete porch and checked the door.

Unlocked.

He smiled then glanced back one last time. No one was watching. Gulmet drew a breath, puffing his chest, then opened the door. The tiny house was clean and organized. A modest but well-made couch rested against one wall facing an expensive-looking coffee table and a television. Through an open doorway, he could see a kitchen, everything in it arranged with meticulous precision. The house smelled of new carpet, a synthetic fruity odor—compliments of the unburnt candles in a wall sconce—and the faint but distinct smell of pot.

A trail of sweat-moistened clothes led down the hall to an open door. Moans and bed creaks came from inside.

Gulmet locked the door behind him and moved toward the sounds, his feet silent on the thick carpeting. He peeked through the door. Quentin's back faced him, the thick muscles rippling with each thrust. Vimiya's slender legs were around him, tightening with the movements, urging him harder. The smell of sex filled the room like a thickening cloud.

He watched for several long seconds, his mouth watering. Amid her cries, Vimiya's gaze moved past her victim, seeing Gulmet. Her eyes narrowed into a scolding glare, and Gulmet turned away. Swallowing his saliva, he returned to the living room.

"Baby, you feel so good," she moaned.

"You're incredible," Quentin grunted. "Amazing."

Gulmet stopped at a narrow shelf, perusing the collection of crystals and polished stones. A sharp, upthrust amethyst cluster stood among them. The moans and grunts grew louder. The bed squeaked as they rolled into a new position.

"Give it to me!" Vimiya cried. "I want it all!"

Gulmet's jaw tightened, anger roiling in his gut. Quentin was his enemy. How dare she feed on him first.

While Gulmet was distracted with his thoughts, Malcolm braved moving a finger. The demon didn't seem to notice. Not allowing himself joy or even thought of his discovery, Malcolm tightened and loosened his fist. He wasn't helpless after all.

Vimiya cried out in an orgasmic whoop.

Malcolm released his limited control just as the demon turned him away from the shelf.

"*Almost time.*" He pulled off his shoes and kicked them aside. The tingle of the upcoming kill returned, mounting faster and faster with bed creaks. Gulmet peeled off clothes and tossed them onto the table.

Naked, his mouth open in heavy breaths, he walked down the hall and peeked again. Vimiya straddled him. The shimmer of her glamoured, outstretched wings filled the room. She held his wrists to the bed, her hips moving, plunging him deeper. Gulmet hardened at the overpowering lust pulsing from the room.

Quentin's face scrunched into a pained grimace of ecstasy. "Oh God! Oh God!" he screamed. He bucked and shuddered, and Vimiya threw her head back and straightened. Her skin seemed to glow with the sudden rush of energy.

Then, with a long groan, Quentin fell still.

Vimiya breathed deep, her glistening breasts heaving with the movement. She crawled off the now unconscious man and gave Gulmet a smile. Her eyes flickered to his erection. "Dogs always like to watch."

An uncomfortable pang needled Gulmet's gut. He'd thought those urges dead with Rajik.

He started to turn away, but she said, "No. Don't hide it." She touched his chest as she moved around him, her nails sliding across his skin. She pressed herself against his back, her flesh hot and smooth. "He's yours, Gulmet," she whispered. "Do as you wish, but keep it quiet. No one can hear."

Gulmet looked over her shoulder. "Why not? We'll be gone before—"

The succubus' claws dug into his shoulder. "Because I say. I have plans."

He clenched his jaw, refusing her the satisfaction of his pain. "Yes, Mistress."

"Good." Vimiya drew her claws out and kissed one of the bleeding, half-moon cuts. "Now have your vengeance, Gulmet."

Blood trickled down his arms. Releasing a breath, he turned to see the succubus strolling back into the living room, her hips swaying with each step. He hated her even more than the unconscious mortal that had trapped him. Gulmet looked back at Quentin, sprawled naked on the damp sheets. "*Well*," he thought, rage mounting, "*maybe not more than.*"

Gulmet stepped inside the room and stretched his arms out. His skin pimpled, and brown-black fur emerged in a cascading wave. Bones groaned, and ligaments popped. The room seemed to warp as his eye sockets shifted. He flexed his lengthening fingers as dark claws extended from their tips.

Malcolm watched, horrified at his own transformation, disgusted by the intoxicating surge of power he felt in his own body. The demon had never let him see this before. But it wanted him to see it. Wanted him to taste Quentin's death.

He stepped closer to the bed and looked down. His prey lay there, unaware of the death above him. Gulmet's lips curled back, a deep growl rumbling from his throat.

Quentin's head moved. His blue eyes fluttered, passing over Gulmet but not registering him. They closed, and Quentin fell back asleep.

"*She fed too much*," he thought. "*He has to fear it. I'm no flesh-eating ghoul. I don't care about the meat. I need the terror.*"

Interesting, Malcolm thought then cursed himself for it.

"*Silence!*" Gulmet crawled into the bed. Hovering just above him, he poised a clawed finger just below Quentin's Adam's apple and pressed.

Quentin winced sleepily and opened his eyes to see the werewolf just inches above his face.

Gulmet growled.

Eyes bulging wide, Quentin opened his mouth to scream, but only a low whine came out. The werewolf opened his jaws, allowing a good look into his mouth. Quentin's chest throbbed with his hammering heart, but he still didn't scream. Gulmet closed his maw and met the mortal's terrified eyes. A string of drool fell from his fangs onto the man's chin. He slid the other claw down the Quentin's stomach.

"Pl ... pl ... I ... no," the man stammered through quickening breaths.

His body tensed, pressing down as if he could somehow will himself thought the bed and on the floor.

Eyes narrowing, Gulmet slid his claws up behind Quentin's scrotum. His teeth parted into a smile, then he ripped and peeled the skin sack off.

Quentin screamed, but Gulmet drove his claw into the man's windpipe and twisted. Blood gurgled and whistled from the hole. Gulmet clamped his hand over Quentin's mouth. The man twisted, trying to escape, but Gulmet squeezed until he felt the jawbone pop.

Frothy blood sputtered and sucked from the ragged hole. Keeping his hand tight on Quentin's broken mouth, he raked the man's thighs, careful to miss the arteries. Quentin writhed and kicked, slinging blood.

Gulmet licked the blood from Quentin throat, tonguing the hole. The painful wounds Vimiya had inflicted on his shoulders healed, but the fear was still lacking. "*It should be more! I knew she took too much of him!*" Angry, he slashed his prey's stomach and slid a finger into the bleeding wound.

Quentin's eyes rolled. Before he could go unconscious, Gulmet latched onto the man's throat, tasting the sweet terror. He thrust his hand deep into the man's entrails and pulled out a fistful of gray loops. He bit down and ripped out Quentin's throat. Quentin flailed and kicked, his blood pulsing with pure fear. Gulmet lapped it up, savoring every drop until the mortal fell still.

Drunk on the thrill, Gulmet cracked the still-hot carcass open and ate its heart, tasting the quickly fleeting emotion.

Somewhere deep inside, Malcolm screamed, his horror mixing with the demon's excitement. He couldn't turn away; he couldn't close his eyes or block it out. All he could do was scream in his own mind as he tore meat from the dead man's bones and ate his fill, savoring it unlike anything he'd ever tasted.

The blood-soaked mattress squished as he crawled back onto the floor. Rising to his feet, he looked back. Crimson dots splattered the baby-blue walls above the torn and mangled form. Gulmet smiled and returned to Malcolm's form.

He found Vimiya in the living room. She sat sprawled on the sofa, her now visible wings draped over the arm and Quentin's revolver in her hands.

"Are you planning to shoot me?" he asked.

The succubus snorted. "That would be a waste." She rolled it over in her hands like a child with a new and strange toy. "When the body is found and this is here, loaded with silver bullets, what will they think?"

"Does it matter?"

"Yes," she hissed, her eyes narrowing. "It does. No one believes anymore, Gulmet. No one remembers the old ways they used to resist us."

Gulmet snorted. "They know silver."

"But no one believes it, you idiot. A man with silver bullets is found dead." She nodded to the sticky blood covering Malcolm's body. "Mauled. People wonder. They suspect their movies may be true."

"They won't know what to think," he said.

"They'll fear, and there's always a market for fear. Someone will start selling silver bullets. Mortals will buy them. Then they'll make bronze, gold, iron, and then what?"

He shook his head. "You're overreacting."

Vimiya sprung from her seat and was on him, her claws around his throat. "No, I'm not! People exploit fear, and we can't let them fear us."

Gulmet swallowed. "My apologies, Mistress. We should take the gun. Dispose of it somewhere else."

Her hard eyes softened. "Yes." She released her hold and turned. "Now that you've had your revenge, leave us."

"What? Should I shower first?"

"Leave the vessel here. Go to your other one."

He clenched his fists. "You said I could keep it until—"

Vimiya wheeled. "And I will keep my word. But I want to play with my mate's killer."

A new terror seized Malcolm. He knew this had been coming but not yet. Then he remembered the amethyst.

"Go," she ordered. "Go to your other vessel. Hunt. That's what you do. Return to this body by sunrise."

Memories flashed though Malcolm's mind. He saw himself at Atabei's container ring, walking away from the wolf's pen. But something was wrong, different than he remembered it. He'd sneezed then stood erect. Shocked, he now remembered removing the silver ring and clothes, and transformed. He'd returned to the wolf pen. The animal rolled onto its back, offering its submission. Malcolm had opened the pen and bit its neck, breaking the skin and lapping the blood. That done, he transformed back, put on clothes, then sneezed again. *You son of a bitch.*

Gulmet smiled inwardly. Yes, yes he'd take his other vessel. The wolf, his truest flesh-form. He'd run and hunt and kill in the bayou, free from this succubus' control.

Malcolm staggered, feeling like some ancient weight had lifted from his bones. The once sweet aroma of blood and death roiled his aching, over-full stomach.

Vimiya stood before him, leathery wings stretching out, blocking the door. "Alone at last."

Malcolm spun. Knocking aside stone and crystals, he grabbed the amethyst cluster. He gripped it like a baseball, the rough base digging into his palm. Before he could turn back, the succubus was on him.

Hissing, she grappled his shoulder. A sweet, musky smell flooded Malcolm's senses. Claws sank into his flesh. He grunted in pain then smashed the crystal down onto her hand. She cried out and released her grip before he could strike it again. Malcolm twisted toward her, ready to brain her with the crude weapon. Her ruffling wings and swinging claws were a blur in the faint light. She seized his throat with a vise-like grip. Her other hand fumbling for his wrist, she slammed him against the wall. The shelves dug into his back then cracked and broke, their contents spilling onto the carpet. The muskiness grew thicker, sticking to his throat with each gasp.

Head swimming, Malcolm brought the crystal down onto her cheek, ripping a pair of ragged cuts through her perfect face. She yowled and slammed Malcolm harder against the wall. Sheetrock crunched as his head hit the wall.

Stunned, he nearly lost hold of the crystal. He tried to smash it against the outstretched arm that held him, but she caught his wrist. She squeezed, earning a squelched cry of pain. The succubus was far stronger than him. Twisting his arm, she yanked it down hard and pinned it against his side.

Blood ran from her cheek, framing her wicked grin. She leaned closer and kissed the claw wound in his shoulder.

A soothing wave rolled from where her lips touched him, rippling out through his body. Malcolm's terror washed away, and straining muscles relaxed. Her choke hold loosened, allowing a gasp. Her sweet scent hit like a drug, and the room shimmered, losing form. His hardening cock throbbed.

"No!" he coughed, trying to fight her grip, but she tore the crystal from his dulled grasp. It thudded somewhere in the unseen room behind her. Malcolm spat into her golden violet eyes.

Vimiya yanked, wrenching him across her body. His arm slammed into the sofa frame as he hit the floor. Malcolm tried to crawl, but his weak limbs wouldn't respond. Her claw grabbed the side his face and pressed him into the carpet.

"Malcolm? Are you okay?"

Groggily, Malcolm opened his eyes. He was on a floor. Why was he on a floor? He rolled his head to see Tasha smiling above him. A new fragrance tinged her citrus perfume, something familiar, but he couldn't remember where from.

"I told you you'd had too much to drink," she giggled.

"Yeah, I guess ..." He pushed himself up onto his elbows, his arm aching at the movement, and looked around. "Where are we?"

"My apartment," she said.

Malcolm nodded, now seeing the cases of cameras and books. "You rearranged your furniture."

She shrugged. "I figured it was time." Tasha helped him up onto the sofa beside him. "So are you all right?"

Malcolm touched his tender throat. "What happened?"

Her brows rose with a surprised chuckle. "You slipped off the couch."

He shook his head. "No, I mean ... how did I get *here*?"

"You sure you're all right?"

Malcolm sighed. "No, I'm good. Just ... where were we?"

Tasha pressed a finger softly against his chest and leaned closer. "The great Doctor Romero can't handle his rum." She laughed.

Malcolm couldn't help but laugh with her. He'd never been much of a drinker.

She leaned closer. Her sweet perfume grew stronger, almost caressing him like a living thing. "We came back from dinner. I asked you to come in." She nodded to the coffee table. "We had some cake, a couple drinks."

Malcolm noticed the two glasses of amber-hued ice on the coffee table beside a plate of half-eaten chocolate cake. His favorite.

"You said it was getting late," she continued, her fingers slowly pushing him onto his back.

Malcolm realized he wasn't wearing a shirt.

"I said you owed me a kiss." She leaned over him, her lips almost touching his. "That's where we were."

Malcolm kissed her. A sudden surge of near-forgotten

feelings rushed though him. He loved her. He always had. She returned it passionately, pressing herself on top of him. His hands moved up to touch her, and he realized she was nude. When had she taken her clothes off?

He was about to ask, but Tasha tugged his lip with hers and pulled his hand to her breast. Her soft, firm skin was perfect. Malcolm squeezed her hardening nipple. He gasped at the sudden, almost painful throb of erection. He pulled her higher up him and sucked and kissed her dark nipples, breathing in the incredible scent.

Moaning, Tasha slid her hand lower. She found his cock and slid it up between her swollen labia, sliding up and down. The hot wetness tingled, almost electric. Malcolm groaned with pleasure, and then she thrust herself down, burying him inside her, and the sensation was more incredible than anything he'd ever felt.

She slid up and down, matching his movements. The smooth tingles stretched further though him with each plunge. They wormed down his legs and along his spine, channeling all his nerves, all his energy into her.

Their speed increasing, Malcolm moaned. The pleasure mounted beyond any threshold he'd ever had. He grabbed her hips, pulling her into each thrust. She was incredible, and her sighs and cries only pushed him further.

"Baby, you feel so good," Tasha whimpered.

"I love you." He wanted to give her everything.

"Mmmm," she cooed. "I want it all."

Malcolm ached, the pressure swelling.

Tasha pulled his hand off her and moved them to the padded armrest above his head. "Not yet, baby."

He let out a long, pleading sigh.

"Shh," she soothed. "Patience, baby." She grinned then pushed his hands together and pinned them beneath one of her own.

Malcolm kissed at her breasts as she reached over to the table beside them.

She drew a breath as he sucked her nipples. Then Tasha sat up, pulling them just beyond his mouth's reach. "Here."

Malcolm looked at the slice of cake in her hand. It seemed to shimmer in the faint light. "What?"

"Open wide."

"Now?" he asked.

Tasha pouted her lip. "Please."

"Fine." He licked his lips then opened his mouth.

"You're going to love this, sweetie." She slipped the wedge into his mouth. A salty taste marred the rich chocolate's flavor. It felt dry against his tongue.

She never could cook, he mused as Tasha pushed the entire piece into his mouth, coating his lips in icing.

"There." She coaxed his mouth shut around the enormous bite then clamped her hand across his lips.

Malcolm coughed as he tried not choke. The cake's texture grew drier, and the sweet tastes soured.

Holding his mouth and hands tight, Tasha continued her thrusting onto him. The air seemed to warble and shift around them. Long wings emerged from the gloom above her, stretching from Tasha's back.

Her breaths grew harder, and suddenly, the room was gone. Malcolm was pinned down beneath the succubus, and she worked herself onto his painfully swollen cock. He tried to scream, but the filthy sock in his mouth muffled the cry. Quentin's sticky blood coated her body where she had rubbed against him, except her nipples where Malcolm had sucked it off. The cuts in Vimiya's cheek were gone, healed by the essence she had already drained from him.

Malcolm fought and bucked beneath her but couldn't escape. The forgotten ache of his over-full stomach had returned. The urge to retch grew worse with each movement. If he puked with the gag in, he could choke on Quentin's remains. She kept riding him, her pelvic bone jarring painfully into him with each drop, and Malcolm felt the energy of his body draining to his crotch.

"Give it to me," she sneered. "I want you all."

Malcolm's breaths quickened, growing desperate as she worked him toward climax. The stink of pure lust repulsed and excited him even further. Bile and Quentin's blood burned up his throat.

Vimiya pounded harder, faster, pulling more of his essence. Tears welled in Malcolm's eyes. He had to resist. Had to—

The orgasm hit like a thunderbolt. He shuddered and writhed in excruciating pleasure as he pumped his life energy into her. It was like a suction drawing everything from his toes to his eyes down electric paths and into her.

Malcolm's vision faded. All he could see were her hateful, violet-gold eyes. He felt heavy, but still, she milked him. Arching his back, eyes scrunched, he screamed as she wrenched the energy from him.

"You like that?" she asked, and then he fell from consciousness.

CHAPTER 18

A squat, fluffy dog charged, yipping, as Gulmet swung over an old picket fence into a back yard, an amused smile on his lips. Fearless, it hopped and barked, angry he was in its territory. A low growl rumbled in Gulmet's throat, and the dog ran away, piss dribbling. It scurried under a dark porch and hid.

Satisfied, he glanced at the house whose yard he'd entered. A woman sat behind the window, her back exposed and watching a television. No one paid attention anymore. Begrudgingly, he admitted the succubus was correct. Mortals no longer feared predators in the night. Hunting was so easy now.

When Gulmet had returned to Malcolm's body, he'd found the mortal drained to near death. He'd had to feed on Quentin's cold remains to heal, like some low-born carrion-eater. A fresh kill could empower him even more, replenish all that she'd stolen. He could kill this woman, taste her blood and fear. But no. He had more important matters at hand. The woman and her brave, idiot dog could wait.

He looked up, searching the night sky for Vimiya. Could she see him now as he contemplated breaking her orders? Matt's blood compass could detect up to one hundred yards. She was far higher than that, he guessed.

Gulmet crossed the yard and swung himself over an ivy-coated chain-link into the neighboring one. Crouching, he skirted a vegetable garden and stopped behind an old clothesline post, its arms buried beneath potted plants. The modest house appeared still. Light shone through sun-faded blinds in one room. The rest of the windows appeared dark save a green glow in the kitchen. Maggie always did go to bed early.

Staying low, he crept closer, stopping beneath a tree. He listened. Insects, the hollow chinks of the neighbor's wind chime, cars on a nearby street, a dog's distant barking. The voodoo queen's house was silent.

Malcolm could only pray the old priestess wasn't home. But where else would she be? After the shotgun incident, Mister Alpuente had stayed there, refusing to be at his home until Malcolm was gone. Was he still here? Malcolm hoped Alpuente had gone back and that Maggie was staying somewhere else, though he didn't dare think it aloud. The air conditioner clicked and whirred to life, dashing any hope that she wasn't there.

He moved to the narrow porch and peeked through the kitchen window. Empty. Gulmet removed the key hidden beneath a square pot and carefully unlocked the back door. Metal rasped as he eased the door open and stepped inside.

Vimiya's instructions were to kill everyone who knew of Gulmet's existence. While Gulmet had urged that they move against Matt and Atabei first, the torment that the old woman's death would cause for Malcolm enticed him to agree.

Excitement priming his muscles, he silently moved through the house, checking each room in turn. The guest room was empty, no sign of Alpuente's things. Gulmet's disappointment nearly overwhelmed Malcolm's sense of relief.

The feelings were short-lived as he turned and moved toward Maggie's door, light peeking out beneath it. Licking his lip, Gulmet touched the knob, and then cracked it open.

Empty.

The bed was still made. Gulmet eyed the floor lamp standing beside the curtained window. Where was she?

Eyes narrowing, he retreated back into the dim hallway and checked the bathroom. Her toothbrush holder was empty.

Malcolm fought back the urge to taunt his captor. Best he let the demon forget he was there, keep his guard lowered.

Jaw tight with anger, he sniffed the air. Beneath the stink of cleaners and food, Gulmet caught a familiar citrus scent.

"Tasha." He tightened his fists. Matt had guessed his move, but how? Their assumption he'd be watching Atabei's house was why Vimiya was saving it for last. And if he was watching Maggie's, where was he?

Fear tingled in his gut, too faint for him to really notice, but Malcolm felt it. Matt had been an accomplished solo hunter years before his Valducan training. If anyone was going to stop him, it'd be Matt.

Gulmet moved back toward the kitchen, about to flee when he spotted something he hadn't noticed before. A black, tubular camera rested on a shelf, peeking out from behind a clutter of framed photographs.

No, Matt wasn't here now. But he was coming. Gulmet smiled. Tonight, Rajik would be avenged.

He stepped out the back of the house and looked skyward. Thrusting one hand in the air, Gulmet pointed his index finger like a gun and moved his thumb like a firing hammer. A shadow darted across the sky, momentarily silhouetted against a cloud, then gone. Vimiya's scheming had prepared them for this, of course. Now, they just needed to lure their prey into the trap.

The all-too-familiar rush of adrenaline returned. No more stalking helpless mortals. This was an Oppressor. Gulmet hopped the neighboring fence and hurried away. He reached the street and stopped behind a decrepit van.

Malcolm felt the mental reigns loosen but didn't risk trying to take control yet. He'd only have one chance, if that. No need to risk it.

Five minutes later, a dark blue car turned up the street and flipped off its headlights. It slowed and stopped one house before Maggie's. Even through the tinted glass, Gulmet could see Matt inside it, wearing a low baseball cap. He'd switched cars.

Matt stepped out, eyes fixed on the house. The light reflected off the bottle in his hand. His other hid inside a brown paper bag at his side. A new satchel hung from his shoulder, the strap tight across his chest. He glanced at the compass, looked around, and then moved toward the house.

Gulmet watched him circle around to the back, staying

clear of the neighbor's porch light. Matt moved with a soldier's grace, smooth and silent, the bagged gun automatically tracking between potential hiding places. The hunter's training was so ingrained he probably didn't even think about it anymore.

Once Matt had vanished behind the house, the mental reins tightened again. Gulmet hurried away, stopping another block from the house and waited.

A moment later, Matt hurried out the front door, compass before him. He searched the street.

Gulmet stepped out from the shadows and stopped. Their eyes met. Matt's arm tightened on the gun, but as Gulmet had expected, he didn't raise it. Too far, too out in the open for a shooting. He smiled. "*Chase me.*" He wheeled and ran.

Gulmet raced down the block and turned at the next street. Vimiya leaned against a telephone pole ahead, casually watching him approach, like she'd been waiting there all night. The mental hold loosened. Blocks behind him, if he was still in range, Matt would see the red bead vanish.

"He's coming?" Vimiya asked.

"Yes."

"I'll prepare the site." She looked off into the distance. "Run him around. Wear him out." Without another word, she strode off down a darkened path between a pair of houses.

Gulmet continued down the street. Behind him, he heard the sound of beating wings. Malcolm fought the urge to look back, refusing to exert any control until necessary. Until then, he was the casual passenger. Gulmet hurried across the street and stopped beside a low, brick wall draped in flowery vines.

Matt slinked around the corner ahead, visible for an instant in the lights of a passing car. He glanced at the compass and peered around. He moved up behind a row of parked cars and lowered from sight.

Wondering if his hold was strong enough to summon the blood bead, Gulmet strengthened his control of Malcolm. Matt didn't step out. Narrowing his eyes, Gulmet searched the shadows. A dark shape slithered beneath a pickup, gun pointing his direction. Gulmet dropped behind the wall as the shot rang. Bits of leaves and flowers blew out over him. Laughing at the brush of death, Gulmet scrambled away and ran.

Weaving between cars and posts, Gulmet sprinted half a block and leaped over a fence and through a yard. Sweat slicked his skin. His heart pounded with the almost long-forgotten thrill of the chase. Oh, he was going to lead this hunter, going to push how close he could come to feeling that cursed bullet, make Matt think he had a chance then deny it. Urakael would die as Matt watched, sweetening the fear.

Jumping another fence, he came out behind a squat convenience store and waited. Once he'd estimated enough time for Matt to find the trail, Gulmet relaxed his control to a minimum and urged Malcolm on.

He hurried down the alley behind the shop and into a weedy vacant lot. He crouched beneath a crop of thin-trunked trees and watched as mosquitoes buzzed around.

Two minutes later, Matt strolled up the streets ahead. He'd discarded the baseball cap and brown bag, his hand now inside the bulging satchel. He scanned the street ahead of him, repeatedly glancing at the bottle before him. Matt stopped just outside the fluorescent glow from the gas station's lights and looked around. His eyes passed over Gulmet's hiding place without response. He checked the compass again. His chest rose and fell with a deep breath, and Matt continued on.

Once Matt had passed out of sight, Gulmet rose from his hiding place and followed. He spotted the hunter at an intersection, looking around as if trying to decide his next move. Shoulders back, Matt looked every part the Hollywood lone gunman.

Gulmet strengthened his hold of Malcolm, sliding into his flesh like a familiar and snug glove. Matt started across the street but stopped and spun. Their eyes met, then Gulmet turned and ran. He raced across the next street then charged through yards and across driveways. He hopped a fence. Dogs barked, but he ignored them and leaped over into the next yard before the enraged animals could give chase.

He stopped near an empty playground and waited, allowing Matt a chance to catch up. Across the park, a group of teens talked and laughed on a set of rusty bleachers. Police sirens wailed some blocks away. Gulmet assumed they were headed to where Matt had fired the gun, but they continued past it.

Once he'd guessed Matt would be close enough, Gulmet started across the park. Something moved in the shadows to the right. Glancing over, he spotted Matt's shape moving between trees, closing in.

"Clever."

Gulmet bolted the other direction, toward the pack of teens. Matt wouldn't take the shot with them in the line of fire. A wiry boy in a gray tank top slapped his friend on the arm and pointed as Gulmet charged toward them with inhuman speed. Gulmet hurdled the low fence separating them, and the teens scattered out of his way. The cover gone, Malcolm expected to feel the bullet between his shoulders, but it didn't come. The metal bleachers pinged as Gulmet ran up and over the four rows and raced away.

Once out of the park, Gulmet led Matt deeper into residential areas, careful to loosen and tighten his control of Malcolm to keep Matt moving in circles. Gulmet never stopped moving, not allowing Matt another chance to circle around him. The hunter had nearly taken him, and the thrill of that close escape excited Gulmet even more.

Playing cat and mouse, Gulmet headed east. Houses gave way to dark and corroded steel buildings. Long shadows cast from the few working streetlights, crossing the narrow streets, making it even harder to see than if there were none at all. It stank of diesel and burnt tar.

Gulmet jogged deeper into the maze of warehouses and factories, past graffiti-coated loading dock shutters and stacks of rotting pallets. Finally, he came to a sheet metal fence. The sliding gate stood open a crack, its padlocked chain hanging broken. Vimiya's work.

Glancing back, the streets appeared empty. But he knew Matt was there somewhere, Dämoren out, closing in. With a smile, Gulmet slipped though the gap and into a wide gravel area. Rusted heaps of scrap metal and stacked poles filled the lot, some standing over ten feet high.

Broken security cameras looked down from the three large

buildings walling off the yard. He searched the sky for Vimiya but couldn't see her. The skeletal frame of a crane arm loomed above. A perfect roost. Gulmet hoped she'd disabled everything in time. They had all night with their prey. Then tomorrow, workers could arrive to find the shredded remains.

Gravel crunched as he crossed the yard. A dusty blue flatbed rested on the far end beside the rear buildings. He leaped onto the top then up onto the metal awning that stretched along the building's face, the scrap yard's name blazoned across the tin in blocky letters. With one final jump, Gulmet grabbed the roof lip and pulled himself up. A dozen box cars littered the train yard just beyond the building. Beyond it, a steep levee wall ran alongside the far canal. Keeping low to hide his silhouette, Gulmet loosened his hold of Malcolm and crouched on the far side of the ridge behind a satellite dish.

A minute later, Matt's head peeked through the open gate. He looked around then quickly sidestepped in. Pistol drawn, he moved through the yard, eyes searching as he passed each pile.

Gulmet smiled, seeing the hunter's tight lips, the mounting paranoia. *"That's right. You saw me enter. There's no exit. Where am I, Matt?"* By now, the compass' range had diminished by half. Gulmet doubted it would sense him at this distance even if he took flesh-form.

Something pinged on one side of the yard. Matt swung Dämoren around and started toward it. Once he'd reached the open area, a dark shape dove from the darkened sky behind him like a giant hawk.

Gulmet grinned, his mind focused on the moment to come.

Seizing the opening, Malcolm took control and stepped from the shadows. He pointed to the sky. "Behind you!"

Gulmet wrenched control back. Instantly, bones stretched and popped. *"Damn you!"*

Matt fired and spun to face the swooping succubus.

Dämoren's slug slammed into Malcolm's gut. He doubled over. The blessed silver burned like molten steel. Blood hissed from the bullet hole, and the freshly grown hairs around it thinned, but it wasn't enough to stop the transformation.

Vimiya shrieked and screamed. Another shot boomed,

echoing off the building walls. Gulmet looked up to see Matt on his back, pistol raised, and the succubus flapping away.

Gulmet's clothes tightened and tore like tissue. He rose, his claws clacking on the metal roof.

Matt looked up at the sound. On his back and upside down, he raised the gun and fired.

Gulmet ducked as the bullet whizzed past. Injured and alone, trying to take the gunman would be suicide. He clambered to the rear edge of the roof and dropped, landing in an overgrown rock pile butted up against the back of the building. The fall couldn't hurt him, but the sudden jolt shot pain though the bullet wound. Silver slugs he'd felt before. Feeding would push them out as he healed. But Dämoren's bullet burned differently, twisting inside him like a live thing made of embers. Rolling to his feet, he hurried toward the rows of tracks, one claw clutched across his bleeding stomach.

He hobbled behind a pair of box cars and let out a pained wheeze. A pale, bald patch surrounded the wound, nearly five inches across. His hold of Malcolm was slipping. Even now, he felt the mortal thrashing inside his mind, struggling to evict him. *"Need to dig it out."*

Gnashing his teeth, he slid a claw into the hole, fishing for it. The pain was unlike any he'd felt. Before, it was merely sensation of his body, but the agony the bullet gave was real. He hissed hard breaths as he probed deeper. He just needed to hook it out.

"You!" Vimiya shrieked from above, slamming into him.

Gulmet fell against the jagged rocks. He moved to turn, but the succubus seized the back of his head and bashed it against the train wheel.

"How dare you betray me!" Her grip tightened to smash his head again, but Gulmet grabbed her wrist and wrenched her over his shoulder.

"It wasn't me," he panted. "The mortal took control. He warned Matt."

Vimiya's narrowed eyes stared hatefully from behind her black hair. "You idiot," she spat. Blood oozed down her leg from a deep gash in her hip. A bullet hole perforated the apex of one wing. "You lost control?"

"Apologies, Mistress, I—"

She sprang, her claws reaching for his throat. He fell backward, the succubus on him. They rolled across the gravel, snarling and thrashing.

The bullet burned with each movement. Gulmet clutched her wrists, desperately pulling them away. Vimiya's claws raked his skin.

"I should have killed you when we met!" she hissed, her face contorted with rage. Vimiya flapped her wings, giving a boost as she wrenched herself on top of him. "Useless." She drove her weight down, grabbing Gulmet's neck. Her iron-like fingers squeezed, claws breaking skin, threatening to tear out his throat. She grinned wickedly down, a drop of spittle on her lips.

The side of Vimiya's head exploded, spraying brains and blood. Purple fire erupted from the hole as the shot's report echoed though the train yard. She fell limp. Her outstretched wings came down around her like a spidery parachute.

Gulmet heaved the flaming corpse off him and looked up to see Matt atop the scrap yard building, gun before him. Light from the burning blood along Dämoren's blade flickered across the hunter's face. Orange flashed.

The shot took Gulmet in the side.

His flesh-form dissolving, Gulmet scrambled back for the cover of the box cars as a third shot pinged off the white rocks beside him. The twin slugs seared his insides as he ran, stumbling alongside the cars. His vessel was dying, and if he was in it when it happened, he would die with it. The thirty feet from the roof to the train yard would be too far for Matt to jump. Gulmet just needed to get away long enough to move bodies.

Reaching the end of the line of train cars, Gulmet raced across the open ground past the other tracks to where more cars rested. The pads of his feet had already dissolved to human, and the sharp rocks stung his bare soles. He expected to feel the bullet hit his back, but it never came. *"I must be out of range."* Gulmet reached the row of still cars and dove though the hitched gap to safety.

Panting, his body panged with each breath. Gulmet stopped

behind a spray-painted cattle car and allowed his flesh-form to return to human.

Malcolm's knees buckled as the demon's weight lifted away. The burning pain of the blessed slugs dimmed, feeling numb in comparison to how they'd hurt before. He gasped and pressed his arm against the hole in his side, and his hand across the caked belly wound. Wisps of Vimiya's fiery blood still burned along his chest and ragged shirt. Malcolm tried to wipe them off, but they only smeared, their light faded.

He was dying. The demon knew it too. It'd left him here to bleed out. "Good shot, Matt." Malcolm coughed.

A soft breeze coursed down the valley of tracks, cooling his sweat-soaked skin. He brushed the hair from his face to feel it on his forehead. Malcolm smiled. He had done that. Ever since Atabei had cursed him, he'd never had full control of anything. Now, as he died, he had it back. He could make his own decisions, think his own thoughts.

His mind wandered to Hounacier. Did she miss him? Was Atabei treating her well? *I want to see her*, he thought. *One last time.*

Wincing, Malcolm pulled himself up and started walking. Atabei's house was only a few short blocks across the canal. He clutched his wounds and started toward the drawbridge only a hundred yards away. His death was inevitable. Dämoren's bullets had seen to that. Removing them might save him, but Gulmet would only take him again. If he was going to die, Malcolm was going to express his newfound freedom the only way he could. He would die by Hounacier. He could make that walk, and if he couldn't, he'd at least die trying.

Malcolm staggered over the rocks but managed to find momentum. He didn't look up, just one foot in front of the other. He could make it. Car noise hummed ahead, growing closer.

The bleeding seemed to have slowed. At least the jelly-like clumps had stopped growing as fast. But the external bleeding was only a small part, and he tried not to think of the blood and fluids pouring all though his shredded insides. Probably why he was so thirsty.

Before he knew it, he'd reached the trash-strewn underpass.

It stank of smoke and piss and cigarettes. Grimy faces watched him from the shadows. He continued though, pretending he couldn't see them.

"Malcolm."

He looked up, seeing a bearded man in a threadbare T-shirt hobbling toward him.

The stranger held up a hand. "Malcolm, wait."

"I can't," Malcolm said to the unknown loa.

Another figure stepped out from behind one of the square, concrete pillars. He popped a lens from a plastic pair of sunglasses and put them on. "Milky, you're hurtin'."

Malcolm met Papa Ghede's single eye. "I'm going to Hounacier then to Ulises."

"Who did this to you?" the first loa asked. Malcolm now recognized Legba's lilting accent. "We can help."

"Atabei." Malcolm shook his head. "And you can't."

"We can help you," Ghede pleaded.

Malcolm kept walking. Reaching the opposite side of the underpass, he started up the slope. He looked back at the two loa still standing there. "Goodbye."

Legba said something after him, but the rumble of traffic drowned it out.

Malcolm clenched his teeth and followed the footpath up to the bridge. Cars raced past, their lights blinding. He crawled over the low concrete wall onto the road and started across, the oncoming cars to his back. They whooshed past, not even slowing. He must have made a pitiful sight, barefoot in shredded, filthy clothes, hobbling along the foot-wide shoulder. The thirst was worsening, but he continued, one foot in front of the other. He still expected to feel the next bullet come—maybe he wouldn't even feel it—but it didn't. He crossed the dark canal and over into the Ninth Ward.

Once finally reaching the bottom, he looked back, but Matt wasn't there. Didn't matter anyway.

He'd made it halfway to Atabei's now, and faint renewal sparked in his tired legs. He could make it. He could see Hounacier one last time. "Kuquo," he muttered, speaking her name for the first time.

The streets off the main road were dark. The gut shot had started bleeding again, running down Malcolm's leg. He walked, barely noticing his surroundings. He should, he thought. This was the last street he'd ever see. He should take it in, but he couldn't. Instead, he thought of how much he wished he could thank Jim for taking him in, tell Maggie goodbye, and thank Matt for getting Maggie and Alpuente out of that house and also for setting him free. Most of all, he wished he had bothered to tell Tasha how much he still loved her, how much he regretted breaking her heart when he left and how he hoped she might forgive him one day. Soon, he'd meet Bondye, God. He'd meet Ulises beyond the crossroads and apologize for being such a poor son. He'd see Colin, Marcus, Ben, and so many friends now gone, so many he'd had to kill. He hoped they forgave him.

Faint drumming worked into his consciousness as he drew closer. Malcolm looked up to see smoke rising from behind Atabei's fenced block ahead. From the sounds of it, the priestess had company. *At least I get to crash one final party.* He smiled at the dumb joke.

He shuffled across the street and followed the earthen path that served as the sidewalk around to Atabei's castle-like home. Whoops and shouts accompanied the rapid drums beyond the high fence. A single yellow light burned above a door beside the car gate. Malcolm stopped, rose to the highest he could, and knocked.

Metal rattled, and the door cracked open. Sadie peered out, and her narrow-spaced eyes widened.

Malcolm slid a foot though the gate door before she could slam it shut. "I want to see Atabei."

The chubby woman stepped back, mouth open, then ran. "Mama Atabei! It's here, Mama Atabei!" The drums faltered then stopped.

Malcolm pushed his way through. Figures stood silhouetted against a high fire beside the carved post. Many rose from a row of benches to one side while others sat and watched Malcolm's slow approach.

Sogbo and Bade stood far to the side, leashed to a post, watching. Maybe they still remembered the monster they'd seen and wouldn't bark. The crowd parted as he neared, and Atabei stood at the heart of the ring, firelight flickering across her white dress and glinting off Hounacier's blade in her hand.

Malcolm squinted, smoke stinging his eyes. "I'm ready."

"He killed Peewee," a woman said.

Atabei's cold eyes watched him near. She raised the machete beside her, standing proud, but Malcolm only watched the blade. He should have felt hatred for her, but he couldn't. All he felt was the joy of seeing Hounacier again.

The worshipers peeled away from their circle, moving behind Atabei.

Malcolm stopped at the edge of the chalk-drawn ring. "Do it," he coughed, his eyes still on the machete. "Set me free." Then he whispered, "Kuquo."

"So you admit I am Hounacier's master?" she asked, taking a step.

"I admit she is no longer mine. But no one is her master."

Her lips drew into a satisfied sneer. "Kneel, demon."

Malcolm stood tall, his knees threatening to buckle. He would not kneel for her. He lowered the hand from his gut, letting the blood flow. It didn't matter now.

Atabei stepped closer and raised the machete high. A drum began beating, followed by another. Malcolm lifted his chin, readying for the blow.

"This is for Hercule!" She swung. Hounacier's blade stopped a foot from Malcolm's neck as if it had hit a tree trunk. It quivered, resisting her the way it resisted him when giving a blessing. She took it in both hands, fighting the blade, pushing it toward him.

In that moment, Malcolm realized his mistake. Hounacier had never renounced him. She hadn't broken the bond. Gulmet had hidden it from his mind. She loved him still and fought against killing him. The demon's deception had worked. Somewhere deep inside, he heard Gulmet's laughter.

Malcolm found his anger.

Atabei swung the machete again. The blade slowed but came down. Malcolm tried to move but fell back onto the packed ground. In a frustrated grunt, she thrust down at him.

The blade bent, missing his heart, but still bit into his left arm.

Malcolm cried out. He tried to crawl away on his back, but he was too weak. If Hounacier still loved him, then there was hope, but he couldn't make himself move. Darkness wormed at the edges of his vision. He'd lost.

Atabei screamed, raising the blade point down, ready to drive it into him.

An engine roared.

The priestess stumbled back as a blue flat-bed pickup smashed though the perimeter fence, its headlights cutting twin beams through the smoky yard. The truck's doors flew open, and the homeless Papa Ghede hopped out, laughing like a madman, followed by Legba. Matt swung from the driver's seat, Dämoren in one hand and the Mac-10 slung over his shoulder. He leveled the machine pistol at the white Lexus twenty feet beside him. A foot-long flame spewed from the barrel in a loud rip.

Screams erupted as the worshipers, even Atabei, scattered.

Matt strode across the emptying yard, smoking Mac-10 leveled before him, and Dämoren trained on Malcolm.

"There you are, Milky," Ghede said, sauntering up. "You ran away."

Legba came around the side and knelt beside Malcolm. Sores pitted the homeless man's cheeks and forehead. "He is weak. We haven't much time."

"Hounacier ..." Malcolm mumbled.

"He's dying," Matt said. "He's in pain."

The firelight reflected in Ghede's single lens. "Pain tells us we're alive."

Malcolm blinked, trying to focus on Matt. "The bond ... still there."

"We can save him," Legba said. "But we must go."

"Spencer, you get him in the truck." Ghede rose to his feet and hurried off. "I'll get the mask."

CHAPTER 19

"You sure this will hold him?" Matt asked, tightening Sogbo's leather collar around Malcolm's wrists.

"He ain't going nowhere." Papa Legba scratched the now docile Rottweiler behind the ear. "Is he, boy?"

Malcolm grunted in pain as Matt heaved him up into the truck's cab and moved him into a sitting position on the bench seat. The engine still rumbled. He looked up to see Ghede prancing out Atabei's back door and down the steps, bottle in one hand, silver wolf mask in the other.

"I got 'em," he said, grinning.

"That's not the ghoul mask," Matt said.

"Don't need it. Don't worry, Spence, ain't like it can walk away."

"What if she takes it?"

"Then we'll know where to find it." Ghede grinned. "Stop worryin' about it."

Papa Legba snapped his fingers and pointed to Bade, still chained across the yard. "Go." Sogbo ran where the loa ordered. Legba turned to Matt. "You too. The others should be there by now. I'll go to prepare." His eyes rolled back. He staggered back, nearly falling. Shaking his head, he looked around. "Where...?"

"Go on home, Jeffrey," Ghede said.

The man looked up to see Malcolm bound and bleeding in the truck. Then his gaze locked on Matt's gun. "Shit!"

Ghede laughed as the man ran away. "And stop stealing

Tishaun's smokes!" He swigged his rum and turned to Matt. "Get in. I'll drive."

"Where are we taking him?" Matt asked.

"The crossroads. Get in." He ran around to the driver's side and climbed up into the seat beside Malcolm. He reeked of body odor.

Matt squeezed into the passenger seat on the other side. He held Dämoren across his lap, pointed at Malcolm. "Don't try anything."

Malcolm eyed at the gun and snorted. "Don't ... worry ... about me." He rolled his head toward Ghede. "Can ... you drive?"

Grinning, the loa took the wheel. "Never had to before."

"Wait," Matt said, his voice rising an octave. "You can't—"

Papa Ghede threw the truck into reverse and slammed the accelerator. Malcolm jolted forward, nearly coming out of his seat as the truck bounced over the broken fence and into the street. Papa Ghede cackled in unbridled joy as he wrenched the wheel around and mashed the brakes. "Hold on!"

Malcolm pressed his weak legs against the floorboard as the loa found the gear, hit the gas, and took off down the dark streets. His sweat-slicked hair whipped in the wind from the open windows.

"Jesus!" Matt fought with his seatbelt, trying to buckle it one-handed.

"Not quite," Ghede said. Tires squealed as he slung the truck around a hard turn and clipped a mailbox. He wrestled with the wheel, jerking them side to side, before leveling out and continuing on. "Lucky we found you, Milky. Why'd you leave?"

"I ... I didn't know Hounacier still loved me."

"'Course she loves you. Till death do you part, and the baron hasn't come for you yet. But he will unless we get you to him first."

"Baron Samedi?"

"He's the only one that can save your life." Papa Ghede knocked back his rum, spilling some down his chin. "But you have to save your soul."

Malcolm nodded absently, unsure what the loa meant. "Why... didn't you get Hounacier ... from ... Atabei?"

"Why?" Papa Ghede shot an insulted glare. "You're her husband." He shook his head and laughed. "That's your job."

"Will you watch the road?" Matt hissed, clutching the handle above the door.

"Don't worry, Spence." He hooked a right onto Claiborne. A car horn blared, the driver's mouth an angry "O."

Ghede thrust his head out the open window and yelled back, "You watch that mouth, Timothy, or I'll tell your mama about what's hidden in your closet!" He laughed.

Malcolm watched his bound hands in his lap, not wanting to see the road. Fresh blood pooled in the nook of his wrist. If Dämoren's bullets didn't kill him, the loa's driving surely would. He imagined the police response to that wreck. Stolen truck, homeless drunk at the wheel, Malcolm's hands bound with two silver bullets in him, Matt with an antique revolver and a machine gun. Headline material if there ever was.

"Now, as I was saying, don't worry. I'll get you home to Luiza before her titties get all plump."

"What?" Matt asked.

"Her titties." The truck started the incline up the bridge.

"How do you know all this? How did you know she's pregnant?"

The loa roared with laughter. He leaned down, his face close enough to bathe Malcolm in rum-soaked breath. "Oh, he's fun. You never told him about Papa Ghede?"

"Sorry," Malcolm mumbled. Darkness worked at the edges of his vision.

"Milky and I go way back. I was there when he met his lady."

Malcolm's head sank lower. The roar of the wind and traffic grew distant.

"Why do you keep calling him that?"

"Why don't you, Spencer Mallory?"

Malcolm closed his heavy eyelids.

"That's not my name anymore?"

"Your name is your name," Papa Ghede chuckled. "That reminds me of ..."

A cool numbness rolled up Malcolm's body like sliding into a still, black sea ... floating ... the shore growing distant, its lights sinking below the horizon.

"Malcolm!" Ghede screamed in his ear.

Malcolm bolted upright, eyes wide.

Ghede shook his head, his single visible eye narrow. "Don't you be doin' that. We're too close now."

Licking his lips, Malcolm looked out the window. *How long was I out?* They were barreling toward the I10. Matt watched him with hard eyes, his jaw tight. He looked terrified, and Malcolm didn't blame him. "I'm sorry ... about attacking you. It wasn't ... in control. I didn't even know it, and when I did ... I couldn't stop it."

Matt just looked at him. "Are you in control now?"

"Yes."

"Are you sure?"

Malcolm's lips parted to answer, but he looked away. "No."

"Move!" Papa Ghede shouted, blaring the horn as he ran a red light. They shot up the on ramp and onto the highway. "Now we're movin'." He slapped the wheel like a child with a drum.

Still not wanting to see the road, Malcolm focused hard on the dash before him. How had he been so fooled into thinking Hounacier had broken her bond? He should have known. If he had, he'd ... what? What could he have done? The demon had controlled every move he'd made since it'd taken him. *No, not every move.* He'd taken control. If he'd known, Malcolm could have fought Gulmet harder. Hounacier still loved him. Malcolm had to live.

Ghede was yammering away about tits and laughing at his own jokes. Malcolm kept his eyes on the dash, ignoring him, and trying to keep his breath steady. Finally, Ghede hung a hard turn onto Jackson, and Malcolm realized where they were going.

A few blocks later, they turned onto a narrow street. The stained-glass windows of Saints of Light Church were dark, but nearly twenty cars filled the little lot. Figures hurried in and out the gymnasium doors, silhouetted by the lights inside.

"Looks like they're here." Ghede pulled into the gravel drive and slid to a stop beside a police car. "Family reunion, Milky." He mashed the horn. "He's here!"

People rushed to the truck as Matt and Ghede stepped out. Malcolm felt more than saw the hands pull him from the seat. He tried to stand, but his legs wouldn't move. Everything slipped and warbled in and out of focus.

"Get him inside," a man said. It took a moment before Malcolm realized it was Earl Warren, shirtless and in jeans.

Arms cradled from either side as they carried him on his back toward the door. Drums and voices sounded from within. Malcolm lifted his chin to his chest, trying to see. Between his bare feet and the moving bodies all around him, he saw the doors open wide into a large room lit with candles.

"Bring him to me," a voice boomed.

The figures parted, revealing a giant man in a top hat and long tuxedo jacket. A thick cigar smoldered between grinning teeth. Baron Samedi.

"Set him down," the baron ordered.

The carriers lowered Malcolm to a dirt floor. The baron knelt beside him and leaned close. It was Jim Luison, but there was nothing about Malcolm's old friend in those piercing eyes. He plucked the cigar from his lips and smiled. "Malcolm Romero," he cooed, smoke curling from his mouth. "Long time."

"Baron," Malcolm mumbled.

Baron Samedi leaned close and sniffed, his nostrils flaring wide. "You got death on you, Malcolm." He inhaled again. "But your soul is cursed. I can help your body," he sucked the cigar. "But I can't remove the curse. Do you want to live?"

"Y ... yes."

"It ain't free, Malcolm. You willin' to pay the price?"

Malcolm nodded.

The baron smiled. "You gotta say it, Doctor."

"Yes."

"Good." He looked to the side. "Do it. Quickly!"

A goat bleated nearby, followed by shuffling movement. The drumbeats grew louder.

"That's right," Baron Samedi said. "Good. Bring it here."

He accepted a shallow bowl and lifted Malcolm's head. "Drink this."

The smell of blood tickled Malcolm's senses before he saw it. Hunger awoke deep inside him as the baron urged his lips to the rim.

"Drink it."

It was hot. The salty, metallic taste flooded his mouth. Repulsed, he wanted to gag, but was too weak to fight the sudden primal urge. The heat flowed down his throat with each shallow swallow, spreading through his veins.

Malcolm gasped and choked on the blood as the numbness washed away. The sounds of drums and voices exploded in his ears. The scrapes and even Hounacier's cut mended. New blood belched from the bullet wounds as Dämoren's twin slugs burned with renewed fire.

Baron Samedi drew the bowl away before Malcolm's writhing could spill it.

Malcolm twisted as the bullets seared his renewed organs. "Burns!"

"Hold still," the baron ordered, pressing him down with a huge hand. With his other, he traced the bleeding gut wound then rammed his fingers into the hole.

Malcolm screamed, but the firm hand pressed him in place. The baron grinned around his cigar. "There it is." He withdrew a steaming, deformed slug. Crimson lines of blood marked its etched surface. He eyed it appreciatively then dropped it on the ground. Accepting the bowl from outstretched hands, he lifted Malcolm's head. "Drink."

Again, the healing waves rushed down Malcolm's throat. This time, he could sense the power inside it, not unlike the power Gulmet tasted in his victims' terror but different. Heat surged into the remaining slug. Malcolm fought back a scream.

Handing off the bowl, Baron Samedi rolled Malcolm onto his side. Again, he traced around the hole and then plunged his fingers inside.

Malcolm wailed, feeling the think fingers burrowing deep, the nails raking his inside as the inched toward the searing hot bullet.

"Here we are." The fingers thrust deeper then withdrew, taking the slug with them. He rolled Malcolm over and pushed the bowl again to his lips. "Drink."

Greedily, Malcolm gulped the blood down, savoring the warm power. The baron raised it higher, letting him have all that was inside. It ran at the corners of his mouth, down his cheeks and onto his neck and ears.

"There." The baron set the bowl down and smiled. Withdrawing the cigar, he tapped the clump of ash from the tip.

His vision clear, Malcolm realized it was Maggie kneeling beside him who had brought the bowl of goat's blood. Her lips were flat and emotionless. A hard sadness marred her eyes. Most of the other faces he also recognized as priests and priestesses throughout the city, many he hadn't seen in years.

A stickly thin man with a trimmed goatee and a white straw hat stood behind Maggie, leaning on a cane. He gave Papa Legba's elegant smile. "Now for your part, Doctor."

A gun clicked. The crowd parted, and Matt stood at Malcolm's feet, Dämoren trained on him. Now that he was healed, Gulmet could seize him at will.

"Take him to the crossroads," Legba ordered.

Hands whipped down from above him. Malcolm caught the glint of silver; then a slender, metal chain wrapped his throat. The drums began to thump with a slow cadence as the followers lifted Malcolm and carried him.

In the heart of the room, loa slowly circled within an elaborate ring of white dust on the floor, a small gap on one end. A dark, polished pole stood at the circle's heard. Tasha was among them, a bright scarf of red, gold, and blue about her head, but it wasn't Tasha. Erzulie had taken her.

They carried Malcolm into the ring and stood him against the pole. They lashed his ankles and tied his wrists above his head, cinching them tight. The drums' loud pulse continued as the non-mounted left the incomplete circle. Then Papa Ghede stepped inside, the silver wolf mask in his hands.

He set it on the ground before him and met Malcolm's eye. His joviality was gone. "I believe in you, Milky. Make me proud."

Malcolm looked at the fearsome mask. "I can't."

"You better," the baron answered, stepping around him. "This is your part. And you still owe me a debt."

"I can't draw it out."

The baron gave a wide grin. "You better, because that," he pointed to Matt standing outside the ring, arms crossed across his chest, Dämoren in hand, "that there's the judge. He says if you live or die. Better make him happy, or I'll be digging your grave before sunrise."

The tight, silver chain dug into his neck as Malcolm shook his head. "I can't do it."

"We'll see." He puffed the cigar, and he turned back to where loa painted the circle closed. The drums quickened. "Oh ..." Baron Samedi looked back with that toothy smile. "I nearly forgot." He reached into his tuxedo jacket and withdrew a pair of ornate, silver pins. One looked like a dragonfly. The other, a flower of white stones. "These might help."

The baron reached up and drove one of the pins though Malcolm's left palm. Malcolm howled in pain, unable to escape as the needle slid all the way through his hand and buried into the pole.

Laughing, the baron pushed the other pin through Malcolm's right hand, nailing it to the wood. "Now, Malcolm," he roared over the rising drum beats. "Now *be* the groom." He drew a long puff and blew the smoke into Malcolm's face. "Win back your lady or *die*."

Malcolm scrunched his eyes, fighting the pain. Loa danced within the large ring, shimmying and twirling. Others, those not mounted, danced along the outer edge, staying clear of the gunman. To the side, clustered on benches, four drummers pounded out the rising beat. Corporal Duplessis was among them.

Swallowing, Malcolm tried to recall Atabei's chant. He'd replayed it countless times, but never could remember it. A tingle buzzed in his palms. Then he could see he her, hand outstretched, clearer than he could before. The silver. The silver piercing him was fighting Gulmet's influence back, protecting his memories. He tried to hear the words, focus on them, but all he could hear was the drumming around him.

"Mayas … notem … mreshti." He shook his head. "I can't."

"Yes, you can."

Malcolm lifted his gaze to see Tasha-Erzulie before him. She caressed his cheek. "I love you, Malcolm. Tasha loves you." Erzulie kissed him. An aura of pure love encased her, not like the succubus' lust but true and warm. "Come back to her."

"I don't know how," he pleaded. "I don't know the words."

"Don't know the words," Earl Warren shouted as he pulled Erzulie back. He wrapped an arm across her shoulder and clutched a black machete in his other hand. It was Ogoun. "I can't," he yelled in a mocking scowl. "Bullshit! You're a warrior. Be a warrior! Act! Do it!" Ogoun smiled and slid his hands over Tasha's body. She leaned back into him, writhing against his bare chest. He squeezed her breasts, and she gave an appreciative gasp. "Do it, Malcolm! Do it, or I fuck your woman."

Erzulie reached back behind his head and pulled his cheek to hers.

"She wants a *man*. A warrior."

"Fuck you," Malcolm spat.

Ogoun laughed, his eyes challenging. He pulled Erzulie away and stepped closed. "Then stop crying!" He slapped Malcolm with the flat of the machete. "You're no root-worker witch, you're husband of Hounacier." He slapped him again. "Bokor!" Ogoun slammed the machete into the pole, nicking Malcolm's raised arm. "Be the warrior!"

Malcolm glared into the loa's eyes, rage mounting.

"Good," Ogoun purred. He wrenched the blade from the post.

Malcolm held back the wince of pain. He felt the blood trickling down his tricep.

"Now do it." Ogoun twirled away, joining back into the throngs of circling loa.

Do it, Malcolm thought. *Do it.* Ogoun was right; Malcolm wasn't some two-bit sorcerer. Hounacier had chosen him because he was more. He had to prove her right. Closing his eyes, he replayed Atabei's chant above the werewolf. He couldn't remember the words but could see her lips. Malcolm focused on that memory, holding it tight. "Holloo … mreshti. Mayas … karri notem."

That was closer. Malcolm pushed aside everything, the pain, the bleeding cut, the drums, the shuffling feet. Matt watching him like the Angel of Death. He pushed it aside and focused on Atabei's lips, remembering himself mouthing the words with her. "Holloo mreshti. Mayas karri notem. Ohma ahsa … rae."

There! Something twisted inside him. Gulmet was here. He was fighting him. Malcolm had to be close.

"Holloo mreshti. Mayas karri notem. Ohma ahsa ah rae."

The demon bristled within him. The silver pins grew hot.

"You can't do it."

Malcolm ignored it. "Holloo mreshti. Mayas karri notem. Ohma ahsa ah rae."

"I'll kill you," Gulmet growled. *"I'll transform you, let that chain cut our throat."*

Do it. Matt will shoot you in the face the moment you show it.

The anger writhed, but Malcolm kept chanting. The demon's fear pushed him harder.

He continued the chant, his voice rising. The beating drums seemed to fall in line, matching his rhythm. The words flowed smoother. Malcolm released the image of Atabei and focused solely on the words.

A rush of wind ruffled his hair. Then a shudder rolled though him, bringing a sense of weightlessness. But there was a weight still. Something dense and heavy slid though his veins like tar. It thickened as Malcolm's chanting grew louder, becoming cold. The demon. He'd isolated it.

Reaching with his mind, Malcolm felt the coagulated energy at the tip of his toes and pulled it up. It moved hesitantly up his leg.

Excitement mounting, Malcolm pulled the demon's energy up from his other leg, but in the moment of losing concentration, it oozed back down his first. He caught it before it had escaped too far then pulled it back up, inching it in time with the drums' rhythm. Once he'd worked it up to his hip, Malcolm started on the next, keeping the roiling ball of cold energy from escaping. The wind howled in his ears, whipping around him like a cyclone.

He gathered it, joining the two balls as one. Malcolm allowed a grin of triumph. He could do this.

Lifting his head toward his hands, he started working the energy down from his fingers. Then his eyes opened a crack, and he gasped.

The wooden pole didn't end just above his hands but stretched, seeming forever upward, through the heart of a tornado, almost curving at the distant horizon. The wood was dry and gray, lined with deep cracks like some dead, barkless tree trunk or a giant fencepost alongside an ancient and forgotten highway. Thousands of spokes intercepted it, branching off into the cyclone's walls, each its own world, a different band of color. The rainbow serpent. Faint shapes moved along the bridges, some small, others larger than the largest whale. Malcolm couldn't tell if he were looking up or down, and his head spun with a sudden vertigo.

He looked away only to see the floor was gone. The pole descended eternally downward, studded with linking spokes. The circling loa no longer danced on any surface, but flew and spun around him like joyous angels. The edge of the ring had become a swirling wall of light, separating them from the world outside. Drummers drummed, and mortals danced, and Matt stood like a statue, pistol across his arm. But it wasn't Matt. He could see him, but there was another figure simultaneously in the same place. It was tall with icy blue skin over powerful muscles. Urakael. Its silver-black eyes seemed to register him, and Urakael smiled.

A figure stepped before him. He was old, his back hunched. Light glowed within his long beard. It was Papa Legba, but no longer the skinny man with the goatee. It was truly him. Wisdom shone in the loa's eyes like a physical force so much that Malcolm wanted to shy away but couldn't. "Welcome to the crossroads, Malcolm."

Malcolm croaked, the words lost in his throat.

"Do not stop!" Baron Samedi sailed into view. His head was a gleaming, white skull. Orange embers smoldered in his eye sockets like the end of his cigar. Vaguely human shapes writhed in the trailing smoke. "Do not stop now!" he roared.

Malcolm blinked. He'd lost focus, and the demon's energy had almost refilled his legs. Cinching his eyes to block out the sights, he continued the chant and pulled the demon's essence back up.

"Holloo mreshti. Mayas karri notem. Ohma ahsa ah rae."

He worked it down his arms. The demon fought him, screaming and roaring in his mind, but Malcolm continued the mantra. Starting with his forehead, he peeled the demon's essence down, tearing it from his brain and eyes. The screaming stopped, but the growing ball of energy pulsed and kicked in his gut.

His mind finally clear of the horrible parasite, Malcolm screamed the chant, kicking his bound feet. Focusing all his will, Malcolm forced the writhing ball up his throat. It moved like barbed paste, grabbing and tearing, but Malcolm continued to push. He roared the chant, and it inched up. Then with one final surge, Malcolm shoved it out.

Tattered ribbons of crimson flame erupted from Malcolm's mouth. He choked as it poured from him like cheesecloth ectoplasm from a charlatan medium. It surged faster, issuing from his nose and the corners of his eyes. Unable to breathe or see, Malcolm continued the chant. The flowing demon essence finally petered out as the last of it left his body.

Malcolm opened his teary eyes. A pulsing orb of red flame seethed and spun an inch from his open right hand. A single tendril stretched out from the ball and then retraced as the wolf's soul was released.

"Bring the mask," he shouted, breaking the chant for only a moment.

Papa Ghede stooped before him and picked up the silver wolf mask. The one-lensed sunglasses were gone. Galaxies spun within the infinite blackness of the old man's empty eye.

Grinning, Ogoun hacked his machete, severing the ropes that held Malcolm's wrists. Still chanting, Malcolm tore his pinned left hand from the post and reached for the mask that Ghede lifted toward him.

It shocked at his touch, and the demonfire coursed down Malcolm's arms and into the mask. The metal glowed and buckled, but the fire continued to pour. The bestial visage grew sharper as if worked by invisible hands. Once the last of the spirit had poured into it, the glow faded.

"You did it," Papa Ghede laughed. He was no longer the loa but the homeless man in broken glasses.

"I knew the warrior would win," Ogoun said with a nod.

Malcolm nodded. "Get me off of this thing."

The loa grinned then chopped the rope at Malcolm's ankles. Gritting his teeth, Malcolm tore his right hand free of the post.

"Here." The baron took Malcolm's hands and withdrew the impaling pins. Blood welled from the holes, but Baron Samedi merely wiped his thumbs across them, smearing the blood but leaving them healed. "Jim will want these back."

Paula, dressed in a white and yellow shawl signifying Ayizan, unwound the silver chain from Malcolm's neck. "You made us proud."

"Now for the judgment, Doctor," Samedi said. He set a hand on Malcolm's shoulder and swept the other forward, parting the loa to where Matt waited. A nervous apprehension twitched at the edges of his once-hard eyes.

Rubbing his neck, Malcolm let the baron lead him to where Matt waited.

"You are a husband yourself, Matthew Hollis," the baron said. "Come to pass judgment on our wayward bokor. Now judge. Does he live, or do I dig his grave tonight?"

Matt swallowed. He looked at the water bottle in one hand. Its red bead pressed in the mask's direction. He met Malcolm's eyes. Suspicion still lingered. "Dämoren will be the judge."

The baron roared in laughter. "Good. I like you, Matt Hollis."

Keeping his gaze on Malcolm, Matt opened the revolver's loading gate and pushed out a single shell. Thumb on the hammer, he spun the gun's cylinder. It whirred, and Matt clicked back the hammer. He raised the gun, aiming it at Malcolm's heart.

Malcolm didn't break eye contact. He puffed his chest. "Do it."

The gun clicked.

Malcolm released his breath and smiled.

"Welcome back." Matt holstered the gun and offered a hand. Malcolm pushed it aside and hugged him. "Thanks, brother."

"Yeah," Matt said, hesitantly returning it. "I'm not entirely sure what I just watched, but it was definitely interesting."

Malcolm laughed. "I'll tell you all about it." He looked at the silver mask glaring hatefully from Papa Ghede's hands. He was free.

"So what's the plan?" Matt asked.

The old anger rekindled inside him. "I get Hounacier back." Malcolm turned to Papa Legba. "Do you know where she is?"

The thin man leaned forward on his cane. "Now, who do you think I am, Malcolm? Of course I know. Let us take you to her."

CHAPTER 20

A moist breeze coursed down the streets, cooling Malcolm's skin. Matt walked to his left, unmoved by the drums and rattles. Papa Legba kept to his right. He shimmied and danced, tapping his cane in time with the rhythm as they marched across the nighttime city.

Nearly forty members made up the strange parade. Business owners, police, vagrants, mothers, fathers, killers, and lawyers. The loa made none of those distinctions in whom they favored.

People watched as the procession passed. Some cheered. Some joined for a short while, dancing and speaking to the living spirits. Papa Ghede told jokes and made obscene gestures to some of the women. But he did stop and talk to one sad-looking girl for a while, his hand on her shoulder as he imparted some grandfatherly wisdom. He caught up a block later, grinning and swigging his rum, and again the merry prankster. But the procession never slowed, never deviated.

"What's this for?" one man yelled from across the street, jigging parallel to them.

"A funeral," the baron answered. "But don't worry, Brian, it's not for you."

The young man's face went slack. Baron Samedi laughed, and the procession continued onward.

They passed parks, bars, shuttered businesses, and homes. The refreshing wind moved with them, urging them on. Malcolm paused from the dance once they reached the canal bridge.

How had they gotten here so fast? It had only felt a few minutes, not hours. Almost a dream.

"Don't slow now, Milky," Ghede called from behind him. "We're almost there."

Resuming his dance, Malcolm started up the bridge. Cars slowed behind them, hesitant to pass the outer lane out of either respect or superstition. Dark drops of dried blood speckled the path Malcolm had taken just hours before, that time to die, this time to kill.

The Ninth Ward was still as the march wormed its way up the dark streets. A few windows lit as the drummers passed, but most houses didn't stir.

A police car sat before the smash-through gap in Atabei's fence. Another pulled around the corner ahead and stopped in the street. Their lights erupted in angry blue and red flashes as the parade neared.

An officer stepped out of his car, hand on his pistol. "Stop right there!"

The other policemen came out of their cars. One of them held a shotgun. From the corner of his eye, Malcolm noticed Matt's hand inching toward the slit in his shoulder back. It was about to get bloody very fast.

Malcolm stepped forward, his hand out to his sides. "Yes, Officer."

"Are you Malcolm Romero?" the first officer asked.

"I am."

The gun came up. "Get down on the ground! You are under arrest."

Baron Samedi roared with chilling laughter. "Or what? I know you don't plan to arrest him, Seymour. You're goin' to dump his body and let the gators eat it."

The officer stepped back then aimed the gun at the baron. "How do you know my name?"

The baron laughed again. "Oh, I know much more than that. I know everything about you, Seymour Hendricks. I know you sold your soul to a witch because so you could gain a little luck. I know you pay for it every month, giving Atabei the money that should be goin' to your little girl's college fund. And you,

Randy Brauduc." He stabbed a finger at another officer. "I know your mama's ill and that you'd do anything to help her. So you sold yourself too. All of you did." He sucked a puff of his cigar. "Do you know who *I* am?"

"Luison," Officer Brauduc said. "You have that antique shop."

"Not quite." The baron pulled back his tuxedo sleeve and stubbed his cigar out on the back of his wrist, raining red embers onto the asphalt. "But you go to his shop tomorrow and ask Jim how he got this mark; he won't know. But *you* will." He dropped the butt on the street and stood straight. "Now do you know who I am?"

The officer's gun lowered as if it had suddenly grown very heavy. "Baron Samedi."

"Indeed." The baron lifted the brim of his top hat in a little bow.

The other policemen seemed hesitant, their resolve softening.

"Now that you know who I am, let me tell you boys something. You made a pact with the darkness, and you know it. You feel that shame, but you're slaves to it. Now this man, Malcolm Romero, see, he's here to save you, bring you back to light. And all you have to do is let us pass, and you'll be free. You can stand tall, look yourselves in the eye again, and know that the darkness is over. This ... witch." He pointed to the house. "She's crossed us, pretended she's acted in our names. Now, I'm not a man to cross. So you can either let us by and save you, or you can cross us and suffer her fate with her. And if you join us, I can promise you that long after you're old, and gray, and I dig your grave, and take you to the other side, you'll remember what happened when Malcolm Romero came calling. So what's it goin' to be? Will you let us pass, or will you join in the debt Atabei is about to pay?"

One by one, the policemen lowered their weapons.

Baron Samedi turned to Malcolm and swept his hand, gesturing him on.

Malcolm continued though the drums and rattles no longer played. Some of the loa and procession members went through the broken fence, but most followed Malcolm as he circled around to the front of the house.

Light came from a few of the second-floor windows, but he saw no movement within. Malcolm marched up the front steps, Matt at his side.

"Atabei Cross!" Malcolm called, pounding on the heavy wood door. "I've come for Hounacier!" He shouldered the door, but it didn't move. He hit it again and again, driving his weight in. Shoulder aching, he pushed aside the pain, focused on the rage, and hit it again.

Matt grabbed his arm. "Stop!"

Malcolm snapped his head toward him, the anger near blinding.

"You're no good with a broken arm," Matt said. "We'll do it together."

Malcolm nodded. He moved to the side, allowing Matt enough room beside him. "Okay. Ready on one ... two ..."

The door bolt clicked.

Malcolm stepped back, ready for whatever was about to come through.

A slender man opened the door, and it wasn't until his apprehensive eyes met Malcolm's that he recognized him as Gary, now cleaned up. "She went out the back door."

Malcolm hesitated, but Gary seemed to sense the question.

"It was wrong what she did." A needy hunger twitched at the corner of his lips. He still thought Malcolm was possessed. He wanted to appease the monster, earn its good graces.

Dogs barked beyond him. She'd unleashed the Rottweilers.

Pushing past the demon-addict, Malcolm charged into the house and down the long breezeway toward where the backdoor stood open. He raced outside to the sounds of clanking metal.

Atabei was in the yard below in a machete fight with Ogoun. The obsidian mask in one hand, she swung Hounacier at the loa with a vicious proficiency. Malcolm had witnessed several machete duels in his time, and Atabei's technique, elbow down and bent front leg, showed she was no stranger to them. And while Earl Warren had the soft hands of a businessman, Ogoun had all but invented the art. He danced around, dodging and deflecting her blade, pushing her back. He could easily take her but didn't. He was stalling her.

Three more of the loa and five of the followers, Duplessis among them, formed a semicircle behind Ogoun, herding her back. Papa Legba watched from the side, petting Sogbo and Bade as if nothing important were going on.

"Atabei!" Malcolm roared, coming down the steps.

She turned at her name. Ogoun stepped back, melting into the human wall.

Atabei's eyes widened. Still panting from her fight, sweat glistened across her narrow, ebon face. She raised the mask toward Malcolm as he neared.

He grinned as the realization dawned on her that it wasn't working. "I've come for Hounacier."

"No." She raised the machete toward him. "It is mine."

"She," he corrected, moving closer.

Atabei stepped warily to the side, and they began a slow circle.

His followers gathered behind him, forming a ring around them. None, not even Ogoun, made any move to assist. Hounacier was his to win and theirs to witness it. It didn't matter. Malcolm felt the bond as he watched the blade. She wouldn't hurt him.

Atabei's nostrils flared with each breath. She was trapped, and she knew it. With a scream, she lunged, hacking the machete. The blade hesitated for a moment, and Malcolm seized the opening.

He sprung toward her, grabbing her wrist and the back of the blade. Malcolm twisted it down as he drove his side into her.

Atabei cried out and stumbled back. She fell onto her ass at the loa's feet.

Malcolm squeezed Hounacier's bone grip, savoring the feel of it. He released a weeping breath, the weight of her absence lifting away. She was his once more. *I'll never lose you again. I swear it.* He glared down at the fallen priestess, his anger returning.

Atabei clutched the mask to her chest as if it might offer some protection. She glared hatefully up at him and spat.

"For Ulises." Malcolm raised Hounacier high, ready to deliver the killing stroke.

"Malcolm, stop!" Papa Legba boomed, his voice louder than could be imagined by such a scrawny man.

He scowled. "Why?"

"Our agreement was to help you reclaim Hounacier, which you have now done."

"She murdered Ulises."

Legba dolefully nodded. "Yes. But you are not a murderer. And Atabei has done more than that." His fatherly tone sharpened as he looked down at her. "She has used our name in vain, guiled, and passed herself off as one of *our* priestesses. So *we* will judge her for her sin."

"You," Atabei said with a hateful glare. "What's your name worth? You were there when Ulises killed my husband. What did you do? What did any of you do? You let him die then you *wept*! As if your pain could rival mine. I can cure the possessions. I save lives. Lives you would take." She held up the obsidian mask, shaking it before them. "This! This is what I did. No one died. No children lost their parents. No wives became widows. So don't pretend that your name means *anything* except death and pain!"

"Those masks only delay the problem," Papa Legba said. "They are only a sleeping volcano, waiting to unleash itself when no one expects it."

"Not if you put it on an animal. Then Hounacier can kill the monster but not a person."

"And how many animals did you slay while you had Hounacier, Atabei?" He shook his head. "None. You kept them both for your own glory. The only time you tried to use Hounacier was to kill Malcolm. But then you pretended it was in our name that you made your gris-gris and worked your spells, taking people from our path and into your own." Papa Legba drew a resigned breath and tapped his cane three times. "Give her what she has earned."

Baron Samedi smiled wickedly. "Time to pay your debt."

The loa descended upon her, swarming, and holding her down. Atabei screamed and thrashed. Tasha-Erzulie took the obsidian mask from her while Adjasou pinned her arm. Papa Ghede pushed his way through until he stood above her head, the silver wolf mask in his hands.

"No!" Atabei screamed, her eyes white and locked on the descending mask. "No! No! No!"

Baron Samedi howled in laughter.

Despite his hatred, Malcolm felt a moment's sympathy as Ghede pressed the mask onto Atabei's face.

Instantly, her writhing ceased. Redness glowed beneath the mask, casting ruby light down her neck and chest and filling the eye holes with swirling, liquid light. She shuddered, and loa backed away. She spasmed and shook with that unnatural speed. The mask crinkled and warped, cracking and pressing itself even more against her screaming face.

Fur erupted along her lengthening limbs. Fabric ripped, and claws sprouted from the toes of her slippers a moment before the bestial feet tore through. Bent and broken shards of silver fell from her face, tinkling to the ground as she rolled onto her hands and knees. Her back arched, the vertebrae popping in succession.

Malcolm squeezed Hounacier's grip. He held his ground as all but Matt backed away.

"You got this?" Matt asked.

Malcolm nodded. The tingling excitement danced across his shoulders.

She howled, her face lengthening. Gulmet rose, clothed in the tattered and dusty shreds of Atabei's dress.

Malcolm charged.

The werewolf leaped to the side. Malcolm spun as the beast swiped its claws. He ducked and thrust, but Gulmet twisted away from Hounacier's tip.

Snarling, the werewolf backed away and dropped to all fours. Malcolm held Hounacier before him as they circled one another. Drums began to play.

It looked around desperately as if searching for an escape. Matt stood at one end, Dämoren ready. Erzulie watched from the other, the ghoul mask clutched to her chest. The beast roared and sprung for Malcolm, claws grasping for his throat.

Malcolm hacked as he sidestepped, severing the claw at the wrist. Howling, Gulmet slammed the bleeding stump against

Malcolm's arm. He stumbled but found his footing before the other claw came down at him. He ducked and moved around the frenzied charge like in a dance then rammed Hounacier into the werewolf's back, up and under her ribs. Gulmet lurched forward, and Malcolm twisted and yanked, pulling the bloodied blade free.

Falling to her knees, Gulmet twisted around. She raised her arm in a pitiful attempt, but the blade came down on her neck, and she crumpled. She gave two ragged gasps, her single paw scratching the ground; then crimson fire burst from her wounds.

Panting, Malcolm watched the fire spread across the corpse. Hounacier trembled in his hand and rose of its own volition. Fiery blood flickered along the blade as it moved toward Malcolm's left hand. He smiled and rolled his palm upward to meet it. He winced as she bit into his skin, and the fire surged into him. A familiar half-lidded eye glowed in his palm for only a moment then faded away.

"Thank you," he whispered.

The surrounding audience stood silent, watching the werewolf's fire. None seemed saddened.

"You," Baron Samedi called to Officer Hendricks. "Take her, and feed her to the gators. She deserves no burial." He strode to where Malcolm stood and nodded. "You did well, Doctor. But ..." He raised a finger then lowered it at him like a knight's lance. "You still owe a debt for your life."

Malcolm swallowed. "I remember."

"You are our bokor, and it's time to honor our queen's decree. Do you understand?"

He nodded.

"Say it."

"I understand."

"Good. Now, you take care of yourself. And you take care of our people." He grinned that skull-like grin. "I'll be watchin'." Then his eyes rolled back, and he shivered.

Jim stumbled back, and Malcolm grabbed him by the tuxedo jacket, getting some of his blood on the shoulder. Jim looked up in confusion, then the recognition flashed in his eyes. "Mal?"

"It's me."

Jim touched the jacket and looked back. He jumped as his gaze found the burning demon. "What the...?"

"It's okay, Jim." Malcolm squeezed his shoulder assumingly. "It's dead."

Papa Ghede sauntered up, a smug smile across his face. "Don't worry there, Jimmy. Milky got it under control."

Jim lowered his head in sudden reverence. "Papa Ghede."

"You're late to the party, Jimmy. I was just about to go. My brother says you've been buyin' those cheap cigars again. Told me to tell you he expects to find better ones in the pocket next time he wears your jacket."

"Of course, Papa."

Ghede beamed at Malcolm. "You made me very proud, Milky. I know Ulises is too."

"Thank you," Malcolm said.

"You won your lady back. Careful not to lose her again."

"I will be," Malcolm said, but the loa's visible eye had already rolled up.

Most of the other loa were all leaving as well, their hosts staggering. Yelps of surprise and fear erupted as all eyes found the corpse that was Gulmet and Atabei.

The homeless man now standing before Malcolm in a pair of broken sunglasses started screaming. He stumbled past Malcolm, trying to escape the monster and the terror of not knowing where he was or how he got there, and ran off.

"My children," Papa Legba yelled in that commanding tone, banging the tip of cane down like a gavel. "Calm yourselves." He looked around, silent as the priests and priestesses realized who was speaking. "This creature murdered and stalked your streets, and it would have kept on doing it until the end of time, and there's nothing none of you could have done to stop it, save this man." He gestured to Malcolm. "Doctor Romero is our sword-bearer. Hounacier is his bride. He has walked the darkness beyond what any of you will ever know, and now, he's come back to the light to save you from it. Treat him with respect for the sacrifices he makes." He nodded to Malcolm, then his eyes rolled back as the loa left its body.

Malcolm pushed his way through the closing crowd until he found Tasha near the back, huddled with Maggie.

Tasha wrapped her arms around him as he came close. "Is it over?"

He held her against his chest. "It's over." Malcolm squeezed her tight. She smelled like sweat, candle smoke, and dust. "I love you."

She pulled back, that angry fire smoldering behind her tears. "Don't say that. Don't you say that and then leave me again. I won't do it."

Malcolm glanced at Maggie, watching them, and then shook his head. "Don't worry. I'm not going anywhere."

NOLA FIELD REPORT AND NOTIFICATION OF REASSIGNMENT

To: <Alexander Turgen>; <Sonu Rangarajan>; <Max Schmidt>
From: <Malcolm Romero>
Subject: NOLA Field Report and Notification of Reassignment

I apologize for the delay in this field report. I've attached it as well as an assessment of information I gleaned while possessed. Please regard this second item with the highest importance. We have never had opportunity to observe these entities as closely, and the information is quite disturbing. The summary is:

Werewolves, if not all werebeasts, can completely control a victim without having to physically manifest or without the victim's knowledge of its occurrence. Even Matt Hollis' blood compasses cannot detect this limited manifestation.

We have incorrectly assumed that demons like werewolves consumed flesh or blood as nourishment. However, the flesh is merely a means to consume their true sustenance, which is energy. In the case of werewolves, that energy is terror.

Most disturbingly, demons are able to propagate themselves. While this theory has been proposed numerous times before, it has never been proven. After recent events in Italy, we incorrectly assumed that demons were spawned entirely by Tiamat. I can verify that the 1783 field report from Sir Tomas Jansen's expedition to Greece correctly identified a pregnant female werewolf and her mate.

However, the reason for my delay in sending this report and my findings is of a very personal nature. While it has been a great honor to have served the Order as a senior knight and Team Leader, recent events have forced me to accept Hounacier's calling, and I must step down from this position. As payment for my life, I have agreed to the loa that I shall stay in New Orleans to continue Ulises' work. While I would prefer to say that this was a difficult decision, I cannot. My possession was not without repercussions, and a small piece of my soul was lost with it. Hounacier has filled that void. Our bond is now greater than it has ever been, and I feel her calling for me to stay. Please understand that I do not wish to leave the Order, but merely change my responsibilities. I am, and always shall remain, a Valducan knight. Obviously, this creates a hole in the leadership structure. It is my opinion that Luiza Hollis is the most capable of filling that position. However, due to her current pregnancy and soon-to-be motherhood, I do not know if she will accept it. If not, the next choice should be to reassign Luc Renault to the Americas and promote Uwe Rachow to lead the Western European teams. While such a change might appear dramatic, with Taras Orlovski's current medical condition, I do not feel that anyone else is capable of filling that role.

Matt Hollis, while still unqualified to fill a Team Leader rank, should be considered as Arms Master. While Luiza currently serves that position, and may choose to continue it if she declines promotion, Matt is a superior candidate. Not only is Matt's knowledge of weapons considerable, his abilities as a New World hunter are beyond compare. Having seen him operate alone in the field, I believe he would be an exceptional teacher for not only New World hunters, but all Valducans, since our ranks have been so reduced. Because of personal history, I suspect he would be more amenable to such a promotion if he were not told that I recommended him for it.

Thank you all for the opportunity to have served as a Team Leader.

I hope nothing but the best for you and for the Order.

Sincerely,
Sir Malcolm Romero, PhD

CHAPTER 21

"Wise one, patient one, Papa Legba take my gift and help me find the way." Malcolm kissed the needle and worked the final stitch into the red leather. He looked at the little photograph of a big-eared kid named Troy Miller, repeated the prayer, and tied off the white thread.

Tasha's laugh carried in through the door as Matt shared one of his many stories. With their mutual interests in movies and antiques, the two of them got along wonderfully, which made Malcolm a little nervous. He didn't know why it should, but it did, and that made him even more nervous. So he tried not to think about it.

He set the gris-gris to the side and blew out the six candles. Rising from his desk, Malcolm eyed the growing stack of pictures and little baggies of personal items for more gris-gris. After Rochelle Duplessis' prompt and generous promotion, he had become very popular, especially with police, whom he readily accepted.

Malcolm stepped out of the office, now quickly filling with candle smoke. The smell of coffee helped mask the lingering odor of new paint and carpet.

Tasha smiled from the kitchen table, still chuckling at whatever Matt was saying. "Morning."

"Morning." Malcolm walked in and gave her a kiss. "You leave any coffee for me?"

"Just made a fresh pot," Matt said.

"Perfect." Malcolm noted the two suitcases in the corner beside Matt, one a blue hard-side meant to carry the obsidian mask. "All packed up?"

Matt nodded. "Yup."

Malcolm poured his coffee and opened the fridge. An array of mismatched dishes, their contents and makers scrawled across their foil and plastic wrap coverings, filled the shelves. Neighbors and prospective clients, hoping to make a good impression and welcome him, had provided the near endless bounty. He scoured the selection, hoping to find at least something he wasn't tired of or at least remotely in the mood for. Malcolm sighed and closed the door.

The coffeemaker's green clock read, 7:26.

"What time do we need to get you to your ship?" he asked.

"They said eleven," Matt said

"Then let's take you out. Get some breakfast, couple drinks."

"Tired of casserole?"

"No," Malcolm said, an unintentional defensiveness in his voice. "It's just it'll still be here this evening, and tomorrow, but you won't. Let's go out."

"I'm down," Tasha said.

Matt nodded. "Sure."

"Perfect," Malcolm said. "Let me just get some—"

A knock came from the door.

Tasha gave a wide "every single time" smile and gestured toward it.

Expecting a new well-wisher or client, Malcolm crossed the little living room, drew a breath, smiled, then opened the door.

Earl Warren, dressed in a blue suit, beamed at him. "Morning, Malcolm."

"Good morning. Come on in, Earl."

"Hi, Earl," Tasha called from the table.

"Morning. I can't stay for too long," he said, stepping inside. "I have a showing down the street and figured I'd drop by, see how things were coming." Earl looked around with an approving nod. His gaze lingered for a moment on the obsidian mask on the facing wall. "Like what you've done. Tasha, you've done a good job."

"Why does everyone think it's her?" Malcolm asked, following him into the kitchen. "I'm the one that lives here."

The priest smiled knowingly. "My mistake."

"No, it wasn't," Tasha said.

"I didn't think it was." He bent and gave her a hug. "And how are you, Mister Hollis?"

"Fine. You?"

"Can't complain." Earl nodded to the suitcases. "So you leaving us?"

"Yeah," Matt said. "I need to get back home."

"I understand. Well, it was a pleasure to meet you." Earl scratched his cheek. "The other reason I dropped by, Mal, is we're having a little barbeque picnic next Saturday. The church's third anniversary. And I wanted to extend an invitation to both of you."

"Well, thank you. Sure."

Earl smiled. "Perfect. Maggie will be there, of course, and if you don't mind, I'd ask that you not mention it to Jim until after I've given him the invite myself."

"Of course," Malcolm said. "How is, um, Gary working out for you?"

"Gary? He's doing fine. I got him working on some odd jobs around the church. Couple of the members have been finding other work for him."

"Good. Anything … unusual?"

"Nothing that I've noticed. He'll be at the picnic too. You can see for yourself." Earl checked his watch. "Anyway, I just wanted to drop in, see how you were, and pass the invitation along."

"Well, thank you," Tasha said. "Let us know what we need to bring. And good luck at your showing."

"Appreciate it." he shook Matt hand. "Take care, Mister Hollis."

"You too."

Malcolm led Earl back to the door. "I'll see you next Saturday."

"Have a good day."

Malcolm shut the door and walked back into the kitchen,

where Matt was grinning like a school boy who knew the principal's fly was down. "What?"

"Picnics?"

"Don't be jealous."

Matt chuckled. "I just wouldn't have believed it."

"He's just making nice," Tasha said. "Very sweet of him to extend the offer."

Matt shrugged. "If you get too soft, I'm going to shoot you again."

Malcolm snorted. "You got too much enjoyment out of that."

"So much that I did it twice." He gave a little smile.

"Well, don't worry. I think I'm going to be plenty busy. Now, come on. Let's get some breakfast and get you home to Luiza."

ABOUT THE AUTHOR

Raised in the swamps and pine forests of East Texas, Seth Skorkowsky gravitated to the darker sides of fantasy, preferring horror and pulp heroes over knights in shining armor.

His debut novel, *Dämoren*, was published in 2014 as book #1 in the Valducan series; it was followed by *Hounacier* in 2015, and Ibenus in 2016. Seth has also released two sword-and-sorcery rogue collections with his Tales of the Black Raven series.

When not writing, Seth enjoys cheesy movies, tabletop role-playing games, and traveling the world with his wife.

Visit Seth's website: http://skorkowsky.com/

Curious about other Crossroad Press books?
Stop by our site:
http://store.crossroadpress.com
We offer quality writing
in digital, audio, and print formats.

Enter the code FIRSTBOOK
to get 20% off your first order from our store!
Stop by today!

Manufactured by Amazon.ca
Bolton, ON